"I need to find my friend," I whispered.
"Can you help me?"

Something—pity, maybe—crossed his face. "Sit back," he said, his hand closing gently over my throbbing shoulder. "Close your eyes."

"I really need to find her." I settled back as his fingertips brushed against my forehead, feather light. He murmured something I couldn't catch and didn't care about.

"Her name's Verity Grey. Have you seen her?" I asked. His hands paused in their tracings, my skin pleasantly warm where he'd touched, the pain softer edged. I opened my eyes. His expression was stony, mouth tight and eyes hooded.

"Verity's dead," he said shortly.

"What? No. No. *No.*" My voice rose, turning into a wail, and he clamped a hand over my mouth. I struggled against him, trying to explain why he was wrong. She wasn't dead. She was the most alive person I knew—laughing, clever, charming Verity, bright and bold and reckless enough for both of us. She couldn't be dead, because there couldn't be a world without her. I shook my head against the pressure of his fingers on my lips, my tears splashing down over his hand. If I said no enough times, Verity would still be alive. This wouldn't be real. I wouldn't be alone.

TORN

ERICA O'ROURKE

KENSINGTON PUBLISHING CORP.
www.kensingtonbooks.com

K TEEN BOOKS are published by

Kensington Publishing Corp.
119 West 40th Street
New York, NY 10018

All Kensington titles, imprints, and distributed lines are available at special quantity discounts for bulk purchases for sales promotion, premiums, fund-raising, educational, or institutional use.

Special book excerpts or customized printings can also be created to fit specific needs. For details, write or phone the office of the Kensington Special Sales Manager: Kensington Publishing Corp., 119 West 40th Street, New York, NY 10018. Attn. Special Sales Department. Phone: 1-800-221-2647.

Kensington and the K logo Reg. U.S. Pat. & TM Off.
K Teen is a trademark of Kensington Publishing Corp.

ISBN-13: 978-0-7582-6703-0
ISBN-10: 0-7582-6703-7

First Kensington Trade Paperback Printing: July 2011
10 9 8 7 6 5 4 3 2 1

Printed in the United States of America

For Danny,
The truest thing I know.
And for my girls,
The best thing I ever did—times three.

ACKNOWLEDGMENTS

I have a terrible time remembering to turn off the coffee-maker when I leave the house, so the odds I will remember everyone who deserves to be mentioned here are slim. Bringing this book to life has been the work of many hands, and if I've forgotten you, I apologize.

My editor, Alicia Condon, and her team at K Teen have been supportive and enthusiastic. From the very beginning they have understood Mo and this story in a way that most authors dream about. I would never have believed that my life could change so much from one phone call. Thank you.

Joanna Volpe, Nancy Coffey, Sara Kendall, and the rest of the NCLMR family have been both champions and mentors. Without their sage advice this book would be a far lesser thing. I am grateful, every day, for the privilege of working with you.

The amazing members of Chicago-North RWA have provided information, good counsel, and chocolate at every turn. Marilyn Brant read the earliest version of this manuscript and offered advice; Karen Dale Harris gave me invaluable feedback and support; Ellen Wehle helped me see my characters more truly. Simone Elkeles, Heather Marshall, Sara Daniel, Erika Danou-Hasan, and June Sproat have kept me sane and made me laugh. Margaret Watson has bolstered me every step of the way and when I grow up, I want to be exactly like her.

K. C. Solano has been there from the very, very beginning, always ready to bounce ideas across the continent and discuss cute boys. Paula Forman has loaned me her kitchen and her dog when I needed a place to write. Genevieve O'Keefe, Lisa McKernan, Amy Hebbeln, Lexie Craig, and Amy Schneider have offered unflagging encouragement for as long as I can remember. Lisa Tonkery knows exactly what to say, every time.

Everyone should have an Eliza Evans in their life, but you will have to get your own, as I am not inclined to share. Truly, I couldn't ask for a better friend, reader, or partner in crime. I am proud and privileged to know you.

I can't imagine having written this book without my parents. The reader, the writer, the person I am today is a direct result of their love, patience, and unwavering support. My sister Kris has offered encouragement and first-aid tips and is my go-to girl for outstanding food.

My three daughters are strong, smart, independent girls who have cheered me on without fail. They've made it possible for me to achieve this dream, and I am proud to be their mom.

And then there is Danny, who deserves far greater thanks than I could ever express. For everything, for always, the boy of my heart.

CHAPTER 1

I woke up to the smell of Lysol and the end of the world. In my defense, I didn't know it was the end of the world at the time. I didn't know anything, and it was better that way. There's a *reason* people say ignorance is bliss.

The room looked like every crappy emergency room I'd ever seen on TV, with the notable difference that I was in it— light blue curtains for walls and rolling supply carts labeled with black marker and masking tape, a ceiling of water-stained acoustic tiles and flickering fluorescent lights. The clock on the wall read 12:38 AM, and the ER was just gearing up for the night, the clatter and bustle clearly audible through the curtains surrounding me on three sides.

I struggled to sit up in the hospital bed, which turned out to be a bad idea, and slipped back with a gasp. The pain was everywhere, waves of it crashing through my body like Lake Michigan during a storm, and the room turned inky around the edges. I tried to draw a breath without whimpering, and failed.

Moving was out, and breathing seemed dicey, but I needed to find Verity. If I was here, she was, too, and worse off than me. *That,* at least, I remembered.

Swirling black descends like ravens, large enough to block the glow of streetlights and neon shop signs. A dull roar

*starts like a train on the "L," a faraway rumbling that grows
louder as it pulls closer, until it's directly overhead and you
feel it in your chest, except this doesn't pass you by. Verity,
white faced and eyes blazing, shoves me, shouting through
the din, "Run, Mo! Run, damn it!" And then a scream, and
when I wake, she is on the ground, the copper scent of blood
and fear filling the air, my hands stained red to the elbows.
"Hang on, Vee, don't go, don't you go, someone please, God,
help us, please don't go . . ."*

"No visitors until the doctor's cleared her," said a woman
in the hallway, jerking me back to the ER. Two pairs of legs
halted outside my room, their feet and calves visible below
the curtain's hem. Pink scrubs and white Nikes stood on the
left, navy pants and scuffed, sturdy black shoes on the right.
"Besides, she's still out."

Without thinking, I shut my eyes. The curtain rustled, then
snapped, like it was yanked open and closed again. "Satisfied?" huffed Pink Scrubs. "She'll wake up soon. I'll notify
you myself."

"Did you see the other one?" Navy Pants said, with a
gravelly South Side accent. Their voices grew softer as they
walked away.

I opened my eyes and strained to hear them. Pink Scrubs
was silent.

He spoke again. "Seventeen years old. *Seventeen.* The guy
is still out there. And you want me to sit around while he
does it again? To some other little girl?"

Verity. She was here, and these two knew where. I ignored
the pain in my shoulder and slowly, slowly pushed up to sitting, biting down hard on my lip to keep from crying out. A
black plastic clamp was attached to my finger, wires trailing
to a blinking monitor nearby. If I took the clamp off, they'd
know I was awake, and Navy Pants would want to talk with
me. I needed to talk to Verity first.

The memory of her made something catch in my throat. For a minute, all I could do was stare at my hand, swathed in layers of gauze. Farther up my arm, rusty streaks had dried, flaking off on the white blanket. The sight made me queasy, and I rubbed with a corner of the blanket until the marks were mostly gone. I eased one leg over the side of the bed, planning to drag the monitor on its wheeled cart along with me, when a nearby voice drawled, "Best you not be doin' that just now."

I whipped my head around. Black fuzz appeared again, and I blinked until it dissipated. In the corner of the room stood a guy dressed like a doctor, hands tucked in the pockets of his lab coat, slouching against a supply cart.

Silently, fluidly, he moved closer to the head of the bed, stopping a few inches away. Even though I was in so much pain my molars hurt, I could see he was hot—nothing wrong with my eyesight except for the fuzz. He looked way too young to be a doctor, except for his eyes, which looked ancient and . . . angry, somehow. They were startlingly green, like you'd read in a fairy tale. But this guy wasn't a prince— he was probably a med student. And it didn't matter what he looked like. He could have horns and a pitchfork, for all I cared, so long as he knew where Verity was.

"I need to find my friend," I whispered. Farther down the hallway, I could see Navy Pants's feet pacing back and forth. "Can you help me?"

Something—pity, maybe—crossed his face. "Sit back," he said, his hand closing gently over my throbbing shoulder. "Close your eyes."

"I really need to find her." I settled back as his fingertips brushed against my forehead, feather light. He murmured something I couldn't catch and didn't care about.

"Her name's Verity Grey. Have you seen her?" I asked. His hands paused in their tracings, my skin pleasantly warm where he'd touched, the pain softer edged. I opened my eyes. His expression was stony, mouth tight and eyes hooded.

"Verity's dead," he said shortly.

"What? No. No. *No.*" My voice rose, turning into a wail, and he clamped a hand over my mouth. I struggled against him, trying to explain why he was wrong. She wasn't dead. She was the most alive person I knew—laughing, clever, charming Verity, bright and bold and reckless enough for both of us. She couldn't be dead, because there couldn't be a world without her. I shook my head against the pressure of his fingers on my lips, my tears splashing down over his hand. If I said no enough times, Verity would still be alive. This wouldn't be real. I wouldn't be alone.

His eyes met mine, and I recoiled from the fury in them. "Yes. Listen to me. Verity's gone."

A sound—an awful, wounded-animal sound—filled the room. It was me, I realized, but he kept talking. "She was gone before she got here, and if you want to help her now, if you want to be her friend, you need to be keepin' your mouth *shut*. Nod if you understand me."

I bit his finger, hard, and he snatched his hand away. "Damn it, I am tryin' to help you!"

"Who are you?"

"A friend. And I ain't got a whole lot of time, so pay attention. Verity's dead, and the rest is flat out beyond you, Mouse."

The air rushed out of my lungs all at once, the room going hazy again. Only Verity called me Mouse.

Before I could ask him about it, he took my injured hand and swiftly unwrapped the gauze. A large gash across my palm was oozing blood, and I looked away. It should have hurt, but all I could feel were his words, each one like a blow.

"In a few minutes, this room is gonna be lousy with people asking you 'bout what happened in that alley." His fingers hovered over the injured skin, pressed against my wrist, and he murmured again, impossible to hear over the rushing sound in my head. "Don't tell them. Say it was a mugger, say it was a gang . . . say you don't remember."

"That's the truth." Mostly. I frowned at him, swiping at my eyes with my free hand.

He looked up approvingly for a second. "Say it just like that. You might be able to get out of this after all." He rewrapped my hand and stepped back.

Get out of what? I tried to ask, but the question was crowded out by what he'd said—Verity was dead, and everything in me felt frozen, the pain I'd felt before a shadow compared to the shards of ice gathering in my chest.

He turned to leave, and I was finally able to speak, the words ragged. "Why? Why Verity? Who would—"

He cut me off. "Too many questions. Best for everyone not to ask." He paused and cocked his head toward the hallway. I could see Pink Scrubs's feet approaching, Navy Pants following close behind. "Time to go, Mouse. Remember to forget, hmn?"

Pink Scrubs—a harried, middle-aged nurse—dragged the curtain aside. Right behind her was Navy Pants, a rumpled, bearlike man with a receding hairline and stubble that was emphatically not a fashion statement. I turned to look at the doctor, but he was gone.

"Maura Fitzgerald?" Navy Pants asked as the nurse moved to my side, snapping on gloves and pulling out a small penlight. I nodded dumbly.

"Glad to see you're awake," Pink Scrubs said cheerfully, shining the light into my eyes. She gestured to my forehead. "That looks better already. How are you feeling?"

"Where's Verity?" I croaked, swiping at tears again.

They exchanged a look—the look adults give each other when they're trying to figure out the most effective stalling tactic. I knew that look. I'd seen it before, more than once. It always meant life was going to suck, very badly, for a very long time.

"I need to check your vitals," the nurse said after a moment. "The doctor will be in soon, and she'll answer your questions, okay? Your family's on the way."

She. Not he. I watched the nurse's hands, in their purple latex gloves, reach for the blood pressure cuff, and a wild hope sprang up in me. The green-eyed guy wasn't a doctor, obviously. He'd never put on gloves, had never looked at my chart . . . he hadn't even worn a stethoscope, for God's sake. Not to mention he'd been way too young. He must have been some sort of nut job imposter, and he didn't have a clue about Verity. Which meant she was alive. I sank back and let the nurse wrap the black strap around my arm.

Navy Pants flashed a badge at me and brought out a small notebook. "Detective Kowalski, Miss Fitzgerald. I need to ask you some questions."

"Where's Verity?" The blood pressure cuff tightened on my arm, but I ignored it.

Kowalski looked at the nurse again. She checked her watch, made a notation on the chart resting on the counter, and said quietly, "We can't release patient information unless you're family."

At the sympathy in her tone, and the small shake of her head, all that wild fluttering hope collapsed. Mystery Doctor was right, and the frozen feeling swallowed me up again.

"Miss Fitzgerald," Kowalski said. "Maura. I need you to tell me what happened tonight."

"It's Mo," I corrected him, stomach clenching. Nobody calls me Maura, not unless I'm in trouble, and since I've spent the last seventeen and a half years *avoiding* trouble, I don't hear it very often. Mystery Doc had called me Mo, right off the bat. And he'd been straight with me about Verity; this guy was just giving me a measuring stare and asking questions. Screw that, I decided. If the cop wasn't going to tell me anything, I didn't have to share, either.

"Okay, Mo." He raised his eyebrow, clearly humoring me. "What can you tell me about this evening?"

I fiddled with the blanket. "Nothing."

"Nothing? Where were you and Miss Grey going?"

"For ice cream," I said. August in Chicago is like living in a bowl of chicken broth, the heat and humidity making the air oily and oppressive. Air conditioning and ice cream are the only cures.

"Which shop?"

"Martino's."

He smiled, like a coconspirator. "Just down Kedzie? My wife says I gotta lay off their butter pecan."

This must have been the good-cop part of the routine. When I didn't smile back, or say anything else, he wrote something down in his notebook. "What time was this?"

"I don't know. Nine o'clock, maybe? Ten? I wasn't really paying attention. We had a lot to talk about." Like Verity blowing off our college plans for absolutely no reason. I shoved the thought away.

"So you left Martino's, and then what?"

I had another vision of those leathery black shapes and shuddered before I could help myself. My rib cage protested sharply. "I don't remember."

Kowalski's eyes narrowed. "Try."

"I don't *know*." My voice cracked. "They came out of nowhere."

"There was more than one?"

"I . . . think so." Too many to count, especially after the first blow.

"Then what?"

Gingerly, I folded my arms over my chest, as if it would protect me from his questions. "I don't know."

Kowalski sighed wearily. "Mo," he said, "I have been a

cop for twenty years this March. I have four daughters, every one of them my pride and joy. My youngest is just about your age. And even though I've been on the force her whole life, she still thinks she can put one over on her old man. She's wrong, which is why she's spent more time grounded than a Cubs pitcher on the disabled list. Now, you look like you've got more sense than my Jenny, so why don't we skip the part where you jerk me around."

I wondered if poor Jenny had to sit on the receiving end of a lot of lectures like this. Probably. "It was dark. Someone hit me. I don't remember anything after that." *Verity's scream, beneath the roar.*

"Someone did a hell of a lot more than hit you. The doc says you've got a cracked rib and a dislocated shoulder, for starters."

That felt about right. I shrugged with the good shoulder.

"You recognize anyone?"

I shook my head. It sounded crazy, especially in the bright light of the ER, but I wasn't sure they had faces, much less any I knew. But saying so didn't seem like a great idea.

"They say anything?" Words I couldn't understand, more guttural than German, and whatever they were saying wasn't, "Welcome home." Verity's words—the few she'd been able to shout before they cut her down—were nothing I'd heard before, either, something fluid and silvery in the dark of the alley. I took too long to answer.

"Mo. What did they say?"

"I don't know." True enough. And I didn't know why I was stonewalling Kowalski. Maybe I thought he wouldn't believe me. Whatever had come after us in the alley was un-believable, but I had the bruises to back up my story. Maybe I thought he'd blame me.

Maybe he should.

But Mystery Doc had been honest when I asked about Verity, and Kowalski had just ignored me, so round one went to Mystery Doc.

Kowalski tapped his notebook against the bed rail, and I tuned in again. "Your uncle is Billy Grady, right?"

I scowled at the change of subject. "He's my mom's brother."

"You two close?" A commotion was building down the corridor.

"He owns the bar next to my mom's restaurant. I help out sometimes. So?"

"Your father worked for him, too?"

My hands clenched the blanket, and I forced them to straighten again. "My dad?" Seriously, who cared about my family right now? The only family who mattered was Verity, and she was dead. Kowalski was worried about my dad? My father was a lot of things—absent, selfish, and a felon, to boot—but he sure as hell wasn't in that alley with us.

The curtain was ripped aside with a harsh rattle. "Don't say another word to this man, Mo."

Uncle Billy, in the flesh.

CHAPTER 2

I dropped my head back against the pillow in relief. Uncle Billy brushed past Kowalski, full steam ahead, but the sight of me stopped him short. I wondered how bad I must look to put that stunned look on his face.

"Jesus, Mary, and Joseph," he breathed.

Pretty bad, then.

Without taking his eyes off me, he called out, "In here, Annie," and my mother appeared, looking decades older than she had at the restaurant this afternoon. Another cop, younger, in a uniform, followed her in.

"Maura! Oh, Mo! Oh, my baby!" Eyes welling, she rushed to me. "Oh, sweetheart," she cried, pushing my hair back with trembling hands.

I love my mother, but she is not at her best in a crisis. Still, the sight of her, in her sensible khaki skirt and blue blouse, her hair scraped back into a bun, her wedding band worn and glinting dully on her hand, made everything too ordinary not to be real, and my tears began again. "Mom?"

"What happened?" She kept smoothing my hair back, like she did when I was a kid, and she smelled like violet hand cream and tea. "I was in bed for the night—you know I'm working the morning shift tomorrow—and then the hospital called, and so I called Billy, and we came as fast as we could.

Do you *know* how I felt, Mo? I've been dreading that call. Every parent has nightmares about it. It was horrible—just horrible—I was frantic, absolutely frantic. I said rosaries all the way here." Also typical Mom. She asks me a question and answers before I can get a word in.

She paused for breath, and Uncle Billy cut in. "What happened?"

Out of the corner of my eye, I saw Kowalski pause in his conversation with the other cop, shift his weight, and turn his head to catch my response.

"It's all a blur," I mumbled. "My head . . ." My head really did hurt, and with each new visitor in the already-crowded room, the ache spread and deepened.

"Are you in pain? Can they get something for you?" Mom held her hand against my cheek for a second, grasping my good hand as if I might slip away. "Tell me what you need."

"They won't tell me anything about Verity." I choked out the words.

"Oh, sweetie," she said, her voice falsely bright. "Don't you worry about it right now. Concentrate on getting better."

Ah. One of my family's patented nonanswers.

"Mom, *please.*"

She looked helplessly at Uncle Billy. "Mo, the thing is . . ." She shot another glance at him, a woman going under for the third time, and he rescued her.

"She'll be fine, darling girl, just fine, but you can't see her now. Your mother is right. We need to get you well again, and away from here." He glared at Kowalski.

They were lying, all of them. The one thing I knew, with perfect clarity, beneath the ice encasing me, was that Verity was totally, completely, not fine.

My mother started weeping silently, and Uncle Billy, never a fan of drama, seized on Kowalski as an escape—and a target.

The first few times they meet him, people tend to underestimate Uncle Billy, with his shock of white hair and wiry little body. His blue eyes crinkle when he laughs, which is most of the time. He's a good fifteen years older than my mother, and he looks it. He's a cheerful, crackling guy, always fidgeting, always moving. But piss him off, and he goes still, all that energy coiling up inside him, tighter and tighter, darker and darker, like a summer storm. Anyone stupid enough to keep pushing would be better off taking their chances with an actual lightning strike instead of Uncle Billy's wrath.

The men's voices were hushed, but I could hear them underneath my mother's crying and fussing. "The girl's been traumatized, you horse's ass! What are you on about, questioning her now?"

"She's a witness," Kowalski said blandly, hitching up his pants. "So far, she's my *only* witness, unless you want to make a statement. Anything you'd like to shed some light on, Grady?"

"She's a minor. And if you talk to her again without a lawyer and her mother's consent, I'll have your badge. Wouldn't that be a shame, Joseph, so close to retirement?" Uncle Billy was giving Kowalski the same look that sent Teamsters packing, but he caught my mother's expression and, like one of those storms, it stopped as quickly as it started.

"Mo, my love," he said, coming around the other side of my bed and dropping a kiss on the crown of my head. "Whatever you need, name it."

I needed Verity back. And Uncle Billy would do it if he could, the same way he'd taken care of me and Mom for the last twelve years, but even he couldn't raise the dead. I'd known Verity my entire life. We'd started kindergarten together in blue plaid skirts and knee socks. We'd made our first communion together, giggling nervously in puffy white dresses. We'd shopped for training bras and Homecoming dresses. We'd read college brochures and crammed for the finals on the floor of her bedroom. Everything I'd ever gone through—mean teachers, giant zits, first crushes, my father's trip to prison—she'd been there, making all of it better. Everything bad that had ever happened, she'd carried me. Now it was the worst thing, and she couldn't help me, because I hadn't helped her.

I hadn't totally lied when I'd told Kowalski I couldn't remember. Some of it was a hideous blur, the black shapes and the screaming, and a lot was simply lost, but one thing I could recall perfectly. The thing I wasn't ever going to tell him. Verity had told me to run, as those things were settling around us, and I had.

I looked down at my bandaged hand, at the blood still flaking off my skin, trailing up my arm and across my once-green T-shirt. Verity's blood. Not mine. Verity's blood on me. The room started to narrow and go black, and my breath came in short, quick pants.

"Mo," warned my mother, squeezing my hand more tightly, "Breathe, sweetheart."

"I want to see Verity," I gasped against the darkness. "Right now, Mom. Please."

"You're making a scene," she said. "Come on, honey. Big, slow breaths. In and out."

Right. The eleventh commandment of the Fitzgeralds— thou shalt not make a scene.

The doctor—the real one, this time, a dark-haired woman with a low, musical voice—parted the curtains and proceeded to kick everyone out except for my mom. She removed the black clamp from my finger and checked me over, making a puzzled noise. She scrawled a note on the chart. "How are you feeling?"

"Like crap," I said.

My mother's mouth thinned. "Mo!"

"We'll get you something for the pain now that you're awake," the doctor said, smiling. "Mrs. Fitzgerald, may I speak to you outside?"

They probably wanted to discuss all the things they didn't think I was strong enough to hear. When they came back, Mom's eyes were watery and frantic, the doctor's gaze speculative.

"Can I go home?" I demanded.

"Soon," said the doctor. "I've ordered a few more tests, and some pain meds. Your mother and I have been discussing your injuries. You were very fortunate, Mo."

I would have laughed, but it hurt too much.

The doctor's definition of "soon" was as accurate as her estimate of "fortunate," because the night stretched out endlessly. Mom dozed in a nearby chair, Uncle Billy kept going out to the lobby to use his cell phone—for what, I had no idea, and decided it was better not to ask—and the ER staff forgot I was there.

All the while, Kowalski and the other cop hovered over us. They should have been out looking for clues.

I am not a people person. Verity was the one who could read people. She had a talent for picking up undercurrents and false fronts. She did it all through middle school and high school, somehow managing to avoid the cliques and the mean girls to be one of those people everyone liked, A-listers and geeks both, while I followed her lead.

Still, it didn't take a psychic to feel the seriously bad vibes between my uncle and Kowalski, like the detective *wanted* him to be responsible. Uncle Billy was no saint, sure, but he'd always looked out for me and my mom. Kowalski, on the other hand, was not exactly inspiring a whole lot of confidence, particularly as the hands on the clock inched toward morning.

The ER hadn't calmed down much—every few minutes I could hear someone run past, or cry out, or throw up, or deliver bad news in a low, solemn voice. It was making me crazy, hearing so much of strangers' lives and not getting answers of my own, so I decided to go and find some.

I waited until my uncle had left to take another phone call, and coughed softly, to make sure my mom was still asleep in her chair. My meds had kicked in, making it slightly less painful to swing my legs over the side of the bed and ease up to standing. Careful not to bump into any of the now-silent monitors, I slipped through the curtains into the hallway.

Someone grabbed my good arm. "Aren't you supposed to be in bed?"

I whirled, nearly falling over. It was Mystery Doc, which should have surprised me more than it did.

"If you were a *real* doctor, you'd know," I shot back, and he looked just the slightest bit ashamed. I moved down the corridor, away from the nurse's station. "I want to see Verity."

"Won't do any good." His accent, even more pronounced than it had been earlier, was a rich, melting drawl, the words blending together like music. But laced through it was an unmistakable note of bitterness. His hand still gripped my elbow, impossible to shake off. People seemed to pass by without seeing us, like a blood-spattered girl and a guy in a stolen lab coat arguing in a hallway were everyday occurrences. Around here, maybe they were. He steered me around a shelving unit filled with boxes of supplies.

"I'm going to find her."

"How are you gonna do that? You can't hardly stand up." His free hand touched my side lightly and he muttered something under his breath. I assumed it was an insult.

His fingers felt warm, curving around my rib cage, and I twisted away. "Quit it! Who are you, anyway? You don't work here. How do you know Verity? And don't tell me not to ask questions, or I'll start screaming for security."

He kept the steadying hand on my arm but took a step back. "Told you before, I'm a friend."

"Of Verity's?"

He nodded, and I rolled my eyes. "What's your name?"

"Luc." When I continued to stare, he sighed. "DeFoudre."

"Yeah, well, she never mentioned you. And she would have told me. Verity told me everything."

"You so sure 'bout that? You one hundred percent certain?"

Verity winds a lock of smooth blond hair around her index finger and uncoils it again, like she always does when she's upset. "I'm sorry, Mo. I really am." She reaches for my hand across the table.

I draw back. "You promised. We promised." This can't be happening. Verity can be flaky, but she wouldn't back out on something so important.

She looks miserable, eyes dull and mouth wobbly. Her mocha almond ice cream is melting down the sides of the cone, dripping everywhere, and she doesn't even notice. "I know."

"There's no way my mom will let me go to New York on my own!" My voice is loud in the crowded shop and heads turn. For once, I don't care.

"Maybe if you explained everything to her," she suggests.

"Maybe if you did. To me. Why are you doing this? What happened to you down there?"

"I . . . can't. But we'll talk every day, I swear. We'll text each other nonstop. Our thumbs will fall off."

I throw my own cone—raspberry sherbet—into the trash. It doesn't even taste good anymore. "Why the hell would I want to do that?" I shoot back, and stalk out into the humid August night.

I leaned into Luc, suddenly light-headed.

"Everyone's got secrets," he said. His expression, so smug

when I was so unsteady, infuriated me. I grabbed the shelf for balance and tried to give him the bored, dismissive look so many of the girls at my school have mastered.

He was taller than me, lean and broad-shouldered beneath the stolen lab coat. Tousled black hair and glittering eyes and a mouth that smirked too much. He was totally Verity's type—a little dangerous, a little arrogant, a lot different from the boys at church we'd known since we were five.

"She probably thought you weren't worth mentioning," I lied.

"Must be it." He grinned, then sobered. "Go home, Mouse."

The familiar nickname rankled. "Don't call me that!"

He shrugged elegantly. "She said you'd say that. You do a piss-poor job of followin' directions, you know that? Told you to forget all this, but here you come, bold as brass, stirring up trouble when there's already plenty to go around."

"I only want to see her. You know where she is, right? *Please.*" If I had to grovel, then fine, I'd grovel. No way I'd find Verity on my own, and it was suddenly crucial to see for myself what no one—except this guy—had been willing to tell me. "Just for a minute."

He shook his head. "You don't want to do this. Sooner you forget it, the better."

Rage flared inside me, breaking through the awful frozen feeling, and I shoved at him. "Forget it? Are you *insane?* Look, I don't know who you are, or how you *say* you know Verity, and I don't really care. All I care about is my best friend. I will not forget her. *Ever.* She died trying to save me, and I'll be damned if I walk out of this building and forget that. So you either help me find her, right now, or go to hell!" I ended out of breath, half-sobbing, half-shouting, and no one even turned to look at me.

Luc did, though, for a long time. Whatever he saw must have changed his mind, because all he said was, "This way."

He rested one hand on the small of my back, kept the other on my elbow, and guided me down the hall to a room at the end, with real walls and swinging doors instead of curtains.

"You're sure about this?" he asked.

I nodded, and pushed through the doors.

CHAPTER 3

The room was silent and painfully bright. Our footsteps echoed on the tile floor. In the center was a table, darkened monitors clustered at the head, a sheet covering the figure lying there. A few tendrils of blond hair hung down below the edge of the sheet, and I lurched forward.

Luc's grip on my arm tightened. "Satisfied?" he asked. "Let's go."

I shook him free and kept moving.

The sheet was splotched red in places, and my hands clenched at the sight. I squeezed my eyes shut and breathed in, because I needed to be ready, and I was stupid enough to believe that anything could make me ready for this.

I opened my eyes. The sheet was cold and rough under my fingers as I drew it down.

For a moment, it wasn't Verity. The girl on the table was too still. Verity was always moving—laughing, talking, kinetic, luminous. The girl on the table was so terribly, terribly still, no glow at all. For the tiniest moment, one heartbeat, no more, it wasn't Verity.

Except, it was.

She lay there, pale as wax, even though she'd come home from Louisiana gold-skinned from the sun. Her lashes were dark smudges against her cheeks. Blood smeared against the corner of her mouth, and three ragged cuts marred one cheek. I moaned, my knees buckling.

Luc was behind me, his arm gentle around my waist, his voice rough. "That's enough, now."

I leaned in and touched her other cheek. It was smooth, uninjured, but the skin had an odd bluish cast. The sheet slipped lower, revealing the ugly gash along her throat, dried blood matting her hair. I sagged back, suddenly grateful for Luc's presence.

"Oh, God," I whispered, fumbling for her hand under the sheet, startled by the weight of it. Her nails were broken, her fingertips bloody. I'd never felt anything as icy as her skin, and I tried to warm her hands in mine. "I'm sorry. I'm so sorry."

I tried to tuck her arm back under the sheet—the room was chilly, and it seemed important that she not feel cold— but instead, it slipped off, hitting the edge of the gurney with a thud, swinging limply. I screamed, the sound tearing through me.

Luc spun me around and crushed me to his chest. Behind me, he hastily rearranged her arm, but the image of her hand, fingers splayed as if reaching for help, was seared into my sight.

"They butchered her," he said against my hair, the words harsh. "And you would've been next, just for fun. There was nothing you could have done to stop it, Mouse. Nothin' at all."

I pulled back a little. His lab coat was wet with my tears, and I stared at the splotch, digging my fingernails into my good hand, relying on the pain to make me focus. "Why would someone *do* this?"

"Ever seen a cat with a mouse? They like to play with it a while, first."

The shock was wearing off, nausea taking its place. I battled it back, swallowing hard against the sour taste flooding my mouth. Luc's face was set in rigid lines, only a muscle in his jaw working as he looked past me. Something in his eyes went beyond the grief and fury I'd seen there before, into a sort of bleakness that reminded me of February, with its endless cold and endless gray, like the sun was never coming back.

I felt the same way.

"Who?" I asked. The word felt iron-hard in my mouth.

"No one you'd know. Like I said, it's better if you forget."

"Oh, right!" I practically spat. "I'll just go back to my life and forget about my best friend lying on the table over there! No problem!"

He took me by the shoulders and shook me, making my teeth clack together. "Things are happening here you don't understand. Things bigger than you. It's for your own good."

I'd heard that before, and it was *never* true. "I don't care. Explain."

He laughed at me, a bitter ancient laugh. Bastard. "I can't."

"That's what Verity said."

"'Course she did. She loved you. She knew what was coming down that alley, knew how bad it would be. She warned you off to save your life. You go chasing after shadows, you're gonna make that all a waste. Be a dishonor, really."

"So I should pretend everything's normal? I don't think so. Whoever did this—" I turned back to the body on the table and rested my hand on her forehead, the sheet between us. "I have to find them. I have to make them pay."

As I said the words, the truth of them settled below my skin, below the ice enveloping me, into my blood and my bones. Whoever had attacked us in the alley had swept me up in a wave of bone-liquefying terror I never wanted to feel again. But it didn't matter. I would get justice, I vowed, not taking my hand from the sheet, willing Verity to hear me. It wasn't what I should have done—I should have stayed and fought—but it was all I could do for her now.

Luc drew me away from the table. "They will. I promise. But you can't be part of it."

Watch me, I started to say, but he cut me off. "Bad idea to stay here. People are gonna be missing you." He was right. Normally, I was the girl no one noticed, but tonight was anything but normal. I needed to get back to my cubicle before my mother woke or my uncle returned. Luc guided me out, and I turned to see Verity one last time.

She lay silent and unmoving on the table, and my knees gave way again, pulling Luc off balance.

"Oh, hell." Scooping me up like I was a child, he pushed his way out through the swinging doors. "You ain't going to make this easy, are you?"

I remembered Verity's face, grim and terrified, telling me to run. I remembered her screams rising up as the blackness swarmed over her, and bright red blood on a bone white knife, wet in the glow of the streetlight. I remembered holding her up in the dark of the alley as her life leaked away. All those memories coalesced into a cold, hard ball lodged directly behind my sternum.

"Not a chance," I said, as he carried me back to my room.

CHAPTER 4

We buried Verity on a windless August morning. By ten o'clock, the temperature was in the nineties, a still, oppressive day that begged for a storm to break the heat and scrub the world clean. The sun beat down, and I could feel my too-fair skin turning pink with sunburn, preparing to freckle like crazy. Despite the heat, the service was packed. As Father Armando droned on about accepting the mysteries of God's will, I kept my sunglasses on and scanned the crowd nonstop.

It seemed as if everyone Verity had ever known was there—girls from St. Brigid's, guys from our brother school, St. Sebastian. The volleyball team stood in a tight knot, holding hands and weeping. Part of me wanted to go and stand with them, to feel less alone, but I knew the feeling was an illusion. They hadn't been there. They hadn't seen what I saw. They hadn't held Verity and begged her to stay. And they didn't—they couldn't—crave justice the way I did.

There were friends from the neighborhood and church, too, clad in black and fanning themselves. The ivory programs looked like moths against their dark clothes. The reporters who had hounded me for the last week hovered at a semirespectful distance. Detective Kowalski stood at the edge of the group, head bowed and hands clasped, oblivious to the stares and whispers of the mourners who looked from him to my family and back again. And somewhere in the teary-eyed crowd was the person who'd killed Verity.

In every mystery I'd ever read, every episode of *CSI* I'd ever seen, the killer showed up at the funeral. Accordingly, my plan was to watch for mysterious figures lurking behind gravestones, track them down, and tell Kowalski. It wasn't the most sophisticated approach, but it was all I could think of.

The cemetery, one of the oldest and largest in the city, was carefully designed to look like rolling English countryside. Sheltered by a ring of mature oak trees, dotted with hedges and hills, it seemed impossibly green and fresh. Verity's grave was near a small pond. The water was still and glassy, no wind to ruffle the surface. When the service was over and everyone went back to their lives, this spot would be lovely and peaceful.

I wanted to burn it all down.

Father Armando finished up, but I kept studying the array of faces, unsure exactly what I was looking for. There was no one suspicious, only a bunch of people bewildered by grief. One by one, they filed past the casket, placing white roses on top, hesitant to approach Verity's family.

The Greys huddled together, but after a few minutes, Verity's mom motioned me over, taking my hand in hers. "Mo, sweetie. Thank you for being here."

"Of course." I tried not to crumple when she hugged me.

"Do you remember my aunt? Evangeline Marais, this is Mo Fitzgerald."

Evangeline nodded politely, linking her arm with Mrs. Grey's. Verity's mom had aged so much in the last week, they looked more like sisters than aunt and niece. Evangeline was composed and elegant, though her hand seemed to tremble as she patted Mrs. Grey's arm, and her skin was so pale with grief it looked like parchment. "It's nice to see you again, Mo. I wish it were under better circumstances."

Her voice held only a trace of a southern accent, nothing as strong as Luc's velvety drawl, but still a reminder that she'd been in New Orleans with Verity a week ago. Surely she had some idea of what Verity had been up to. I wondered how to politely ask if she'd ever met a green-eyed, black-haired fake doctor with a talent for avoiding questions who might have been dating her dead niece. Somehow, it didn't seem like the right moment.

Verity's fourteen-year-old sister, Constance, stood nearby, arms wrapped around herself.

"I keep thinking she missed her plane," she said to her father, misery plain in her eyes. They were the same deep, dark blue as Verity's, so red rimmed and puffy my own filled up again. "From New Orleans, you know? That's why she's not here. I keep thinking she missed her plane and the cab's going to drop her off and she'll be home again. And this could all be a mistake."

Her dad nodded, stroking her hair, too broken to respond.

"How are you doing, Con?" It was a stupid question, the same one I kept getting from adults, but she looked so lost, and so young, despite being only a few years behind me, that the words slipped out. "Do you . . . need anything?"

Her lip curled as she looked at me. "Not from *you*."

Mr. Grey gave me an apologetic glance over the top of her head, putting a restraining hand on her arm.

I drew back as she turned to him again, and he held her tightly, face wet.

Maybe it was a natural reaction for her to be so angry with me. I'd survived what her sister hadn't . . . who could blame her for feeling cheated? She'd always tagged along after Verity and me, imitating us, spying on us . . . generally driving us crazy. It was like having a little sister of my own. Now I'd lost her, too.

Feeling like an intruder, I stepped away for a better view of the crowd. My mother and Uncle Billy were busy with people from church. Mom shook her head and dabbed at her eyes while she stood with the women, and my uncle held court with the men, looking solemn and resolute. They'd be busy for a while. I slipped farther back into the cemetery, past a big, impressive monument to someone who'd died a hundred years ago. No one seemed out of place, no one wore a sign proclaiming their guilt, and I was beginning to realize how naive my plan was. Frustrated and sweaty, I pulled my hair— nut-brown and way, way too long for this heat—into a knot at the base of my neck. The humidity made the wisps around my face spring into curls, and I swatted at them irritably.

Kowalski ambled by and stopped a few feet away, reading the inscription on the monument. "How are you holding up?" he asked.

It was the same thing I'd asked Con, so I tried to be polite. "Fine, thank you. Shouldn't you be looking for clues?"

"Who says I'm not? The way I figure it, there's plenty of suspects right here." He swiveled toward me. "Your speech at the church was real nice, by the way."

"Thanks." My eulogy had been nice, all right. Nice and shallow, like a greeting card, filled with clichés about living life to the fullest and honoring Verity's memory. The whole time I'd been speaking, all I'd felt was a black, splintering rage. It was a wonder I hadn't been smote right there, although it seemed like a smaller sin than killing Verity. Apparently God was not as into smiting as we'd been taught.

Kowalski spoke again. "I hear you're a good student. You're probably used to speaking in front of people, huh?"

"Nope," I said, not taking my eyes from the crowd. He wanted me to know he was looking into me, so I would slip and give him something. I had nothing to give.

"Listen, Mo. There's some pictures down at the station

we'd like you to look at. Mug shots, that kind of thing. How's tomorrow sound?"

"I don't think I can help you," I said, trying my best to sound apologetic. "It was too dark to see anything."

"You never know," he countered. "The pictures might jog your memory. Or you could recognize someone you've seen before, maybe at your uncle's place? Hanging around the diner?"

I rolled my eyes, confident the sunglasses would hide it. In the days since Verity's death, Kowalski had hinted at a connection between her murder and Uncle Billy's business countless times. I wasn't surprised. When your father goes to prison for embezzlement and money laundering, everyone in the family business gets painted with the same *Sopranos*-colored brush. I'd heard it so many times I didn't care anymore, but now it was pulling Kowalski's attention away from finding the real killer. And his lumbering, polyester presence was drawing attention to me at the very moment I needed to be invisible.

If Kowalski had actually been on the right track, I wouldn't have been so angry. But he was wasting time harassing my family when he should have been looking for Verity's killers, and today of all days, you'd think he could have let up. But I didn't call him on it, because to do so would have violated my mother's golden rule: Don't make a scene. Instead, as he rambled on about what to expect at the police station, I tuned him out and studied the crowd, looking for something—for someone—that didn't fit. With a start, I recognized Luc, standing in line to speak with the Greys. I hadn't seen him earlier, but now was the perfect time to find out more—about him, about Verity's trip, and about all the answers he kept trying not to give me.

"My uncle hired a lawyer," I said to Kowalski, turning away. "He says you should talk to her, not me."

By the time I reached him, Luc was shaking hands with Verity's dad. Mr. Grey's brow was furrowed, and I caught snatches of his words: " . . . so familiar."

Luc froze for the tiniest instant. "I was on duty that night," he said, not quite looking up. "And I just wanted to tell you, sir, she was a fighter. She hung on for as long as she could, fighting to get back to you. She must have loved you very much."

My hands curled into fists. He was lying to them, minutes after we'd put Verity in the ground. I'd replayed the fragmented memories of that night over and over in my mind's eye and I knew, absolutely, that she hadn't made it to the hospital alive. There'd been no fight left in her at all. The only thing stopping me from making a scene was the sudden realization that I was lying, too. I had good reason—Kowalski wasn't interested in the truth, just settling a score with my uncle—but it was a still a lie.

Mrs. Grey caught sight of me. "Mo—" She gripped her husband's arm so tightly, the tendons on the back of her hand stood out. "This is Doctor . . ." She trailed off vaguely.

"Doctor Smith. You're looking well, Miss Fitzgerald." He took my hand and gave me a small frown. His accent, the lazy drawl that made me think of a slow-moving river, was gone. "You probably don't remember much."

"Bits and pieces," I replied. "I can't quite put it all together. Yet."

His pressure on my fingers increased. Behind us, the other mourners were lining up, shifting restlessly.

"Will we see you at the luncheon?" Mrs. Grey asked Luc. You could see her struggling, forcing herself to remember what she was supposed to say.

Luc—Dr. Smith—whoever—exchanged a glance with Evangeline. She gave an almost-imperceptible head shake, and Luc smiled regretfully at the Greys. "No. I need to be going, in fact."

Well. That answered whether Evangeline had ever met Luc. He'd been telling the truth about knowing Verity in New Orleans. And now he was going to disappear again, damn it, taking my answers with him. I turned as if to leave and made myself stumble into him.

Lightning-fast, his arm was around me. "Easy," he said, as Mrs. Grey exclaimed softly.

"I'm not feeling very good," I mumbled, clutching his arm. Unlike Kowalski, his suit was definitely *not* polyester. "Maybe it's the sun."

"We should send you on your way, then," Luc said, false sincerity ringing through his voice. He attempted to pull away, but I hung on and tried to look pitiful.

Evangeline stepped forward. "Perhaps Doctor Smith can take care of you? I'll tell your family, Mo."

"That would be great," I said, hooking my arm more firmly around Luc's. I could practically hear him grit his teeth. I might not know much about the guy, but it was pretty clear he didn't do anything unless he felt like it. And yet, a look from Evangeline, a few pointed words, and he gave in. I tucked it away to study later, when I could think straight.

"I'll make sure she stays out of trouble," he said, the faintest note of warning in his voice as he spun me toward the cemetery drive. I was pretty sure he was talking to me.

CHAPTER 5

Luc led me away from the cluster of people, along the curving asphalt road gone sticky in the heat. When we were out of earshot, he leaned down, his breath warm against my ear. "Your swoonin' needs work." His accent was back.

"So does your alias," I snapped. "Dr. Smith? Seriously? Why not John Doe? And how is it that everybody around here seems to buy that you're a doctor? You don't look old enough to drink, let alone practice medicine."

"People see what they want to. You should try it." He yanked his arm away and bowed, mockingly. Ahead of us, the driveway split in two, one path leading back to the wrought-iron entrance, the other farther into the cemetery. Luc started toward the gate. "Take care, Mouse."

"Wait! You can't *leave!*"

"Just did," he said over his shoulder.

I chased after him. "I need to talk to you."

"There's nothin' to say."

"That's so not fair!" Inspiration struck. "I'll scream! I'll tell them I remember you were in the alley, and they'll check out your story. Kowalski's right over there."

Luc glanced over, then turned toward me. I couldn't help feeling a little smug.

"This ain't a game," he said, his face darkening with temper.

"No kidding. Listen, I've stuck to my story, the way you said to. Now I deserve some answers."

He studied me for a long moment. Lines furrowed across his forehead, and smoothed out again. "Fine. C'mon." He caught my elbow and steered me across the lawn, away from both paths.

I should have felt triumphant, but instead, every nerve prickled with wariness. The sensation only increased when he slowed his pace, allowing me to catch up as we crossed into an older, richer part of the cemetery. We wound our way through marble crosses and mournful saints, Luc towing me along.

I watched him, acutely aware that my face was flushed and sweaty. The back of my plain white shirt stuck damply to my skin. Naturally, Luc looked like he'd just stepped out of the pages of GQ. He looked like he knew it, too, which should have made him less gorgeous.

It didn't.

Which was irrelevant, I reminded myself. My interest in Luc was limited to learning more about Verity's time in New Orleans. Time she'd spent with him.

He started up a small hill, his grip firm but not painful. At the top was a white marble mausoleum, standing alone like a Greek temple. Rose-filled planters marched up either side of the stairs, the scarlet flowers overblown and drooping. I tugged away and sat on a marble bench a few feet away, the stone cool under my fingertips. Luc kept his back to me, one hand braced against the corner of the tomb.

"Why did you come today?" I asked, rubbing my elbow where he'd gripped it.

For a moment, he just stood silently. Without turning around, he said, "Same as you. To say good-bye."

I didn't bother to tell him I'd said my good-bye at the hospital. From the tension in his shoulders and the way he kept so still, it was obvious he was looking at something. From my spot on the bench, I couldn't see what it was, but I didn't envy his target.

I scowled at the back of his head. "You lied to the Greys." I raised my voice, remembering the body on the gurney. "She was dead before she got to the hospital. You don't know how she fought."

"She did fight, though." His voice was soft, but what it lacked in volume, it made up in intensity. "You saw what they did to her. You saw how hard she hit back."

The memory of Verity lying in the ER, her hands scraped and bloody, made my own hands tremble. He continued, still looking out over the hill. "She lost 'cause they were stronger, and there were too many of them, not because she didn't try hard enough. Everything I told them was true."

"You're not a doctor," I pointed out, trying not to think of Verity fighting off the darkness alone.

He raised his chin, arrogant even in profile. "Never said I was. They filled that in themselves."

"You let them believe it."

He shrugged. "Why'd you give that speech?"

"Mrs. Grey asked me to."

A wry smile curved along one side of his mouth as he turned. "You don't like people looking at you. Shy as a mouse, Vee said. Told me you were the only person she knew who worked as hard to stay out of the spotlight as most people did to get in it."

I didn't know how to respond. It was embarrassing to think she had told him so much about me, and unfair, too. I knew nothing about him. "So?"

"So, you didn't want to get up there. But you did, and you said those things to make her family feel better." He smiled again, bitter and knowing as he walked toward me. "You don't believe you can keep Verity alive in your heart or any-place else. But you knew it would help her folks if they heard you say it."

I wanted to tell him he was wrong, but I couldn't. In that moment, when he'd analyzed me so neatly he could have gift wrapped it with a satin bow, I hated him. Not just for seeing me so clearly—though that was enough—but for knowing how meaningless my words had been.

"It worked," he said softly, before I could deny it. "What you said. It gave them a little bit of comfort when they thought they didn't have any. I did the same thing, is all." He reached a hand out, like he was going to touch my hair, and let it fall away. It was harder to know, to be the one without hope or comfort. He knew it, too, and it separated us from everyone else in the church.

Now it was my turn to look away. I didn't want that sense of connection, especially not with him. Bad enough I was be-coming as big a liar as he was. Standing abruptly, I pushed past him toward the mausoleum, and realized what he'd been staring at.

Verity.

The hill overlooked her grave and the small, shallow pond nearby. The crowd had left, and my family was probably looking for me. But seeing the stark black rectangle of earth made everything hurt all over again, as sharp and raw as the moment I'd seen her body. I hugged myself to ward off the pain and breathed in humid, rose-scented air, waiting until the urge to scream had passed.

And something shifted.

A stirring at the corner of my vision. I cut my eyes toward it, worried a too-sudden move would make it vanish. At the edge of the woods bordering the cemetery, four cloaked fig-ures appeared, the lead one clad in pale cornflower blue. It was the fluttering of the robes that had caught my notice. As deliberately as a wedding procession, they paced toward the pond, the one in blue leading them. Behind each of them trailed more robe-clad figures in neat lines.

The figure in blue knelt at the edge of the pond, regal and solemn, and reached toward the water, one hand hovering over the surface. The other three did the same. As the breeze picked up, light gleamed fiercely on the millions of tiny waves, setting the surface aflame. Almost without realizing it, I started down the hill, wanting a closer look.

Luc wrenched me around and dragged me behind the mausoleum.

"Hey!" I tugged loose. "Let me go!"

"What do you think you're doin'?" he hissed.

"I need to go down there! Who are those people? Do you know them?" I tried to push past him, but he blocked my way. "Let go of me!"

"Settle down," he snapped. I took a swing at him. With a snort of derision, he grabbed my wrists, muttering something I'm sure was unflattering.

"I want to see them!"

"See who?"

"The people! By the water! You saw them, too, I know you did!" I struggled against him, trying to get free.

He shook his head, his grip like iron. "Nobody's there."

I froze. "What? Yes, there *is!* Look. Just look!"

Twisting away, I dashed around the side of the tomb. The sun flashed brilliantly on the white marble walls, blinding me. When the spots cleared, Luc was next to me, face taut and grim.

"You see anyone now?" he asked.

He was right—the pond was still, and there was no one in sight, in robes or anything else. The woods were dark and quiet, the air quavering in the midday heat.

"I saw them. I *did.*" I rubbed my forehead, disoriented.

He slipped an arm around my waist and guided me down

the hill. "You keep seeing things that aren't there, Mouse, eventually they'll see you. And trust me, you do *not* want that."

"You should have let me go."

"Why? There's nothing here for you." He stopped. "If you saw something—and let's be real clear, you most assuredly did not—but *if* you did, maybe what you saw were the good guys. Her people. And maybe they were coming to say good-bye. Be nice if you could respect that. Everyone should get the chance to say good-bye."

"Did you?" I asked without thinking.

He paused. "Not like I should."

"Why not?"

He raised an eyebrow. "Something came up."

Something being *me*. No wonder he'd been so angry when I'd insisted we talk. We continued deeper into the cemetery, where the trees were massive and gnarled with age. "You said they were the good guys. Are there bad guys, too?"

"There's always bad guys. Don't you know that by now?"

"Which one are you?"

He looked at me, clearly insulted. "You can't tell?"

I threw up my hands in exasperation. "You won't help me. You won't tell me anything *useful*."

"Useful how, exactly? What Verity was tangled up in . . . you've seen how dangerous it is. You'll get yourself killed."

"I don't care." The words slipped out before I could stop them.

"You should," he said firmly. "Leave it alone, Mouse. This isn't for you."

"What does that even mean?"

"It means you're a nice girl. Go off to college. Marry a nice boy. Have some nice kids and live a nice, quiet life in the suburbs. Walk away now, you can still have all of that. You can have whatever kind of life you want, and that's a damn blessing."

I shoved him away. "A blessing? I watched my best friend *die*. What the hell is so blessed about that?"

The look he gave me was cold and contemptuous. "You lived. Isn't that enough?"

"No. Not without her." I could feel the tears starting, but pushed on. "Don't you get it? I would do anything to have her back. *Anything*. It's impossible, I know. But she's gone, and I need . . . I need to make it up to her."

"Quit crying," he said, but there was sympathy in his tone. "It wasn't your fault."

With the heel of my hand, I wiped the tears away. "You don't know that."

"Sure I do." He tilted my face up to his. Up close, his eyes were luminous, like gold-flecked jade. It was hard to see anything else when he looked at me like that. "Verity was fated to do big things, and the people who did this . . . they wanted to keep her from doin' them. They're the ones to blame, not you."

He was trying to make me feel better, but I needed leads, not pity. "Then tell me who. Please. Just a name, that's all. You have to help me."

"There's a lotta things in this world I have to do, but helping you ain't one of them. Besides, you are not exactly bringin' a lot to the table right now." He gave me an appraising look before walking away. "That changes, be sure to let me know."

Mind racing, I called after him, "Like what? What could I possibly have that you'd be interested in?"

He turned, seemingly nonchalant. "Vee bring anything back from her trip? I'm a sentimental guy. Might be nice to have a souvenir."

His casual tone was hiding something more urgent. He was after something, and if I found it first, he'd have no choice but to help me out. Leverage was a concept I'd understood since I was old enough to ask for dessert. "What if I find something? A clue, or a lead, or . . . a memento? For you?"

"I'll be around, now and again." He pushed his way through the branches of an enormous weeping willow. "Have to say, Mouse, I was not expectin' you to be this much trouble."

"I never used to be," I muttered, shoving past the curtain of silver-green leaves to follow him. But Luc had disappeared.

I might have changed, but my family hadn't. That much was obvious when I returned to the parking lot and found them waiting next to my uncle's car. To the untrained eye, my mother and uncle appeared to be having a pleasant conversation. About the construction on the expressway, maybe, or whether the White Sox would go all the way this year, or if tomorrow's special should be blackberry pie or rhubarb. Nearly eighteen years' experience revealed the truth, though. Those splotches of red high on her cheeks, the way she twisted her wedding band, my uncle's reassuring hand pats . . . Mom was in the middle of a category five freakout, and Uncle Billy was trying to calm her down.

"Where have you been?" She rushed over to me, glancing around before continuing. We were alone, but she still kept her voice low. "We have been beside ourselves! Someone said you fainted!"

"I'm fine." I pried her fingers off me. "I was a little light-headed, that's all."

"Why didn't you wait for us? I've been calling your cell every five minutes! We thought . . . I can't even tell you what I thought! How could you scare me like that?"

Uncle Billy pressed a tepid bottle of water into my hands, his expression mingling concern and suspicion. Once I'd talked my mom down, he'd want answers, too. I took a long drink, partly to cool off and partly to buy time while I worked out a story. How did Luc manage to lie so smoothly?

Pasting an embarrassed smile on my face, I pulled out my phone and offered it to my mom. "I turned it off before the service. It didn't seem right to let it ring here." True, actually. And also convenient, since my mother's greatest fear was that I might make a scene. The very suggestion was like my own personal "get out of jail free" card.

"Well," she said, mollified. "That's understandable. Are you sure you're feeling better?"

"Completely. I just got a little woozy."

"That could be serious, sweetheart! A concussion! Maybe we should take you back to the hospital. Billy? What do you—"

Uncle Billy opened her door and helped her into the Cadillac, his voice lightly chiding. "Now, Annie. If the girl says she's fine, she's fine. She probably just wanted to escape for a little bit, like Patty's aunt said."

Evangeline hadn't mentioned Luc was with me, then. Which one of us was she protecting?

My mother waited until I was buckled in, then twisted around in her seat and picked up where she'd left off. "You can't disappear like that again, Mo. Haven't you learned anything? Something could have happened to you."

"But it didn't!"

"This time," Uncle Billy said, tapping one finger on the steering wheel as we headed for the Greys'. "If you're going to wander off like this, Mo, we'll have to keep a better eye on you."

Mom nodded vigorously. If Uncle Billy had suggested we put an invisible fence around the house, she'd have me fitted for the collar by the end of the day. I slumped back in my seat, and we were all silent until we arrived at the Greys' beautiful Prairie-style house.

People streamed in and out steadily, so we let ourselves into the light-filled living room. Almost instantly, my uncle was surrounded by people from the neighborhood wanting his advice or his favor. It was always like this, whether it was at church on Sunday or a Friday night at Black Morgan's. Uncle Billy knew everyone and everything in our little corner of the city. He'd never get on Facebook in a million years, but he was still plugged in.

Meanwhile, my mother headed straight to the kitchen with the pies she'd brought, joining the rest of the Ladies' Guild as they set out hams and casseroles and potato salad. People milled around me, their murmurs like an ocean of grief. Other than the occasional pitying glance, I was left on my own, which suited me perfectly. Father Armando caught my eye from across the room, and I ducked away before he could come over and tell me again how our faith would sustain us during this difficult time.

Standing in Verity's house was harder than I'd expected. I saw her in every corner—draped over the edge of the couch, poking at the massive stone fireplace, stretched out on the floor with a bowl of popcorn while we watched bad reality TV. I pressed my balled-up fists into my stomach, trying to hold it together, forcing myself to think about my mission here, a tangible thing I could do to help Verity.

The fraught, silent ride from the cemetery had given me time to think, to analyze Luc's words in a way I couldn't seem to when he was right next to me. I wanted answers, and he'd given me philosophy and warnings instead. But he'd had questions, too, and they were the only clues I had to go on. Verity had brought something back with her from the summer, more than a tan and the decision to bail on our college plans. Whatever that thing was, Luc wanted it. If I wanted his help, I needed to be the one to find it.

Trying to look casual, I edged my way into the family room, searching for Verity's mom. She was standing near the big brick fireplace, clinging tightly to Con's hand, Evangeline talking in low, soothing tones to both of them. Con nodded rotely, but you could tell she wasn't really hearing anything.

It was lousy timing, and a lousy thing to do, but it couldn't be helped. I squared my shoulders and stepped forward.

"Hi, Mrs. Grey. Hey, Con."

Con's head snapped up, her expression twisting into something ugly and sharp for a second before it retreated back into blankness. I bit my lip and looked away, trying to ignore the hurt.

"Mo," Evangeline said. "We were just discussing the upcoming school year. You're a senior, yes?"

I nodded, grateful for the attempt at normalcy. Con turned her head toward the fireplace.

"Mo's an excellent student," Mrs. Grey put in, her voice thin and wispy as cotton. "Very diligent."

Yep. That was me. Diligent and dull, when I wasn't planning to burgle my best friend's house.

"And your hobbies?"

I commit felonies? "Photography. I'm co-editor-in-chief of the school newspaper this year, and I take a lot of the pictures, too. I play soccer."

"Second-string," Con muttered, scowling at the mantel.

"We're so glad you'll be at St. Brigid's, Mo, to help Con. She'll need a familiar face, to show her . . ." Mrs. Grey trailed off. No one pointed out the obvious—Verity was supposed to be giving her the tour and teaching her how to shorten the skirt on her uniform—but the knowledge smothered the conversation like a blanket.

"I can take care of myself." Con wrenched her hand away from her mother, crossing her arms over her chest.

"Constance," said Evangeline. "Don't be so hasty. You never know where help might come from, or when you'll require it."

"Whatever." She stalked out of the room, Mrs. Grey following anxiously behind. Uncle Billy stood aside to let them through.

"Poor mite," he said, shaking his head. He patted my arm and gave Evangeline a sorrowful smile. "My sympathies. Verity was such a special girl."

"Yes. She was."

"Will you be staying in town long?" he asked, interrogation disguised as small talk. *My business,* he always said, *is everyone else's.*

Evangeline tilted her head to the side, eyes bright and sharp like a bird's. "Until things here are settled. I've closed my shop in Louisiana indefinitely."

Uncle Billy nodded. "One of the benefits of being the boss, I've always said."

"Indeed." She held her coffee cup delicately in front of her and offered nothing more. The silence was punctuated by the clinking of silverware on plates and the indistinct voices of the Ladies' Guild in the kitchen as they scraped and rinsed the dishes.

Uncle Billy seemed content to stay by my side, which was unfortunate. I hadn't planned on making my move in front of him, but there didn't seem to be another way.

"Um . . . Evangeline? I left some stuff. In Verity's room. That night." Technically, this was not a lie. My bag, with my camera, my toothbrush and makeup, and most important, the essay I was writing for my NYU application, was still in Verity's room. "I kind of need it, before school starts. Would it be okay if I went up and got it?"

Hopefully she'd attribute my trembling hands and shaking voice to nerves, but Uncle Billy wasn't fooled. He tsk'd, so quiet I barely heard it, but let go of my arm and examined the candles on the mantel.

Evangeline pursed her lips, looking out the doorway Con and her mom had gone through and nodded once. "You know the way, yes?"

I'd climbed those stairs countless times. I could have done it blindfolded. Up the golden oak treads, my footsteps heavy even in black ballet flats. Past the portraits of Verity and Con as grinning babies, round-cheeked toddlers, gap-toothed little kids, and teenagers. Unlike the mantel full of school pictures at my house, there were no awkward preteen pictures of Verity, since she had skipped that phase completely. It would have been irritating if she wasn't my best friend. Actually, it still was, kind of.

There were pictures of Con, too, always the baby, tagging along behind. I remembered suddenly how we used to play Barbies with her, and the way Con never complained when we gave her the dolls with the bad haircuts and the weirdly bent legs. She'd just been happy Verity had let her join in. Now there would be no more pictures of Verity, and Con wasn't the little sister anymore.

I studied the family portraits, too, anticipating the twinge of envy that always hit me when I saw them. It was never enough to stop me in my tracks, and Verity never commented, but it was always there. A quick little twisting in my gut at the sight of them, clustered together year after year, a solid, smiling family. We didn't have those pictures at my house, either. Hard to take a good Christmas picture through the prison's security glass.

Outside Verity's room, I paused with my hand on the glass doorknob, palm slippery and breath shallow. Dread wasn't going to help me. Missing Verity wasn't going to help me. I needed information, and this was my best chance to get it. I opened the door and stepped inside.

The scent of Verity—lemon candles and fancy shampoo—hit me. I breathed as deeply as I could, squeezing my eyes shut. Already, she'd started to fade in my mind, but the smell brought her roaring back, and with her, millions of memories. I couldn't believe I'd forgotten so much, so quickly.

Carefully, I shut the door behind me and circled the room. Aqua blue walls, white furniture, chocolate duvet on the bed. It was the same cluttered, comfortable place we'd left that night. I set her wind chimes jangling against each other and stilled them with a touch.

Verity's desk was still jammed with stacks of magazines, mix CDs, sheet music with her scrawled notations, Playbills from shows we'd seen, an empty rectangle where her laptop had rested. The police had taken her computer. If her secrets were there, they were lost to me now.

But I knew Verity wouldn't have put anything worth hiding on her MacBook, not when Con could sneak in and find it. Her ability to guess passwords was beyond annoying—it was awe-inspiring. In ten years, she'd probably be running the NSA. Between her sister and my mom, it was amazing Verity and I had ever had any secrets. That's what I'd always believed, anyway.

Think. In a few minutes, someone would come looking for me, and my chance would be gone. I turned slowly, trying to see something out of place, something new, something from the summer. Something that didn't fit the patterns of the Verity I'd known. The girl who had died in that alley, I was beginning to realize, I didn't know at all.

Slumped on the window seat was my olive drab messenger bag. I rifled through it to make sure the police hadn't taken anything of mine by mistake, then slung it over my shoulder as I continued searching. Nothing stuck out, but everything in the room felt slightly altered, like it had shifted a few inches to the left since the last time I was here.

"Are you glad to be back?"

Verity shrugs. "Sure." She seems off. Uneasy.

"Did New Orleans totally suck?"

She shrugs again and rolls over on the bed, staring up at the ceiling. "Not totally."

"Hot guys?"

"I guess." She sits up, crossing her legs into the lotus position. "The architecture's amazing, Mo. A lot of it's trashed now, but the stuff in the Garden District is gorgeous. And the music is insanely good."

"Any beads?" I tease. "I've heard what you have to do to get those, you know."

She throws a pillow at me, laughing, and shifts, hanging upside down off the edge of the bed. Her hair fans out, bright gold against the dark duvet. She seems nervous, fidgety and distracted. Every time I ask what's wrong, she smiles, but it doesn't reach her eyes.

She stands and goes to the bookshelf, inspecting the snow globe she brought back.

"I really missed you," she says after a minute. She tips the globe upside down and rights it again. "It wasn't my idea, you know."

"Duh," I say. "I know. But who cares! You're home. Everything will be just like before."

Verity opens her mouth to say something, then closes it and looks away. "Right."

"Except that we're seniors. Best year ever, I'm telling you."

She doesn't answer for one long moment, just taps the snow globe gently and stares at it. "Let's go get some ice cream. I'm sweltering."

"You brought the heat back with you."

"Yeah," Verity says. "That must be it."

I looked at the shelf. There were snow globes from everywhere Verity had been—New York, San Francisco, Mexico, Minneapolis—and from all over Chicago, too. Wrigley Field, the Art Institute, Navy Pier, the Shedd Aquarium. She had one from an apple orchard, another from our eighth-grade ski trip. She had one for every big musical she'd seen—

Wicked and *Legally Blonde* and *Phantom,* just for starters. The neat lines of glass domes were so familiar, I hardly noticed them anymore. But the New Orleans one was missing. I peered closer and finally spotted it, shoved to the back. The bright yellow base and Mardi Gras scene were barely visible through the crowd of glass domes. Why had she pushed it out of sight? The newest globe always had the place of pride, the kitschier the better.

I reached in and pulled it free, careful to keep from clinking the others. Inside was a gaudy harlequin sitting on a treasure chest, leaning against a wrought-iron lamppost. Ugly snow globes were her specialty, but this one was even tackier than usual.

I turned it upside down, swirled it gently, and righted it again, waiting for the glittery flakes to fall.

They didn't. I squinted at it to make sure.

There was no snow.

The stairs creaked, and without stopping to think, I tucked the snow globe into my bag, nestling it in an old Wilco T-shirt. I snatched up a picture of last year's Homecoming dance from the shelf below, trying to look like I was reminiscing.

Evangeline opened the door, looking like a very well-bred bouncer. Her remote blue gaze swept the room, finally settling on my bag.

"You found what you were looking for?" Her voice was steely under the honeyed drawl. Evangeline, I decided, was not someone to mess with.

"I think so." I set the picture down.

She moved toward me, and I took an involuntary step back. But all she did was brush the hair away from the cut on my temple. Without a word, she took my injured hand and studied it carefully.

"This looks to be healing nicely."

I wanted to snatch my hand back and hurtle down the

stairs, but I forced myself to stay still, not wanting to seem guilty. "The doctor said it wasn't as bad as they first thought. She said it's lucky there wasn't nerve damage."

"Luck's a fickle thing," she said, folding my fingers over and releasing my hand. "You should be more careful."

"I'll remember that." The bag's strap dug into my good shoulder, and I shifted. "I should get going. I have to work tomorrow."

"Of course. I'll walk you out."

Careful not to let my bag strike the wall, I trailed down the familiar stairs for the last time, my heart careening in my chest, the scent of Verity's room receding with every step. But her secret was within reach—my fingertips itched with the certainty of it. Luc had said I needed to bring something to the table before he'd help me.

Time to pull up a chair.

CHAPTER 6

Even though he'd been lumbering around like a badly dressed bear since Verity's death, Kowalski moved fast when he wanted to. Which is why, the next afternoon, I met my new lawyer at the police station.

I felt conspicuous sitting in the lobby, wearing Sunday clothes on a Wednesday afternoon—my mother's demand. She'd wanted to come with, but the diner was shorthanded again. Besides, the last thing I needed was her helicopter routine while I was looking at mug shots and pumping Kowalski for information.

I'd expected something grittier than the all-beige waiting area I'd been directed to. Beige plastic chairs, dinged-up beige walls, beige linoleum. Even the blinds covering the windows into the rest of the station were beige plastic. I wouldn't have thought crime-fighting was quite so drab. The air was slightly stale, the lights overhead buzzed, and people passed by me with the briefest of glances. I kind of liked the anonymity.

Tracing a finger over the initials carved into the seat of the chair next to mine, I let my thoughts drift to Luc. Was he Verity's boyfriend? They would have looked great together, Verity all blond and bright, Luc so dark and smoldering. Unlike me, she would have held her own with him. She would have gotten more answers and fewer insults. No insults, actually.

Still, I couldn't make myself believe she'd blown off our New York plan over a guy, even Luc. She wasn't that disloyal. Whatever had happened with them, whatever she'd gotten involved in . . . it was so bad she'd bailed on me. I seesawed between fear and hurt, but both made me queasy.

A woman—midfifties, maybe, with well-cut ash-blond hair; a square, shrewd face; and an expensive suit—strode into the waiting room. Spotting me, she headed over.

"Mo?"

I nodded and stood up awkwardly, hitching my bag over my shoulder. I'd left the snow globe at home, buried in my hamper. Bringing stolen property to a police station seemed beyond stupid, and since my mother only did laundry on Mondays, a pile of dirty clothes was the safest spot in the house. For once, my mother's ironclad routines were coming in handy.

"Elsa Stratton. We spoke yesterday." She shook my hand, her grip strong and her nails perfectly French manicured.

"It's nice to meet you," I said, lying through my teeth. She was completely terrifying, a pit bull in pinstripes and Chanel No. Five. I didn't know what she was charging Uncle Billy, but I already had the distinct impression she was worth it.

"You too. Let's sit for a moment. Has anyone spoken to you since you've arrived?"

"The officer at the desk said to wait here."

"Excellent. I don't anticipate any surprises today. You'll look at some pictures and Kowalski will review the statement you gave at the hospital. If you're not sure about something, leave it to me." She flagged down a uniformed officer. "Tell Detective Kowalski his hour started five minutes ago."

The officer ducked through a door marked AUTHORIZED PERSONNEL ONLY, and Elsa turned to me. "Anything I should know before we go in there? Anything you forgot to mention on the phone?"

I shook my head. There was plenty I wasn't telling her, of

course—the nightmares that woke me at two AM, Luc and his half answers, my own search for Verity's killers—but none of those things fell under the heading of stuff Elsa and my uncle should know. My gratitude toward Uncle Billy for providing what was obviously some high-powered legal help wasn't enough to make me tell him everything.

Kowalski came through the door, looking tired and rumpled even though it was only one o'clock. Elsa would chew him up, I thought, which should have made me more confident. Instead I almost felt a pang of sympathy for the guy. He might be looking for Verity's killer in the wrong places, but at least he was looking. He clutched a coffee cup decorated with "World's Best Daddy" in fading blue ink in one hand, and a bulging file folder in the other. "Afternoon, Miz Stratton," he said, raising the cup in greeting. "Afternoon, Mo. Thanks for stopping by."

He held the door with his foot and ushered us through. At the end of the hallway was a room filled with desks and file cabinets and police officers, chatter and ringing phones drifting toward us, but Kowalski gestured to a side room instead.

We sat down at the Formica-topped table, Kowalski on one side, Elsa and I on the other. Elsa took out a fresh legal pad, set it on the desk, and met Kowalski's eyes coolly. Silence—the awkward kind—stretched out between the three of us.

"You're not a suspect," Kowalski said abruptly, shifting his gaze to me. He put the folder on the table and shoved some papers back into it. "You don't need a lawyer."

"Advise my client to dismiss counsel again, Detective, and I'll bring a lawsuit against the city, and you, that will take everything but your boxer shorts."

I bit the inside of my cheek to keep from smiling. Strange, what struck me as funny these days.

Kowalski scowled at her, then refocused on me. "I've got some books of mug shots, Mo—guys who have a history of violent attacks. Can you look through them for me? Tell me if any of them look familiar?"

The laughter fled. When I answered, my voice sounded small and scratchy, even to me. "I didn't get a good look at them before I passed out."

"Won't hurt to try, will it?"

"I guess not."

He slid the first book across the table to me, and I opened it, paging through slowly. None of the men pictured rang a bell, but even with my memory slowly returning, I still wasn't sure what I'd seen in the alley. I studied the faces—sullen, angry, vacant, every race, every size—but there was no spark of recognition, no flutter of fear, no flickering of memory.

I shook my head. "Sorry."

Kowalski passed me another book. "Don't worry. We've got plenty more to go."

I continued to look at the pictures, wondering how I was going to get any information out of Kowalski, when he spoke again.

"Mo, did you see anything unusual happening in the last few weeks? Somebody new, not a student, hanging around your usual spots? Maybe more than one? Had Verity noticed anything?"

Maybe I wouldn't have to dig after all. "Verity was in Louisiana. If something unusual was happening, I wasn't there to see it."

"I meant here, in Chicago. Was anyone suspicious hanging around? Anyone you didn't recognize?"

"I told you. Everything was totally normal." Which is what I'd been telling him all along. Why wouldn't he listen?

"Nobody new at the diner?"

"She's answered the question," Elsa cut in.

"No," I said through clenched teeth. My temper felt like a fraying rope, and I could imagine each thread snapping with a sharp *ping*. "Nobody new."

"Did Verity hang out at the diner a lot?"

"She'd been gone all summer." He was asking all the same questions, like I might change my answer.

"But she came to the diner that day?"

"Yes." My mom's restaurant is called The Slice is Right, which is cutesy and kind of mortifying, especially if you work there. She makes ridiculously good pies, though, so she pulls it off. It's nothing fancy, just eight booths and a counter that have seen better days, and décor so old it's almost, but not quite, back in style. Verity had popped in that afternoon, golden and glowing, making the place seem a little fresher, a little brighter, tipping it from rundown to vintage, like she always did.

"You're home! You weren't due back for another week!"

We hug and practically dance a jig by table six.

Verity shrugs and shakes her hair out of her face. "I was ready to come home."

I drag her to the counter. "So? Tell me everything."

"There's not a lot to tell," she says, toying with the list of the day's pies. "And I can't stay."

"What's up?"

"Nothing." She shoves the menu back into its wire stand. "I have some things to take care of. What time do you get off work?"

"Five."

"Come and crash at my place tonight, okay?"

Table eight, a mother with two rambunctious toddlers who are wearing most of their strawberry pie, is giving me the frantic hand wave of a woman on the verge of a time-out.

"Totally. I can't wait—you have to tell me everything."

Verity nods, but she's looking past me as she does.

"And you didn't see anyone suspicious?"

Elsa's pen tapped lightly next to me. I rubbed at my eyes, sandy and stinging from lack of sleep. Every time I started to drift off, those black figures swooped in on Verity and she screamed, over and over again, while I stood doing nothing, too small and too scared to stop them. My head pounded from the effort of not crying in front of Kowalski. The cut across my palm was pulling painfully. My chair was hard and seriously uncomfortable. They'd probably done it on purpose.

The walls were plain cinder block, except for the mirror behind Kowalski, leaving me nothing to look at but my own reflection, particularly the hideous yellow and purple bruise at my temple and the circles under my eyes. I was used to looking pretty average. Not gorgeous, not horrifying, just moderately nice. Presentable, my mom would say. But I was really something to look at now, in the same way people stared at pileups on the expressway. I was the beauty equivalent of gapers' block.

"Mo?" Kowalski prompted. "Someone didn't fit?"

"This is a waste of time!" I slammed the book of mug shots closed, anger sweeping through me, clean and sharp-edged. This wasn't me, this girl who lied and stole and shouted. I'd been raised to keep my voice down and do what was expected. But this new girl . . . she'd gotten answers when the old Mo would have gotten only a pat on the head. And I was starting to hope the new girl would stick around, at least for a while. She was the friend Verity had deserved. "No! For the zillionth time, no! Everything was perfectly ordinary. Why won't you listen to me?"

Elsa leaned forward, interjecting smoothly, "My client has already answered this line of questions, Detective. Find a new one or we walk out right now."

Kowalski drained his coffee cup. He started to straighten the papers in front of him, like he was wrapping up, and the tension in my shoulders eased a little at the thought of escape.

"Did Verity know your uncle?"

Beside me, Elsa went still.

"Of course." Verity and Uncle Billy had crossed paths plenty over the years. He was a fixture in the neighborhood and in our church. It would have been strange if they *hadn't* known each other.

"And your families got along okay?"

I made a little noise of impatience, and Elsa gave me a slight frown. I ignored her. "They got along fine. Look, I get it, okay? You don't like my uncle. You'd like nothing better than to connect this to him. But you're wrong. Whoever killed Verity has nothing to do with my family."

"Who did, then? If you have a theory, Mo, or you know something, I'd love to hear it. Really."

"We're done." Elsa pushed back from the table. "We came here in good faith, Detective, to aid in your investigation— not to be badgered. Until you have some questions actually pertaining to my client, or Miss Grey's death, Mo will not be available to you."

I struggled to my feet and grabbed my purse.

Elsa steered me from the room with her hand on my shoulder, back through the dingy, dismal corridors of the station and onto the street. Her hand dropped, and she gestured toward the nearby parking garage.

"You strike me as an intelligent girl," she said as we walked. "I've been impressed with the way you've handled everything that's happened."

I looked up at her. I could no more handle what was happening than I could be one of those acrobats you see in Cirque du Soleil. It took every ounce of willpower I had to get out of bed in the morning. I alternated between a rage that made me want to smash everything around me to bits and an exhaustion that made me want to crawl under the covers for the next ten years.

"Your uncle says you're an excellent student."

"I study hard."

The start of school in a few days was one of the thoughts

sending me back under the covers. Everyone would have questions. Everyone would stare, and whisper, and the weight of it made homeschooling seem pretty appealing.

"I didn't interfere with Kowalski's questioning today, Mo, because I wanted to see where he'd go. Now he's showed his hand, so we need to set some rules."

Oh, excellent. Just what I needed.

We turned into the parking garage, me stumbling to match Elsa's short-but-purposeful stride. "Three simple rules. One, you don't talk to Kowalski, or anyone else from the department, without me. At all. If they want to know which way to Michigan Avenue, you call me. They want to know your dog's name, you call me."

I considered pointing out I didn't have a dog, but Elsa's face had taken on a diamond-hard, all-business look. She continued. "They want to talk about the weather . . ."

"I call you. Got it."

"Rule number two. When we are in an interview, keep your answers short. Yes, no, dates, times. You answer *only* the questions he asks."

"I did!"

"You argued. You defended your uncle. You questioned the progress of the case. That's not your job, it's mine. I'm better at it than you are, and your uncle pays me very, very well to do it, so let me."

We stopped in front of a gleaming black Mercedes, and Elsa pulled out the keys from her Hermès purse. She wasn't kidding about her rates.

"But Uncle Billy didn't *do* anything. And how am I supposed to find out what happened to Verity if I don't ask, and Kowalski's being such a dumb-ass?"

She smiled thinly as she opened her door and gestured for me to get in. "Kowalski's not a dumb-ass. He's a seasoned investigator who is, in this case, on the wrong track. If you want him to get back on the right one, you need to make sure your answers point him there."

"You mean lie." I snapped my seat belt in place and tried to look innocent.

"It's not lying if it helps them find Verity's killer."

I didn't know what the right direction was. All I had was a hunch, about the connection between Luc, Evangeline, and Verity's trip to Louisiana. And a stupid snow globe.

Elsa gave me a fake chummy smile, the one adults use to show that they're really, truly, on your side. It is a look beloved by guidance counselors everywhere, and it worked about as well as it usually did, which is to say not at all. She pulled out of the garage and onto the street. "I know you've said there was nothing unusual going on when Verity came home, and that you don't remember anything further about the attack. But if there was something . . ."

"There isn't," I said, sliding down into the buttery leather seat.

I could have told her about Luc, I guess. He was my one solid link, the part of the mystery that had followed Verity home. He'd made it clear he wasn't interested in helping me, and Elsa was *supposed* to be on my side. And yet something held me back. Maybe it was because Luc, for all his evasiveness, seemed to actually care about Verity, and Elsa had never met her. Or maybe it was because I was tired of doing what I was told. Whatever the reason, I stayed quiet as we crossed over I-57, the traffic below us already starting to snarl as rush hour approached.

Elsa sighed. "All I'm saying is, if there was, telling the police could nudge them in the right direction, and help them solve the case. Isn't that what you want?"

I don't think she meant to be patronizing, but she made it sound like I was a little kid who wouldn't eat her lima beans. Of course I wanted them to solve the case—but for Verity's sake, not Uncle Billy's. He could handle himself, especially with Elsa on the payroll. "So that's the third rule? Tell them what I remember? I mean, *if* I remember?"

Elsa's encouraging smile disappeared. "No. The third rule is, don't lie to me. Lies mean surprises, usually at the worst possible moment. I can handle the police if there's something you don't want them to know, but it's important for us to control the situation. It's all about who's controlling the information.

"Play straight with me and I will do everything I can to help you. Tell me a story, and we're done. I told your uncle as much when I agreed to handle your case personally. I'll kick you down to one of our new hires, some kid who barely passed his bar exam last week. You don't want that, Mo. You want me on your side."

I considered it a victory when I didn't gulp audibly. Did stealing the snow globe qualify as a lie? No one had questioned me about it; no one had asked if I'd turned to theft recently. And since they hadn't asked, I hadn't lied. It was a technicality, sure, but weren't lawyers supposed to appreciate that sort of thing?

Elsa drove like she did everything else—quickly, decisively, and aggressively. My fingers tightened on the door handle. Other drivers seemed to sense it, too, scooting out of the way as she slid up behind them. Cyclists, normally so aggressive they seemed suicidal, veered toward the curb and waited for us to pass.

"I don't understand why he's so fixated on Uncle Billy." Thanks to my father, we were used to police attention. We were practically on a first-name basis with the IRS. But this was different. It went beyond rumors and harassment. Any moron could see Verity's death had nothing to do with my dad or the Outfit, but Kowalski would rather nurse a grudge than look for the truth. The unfairness of it made me want to kick something.

Elsa said nothing, a perfect example of her own advice.

Dread started to unfurl, a few sticky black tendrils in my stomach, and I forced them away. "Uncle Billy hasn't done anything wrong, has he?"

She changed lanes. "Detective Kowalski suffers from an acute case of tunnel vision where your uncle is concerned."

She hadn't answered my question, and I was about to say so when she glanced over. "You want answers, and I can get them for you, but not if Kowalski stays focused on you and your uncle. The best thing you can do—for your friend, and everyone else—is to follow the rules." She careened into a space in front of The Slice is Right, tires protesting. "Are we clear?"

"Absolutely."

"Excellent. I'll be in touch." My feet had barely hit the pavement before she roared back into traffic.

Uncle Billy's bar, Black Morgan's, stood next door to the diner. It was possible, if you were so inclined, to start your day at The Slice, at five in the morning, and finish it at Morgan's, twenty-three hours later, without ever setting foot outside. A door in the back storeroom connected them. I'd grown up running between the two, studying wherever it was quieter, grabbing food from whichever kitchen was open, playing in the back room or visiting the regulars in their usual booths. I'd been waiting tables at The Slice since I could see over the counter. It wasn't always my choice, it was embarrassing when kids from school came in, and I hated having to work the early shift on my summer vacations, but The Slice and Morgan's were as much my home as our orange brick bungalow.

I pulled open the tall, narrow black door to Morgan's, the brass handle cool against my palm. Inside, air-conditioned darkness carried the scent of tobacco and whiskey that had seeped into the ebony paneling over the years. The wooden blinds on either side of the doorway were closed, pinpricks of sunlight leaking through and scattering across the worn oak floor.

Threadbare towel in hand, Charlie, the bartender, wiped down the bar, skirting around the few figures hunched over their mugs and bottles. It was a slow time, too late for lunch, too early for the guys finishing their shifts at the nearby factories, and he used the lull to prepare, setting out fresh bowls of peanuts and pretzels, lining up the glasses near the tap. In the farthest booth, all the way in the back, Uncle Billy held court with a cup of coffee and a neatly folded *Tribune*, waiting for my report on the meeting.

"Something cold to drink, Mo? It's hotter than hell out there." Charlie's broad, homely face lit up when he smiled at me, and he wiped his hands on the white apron straining across his middle. He'd already filled a glass with ice.

I wasn't really thirsty, but taking out my day on Charlie would be like kicking a puppy. "Diet Coke?"

He garnished it with three cherries, as he had since I was a kid. "Here you go, honey. How you doin'?"

I shrugged. "How are you doing?" was rapidly becoming my least favorite question. I heard it, or one of its variations, a million times a day.

"Okay. Uncle Billy wanted me to check in." I tilted my head toward the back.

Charlie's glance flickered to a guy at the other end of the bar. He was as nondescript as any of the other customers, solitary and silent. A mug and a battered paperback sat in front of him.

"Sure, kiddo," Charlie said. "We'll catch up later."

Taking my glass with me, I made my way toward the back. To my surprise, Verity's dad was already there. "Anything you can do," he said, his voice hoarse. "My wife and I . . . we just can't . . ."

Uncle Billy stood, clasping Mr. Grey's hand. "Of course," he said. "She was a lovely girl, and it's a sin they haven't done more. Give my love to Patty and Constance."

I halted as Mr. Grey passed me in the narrow passageway. "Mo . . ." he said, trailing off.

I waited for him to say more, but instead he touched my shoulder for an instant before shuffling out. He looked gaunt and colorless, like a newspaper left in the rain. My throat ached at the sight.

"Sit down, Mo," Uncle Billy said, his voice commanding but kind. "The living carry a greater burden, don't they?"

I brushed at my eyes. "What did Mr. Grey want?"

"Peace," he said after a moment. "And it will be a long time coming, no doubt. Now, how was your interview?"

"I couldn't ID anyone." I sipped from my glass. "It seemed kind of pointless. Kowalski asked a bunch of questions and ignored my answers."

"Questions about me, I'm guessing."

"Yes. Elsa stopped it, though."

"I'm certain she did," he said with a satisfied grin.

"It's like they don't care about who killed Verity." I hadn't meant to say it, but it slipped out anyway.

He waved a hand, unconcerned. "Elsa will get them moving in the right direction, love. She'll take good care of you."

I didn't really need taking care of, but it seemed ungrateful to say so. Besides, it had never stopped Uncle Billy before.

"I want them to get whoever did it."

He nodded. "You want justice. It's a hard thing, though, to stay focused on justice and not seek revenge in its place."

"There's a difference?"

"Justice is about making them pay for Verity's pain. Revenge is making them pay for yours."

"I want both."

"Of course you do. But you need to let others handle it." The compassion in his voice was tempered with firmness.

God, I was tired of people telling me how careful I needed to be. There'd been too much change—Verity's death, Kowalski's prying, Luc's evasiveness—careful and quiet didn't fit me anymore. It was unsettling. Lonely, too. I'd spent seventeen years quietly following every rule in the book. And it had turned out okay, mostly. But Verity's death had cracked my life in two—before and after—and now nothing worked the way it was supposed to. The problem was, the only person who seemed to recognize it was Luc, and he still didn't want to help me.

"Your mother's worried about you."

"She's *always* worried," I said dismissively. "You know how she is."

"Circumstances alter cases, Mo. In this case, I agree with her."

This was new. And unwelcome. "Why?"

He ticked off the points on his fingertips. "You're the only witness to Verity's murder. You've been seen talking to the police, which makes you a liability. And while you are a darling girl, you're not particularly well equipped to defend yourself. Whoever killed Verity nearly killed you as well. Who's to say they won't try to finish the job?"

The air-conditioning raised sudden goose bumps on my arms. "That's crazy. Nobody cares about me."

"I do. Your mother does."

"I mean nobody . . ." I gestured helplessly. "Nobody bad."

"It's common sense. I made a promise to your parents and I'll not go back on my word, Mo. Whether you like it or not, I have an obligation to protect you." He raised a hand, beckoned toward the counter for a fresh cup of coffee.

"Protect me how?" I set my glass down and folded my arms across my chest.

The guy from the bar appeared silently at Uncle Billy's side, his expression cool and steady. He nodded at me once, and turned to my uncle. Seeing him face-to-face, I knew, absolutely, he wasn't just a regular customer. He was a complication. A big one.

"Mo, meet Colin Donnelly. Your bodyguard."

CHAPTER 7

"Close your mouth, Mo. Something will fly in there."
I pressed my lips together and glared at Uncle Billy, at the guy, and back at my uncle again.

"For your own protection," he said soothingly.

I slumped down, unimpressed. I'd barely noticed the guy when I came in. If he was going to protect me, he could at least bother to look intimidating instead of bored. Handsome, in a rough, hardened way, but definitely bored, with a hint of cranky. His light brown hair was cut close, and his eyes, dark and hard, took my measure and seemed to find me insignificant. Even in the heat, he wore cargo pants and a white cotton shirt, untucked, with the sleeves rolled up.

"I don't need protection. I'm starting school again. What's he going to do, follow me around St. Brigid's? He looks a little old for AP Chem." I narrowed my eyes. College chem, or even grad school, maybe. But something in the way he stood, watchful and perfectly still, told me he'd learned from experience, not books.

I studied him, the carved look of the muscles in his forearms and the way the shirt strained slightly across his shoulders. His hands were large and capable looking, nicked and scarred. He met my eyes, and my cheeks heated. Maybe I'd underestimated him.

Uncle Billy nodded. "You can go about your normal life, Mo. He'll take you to school and work, drive you home, and keep an eye on you until you're tucked in for the night."

The blush spread. "Nobody's tucked me in for years."

"Regardless. It's just for when you're out and about. Maybe if you'd had Donnelly with you . . ." He didn't finish the sentence, and I didn't correct him, even though my fingers clenched the glass until my knuckles turned white.

"This is silly," I said. My voice sounded desperate, even to my own ears. "Nobody's after me. It's a waste of time and money. Everyone's going to notice him! How do I explain it to people at school?"

"You don't. Hold your head up and go about your business." He eyed me with the same calculating look he used on horses at the track. "Your name might be Fitzgerald, but you're a Grady underneath, and we don't explain." He was getting the look, the one that sent braver souls than me running for cover.

"What about my privacy? I don't want someone following me—"

"Enough." Uncle Billy slapped his open hand on the table, making the silverware jump and his coffee cup rattle in its saucer. "Your mother is terrified, Maura Kathleen, and you disappearing at the funeral was the last straw. I won't allow my sister to spend her days waiting for the call to come and identify what is left of your body. Until I say otherwise, Donnelly is watching out for you. Not another word on the matter."

Something was off. Uncle Billy was controlling, but this seemed a little over-the-top, even for him. My uncle was used to my mom's overreactions. But he usually talked her down, reassured her—which is the only way I'd been able to go to junior prom last year. If Uncle Billy was hiring someone to watch me, it wasn't because my mom was worried. He had reasons of his own. And I'd bet a summer's worth of tips he wouldn't tell me.

Throughout Uncle Billy's tirade, Colin stood, hands behind his back, eyes fixed on the table between us.

"Now. Shake hands and say hello like the polite young lady you were raised to be."

I was nearly vibrating with fury and humiliation. How dare he treat me like a five-year-old in front of this guy. But I stuck out my hand, and Colin took it for an instant. His skin rasped against mine, calloused and rough. The contact was over before I finished stammering, "Nice to meet you."

"Likewise." The slightest grimace ghosted the corner of his mouth, and it hit me—Colin no more wanted to guard me than I wanted to be guarded. No doubt watching out for a Catholic schoolgirl from the South Side ranked pretty low on the bodyguard totem pole.

I slid out of the booth. "I need to go," I said. "Errands."

"We'll take my truck," said Colin.

"They're close. I can walk."

He shrugged. "*We* can walk."

Uncle Billy stood and gave me a hug and quick kiss on the cheek, his way of letting me know the storm was over. "It's for the best, love," he whispered.

Outside, the heat and light slammed into me like a wall, but I didn't slow down.

Colin kept pace with me, wordlessly.

"I don't need a babysitter," I tossed out as we passed the dry cleaner's on the corner.

"And I don't need the attitude. Listen, kid, I'm not here to make you miserable. Go to the mall, get your nails done, spend six bucks on a cup of coffee, whatever it is you do. I'll stay out of the way. You won't even know I'm there."

Right. Nobody would notice the hot guy with the permanent scowl following my every move. Business as usual.

"I don't go to the mall," I snapped. "And you don't get to call me kid. How old are you, anyway? Twenty-two?"

"Old enough to know it's pointless arguing with your uncle about this. In case you haven't noticed, Billy tends to get what he wants."

"And what I want doesn't matter."

"Depends on what you want, I guess." He glanced behind us as we walked. "Seems like personal safety should be pretty high on your list right now."

Should be, but wasn't. Finding Verity's killers was the highest thing on the list. Everything else was a very, very distant second. I didn't bother to explain that to Colin, though. "And for the record? I don't drink lattes. Or get my nails done."

Colin looked at me for a moment before nodding. It struck me that the people I seemed to be spending the most time with lately were either family or on Uncle Billy's payroll. The thought made me feel even more sullen.

"So this is what you do?" I asked, injecting as much condescension into my voice as I could manage. "Play bodyguard?"

He stepped in front of me, blocking my path, and walked slowly toward me, face darkening. I took an involuntary step back, and another. And another. He kept coming until I was pressed against the wall of the auto parts shop. "I'm not playing. You might be a smart-ass kid, but your uncle's worried about you. Do you really think he'd hire someone who was only playing?"

I swallowed and stared at the collar of his shirt, the pulse beating at his throat. If I'd thought before that he was harmless or average, clearly I was delusional, or he was a hell of a poker player. He zeroed in on me with an intensity that made me forget how to breathe. A spark of fear, and something else, ignited in my chest.

"No."

"Damn straight." He stepped back, and I gulped down air. He gestured toward the bank. "After you."

We started off again, and I discreetly wiped my damp palms on my skirt.

"I work construction for your uncle," he said after a minute, easy and conversational. "Carpentry. When I'm not babysitting."

I tried to match his tone. "Which one is your real job?"

"Whichever one pays the bills at the end of the month." He shrugged a little. "Your uncle's been good to me. He needed help, and I was happy to step up."

Yeah. He seemed thrilled. I wanted to ask how, precisely, Uncle Billy had been good to him, but we'd arrived at the bank. He waved me toward the ATM line. "See you when you're done."

I waited my turn in line, sneaking glances at Colin every now and then. He leaned against a nearby bus shelter, holding an open copy of the *Sun-Times* as his eyes swept the street, pretty much nonstop. I could almost feel his gaze slide over me, but he never made eye contact. I had to admit it—he was unobtrusive.

He followed me through the grocery store but stayed far enough back that I only spotted him when I really looked. By the time I was done, he was already outside again, reading the sports section.

"Here." I thrust the heaviest of the bags at him.

"Not in my job description."

"I can't carry all of them," I said. "If someone tries to kill me, I give you permission to drop the bag."

He snorted. "We done yet?"

I nodded.

"Back to the truck." He jerked his head toward the diner, and I went, handing him two bags as I did.

I'm pretty sure I managed to keep the smirk off my face, at

least until he couldn't see me. For a moment, it felt as if light had broken through the sticky layers of grief and anger suffocating me, like I was a normal girl, joking with a cute boy on a summer afternoon. And then the light vanished, because how could I feel that way with Verity gone?

Colin walked next to me the entire way back to the diner, silent and watchful. He was a problem. How could I track down Verity's killers if he was always two feet away? He'd tell my uncle, and then I wouldn't need a bodyguard, because I'd be locked in my room. Yeah, definitely a problem.

We arrived at the truck, a dented and rusting red Ford, and Colin dumped the groceries in the back, next to a gleaming steel toolbox with a lock the size of my fist. Whatever Uncle Billy was paying him, it wasn't in the same league as Elsa. Apparently keeping me out of jail was more important than keeping me alive. It was a bitchy thing to think, much less say, so I pressed my lips together and clambered into the cab. It was smaller than I expected, and the bench seat was covered with gray cloth. The interior smelled like coffee and wood shavings. On the seat lay a battered copy of a Steinbeck novel.

Colin climbed in a moment later and angled forward, pulling a gun out from the small of his back, under his shirt.

For the second time since I'd met him, my jaw dropped. He did something to the handle of the gun and tucked it into the glove compartment. Settling back in his seat, he put the key into the ignition and pinned me with eyes so dark they looked like obsidian.

"Don't. Touch," he growled. "Got it?"

I very carefully didn't move.

"I'll take that as a yes." He started the truck.

"You have a gun?" Stupid question. It was sitting six inches away from me on the other side of a flimsy piece of plastic. I pressed farther back into the seat. He didn't answer.

"Does my uncle know?" His look clearly implied that if I were this dumb, it might be better to let the bad guys get me.

"Of course he does," I said, answering my own question. "Handguns are illegal in the city, you know."

Colin took a deep breath and gripped the steering wheel, no doubt to keep from strangling me. I tried again. "Guns are dangerous."

"That's the point. It'll be better if you don't mention this to your mom."

"You think?" I snarked. "You know how to use it, right?"

"I've got a pretty good idea." He twisted the key in the ignition, a little more forcefully than necessary.

"Have you ever shot anyone?"

A muscle in his jaw jumped. He didn't answer, which was not comforting. Then again, a gun might be handy when I found Verity's killers. For protection.

I eyed the glove compartment. "Will you teach me how to shoot it?"

"No."

"If people are after me, I should be able to defend myself."

"No."

"But I—"

"Mo." We stopped at a light and he glanced over at me. "If someone gets close enough that you need a gun to defend yourself, they will have gotten past me. And if they've gotten past me, a gun isn't going to help you." His expression was serious but not worried, as if something like that occurring were an impossibility.

The thing was, I'd seen enough impossibilities recently to not feel reassured. The light changed, and he turned instead of going straight.

"You're going the wrong way," I said. "It's faster to take Western to 91st."

He checked the mirrors. "I know."

"Aren't we going home?" I was kind of eager to escape all the coiled-up tension in the car.

"We're taking a different route."

"Why?"

"You take the same way home every day, don't you?"

"I take the bus. I'm kind of stuck."

"You're done with the bus," he said. "And we're going to vary your routes, keep your movements unpredictable."

"You don't know me very well, do you?" I was pretty much the definition of predictable—or I had been, anyway.

"Nope." He smiled thinly as we pulled up in front of the house. "But I'm going to."

I reached for the door handle, unsure how to respond. "Thanks for the ride," I said, when it looked like he was getting out. "I can get the groceries in."

"I need to see the house," he replied.

This guy? In my house? The thought made me panicky. Had I left any underwear out? Bras drying on the shower rod? That issue of *Cosmo* with the article about seven ways to drive your man wild?

Colin pulled the gun out of the glove compartment and tucked it under his shirt again. He wore some kind of holster, the black leather at the small of his back flashing into view momentarily.

"Keys?" He brushed past me toward the front steps.

I pulled the jumble of keys out of my bag, and he plucked them out of my hand.

"Who else has a set?" He ignored my squeak of protest as he let himself in.

"Me. Mom. Uncle Billy, probably." I paused. "Verity."

He looked around, his body blocking my view of the living room. "New locks. Alarm system," he muttered as he prowled through the house. "Exits?"

"Well, the front door. You came in there, so you knew that

one, obviously. . . ." I trailed off as he turned to me and frowned, making a "get-on-with-it" motion with his hand. "There's a back door through the kitchen. We don't need an alarm system. We barely have anything worth stealing."

"You want me to move in?"

My toe caught on the faded Oriental rug. "No!"

"Then you're getting an alarm." He continued his tour through the house as if I wasn't there, examining windows and shaking his head in obvious disappointment.

I tried to see my home through his eyes, an unsettling feeling. I'd lived here since I was born. The rooms were so familiar I could walk through them in the dark without banging into the furniture—quite a feat for a klutz like me. I didn't even see it anymore, really. Nothing here ever changed. I trailed behind him and fingered the hairline crack in one of the windows.

The house was clean, of course. My mom was hell on dust bunnies. School pictures of me were lined up precisely above the fireplace we never used. They never varied—school uniform, brown hair held back in a ponytail or headband, the fake smile and slight head tilt everyone does. There was only one of my father, pushed toward the back. In it, he held me on his lap as we went down a slide at the park. I was about three, and my expression was half terror, half glee.

Colin glanced at the pictures briefly, then back at me. "Your old man?"

I nodded. He looked again, more closely. "You look like him, a little. Same eyes."

That's where the similarity ended, I wanted to assure him. But he'd moved on already, and I tilted the picture toward me, seeing it for the first time in years. My face was toddler round, my eyes scrunched up, but my dad's were perfectly visible, hazel colored and wide set. I'd never spotted the resemblance before.

Our couch had seen better days, the worn spots on the

faded blue brocade carefully hidden by my great-grandmother's needlepoint pillows and the neatly folded yellow afghan my mother knitted when I was a baby.

Along one wall were bookshelves filled with ancient encyclopedias, books about Ireland, back issues of *National Geographic*, and cookbooks galore, crowding around the TV. Potted plants and African violets were tucked in at careful in tervals.

It was all ruthlessly neat and just this side of shabby, and I wondered what Colin thought of it. His careful inventory of the house seemed to note every detail—nothing escaped his attention—but other than his comment about the picture, he had no outward reaction.

He walked back to the kitchen, taking in the Formica counters so thoroughly scrubbed they'd lost their shine, the cross-stitch sampler hanging over the kitchen table, and the small font of holy water next to the back door.

"Do you want something to drink?" I asked, moving to the fridge. "We've got water, lemonade . . . iced tea . . . milk? Diet Coke?"

He shook his head no and continued prowling the room. He stepped out the back door onto the screened porch, with its ancient wicker furniture and porch swing. It was my favorite place in the house. The ceiling was sky blue, the floor a glossy green. Verity and I had painted it ourselves the summer before high school. Even with just a single box fan instead of air-conditioning, it was cool and restful. I could still see Verity there, stretched out across the swing, one leg hooked over the back of the seat and the other rocking her gently. She'd be reading the latest issue of *People*, dissecting celebrity haircuts and which former child star had publicly melted down this week. The pain was so sudden and fierce I had to grab the door frame for support, fighting to get the tears under control.

After a few minutes, Colin returned.

"Your room upstairs?" Without waiting for an answer, he headed for the staircase.

I let go of the door. "Yes. But . . . wait. Can you wait a minute?"

"A minute," he said, but I was already dashing past him, my sandals slapping against the wood.

I flung open the door. For seventeen years, my mother had warned me to keep my room picked up in case someone dropped by, and I'd ignored her. Now, as she predicted, my room looked like a tornado had hit.

I scooped up armfuls of clothing and shoved them into my closet, not caring if they were dirty or clean, then leaned against the closet door until it finally clicked shut. I kicked the incriminating pile of *Cosmo* and *Teen Vogue* under my bed, swept all of the makeup and hair doodads and zit cream into an open drawer with my good arm, and hastily tugged up my pink and green quilt.

"Mo!" Colin called. "Jesus, kid. Are you repainting up there?" His feet were heavy on the stairs.

"Just a second!" On my nightstand was Bogart, my childhood teddy bear with the fur rubbed off and one eye missing. No wonder he thought I was a kid. With a silent apology, I stuffed poor Bogart behind my pillow and settled back on the bed, trying to look nonchalant.

Colin filled up the doorway, and when he stepped into the room, everything looked small and toylike. The white and gilt bedroom set that had been my mom's seemed spindly and flimsy next to his solid, masculine presence.

He checked the window latch, studying the view.

"You sneak out a lot?"

"What? No!" For once, I was telling the truth.

"Let's keep it that way. Give me your cell." He stretched out a hand toward me expectantly.

So much for a getting-to-know-you chat. I sighed. The first

nonrelated guy in my bedroom in seventeen years, and all I wanted was for him to leave.

He flipped open the phone and started keying in numbers. "What time do you leave for school?"

"Quarter to seven." I anticipated his next question. "I get out at three, but there's usually stuff going on afterward. It's kind of unpredictable."

He frowned at the phone and shrugged. "Fine. I'll be at the school at three. Don't leave the building until you see me. Anything changes, you call." He turned the phone to face me. "See? Speed dial one."

"That was—" *Verity.* I shut my mouth with an audible snap.

How could it be so easy to erase her? I sank back down on the bed, my breath wheezing in my chest.

Colin held the phone out, but I waved at the desk and kept my face turned away from him.

I didn't need to bother hiding my reaction, though. He continued to ignore me, studying the room. "Anything changes, you call. Anything weird, you call. If there's trouble, if you need help—"

"I get it. What if you're on a job, though?"

He finally looked at me. "You *are* my job."

"What about—"

"I'll go back to building when we decide you're safe."

"Well, I've decided."

He chuckled, the sound low and warm. "Not for you to decide, kid."

Okay, *enough*. "Stop calling me kid!" He was infuriating—the phone, and the porch, how he hadn't even noticed how special it was, and the way he thought he could just decide for me what was safe and what wasn't. Like I didn't have enough people in my life doing that already? But explaining would take energy I didn't have. The stupid nickname was easier to fight over. Besides, nothing about my life these days was remotely childlike.

He paused, looked at me squarely. "Sorry."

It seemed genuine, but I didn't feel any better. The problem wasn't just that having a babysitter—even one like Colin, all dangerous, capable, and easy on the eyes—was a totally humiliating way to start senior year. Finding out who killed Verity was going to be almost impossible without tipping him off, and he'd turn around and tell Uncle Billy.

"So you're supposed to tell my uncle everything I do, huh?" I fiddled with the walnut jewelry box on my dresser, neatening the trinkets cluttering the top. It was an effort not to stare at the hamper, where I'd buried the snow globe.

"I'm supposed to protect you."

"So the spying's a bonus?"

"Are you trying to hide something?"

The opposite, actually. I'm trying to find something. I turned and gave Colin my best Sunday smile, dutiful and bland and a credit to my mother. "Do I look like my life is superinteresting? Up until last week, I had a very boring life." I paused, thinking back to my perfectly uneventful summer. "I miss it."

The collage on the wall, a gift from Verity for my sixteenth birthday, caught his gaze. He studied it with the same intensity he did everything else. I was relieved to have his focus off me. It was easier to breathe.

"I'm sorry about your friend," he said.

"Do you think the police will find her killers?"

His eyes held mine for a moment more, and then broke away, taking in the room. He hesitated for a moment, looking back at the collage. There was a picture of Verity and me at one of our Friday sleepovers, hair and makeup to the nines, wearing ratty T-shirts and flannel pajama pants. Verity vamped for the camera, cheeks sucked in, lips in a pinup girl pout, eyes laughing at the ridiculousness of it all. We were twelve, maybe thirteen, and behind the goofiness, Verity was already showing hints of how gorgeous she'd be in a few years. I held the same pose, and looked like a little girl playing dress-up.

"They'll try," he said. "Your uncle's working on it."

I started to ask about Uncle Billy, about why everyone was falling over themselves to prove he wasn't involved when the idea was ludicrous to begin with. Then I thought better of it and concentrated on untangling the chain of a necklace.

"Do you have a boyfriend?" he asked.

I dropped the jewelry. "No. I mean, I've *had* boyfriends. Dates, anyway. I'm not a nun. But they weren't serious, either." I was babbling. Colin raised an eyebrow and watched, eyes dark and amused. "I'm not really good at that sort of thing. Dating. And high school boys are . . . well, you were one, right? You know what they're like. They're . . ."

He held up his hand. "No was enough."

"Oh."

He checked the room one last time and headed out toward the landing. I trailed after him.

"School stuff, the diner. Newspaper stuff," he said over his shoulder. "Anything else you're up to?"

I swallowed and studied the line where the baseboard met the wall. "Nope. Very boring. How about you? Babysitting, carpentry, anything else? Girlfriend?"

He jiggled the latch on the bathroom window and started back down the stairs. The inspection was over. "No."

"You don't have to stick around, you know. I'm not going anywhere tonight."

His eyes, iron gray, crinkled a tiny bit at the corners. "You trying to get rid of me? Until the alarm's installed, I stay here. You want me in the truck or the living room?"

"Truck," I said. Nothing good could come from him staying that close by. The idea made my stomach pitch. "Definitely the truck."

"Okay. See you in the morning."

I stared as he jogged down the wide cement steps and back to the truck. He seemed to settle in, leaning the seat back and pulling out the Steinbeck I'd seen earlier.

Great. It was enough to make a girl claustrophobic.

I went back to my room. Colin's truck was directly in front of my window, and as I peered out, he raised one hand in greeting, his eyes never seeming to move from the book.

If he was watching the front, I reasoned, he couldn't see the back. I'd avoided the porch since the attack. It was too hard, and too lonely, and increased my mother's opportunities to hover. It wasn't a refuge anymore, but a grim reminder. I stepped onto the worn floorboards anyway, careful not to look at the jumble of magazines and memories scattered around the room. After easing the screen door shut behind me, I slipped into the alley behind our house, not even sure where I was headed. All I wanted was to be out of Colin's view and away from all the ghosts in my house.

My feet had barely touched the street when my cell rang, unnaturally loud in the still, humid afternoon.

"Hello?"

"Tell me again how you're not trying to get rid of me?" Colin's voice seemed more amused than irritated. Which was fine. I was irritated enough for both of us.

"How did you . . ."

"Next time, pull the shades first. Better yet, let's not have a next time."

Yeah. Colin was going to be a problem.

CHAPTER 8

Stomping past Colin to my bedroom and slamming the door was very satisfying—for all of five seconds. Then I realized I was stuck in my room for the rest of the night. There was nothing to do but study Verity's snow globe.

Under the light of my desk lamp, the dome was perfectly smooth—no seams where it had been cut open, no holes near the base where the water had been drained out and refilled. I shook it again. It must have had snow once, right?

So many secrets. So many lies. I'd always thought there was a difference between the two, but now they seemed to blur into each other. Why hadn't Verity told me the truth about New Orleans? It was clear she'd only been giving me the tourist's version. And the grinning, sloppily painted harlequin wasn't ready to give me any answers.

I could hear my mother as she came up the stairs, her voice cheerful on the surface, but more clipped than usual.

"Mo? Are you up here?"

I shoved the snow globe into my bag. Mom opened the door, not bothering to knock. She was still wearing her usual workday outfit, a knee-length khaki skirt, a cotton blouse sprigged with blue and white flowers, sensible Aerosoles flats. She'd worked the early shift and come home in time to check my homework and start dinner for as long as I could remember. I wasn't sure when the pattern had changed from routine to suffocating.

"We have a guest."

"He's not a guest. He works for Uncle Billy."

Her mouth thinned. "That young man is here as a favor to me. Which makes him a guest."

With my foot, I nudged the bag farther under the desk. I considered pointing out that a favor wasn't something you typically paid for, but it wasn't worth the fight. When it came to my mom, not many things were.

Smoothing the covers of my bed, she removed Bogart from behind the pillows where I'd jammed him. She placed him front and center with a satisfied pat. "I'm glad that's settled. Billy said the police station went well?"

Of course she'd check with him instead of me. "The lawyer seems smart. I couldn't ID anyone, though. What if they don't find the people who did this?"

"They will," she said firmly. "And we'll put this whole thing behind us."

Was I the only one who didn't *want* to put Verity's death behind me? It seemed like abandoning her all over again.

She nodded toward the stairs expectantly. "Our guest?"

Sighing, I followed her down. Colin stood as we entered the kitchen. "I can wait outside, Mrs. Fitzgerald. Sorry for the surprise."

"Don't be silly! We haven't even fed you," she said, trying to wrap her head around the idea of a visitor who didn't stay for dinner. She made a show of peering around the meticulously organized fridge. "I don't have much on hand . . . cinnamon rolls? I made them yesterday, but they're still fresh."

Colin dropped back into his chair. "I don't know if I've ever had them from scratch."

It was the perfect thing to say. He even managed to sound sincere underneath the gruffness. My mom beamed and set them in the microwave to warm, then put on a fresh pot of coffee. As she plated the rolls on the plain white stoneware, the scent of cinnamon and buttery dough filled the room. "Mo? Are you joining us?"

I didn't really want to. My mom had gone into a baking frenzy since we'd come home from the hospital, but even my favorites—the cinnamon rolls, her special brown bread, the lemon bars—didn't taste right. I wasn't in the mood for a lecture about keeping my strength up, though, so I stayed.

When the microwave beeped, I set Colin's plate down with a clatter and slipped into my seat, determined not to talk.

He took a bite, and a second later his eyes widened. "I am never buying those rolls in a tube again."

Mom patted his shoulder, completely won over. "It makes a difference, doesn't it?"

I stood to pour a cup of coffee for myself, but she waved me back. "Milk for you, sweetie. Too much caffeine, especially this close to bedtime . . . that can't be good for you."

"It's four o'clock," I muttered, feeling my cheeks turn scarlet.

Colin's mouth turned up for a split second, his eyes gleaming with what had to be a repressed snicker.

"Better for your bones," she returned, and I wanted to sink under the table. She might as well have offered to put the milk in a sippy cup and cut up my food for me. "You two chat while I start dinner. Colin, you'll eat with us?"

I scowled at him, and he gave a tiny, nearly imperceptible shrug. "As long as it's not a problem. Thanks."

She pulled a container of chicken, leftover from last night, out of the fridge. "No bother at all! Besides, it will give us a chance to get to know each other better."

Colin's gleam disappeared, and now it was my turn to smile. I took a small bite of the roll, letting the icing dissolve on my tongue while he shifted in his seat.

"It's just chicken salad, nothing fancy. Mo, honey, can you toast some bread?" I pulled a loaf from the bread box and started feeding slices into the toaster as she continued. "I hate to turn on the oven every night, with the weather so hot. Do you cook much?"

"A little."

"Don't tell me you're one of those men who live on frozen lasagna and takeout!"

"There's a good pizza place near me."

Mom shook her head, intent on cutting up celery and grapes. "Well, you're always welcome here. It's the least we can do. I haven't seen you at St. Brigid's. Do you attend a different parish?"

"I'm near St. Arden's," he replied, carefully scraping up the remaining frosting. This was not, I noticed, the same thing as saying he *attended* St. Arden's, but my mom seemed satisfied.

"Oh, did you grow up there?"

"Partly." He didn't elaborate.

"My brother speaks very highly of you."

Colin ducked his head, clearly uncomfortable. "He's always talking about your cooking. I can see why."

"Oh, Billy exaggerates," Mom said, but I could see her blushing as she plucked the toast from my hands and started assembling sandwiches.

"Billy says you're a carpenter. And you've known him for how long?"

"Since I was a kid." His voice was quiet but rough, like footsteps on a stony path, and I studied his profile. Secrets and lies. I wondered what mixture Colin held.

"Well, we just can't thank you enough for taking care of

our Mo. When I think about everything that's happened, how close we came to losing my little girl. . . ." Mom wrung a dishtowel in her hands until it twisted back on itself. Smoothing it out again, she continued. "My brother has great faith in you, you know."

"I'm happy to help," Colin said. He didn't sound like he was lying, exactly, but it was pretty clear "happy" was overstating the case.

She finished securing the sandwiches with frilly, paper-topped toothpicks—for Colin's benefit, I guessed—and arranged them on a platter. "There! I think we're ready. There's some lemonade, Mo. Let's have that."

I poured the lemonade and turned, but Colin was right there. Wordlessly, he took the glasses and set them on the table.

We held hands to say grace. Colin's fingers barely pressed against mine, and I mumbled the words from memory, studying him from under half-closed lids. He kept his eyes open, but downcast, and his voice was a low, indistinct rumble.

My mother shook out her napkin and we started to eat, the kitchen falling quiet as the early-evening light coated the room like amber. After a few bites, my mom set her sandwich down, lacing her fingers tightly.

"I spoke to your father today."

I froze in the middle of reaching for a potato chip. Distantly, I heard a soft clink as Colin put down his glass, but I didn't look at him. Instead I stared at my mother's hands, red around the knuckles from all the hot water at the diner, the nails cut short and left unpolished. No jewelry except her plain gold wedding band and her engagement ring, with its tiny chip of a diamond. He'd been gone twelve years, but she wore them every day. I pushed my plate away, what little appetite I had, gone.

"He's very upset, Mo, and terribly, terribly relieved you're okay."

I folded my napkin precisely, using my thumbnail to crease the checkered cotton. "Great."

"He'd like you to visit. This weekend. To see for himself you're okay." She drew her shoulders back and turned toward Colin. "I'm sure my brother has explained our situation to you."

He dipped his head in acknowledgment, turning the lemonade glass in his hand, looking uncomfortable. Had she thought asking me in front of Colin would shame me into saying yes? She'd thought wrong.

She tried again. "He misses you. Don't you remember when we used to go and see him?"

"Kind of hard to forget." Federal prisons tend to make an impression on an eight-year-old. I broke my potato chip into jagged halves, not answering.

"It's been four years since you visited. He's only seen you in school pictures. We should go."

I kept my tone just this side of respectful—not insolent, not enthusiastic, as emotionless as I could make it. "No, thanks."

"He's your father! How you can be so cold?"

I'd stopped visiting the prison when I was in junior high. The other kids had known all about my dad, and they went after me a million different ways. My PE uniform had a habit of clogging the toilet. My lunch disappeared from my locker at least once a week. When I was student of the month, and my picture was displayed outside the office, someone kept drawing bars over my face. For a while, girls would invite Verity to sleepovers, but not me, saying they didn't want their stuff stolen. Verity turned them down, every time.

My father had made his choices, and I'd had to live with them. Refusing to visit him in prison was turnabout, kind of.

I gave my mom the coldest, blankest look I could muster, even though I was boiling underneath. "May I be excused?"

Without waiting for an answer, I dropped my plate in the sink and stalked outside. Behind me, a chair scraped, and Colin's footsteps sounded heavily on the linoleum. I thumped onto the cement steps, tugging a wilted geranium from the white-glazed pot at my feet. The door opened behind me.

"Let me guess. I'm not allowed to sit on my own porch? I don't want to be inside."

"You don't want to do a lot of things," he returned through the screen. "Move so the door doesn't hit you."

I scooted toward the edge, and he turned his body sideways, opening the flimsy screen door as little as possible. Squeezing through, he sat down, back against the white metal railing.

"Don't lecture me," I said, mortified by the quaver in my voice. "I don't care what you think."

He shrugged. "Wasn't planning on it."

He kept to his side of the stoop, leaning forward with his elbows on his knees, those large, beat-up hands dangling harmlessly. Cars were coming home from work, and you could hear people bring in their trash cans, kids playing in the alley behind us. Almost all the houses on our block were bungalows, differentiated by the yard decorations—geese in country garb, windmills, the occasional yard gnome—and the color of the brick. Ours was faded orange, with dark green trim, like living in a pumpkin.

"I'm not going to see him."

"I thought we weren't talking."

"We're not. I'm just saying, I have my reasons."

"Sounds good."

"Reverse psychology won't work, you know. It doesn't work if the person knows you're doing it."

"Mo," he said wearily, turning to face me. "I don't give a

rat's ass if you visit your dad. I really don't. It's not my business, and it's not my problem."

"What did Uncle Billy tell you about him? You said . . ."

"I didn't say anything."

He hadn't, actually. He'd kind of nodded, a little, but he'd been really careful not to answer most of my mom's questions, including that one. I wondered again what secrets he was hiding. "So you don't know anything about it?"

"Jesus," he muttered, looking skyward. "I know what your dad did. Do you?"

"I'm not *stupid*. I was only five when it happened, but I can read a newspaper. And this thing called Google? Have you heard of it? My dad laundered money for the Mob. Then he got greedy and embezzled from my uncle, too. Now he's in prison and my mother is guilt-tripping me into a visit."

He studied me for a minute. "Nice to hear you have it all figured out. Saves me some trouble."

"I am *never* trouble."

Colin snorted.

"Ask anyone. I am smart and quiet and cooperative. I have a 4.0 and perfect attendance since the sixth grade. I am, by definition, a very nice girl." Luc's words at the cemetery echoed in my head. *You're a nice girl. Go have a nice, quiet life somewhere.* Coming from him, it was a dismissal, not the praise I was accustomed to. I crumpled up the tattered blossom in my hand.

He looked back at the house. "You call that dinner cooperative?"

"You said you wouldn't lecture me."

"No lecture. Not my job to solve your daddy issues."

"I don't have daddy issues."

He looked at me, skepticism written clearly over his features.

"He's a terrible father. And husband. He wanted easy money more than he wanted us. It's not an issue, it's a fact."

"A fact that pushes your buttons. Good to know."

"Why?"

He looked away, scanning the street. "It's my job to know you."

Right. Because without the promise of a payoff, who would want to? Not Luc, who was after whatever Verity had brought back to Chicago. And not Colin, who was only interested because of my uncle. Only Verity, and she was gone. Every time I remembered that, the world seemed to come off its axis for a moment. I clutched the step beneath me until it steadied.

The evening was warm but pleasant, even if I did have to share the porch with Colin. Anything was better than being inside my house. The sun was setting, street lamps turning on, and his gaze swept across the neat rows of bungalows. Parents were calling kids inside for the night, but I didn't move.

A hot wind whipped down the street, rustling leaves and stirring my hair. Next to me, Colin's expression changed from slightly bored to very skeptical, as he sat up, tension crackling around him like static electricity about to discharge. "You telling the truth about the boyfriend?"

"What boyfriend?"

He jerked a thumb toward the end of our block, six or seven houses away. Standing in the fading sunlight, the rays like fire as they struck his hair, was Luc. Without thinking, I pushed off the steps and started toward him, the air so heavy it felt like pushing through water. His gaze locked with mine, a mix of curiosity and challenge. I wanted, suddenly, desperately, to be worthy of both.

Colin stepped between us, blocking my view, and loomed over me. "Him. Boyfriend?"

I tried to signal Luc, to tell him we should talk, but Colin was like a boulder in front of me. I finally stood on tiptoe to peer over his shoulder.

Naturally, Luc was gone.

"Not mine." I reached for the screen door, hoping my voice and hands were both steady. The last thing I needed was Colin looking into Luc. "He's Verity's."

CHAPTER 9

Ikept the snow globe with me the next day at The Slice,
which seemed silly, given that it was as useless as actual
snow. I'd shaken the stupid thing like it was a Magic 8 Ball,
and nothing happened. Verity had bought a defective snow
globe, I had decided sometime around three AM. Once she'd
realized that even she had standards for kitsch, and this one
failed to meet them, she'd shoved it to the back of the shelf so
she didn't have to stare at it. Who could blame her? The harlequin's dull eyes reminded me of a painting in an episode of
Scooby-Doo, following me around the room.

Broken or not, I wasn't comfortable leaving it behind
while I worked. Luc hadn't shown up again, and I wondered
if he planned to. Maybe he'd found out, somehow, that I
took the snow globe and was looking to steal it back. He
probably never had any intention of helping me. The ugly little knickknack was my only clue, and I was going to keep it
close.

Working at the diner wasn't really a glamorous job. The
grease from the grill seeped into my hair and clothes, even
though I spent most of my time in front, waiting tables. The
apron—green and white gingham with a *ruffle,* and a little
cap to match—wasn't exactly a look Abercrombie & Fitch
was promoting for the fall. But the tips, especially from the

regulars, weren't bad, and every one brought me a little closer to New York. There was Mr. Nelson, who ordered a poached egg, whole wheat toast, and grapefruit juice every day and stayed until he finished his daily crossword. Father Armando ordered "as the Spirit moved him." Mrs. Ahern always ordered a side of sausage and tucked it into her purse for her Yorkie, Ferdinand, to eat when she got home.

It was no surprise the tips from my classmates tended to bite, but we were far enough away from St. Brigid's that they didn't come in all that often. Unfortunately, St. Sebastian, our brother school, was only a few blocks west. Which meant I waited on a lot of sixteen-year-old boys, who tend to base their tips on how well you fill out your T-shirt.

I didn't get a lot of tips from that group.

In the days since Verity died, Kowalski had become a regular—corned beef hash and a fried egg, which clogged my arteries just looking at it—and he always left exactly 15 percent. He pulled the singles out of his cracked leather wallet and counted out the pennies carefully, placing a perfectly stacked pile on the edge of the table, every time. He liked things neat, which didn't inspire much confidence.

I was clearing booth four when Tim, the cook, shouted from the kitchen. "Mo! Your phone's ringing!"

Over the clanking of plates and cutlery, and the rise and fall of eight booths' worth of conversation, I could hear a snippet of Liz Phair. I dashed for the kitchen, sliding the tray of dirty dishes onto the counter.

"Mo? It's Lena."

"Hey! What's up?" Lena Santos was my coeditor for the school newspaper and middle hitter on the varsity volleyball team. She was blunt, and a little prickly, and definitely hyperactive, but I liked her. She'd been at the funeral, weeping but trying hard to keep it together. No hysterics, which I appreciated.

"Jill McAllister's party is tonight. Are you going?"

The McAllister end-of-summer parties were famous—a St. Brigid's tradition. Five daughters, whose psychiatrist parents routinely spent the summer in Europe, leaving the house empty for a back-to-school party kids were still talking about in December. Only a few underclassmen were allowed in, but every senior in the school was invited. Verity and I had been planning for this since freshman year. Jill was the youngest sister, a senior like us, which meant this was the last McAllister party, ever. But the thought of going on my own made me panicky, the first step into senior year without Verity leading the way.

"I don't think so." There was no way I was ready to go to a party. I tucked the phone against my shoulder while I carted the tray to the dishwasher.

"Mo, come on!"

"I'm not really up for a party."

"You can't *not* go. Everyone will be there."

"Exactly." I started loading dishes into the box.

"And you can't spend the year hiding, either," she said. Lena wrote good stories and better editorials—smart, pull-no-punches columns that said exactly what people were thinking but didn't want to say. Last year, I liked that about her.

"I'm not hiding, just tired," I said. "Besides, everyone's going to ask questions."

"They'll ask questions no matter what. There are a ton of rumors going around. People are saying all sorts of crazy stuff."

"Like what?"

"Like Verity was dealing drugs, and someone came after her? She wasn't in New Orleans this summer, but rehab?"

"That's crap." My voice rose, and I glanced through the swinging door to the front. "I talked to her every day. Do you think they let people in rehab do that?"

"I'm not the one who needs convincing."

"So if I don't go . . ."

"It looks like you're hiding something." Lena paused for a minute. "It would do you good to get out."

"I am out. I'm at work."

"The Slice does *not* count. Come on, Mo. We miss you."

I concentrated on wiping down my tray supercarefully and putting it back on the stack.

"Mo!" called Tim. "Order up!"

"Verity would tell you to go," Lena said. "You know she'd want you to do this year up right. She'd expect you to."

"Mo!" Tim shouted again.

"I'll think about it." I didn't wait for Lena to reply, just flipped the phone shut and tossed it back in my bag, not looking at the T-shirt-wrapped lump in the corner.

I grabbed the western omelet and French toast and backed through the swinging doors, trying to ignore the irritation I felt. Everyone seemed to know what Verity would want me to do. I wasn't so sure. Dropping the plates off with the older couple in booth three, I spotted a new customer at the counter. I headed back to grab the coffeepots off the burner, only to come face-to-face with my mother on the other side of the pass-through to the kitchen.

"Who was on the phone?"

"A friend from school."

"It sounded like you were making plans to go somewhere." Already, my mom's face was taking on a taut, lemony look, her lips thinning and pursing. It was her standard response, right before she said no.

"There are some people getting together tonight. I thought I might go."

Mom folded her arms across her chest. "I don't think that's a good idea."

My stomach tightened in anticipation of the fight to come. "It's just some girls from school." And a bunch of guys from Loyola University, but I didn't mention that. If my mother were a superhero, she'd be Panicwoman, capable of flattening cities with the sheer force of her overreactions, of tensing up so quickly she levitated.

"You're still recovering."

"I'm well enough to work," I pointed out. "If I can pull an eight-hour shift, a few hours at a party should be fine." I didn't even want to go, but I had a sudden vision of my senior year, and college, and the rest of my life. My mother hovering, Colin watching me through the window, Verity gone, and me, stuck here in the diner, safe and sound and bored to death. Compared to that, an evening facing down my classmates' questions about Verity sounded de-fricking-lightful.

"It's not safe. You shouldn't be going out by yourself." She reached up, adjusting the order tickets hanging from the overhead rack.

"I won't be by myself. I'll be with people from school." Colin's truck was parked right across the street, and I waved a coffeepot toward the window. "Colin can take me there and back."

Obviously, I'd lost my mind.

Mom considered that. Colin was a nice Catholic boy who came with my uncle's approval and liked her cooking, whose sole purpose in life was to keep me safe. "Will he be with you the whole time?"

"No! God, Mom! I'm not bringing a *bodyguard* to a high school party." I could only imagine the effect he'd have on my chances of having a normal night—not to mention his effect on the other St. Brigid's girls. Colin might be a pain in the ass, but I wasn't blind. He'd be a lamb to the slaughter. A broad-shouldered, dangerously handsome, gun-toting lamb.

I shook my head to clear the vision of Colin fighting off some of my less inhibited classmates, sans gun.

For a minute, Mom looked like she was actually considering it, closing her eyes and taking a deep breath. Whatever she saw behind the lids made her frown.

"No. I'm sorry, Mo."

"But . . ."

"You're still on the mend, and you don't need to be out after dark for something so trivial. Invite a friend over," she suggested. "You could rent a movie and make some popcorn. That would be fun."

"You can't keep me at home for the rest of my life." I clenched the ruffled hem of my apron to keep from shaking. This was payback for refusing to visit my father, I was sure of it.

"I wish I could," she snapped. "You're all I have."

I'd heard that argument a million times—it's the Fitzgerald girls against the world, we only have each other, we need to stick together. It was my mother's theme song, and had been ever since my father was carted off to federal prison. The tune was getting old, though, and I wanted my own life.

"I'm going."

"You're not." Her face was pale, her mouth set. "Don't push me, Mo. I didn't raise you to speak to me like this."

The bell on the counter rang out.

"You raised me not to speak at all," I hissed, snatching up the orange-handled coffeepot, rattled by my outburst. At the Formica counter sat a guy in a close-fitting black T-shirt, baseball cap tugged down low over his brow, menu obscuring the rest of his face. He'd probably heard everything.

"What can I get you?" I said, trying to sound believably cheerful. "The crumb-topped cherry pie is really good today."

The menu dropped, and Luc grinned up at me. "Well, well," he drawled. "Ain't you the social butterfly? Vee's house, police station, dinner guest, parties . . ."

"Seriously? You're stalking me?" My voice dropped to a whisper, and I shot a furtive glance toward the battered red truck outside. "You're not even good at it. You're going to get me in trouble!"

"You're doin' a fine job of that all by yourself. Such a busy girl, Mouse. How you getting it all done?" He held out the empty coffee cup, and I forced myself to pour it in the mug, not his lap. "I thought we agreed you'd leave this alone. You, *chère,* are showing a real deficiency in the followin' directions department."

"Bite me."

His smile widened, genuine this time. "Careful what you wish for. Slice of that pie sounds good."

I turned to the back counter and cut the pie, hoping that he couldn't see my hands shake. It was a smaller slice than normal, because he was too obnoxious to deserve a full piece.

"I thought you were going back to New Orleans."

"Figured you might need watchin', on account of the aforementioned piss-poor listening skills."

I slammed down a little stoneware cream dispenser. "I've already got a watchdog, thanks. Why'd you show up last night?"

"Did you find what you were looking for at Vee's?"

I nearly dropped the carafe but kept my expression innocent. "I needed to get my stuff."

"Mmn-hmn." His eyes over the coffee cup were sharp green and skeptical.

"What could I possibly be looking for?"

"You tell me. 'Course, even if you found something, no guarantee you'd know what to do with it."

I narrowed my eyes. "I just want to find out who killed Verity. Trust me—there was no signed confession sitting around her room."

Luc took a bite of pie and pointed the fork at me. "Trouble. You go looking, that's what you'll find. Trouble bigger than a girl like you can handle."

A girl like me? I resisted the urge to ask what he meant. "I have to check my tables."

Fuming, I wiped down tables, dropped off checks, refilled

coffee, pocketed tips. The whole time, I could feel Luc, sitting at the counter, acting as if I wasn't there. It was annoying, really. The awareness of him made my skin prickle, uncomfortably warm.

"Go away," I said, when I was back behind the counter. "Before Colin sees you."

"Not sure how much good Cujo'll do you, but it never hurts. You listen to him?"

"Why does everyone think they can tell me what to do?" I scrubbed at a spot of dried ketchup with more force than necessary.

"Because you let them. You going to that party?"

"She said . . ." I clamped my lips shut.

"And you're gonna do what she says? You haven't done a single thing I've asked since I met you."

"She's my *mother*."

In the kitchen, Tim rang the bell again.

"You want an omelet, you gotta break a few eggs," Luc said, taking another bite.

"Yeah, well, I'm always the one stuck cleaning up the mess."

He shrugged. "Guess you got a decision to make. Keep things tidy, or get what you want. Can't have both."

I gathered up the order. When I looked back, Luc was gone, and there was a twenty under the empty mug.

After work, I curled up in bed and examined the snow globe again. Did Luc know this was what I'd taken? Did Evangeline? Maybe she'd ordered him to come after me. It was hard to believe anyone would be interested in such a gaudy little trinket. The harlequin figurine inside leaned drunkenly against a lamppost. It sat atop a half-open treasure chest stuffed with gold coins and ropes of brightly painted gems. A single lonely ruby was nestled against the dull brass hinge of the chest.

It must have had snow once, right? Taking it out had been Verity's idea of a joke—or a clue. I tried to unscrew the glass portion from the base, but it wouldn't move. I tried prying the two apart, unsuccessfully. Turning it upside down, I examined every inch of the base for some sort of plug, but it was completely sealed. There had to be a way to get inside, but for the life of me, I couldn't figure out how. Not before my mom got home, anyway.

My phone rang and I reached for it, still shaking the snow globe.

"So?" said Lena immediately. "You're in, right?"

"I can't. My mom is freaking out."

"We're seniors! You have to!"

I flopped back on my bed, frustrated.

"Blow her off," Lena said.

"She's practically got me under house arrest." I peeked out the window at Colin's truck. "I'm lucky I don't have one of those ankle monitors."

"It'd be a pain come soccer season," Lena agreed. "So, go all Hollywood starlet and sneak out."

I continued shaking, and the chest seemed to shift, jostled open by one of the ropes of gems. "What? I can't do that!"

"Come on," she urged. "You've earned the right to have a little fun."

I was pretty sure the McAllister party was not really my kind of fun. Six months ago, maybe, but not anymore.

"Time to break out, Mo," chided Lena. The phrase made something in the back of my mind flicker. Luc. *Break some eggs,* he'd said.

"I've gotta go."

"But you'll be there, right?"

For once, I acted on impulse. "Yeah. Can you pick me up? Late, though, so my mom will be asleep?" *And so my bodyguard will have gone home for the night?*

"Sure!" She sounded delighted and stunned all at once.

"See you then." The excitement in my voice was genuine, but it had nothing to do with the party.

I bolted out of bed and tripped down the stairs. There was only a little time before my mom got home from the diner, and I really didn't want to explain what I was about to do.

In the kitchen, I hefted the snow globe in both hands and brought it down, hard and sharp, on the edge of the sink.

Nothing happened.

I did it again, two harsh strikes. For my efforts, I left a tiny chip in the smooth glass and a much bigger one in the enamel coating of the sink. Great. I needed something harder—something my mother wouldn't notice if it got dinged up.

The driveway. I rushed out back, through the porch, to the curb. Tightening my grip, I smashed the snow globe on the ground.

The impact sang up my arms. It felt strangely good, but the glass remained unbroken.

"Come on," I grunted, taking another swing, and another. "Come . . . on . . ."

I was never the one to break things. I never made a noise, never raised a fuss. I was such a *nice* girl, just like Luc said, and where had it gotten me? No matter what I did, I was still Jack Fitzgerald's daughter. My being good didn't make him less of a criminal. It didn't make Verity less dead. It wouldn't even get me to New York, where I could start fresh. Being the nice girl hadn't gotten me a damn thing.

Asphalt pebbles scattered around, some flying back at me, but the glass was starting to crack and craze, until finally, I brought the globe up high over my head and swung down, as hard as I could. It exploded, water spraying everywhere. My knees and shirtfront were soaked, and the shattered glass cascaded in a glittering wave over the driveway, catching the late-afternoon light. The harlequin and his treasure chest clung stubbornly to the base, and I turned it over to get a better look, panting.

"What in the hell are you doing?"

I tried to jump up, but my feet got tangled and I fell back-ward, flat on my ass in the middle of the alley. Not for noth-ing did I warm the bench each soccer season.

Colin stood at the end of the driveway, arms folded, as I struggled to stand. The scowl on his face would have been re-assuring if he'd directed it at a bad guy.

"I wasn't sneaking out. I wanted some fresh air."

"You didn't shut off the alarm. In a hurry to get your fresh air?"

"I forgot about it. Sorry."

"Any reason you're busting up . . . what was that, any-way?" He cocked his head to the side and studied the pool of glass-studded water. "You have a thing against snow globes?"

"It was defective," I mumbled.

"It is now. You should sweep up that glass," he added.

"You're very helpful."

"Your uncle said I should watch you, not clean up your messes."

I huffed out a breath I didn't know I'd been holding. "I wasn't asking you to." I needed to get rid of Colin. Again. "I'll clean it up now, all right? Can you stop hovering? You're like my mother."

I stomped back to the house and grabbed the broom, leav-ing the base on the table of the sunroom.

Colin was leaning against the garage when I returned. "You're not telling me everything." He sounded like he was scolding a kindergartener caught in a fib.

"Do I need to?" I swept the glass into the dustpan. "I wasn't going anywhere, except back in."

"Great idea." He waited until I was almost to the porch before calling, "Plans tonight?"

Don't break stride. Don't look guilty. "I've got to finish my summer reading list—more Shakespeare. Big fun. Have a good night."

"You too. Watch that glass."

I wondered for a minute how many jobs like this he'd done. Probably a million, judging from how detached he seemed. He'd never tell me. He'd deflected every one of my mom's questions without her realizing it, and he'd done the same to me. Sighing, I locked the door behind me and reset the alarm. I'd learned one thing, anyway. Colin was monitoring the alarm system.

I used a kitchen towel to knock the rest of the glass around the base into the kitchen trash, and threw some well-past-its-prime cabbage on top. There was only a little time left before my mom came home.

I studied the base in the glare of my desk light. The harlequin smiled vacantly at me, masked and gaudy. Even the paint job was cheap, colors bleeding into each other, nothing like Verity's work. She'd always liked the performing arts best, but she was a talented artist. She'd never have been so sloppy.

The treasure chest was different. The ropes of jewels were carefully painted, each tiny gem strung together so they swung back and forth when I blew on them. The gold coins peeking out along the edges were shiny and minutely detailed. I pried the tiny latches open with a paper clip and flipped the lid back, revealing a solid lump of jewels and coins. I dug at them, scrabbling with the tip of my fingernail. Whatever Verity had put in here—if she really had, and wasn't in the hereafter, laughing at my idiocy—had to be important if she'd gone to this much trouble.

With an audible pop, the false bottom of the chest came away. The little cavern went down to the base, which turned out to be stuffed with . . . fabric. Black, bone-dry velvet, soft and crumpled against my fingertip. I fished around until my nail snagged on a thin silken cord. I tugged, and out fell a tiny black pouch. Trembling, I loosened the top and emptied it into my palm.

A ring. A fine circle of gold, so lovely and delicate I was afraid to pick it up. Centered in the middle was a shimmering cobalt stone, not faceted like a sapphire, but smooth and luminous like an opal. The stone was anchored with four diamonds, like compass points, any one of which would make a very nice engagement ring.

"Jesus." I didn't know much about jewelry, but the ring, intricate and gleaming, had to be expensive—way, way more than Verity had made working for her aunt this summer. Had she stolen it? Was this why she'd been killed?

I turned the ring over and over in my hand, squinting at the illegible engravings on the inside of the band. The stone quietly glimmered, the same blue as Verity's eyes.

The ring was hers. I felt the certainty of it square in my chest. Which, unfortunately, didn't clear up how she'd gotten it.

The bag wasn't empty. I shook it again and discovered a data card, like the one in my camera. As I frowned at it, I heard my mother open the back door.

"Mo, why is Colin sitting outside? You should invite him in, give him a glass of—Maura Kathleen Fitzgerald! Why is there a chip the size of a saucer in my sink?"

Damn. I knew I'd forgotten something. I swept the ring and memory card into my camera bag as she came up the stairs.

"The size of a saucer! What were you doing?"

"I dropped the skillet. I made a grilled cheese, and I went to wash the skillet, and it slipped." It turns out that lying is like anything else. You get better with practice. "It's not *that* big."

"The sink will *rust*. We'll have to get it repaired. I don't understand you," she continued, working her way up to full-on mad. "You treat your camera like a newborn baby, but there's no such respect for my things. And why is there glass piled up in the trash?"

Nothing got by my mother. For someone so good at keeping secrets, she certainly was not a fan of other people having them.

"Mo? The glass?"

I shrugged. "I dropped a bottle of iced tea. Not my best day."

"What am I supposed to do about the sink? The repair won't be cheap."

All I wanted was for her to leave. The ring was sitting in my camera bag, the first actual, tangible clue I had, begging me to examine it more closely. I needed to figure out how I was going to sneak out tonight. Mostly, I just didn't want the fight that was brewing, because it wouldn't have been about the sink, or the party, or anything else so mundane. It would have been the fight we've been having for years without ever saying the words. I don't know when I figured out that my mom expected me to be the perfect daughter, like my good behavior was some kind of atonement for my father's sins. I only knew that I was tired of it.

"Fine," I snapped. "I'll pay for it. It's not like I need the money anyway, since I'm not going to be going anywhere for the next hundred years!"

"Don't take that tone with me. I'm looking out for you. We all are."

I glanced out my window. Colin was sitting in his truck, eating a sub sandwich and reading yet another paperback.

Yep. Everyone was looking out for me, or at least at me. Either way, I hated it. And I hated apologizing for it.

"Whatever. Are we done? I have to finish reading *King Lear*."

Her eyes narrowed and her lips thinned. "Dinner in half an hour," she said, and turned on her heel.

"I'm not hungry!" I shouted, shoving the door shut. I was probably the only teenager in America with no lock on her door. It sucked all the time, of course, but particularly now.

With one ear listening for my mom to come back, I fished the ring and data card out of my bag.

I loved my camera, a digital SLR with a bunch of lenses Uncle Billy had given me for my sweet sixteen. It's miles better than the little point-and-shoot ones most people use. It's great, because what you see in the viewfinder is the exact image you get when you take the pictures. There's no distortion, no lapses, and it's fast, too, so you don't miss anything. It's also the best way I know to be invisible. People spot a big black lens, and they worry about what they're doing, or how their hair looks. Nobody sees the person holding the camera.

I waited for the images to load, thumbing through the shots when they appeared on the tiny screen. Pictures of the Garden District, fancy metalwork and old buildings. And pictures of Luc. Every image held a bit of Verity's vibrancy, her flair. There was a shot of her and Luc, sitting together outside a café, the angle all wonky, like she'd held the camera at arm's length and taken the picture herself. Luc was kissing her cheek, Verity's face was scrunched up in laughter, and they looked totally comfortable together. I swallowed and went to the next shot—Luc, mock-glaring from behind a glass of iced tea. Evangeline's shop, the discreet wooden sign hung from shiny brass chains. Another picture of Luc, standing on a wrought-iron balcony, looking out over the city at sunset. You could tell she'd snapped it without his knowing, because he seemed completely unguarded, comfortable enough to drop the swagger he always adopted around me.

I wanted to believe Verity was trying to tell me something, that she'd meant for me to find these pictures, and the ring, and put them together like a complicated equation set. But for the life of me, I couldn't solve for X.

Aggravation sent me pacing through the room. Why had she kept so much secret? What would she want me to do now? I thumbed through the pictures again, slowing when I got to the ones of Luc. He looked softer. Happier. Of course he did—Verity had been alive. The hard glint to his eye and the set of his jaw were missing, because they'd been together. Their obvious affection made one thing clear—she trusted him. Luc was on my side, or Verity's, anyway.

While I'd been poring over pictures and ignoring my mother's repeated calls for dinner, night had fallen—a late-summer, soft navy darkness. I checked my clock. I'd mumbled an insincere good night when she'd gone to bed an hour earlier, and now it was just after ten. I turned off the light and waited for the low rumble of Colin's truck pulling away.

Once the sound had faded, I changed outfits. I wanted to wear something . . . not me. Something that would prove to people I was okay, even though I wasn't. They were going to talk about me—no avoiding that—but I wanted to avoid outright pity. I finally settled on a short black skirt and a silky green top, topped off with a violet scarf. Verity had always liked this outfit. Maybe it would give me a bit of her strength.

It didn't feel right to leave the ring behind, so I threaded it onto a gold chain I'd gotten for confirmation and dropped it over my head, carefully tucking it under the scarf. The necklace was long enough to hide the ring beneath my shirt, and it rested coolly against my skin like a talisman, as if Verity were still nearby.

I didn't know why I was going. To get back at my mom, maybe, or to test how good Colin was, or to see if I could actually function without Verity, or to keep my promise to Lena. A jumble of reasons, none of which were very good.

Twenty minutes later, avoiding the squeaky treads on the stairs and the loose floorboard in the living room, I stood on the sunporch, resetting the alarm. Even if Colin noticed that someone was messing with it, Lena and I would be gone by the time he made it back to check on me.

I touched the ring, now warmer against my skin. At the foot of the driveway, Lena blinked the lights of her dingy white Malibu, and I hurried to meet her.

"See?" she said, as I climbed in and tugged on my skirt. "It's going to be fine."

I doubted that. What had seemed like a not-terrible idea even a few minutes ago now seemed utterly stupid. I twisted my fingers together, hating myself. What was I doing, going to a party when my best friend was dead? What sort of horrible person did that?

Lena took one look at me and shook her head. "No way," she said. "I'm not turning around."

"I don't feel good," I said, not caring if I sounded whiny.

"You can't hide all year. If you can survive this, everything else will be easy." She clapped her hand over her mouth. "Sorry. Bad choice of words. I didn't mean to . . . remind you."

Touching the necklace, I watched the lights on the passing cars, blurry through a film of tears I blinked away. "You can't remind me. I'd have to forget it in the first place."

When we arrived at the McAllisters' house, I paused.

"Go ahead in," I told her. "I need a minute."

She wrinkled her nose. "You don't show in five minutes, I'm coming back for you. Get ready."

I waited until she closed the door, then sat on the front steps of the elegant red-brick house, queasy with nerves.

Kanye West was audible through the arched oak door, and behind the tasteful window treatments, I could see my classmates dancing, drinking, hooking up with boys imported from DePaul and Loyola. Why date nice Catholic high school boys, the reasoning was, when you could find Catholic *college* boys just as easily?

It was the party we'd talked about since we were freshmen, and now I was here, and Verity wasn't. I fingered the chain around my neck. She should have been here, taking the lead, walking in and parting the crowd with her beauty and her energy and glow, the girl everyone wanted.

I couldn't do it. Verity could have. She *would* have. She

might have been nervous, but she would have gone right in. And I needed to, or I was just as small and weak as Luc thought.

I slipped the necklace off and cradled the ring in the palm of my hand. Even in the dim porch lights, the stones had a curious sheen about them. Everyone kept telling me Verity's spirit was still with me. Why not her jewelry, too? I slid the ring onto my finger, surprised it fit. It caught the porch light again and seemed to flare, a white sunburst running over the indigo stone. I stared, transfixed.

The door opened. Lena, plastic cup of Absolut Mandrin in her hand, dragged me inside.

CHAPTER 10

The party didn't actually screech to a halt when I walked in—the music kept playing, the couples on the couch kept grinding, the alcohol kept flowing—but there was a distinct ripple effect. Each group I passed got very quiet as I walked by. Then, just before I moved out of earshot, they would start to giggle, the gossip humming through the room like the sound of a beehive.

"In here," Lena said, tugging me through rooms filled with antique furniture and sickly sweet smoke. We passed a music room where someone was playing the *Addams Family* theme—badly—on a grand piano. We ended up in the kitchen, and she thrust a plastic cup of something red and fruity looking in my hand.

"Cosmo," she said. "You need it."

"Is it that obvious?" Probably. This was a terrible idea. I tipped the cup back and drank half, coughing a little.

Lena smiled nervously and topped it off. "Liquid courage."

I snorted and took another sip as her smile fell away. "What's wrong?"

"Don't freak," she said, trying to sound reassuring.

I wasn't reassured.

"What?" I set the cup down on the marble counter. My

mom? Oh, God. Colin? I closed my eyes and willed the alcohol to hit my bloodstream.

"Seth's here."

I opened my eyes. "Seth Gibson? Why?"

"Jill decided to invite St. Sebastian's."

"It's a shame all this money can't buy her some taste," I grumbled. "Does he know I'm here?"

"People kind of noticed your entrance," she said weakly, and I reached for my cup again.

Not terrible, I told myself. He'd been my date to the junior prom last year, and we'd gone out a few times over the summer. He was a perfectly nice guy.

"Jesus, he's boring," says Verity. She browses through a rack of vintage clothing, forehead wrinkling in concentration. "It's like he's competing for an Olympic medal in average."

"He's nice." I shake my head at the sheer purple scarf she's found, and she sighs heavily, putting it back.

"So are cocker spaniels. You don't need nice. You've spent your entire life being nice. You need . . ."

"A real bastard?" I suggest.

She swats at me. "Someone . . . with an edge. Someone dangerous."

"Thanks, but no."

"Someone bad. Just a little bad," she assures me, and pulls out a sleeveless blouse of bottle green satin. "Not serial killer bad. Try this on."

"Good to know you've got standards." I take the shirt unwillingly, feeling the cool sleekness of the material under my fingers. It's not my style—too revealing and too impractical. It's more Verity than me, but she shoos me back to the cramped, badly lit dressing room and waits outside.

"Mo, the only guys you've ever gone out with are the ones your mom approves of."

"If she didn't approve, I couldn't go out with them." This

*seems like a reasonable defense. I draw back the curtain and
her face lights up.*

*"Your hair looks fabulous. You're getting it. And this,
too," she says firmly, looping the scarf around my neck. The
ends dangle past my fingers, but it's practically weightless.
"Your mom isn't the one kissing those guys. You need someone who makes you shiver. Can you honestly tell me Seth
Gibson makes you shiver?"*

Seth didn't make me shiver, even when he blasted the air-
conditioning in his Civic.

"Hey, Mo." As if summoned, Seth appeared in the doorway, a cheerful, nervous smile on his face.

Lena shrugged and eased past him. "Find me later," she
said.

"Hey, Seth." I clutched my drink as he approached me.

He gave me a clumsy, beer-scented hug and stepped back a
little. "Sorry about Verity," he said after one of those pauses
that gets longer and more awkward while you try to figure
out the least awkward response. "Unreal."

"That's the word." I studied the pitchers of drinks lined up
on the counter. Cosmopolitan, appletini, strawberry daiquiri,
lemon drop. At least I'd be getting a few servings of fruit.
Scurvy wouldn't be an issue.

"You're okay, though. That's good."

I didn't have an answer for that.

We walked toward the breakfast nook, if you could call a
room bigger than my bedroom a nook. It was decorated in
blues and yellows, the kind of French country farmhouse no
farmer could afford. I stared at a collection of rooster plates
instead of meeting Seth's eyes. They were a little too bright,
full of questions. His face was ruddy. Drunk, but not sloppy
drunk.

My cosmo was already hitting me, since I'd skipped dinner. Now I regretted it. Avoiding Seth would be easier if I
wasn't weaving.

"I went to the funeral," he said. "Why didn't you come and stand by us?"

Because I was keeping an eye out for a murderer? "Family stuff."

"We all went over to Anderson's later. You should have come."

Of course. They went to Verity's funeral, then had a kegger in her honor. I tugged at my skirt again, trying to figure out the best way to escape.

"I should find Lena."

Seth talked over me. "You were there, right? When it happened?"

My mouth tasted sour. I took another sip to make it go away. "Yeah."

"You're so lucky, Mo." He took a step closer. "It totally could have been you."

He meant well, I reminded myself.

He touched my elbow lightly. "I didn't call after, you know. Because I thought you might need some time."

I didn't point out it had only been two weeks. I stared into my cup as he barreled on. "I was wondering if you wanted to go see that new movie—by the guy who did *Shutter*? Maybe grab some dinner after?"

A slasher flick? Really? I took a tiny step backward. "Wow. That's . . . um . . . really sweet, Seth. I'm not sure I'm ready, though."

"You look nice. Like you're okay, I mean."

Nice. I was starting to hate the word.

"Next Friday? Good way to start off senior year," he added. He moved closer, running his hand lightly over my bare arm, and that was it. The hell with nice.

I shoved his hand away. "I have to find Lena," I said, and fled the room.

It was stupid to come. Stupid to think I could go back to my old life when it had been smashed worse than Verity's snow globe. I stumbled through the house, and this time, if people whispered, I didn't notice.

The good thing about a house like mine is, while it's the size of a shoebox, you can't get lost, no matter how many drinks you've had. Not so with the McAllisters'. I was looking for freedom but ended up in the backyard. The pool threw off a wavering light, the scent of chlorine and pot mingling unpleasantly. Paper lanterns dotted the patio and lawn. Clusters of furniture were scattered throughout, with people perched on them, and the music was so bass heavy my teeth vibrated. Exactly what I had wanted to avoid. I saw a lone chair peeking out from behind a hedge and practically dove for it.

A crowd was gathered on the other side of the hedge—Jill McAllister, surrounded by admirers. At first I couldn't hear what they were saying, but then the music shifted from electronica to indie-pop, and the conversation carried perfectly.

"You know what they're saying, right?" Jill, no doubt preening. "The killers were after Mo, not Verity."

Audible gasp. "Seriously?"

"No way," someone scoffed. "Mo? They'd have to notice her first." A chorus of giggles.

I bit my lip as Jill said, "It's true. It's all about her uncle. He's a mobster, you know."

"That's right," a voice agreed. "Her dad . . ."

"Was just an accountant." Jill cut the other girl off—no way was she going to let anyone else get the credit for her scoop. "He laundered Mob money, but her whole family was in on it, even her mom. He's getting out of prison soon, too."

"Oh, my God," another voice shrilled. "Can you imagine?"

You could hear the smirk in Jill's words. "Think he'll wear his prison jumpsuit to graduation?" The group snickered as she continued blithely. "My dad plays tennis with the State's Attorney, and *he* said the police think the Mob was trying to,

like, intimidate Mo's uncle, or something. They were probably only supposed to rough her up."

"No," breathed a groupie. "And they killed Verity instead?"

Someone else spoke. "Were they blind? How do you mix
up those two?"

"I *know*." More cackling. Still, I didn't move, frozen by
the need to hear more.

"Is someone still after Mo? I mean, if she's in danger, doesn't
that mean we would be, too?" They murmured, gauging the
impact such danger might have on their popularity.

"Probably not," said Jill, loving every second of her time
as the star. She was such a bitch. Always had been. I knew
Verity's death wasn't connected to my family—that much, I
was certain of. But the rest of her poisonous little show made
a sort of horrible sense. Kowalski's interest in Uncle Billy,
Elsa's pit bull tactics, Colin's constant hovering, my mother's
increased paranoia—they were all overreacting because they
believed there might be a connection. And they would only
believe that if the rumors about my uncle and the Mob were
true.

I dug my fingernails into my palms and stayed quiet as she
spoke again. "They made their point, right? Besides, one
dead girl could be random. Two means a lot of media."

She sounded so smug, so smart, and I wanted to reach
through the hedge and yank her bottle-blond hair out by the
roots. She was parroting what she'd overheard, embellishing
it to get more attention. She'd never liked Verity. She'd been
jealous of how someone with less money and less status
could be genuinely popular when Jill herself was more feared
than liked. Still, I didn't say anything. I stayed in the shadows, just like always.

"Does Mo know?" someone asked.

"Of course! Why else has she been so quiet? She hasn't
given any interviews, she has some eight-hundred-dollar-an-

hour lawyer whenever she talks to the police, and you saw her at the funeral—she wouldn't even talk to us. It's her fault, and she knows it."

Enough. I had to get out. I stumbled away, not caring if they heard me. Lights blurred, the walls and floors canting at strange angles. People stared as I shoved my way through crowded rooms, looking for Lena, feeling the effects of my drinks. Rounding a corner, I slammed into Seth. His face brightened and he reached for my hand. I jerked away and darted down another hall, desperate for escape. Forget about tracking down Lena—I'd find another way home. Finally, I found the front door and half fell down the steps, gulping fresh air as I walked. It didn't matter where I ended up, as long as it was away from the party.

Jill's story wasn't true. I mean, the part about my dad, sure, but they'd never proved Uncle Billy was connected to any of the money-laundering charges my dad had been convicted of. My father was a crook, and a lousy one at that, but Uncle Billy was clean—or as clean as anyone in Chicago could be. He'd never do anything to harm our family. He'd *promised* me. I'd *believed* him. Until today.

Verity would have stood up to Jill. She wouldn't have hidden behind a bush and let a catty trust-fund bimbo, a Paris Hilton in training, trash her family and her friend. But once again, I'd failed her. I couldn't be like Verity. I couldn't even come close.

I glanced at the ring, at the white sunburst slipping over the deep blue surface whenever a streetlight struck it. It fit me perfectly. Maybe that's why Verity hadn't been wearing it. For safekeeping, until she could get it sized. Who knew why she'd done anything these past few months? Not me, for sure.

The night, at least, was beautiful, the air cool against my overheated skin. The moon was nearly full and a brilliant white. The neighborhood was filled with large, gracious homes, mature trees, plenty of streetlights. I could walk for a while and clear my head, then go back and wait for Lena at her car.

The temperature dropped as I wandered the well-lit sidewalks. I shivered slightly in the breeze, wishing I'd brought a sweater, and crossed the street to a small park. There was a baseball diamond and bleachers, and an aging metal playground with slides, swings, and a geodesic dome. I fumbled in my purse for my cell, looking around for a street sign. I could call Lena. She'd pick me up, if I could figure out where I was.

Or I could call Colin. He'd find me no matter what. Lena was less likely to yell, though.

The breeze kicked up, and the moonlight on the jungle gym cast checkered patterns on the wood chips underneath. The swings knocked together gently, chains creaking. Sitting down seemed like a good idea, so I started toward a metal spinner, only to catch my heel on the edge of the sidewalk, my ankle turning under me with a quick, agonizing wrench. Perfect.

I hobbled over and sank down, resting my head against the metal grab bar. The pain in my ankle faded to a dull throb, and I massaged it, keeping my other foot firmly planted. My shoes, black open-toed sandals with a spiky heel, probably weren't the best for making a hurried, drunken escape. If my mom were here, she'd make some pious comment about the dangers of vanity. Right after she strangled me.

The floating effect of the cosmopolitan couldn't quite erase the heavy feeling Jill's words had left. I'd heard rumors about Uncle Billy, but never put so bluntly. Never about me. Even knowing Verity's death had nothing to do with us—Luc had made it crystal clear there was no connection, and he seemed intent on keeping it that way—didn't ease the shock and anger coursing through my body.

When school started, I'd be facing down entire classrooms

of people who thought I was the reason Verity was dead. The realization made my stomach roil. All those eyes on me, not knowing the truth, judging me anyway. If I'd been an outsider before, it was nothing compared to what senior year had in store for me.

Suddenly, the entire park went black and cold. I stood just as the spinner started whirling, sending me face-first into the wood chips.

Ignoring my ankle, I scrambled up, brushing myself off and looking at the sky. The moon flashed into view, disappearing as something leathery rushed in front of it.

I screamed.

The black shape swooped in. I raced for the houses across the street, slowed by my bad ankle.

He leaped, not gracefully, but powerfully. He landed in front of me, so massive that his shadow blocked my view of the cozy brick homes. I backpedaled, running for the swings.

He gained on me, hissing and guttural, seeming to chuckle. Desperate, I shoved the rubber-seated swing at him and kept going.

The thick chain caught him across the chest, knocking him back a foot. I'd never get past him. He was too fast. Instead, I took off toward the iron dome, the only thing that gave any cover at all. Made of thick metal bars, it was heavy enough to keep him off, and the openings were sized for elementary kids, not freakishly tall killers. If I could buy some time, I could call 911.

I glanced back. Mistake. He was still coming, enormous, easily two feet taller than me and swathed in black leather. The coat sleeves flapped like wings as he reached for me.

As my fingertips brushed the bars of the dome, he snagged the back of my shirt, sending me to the ground, my purse tumbling away. Grabbing my foot, he hauled me closer, wood chips scraping my bare legs and arms, Verity's scarf tightening around my throat. His hand felt spiny and sharp against my ankle, the fingers thin but steely and rough. I sobbed and kicked, bucking wildly, and the heel of my shoe—the one he wasn't holding—connected with his hood. There was a squish and a crack, and he fell back, howling.

Half crawling, half running, I made it to the dome and wriggled through an opening meant for a third grader. My breath sounded painful and harsh as he prowled around the outside of the dome.

He stretched an arm between the bars, but I scooted back out of range. And then I spotted my purse. Behind him. Ten feet away.

I was trapped, and the only thing left to do was scream.

He snarled, jumping on top of the dome in one massive leap, reaching down for me. I flattened myself against the ground, hands covering my face. The ring felt searingly hot.

Verity's ring.

He snarled and I froze, my terror swept away by fury. He was Verity's killer, or he was one of them. He had to be. I held out my hand, flashing the ring. The moonlight seemed weaker than before, but even so, the stone was brilliant, like it was lit from within. "Is this what you wanted? Is this why she's dead?"

He went berserk, slamming against the dome, denting the bars.

"I'll give it to you, okay?" Like he wasn't going to kill me anyway.

He must have carried a knife. A metal screech filled the air as he began sawing through the bars. "Come on," I said. "Let's make a deal. You get the ring. I go home. Everybody wins."

He didn't need to make a deal. No one was responding to my screams. I couldn't call 911, not with my phone on the other side of the dome. It might as well have been ten *miles* away.

He might not bargain for the ring, but maybe it could buy

me some time. If I threw it in the opposite direction, there might be enough time for me to dart out, grab the phone, and get back safely. I could call the police. It might be enough to scare him off.

He finished sawing through the first bar and started on the next. He was cutting a doorway. The scraping sound resonated in my teeth, in my bones, and I started to quake. I would lose the ring, but no jewelry was worth my life, right? Verity would understand.

I tried to tug it from my hand, but it wouldn't budge. The second bar tumbled down, missing me by inches. The screech filled my ears as he started on a third. He'd be through in a few more seconds. I yanked harder, my breath coming in sobs.

"*Really* wish you wouldn't do that, Mouse," came a familiar drawl.

Luc stepped onto the playground, calling out something in another language, and the moon came back.

And whatever was on top of the dome, about to come after me . . . it wasn't a guy. It was a nightmare.

The thing—*not a guy, a thing,* I told myself over and over again—stopped sawing and turned toward Luc, like he was scenting new prey. I sagged back against the wall of the dome, panting.

"You'll be wantin' to keep your jewelry on," Luc called to me, his eyes never leaving my attacker as he dropped into a crouch. "Least for the next little while."

"He's got a knife!" I cried.

"More'n a knife," he replied. "How 'bout you sit tight, hmn?"

Suddenly, the thing lunged for Luc, who jumped out of the way and pulled from behind him—I swear to God—an actual sword. It gleamed where the moonlight touched it, intricate patterning all the way to the handle, and Luc looked crazy-comfortable with it, his whole body lithe and relaxed and ready. Relief poured through me as I watched, but terror shoved back against it.

Luc lunged and parried, the blade flashing like lightning. I could hear him muttering, and the harsh, sibilant cries of the creature as it lashed out with vicious strokes.

"He killed Verity! He's one of them!" I shouted, gripping the bars. They bit into my skin, icy cold despite the warm night.

Luc ignored me, busy attacking, retreating, chanting. I strained to hear the words over the sound of clashing metal and my own ragged breaths. The wind picked up. With a grunt, he hacked at the thing's arm, and it fell away as screams filled my ears.

There was no blood, only a rush of foul air, like something was rotting. The coat had torn away and I could see, not an arm exactly, but something that, long ago, might have been an arm. Now it was just bone, patches of decayed flesh, tatters of leathery skin. I pressed a fist to my mouth as bile rose up.

Luc vaulted backward as the thing lashed out with its remaining arm, and one talonlike finger caught his shoulder blade, slicing deep. He gave a sharp cry, falling back for an instant, but kept fighting.

"Mouse, need you to come on out," he called, his voice sounding strained for the first time.

He'd circled around, putting himself between me and the thing, almost close enough for me to touch him through the bars. Crimson bloomed across the back of his shirt like a crushed flower.

"But . . ."

The thing screamed raucously. The moon disappeared, plunging the park back into darkness.

"He's calling his friends," Luc growled. "Now, Mouse."

I crawled out, banging my shoulder and tripping. I landed on my hands and knees, so weak I had to use the bars to pull myself up. Luc kept moving with a grace and intensity that would have been breathtaking if I wasn't so afraid of dying.

He raked a glance over me, nodded once, and beat the thing back, burying the blade in its chest, pulling it out with a revolting sucking sound. It crumpled to the ground, writhing. Whirling, he chanted and slashed at the air with the sword—one, two, three times. The blade flared and where he had cut, a line of ruby-gold flame appeared. The flickering lights hovered in the air, nearly as tall as me, creating a shape like a doorway. Outside the lines, the playground stood in shadow, but inside was an inky, unnatural darkness. Even the flames, blood red at the center fading to orange-white edges, couldn't illuminate it. It crackled and snapped, like a real fire, but I didn't feel any heat coming off it at all.

The creature staggered upright, heading for Luc. I screamed a warning. Luc cursed and hacked at it again, a violent burst of speed forcing it back. With the blade still gleaming strangely, he grabbed my wrist, yanking me toward him.

"Don't let go," he said. "No matter what."

The thing howled behind me, and I looked over Luc's shoulder—two more figures had appeared out of the shadows. I clutched Luc's arm. His fingers wrapped more tightly around me. We fell through the door of flame.

CHAPTER 11

I fell—just like in a nightmare, falling and falling into endless black. I flailed for something to slow myself, but my
arm was held fast, and the tumble into nothingness continued.

People say if you fall in your dreams and hit the bottom,
you'll never wake up. So when we landed, and I slammed
into the bottom of my nightmare, I was convinced I'd died.

I lay for a moment, facedown against something cool and
smooth, my eyes squeezed tight. Next to me, something
moved, and I curled into the tiniest ball imaginable. Dead or
alive, it was better not to be seen.

Luc's voice was ragged. "Take off the ring."

I opened my eyes and saw polished wood underneath me.
There was hardwood flooring in the afterlife?

"The ring, Mouse. Off. *Now.*" He reached for my hand.

"Am I dead? Are you dead, too?"

"If you don't get that ring off in the next five seconds,
yes."

Weakly, I tugged at it. The shining circle slid easily off my
icy finger.

He held out his hand—the one that wasn't gripping a
sword.

"Uh-uh." I curled my fingers around it. "Not yours." A

wave of nausea hit me, and I must have turned a really nasty shade of green, because Luc dropped the sword and half hauled me through the darkness, depositing me in a white-tiled bathroom. I heard him speak in that silvery language, and a light came on.

I held myself together for as long as it took Luc to flee back down the hallway, and then I sank down to the toilet and promptly threw up everything I'd eaten in the last month.

When I was finally done, shaky but stronger, I rinsed my mouth out and washed my face, trying to figure out what had just happened.

I wasn't dead. I'd been in the park, and then those . . . *things* were there, and then *Luc* was there, and then I was *here*. Wherever *here* was.

Luc knew. He knew all sorts of things. The answers to my questions, for example. I reached for the side of the sink, unsteady but with a new resolve.

Carefully, I unwound the scarf, wincing at the spots where it had rubbed my skin raw. The ring was still clutched in my hand, leaving a perfectly circular red mark. I slipped it back onto its chain and let it dangle around my neck in plain view. True, it highlighted my complete lack of cleavage, but it was also my only bargaining chip, and I wanted it on display. I had a feeling Luc wouldn't dismiss me quite so easily while I had the ring. I took one last look in the mirror, shook my head at the disaster reflected back at me, and shrugged. It could have been worse. The thing in the park might have gotten me.

I shuddered, and went to find Luc, limping on my bad ankle.

The living room we'd passed through earlier was empty, and a soft, humid breeze scented the air with something sweet. Despite the heat, a small fire burned in a marble hearth. I brushed my fingers over a polished ivory statue sitting on a narrow table. The furniture was a mix of well-worn antiques and sleek modern pieces. Scattered about the room as carelessly as I dropped magazines were sculptures and art pieces, both classical and primitive, from around the world. Everything in the room was a strangely harmonious, clearly expensive mishmash.

I found Luc standing by a set of half-open French doors. His expression was impossible to make out. For a moment, I wondered if he'd spotted the things from the park, if they'd followed us, but the way he stood didn't seem to show any kind of fear. Exhaustion, yes, and so much tension he practically vibrated where he stood. But nothing that hinted we were about to be attacked again.

He turned toward me. Light from the fire threw shadows across his face. The sword was gone. He'd changed into a black linen shirt, open at the throat, and threadbare jeans slung low on his hips. His hair fell damply into his face, jet strands contrasting with his tawny skin, making him look as exotic as the rest of the room.

"Feeling better?" He took my arm, like an old-fashioned gentleman who also happened to be a pirate.

I knocked his hand away. "What in the *hell* was that?"

He looked down at his arm, deliberately misunderstanding me. "Where I come from, we call it manners."

"Don't give me the aw-shucks routine," I snapped. "The thing, in the park. What was that? Why did you have a sword? How did we get here? And where are we, anyway? I want answers. *Now.*"

He took my arm again, less gently, and propelled me across the room to the couch. "Sit."

"No. I am done following instructions, sword-boy. Start talking."

He shrugged. "Suit y'self."

After walking over to an intricately carved sideboard, he poured a glass of something the same pale gold as his skin.

He raised the glass in a mock toast and took a healthy swallow. I stood fidgeting while he studied me like a scientist would examine a specimen pinned to a board. The silence stretched thinner and thinner, until I broke it. "You owe me an explanation."

"Your concept of gratitude needs a little refinin'. I just saved your life." He shook his head, smug again.

I started toward him, fists clenched. Sword or no sword, I'd get the truth if I had to beat it out of him.

When we were almost toe-to-toe, he smiled, slow and easy. "You interested in a trade?" His eyes slid to the ring around my neck. "I'm partial to jewelry."

I didn't even think. "No way."

"You were ready to deal in the park."

"Because that thing was trying to *kill* me."

He smiled again, and there was nothing easy about it. I crossed my arms and stared back.

"Nothing in the world is free. If you ain't learned that yet, you're dumber than I thought." He took another drink, looking as if he hadn't thought me very bright to begin with. "Something about you don't add up, you know that? How 'bout this: answers for answers, Mouse. Final offer."

"How will I know you're telling the truth?"

"Because you'd like a lie better. We got a deal?"

I didn't trust him. I didn't like him, either, with his smugness and his secrets, no matter how enjoyable he was to look at. Then again, he'd saved my life. He cared about Verity. And since I didn't actually know anything, I'd be coming out ahead.

I stuck out my hand to shake. Instead, he brushed his lips over my knuckles, keeping those jade-colored eyes on mine.

"Pleasure doin' business," he murmured.

It was the breeze from the balcony making me shiver.

"I'll go first," he said. "Where'd Vee hide the ring? We've been searchin' everywhere."

"In a snow globe," I admitted. "She collects them."

He laughed, the sound startling and genuine. "Cheap-ass-lookin' thing? So ugly they should've paid her to take it, not the other way 'round?"

I nodded, smiling despite myself. "You knew about it?"

"She said it was too nasty to buy. Said Evangeline would drop dead before she let that thing into her home." He shook his head. "And you figured it out."

"I know the way she thinks. Thought," I corrected myself. The easy moment evaporated. "My turn."

He strode into an adjoining kitchen. "Fire away."

"What were those things in the park?" I sat down on the couch, crumpling the scarf in my hands, then setting it on the nearby table. Finally, I said what I hadn't allowed myself to think since the night of the murder. It was easier to ask when I couldn't see his face. "They weren't human, were they?"

I heard him rummaging in the cabinets, but he didn't respond immediately. "Once, maybe. Not anymore. They're Darklings."

"Darklings?" A bubble of hysterical laughter broke loose. "Like, what, nocturnal ducks?"

He came back with a plate in one hand, a teacup and saucer in the other. "Think of them like the monsters under your bed when you were little."

"Not real?" I asked, candy sweet.

He scowled. "How's your ankle? Feel like something real got hold of it? Darklings are nightmares. Doesn't mean they aren't real."

I didn't move.

"You saw what *one* of them can do. How many were in the alley with you and Vee? Six? Seven?"

"I don't know," I whispered, wishing I didn't believe him. "Lots."

"That many Darklings on a hunt, it's a miracle you survived." He handed me the cup, raised his glass. "To miracles," he said, eyes on mine.

"To . . . miracles," I echoed, and tasted the strong, sweet tea. For a split second, the air around us seemed to quiver. I tightened my grip on the cup. "Verity tried to fight them. She knew they were coming, I think."

"She would have felt them going Between."

"She knew about them?" Another one of Verity's secrets. Darklings, Luc, jewelry that probably cost more than a car. "What happened to her this summer? She was fine before. Everything was fine. We had plans. She went down to New Orleans, and everything changed. What did you *do* to her?"

"Nobody did anything. It's who she was."

"She was a teenage girl!"

"She was meant for more, and more's what got her killed." His hands curled into fists and flexed open again. "You're so desperate for the truth, Mouse? Here it is. The Darklings ain't human. Verity wasn't just some girl. She had magic, and a destiny, and she came to New Orleans to claim 'em both. Somebody was trying to stop her, set the Darklings on her. They killed her, and now we all pay."

I stared at him, every rational cell in me fighting against his words, my heart stuttering in my chest. "There's no such thing as magic."

His voice was laced with scorn. "Yeah? How'd we get here?"

"A cab, maybe? Your car? The details are a little fuzzy."

He shook his head. "Look outside."

I walked to the French doors and stepped onto the balcony. The second-story porch overlooked a street filled with sidewalk cafés and tiny shops. Couples strolled along, laughing, swinging shopping bags and holding hands. Breezy accordion music spilled into the night. I'd seen this view on Verity's data card. Luc, standing on the balcony, the city behind him. She'd stood here, this exact spot, and taken the picture. My knees loosened, and I clung to the railing. Then I limped back inside. Anger felt more comfortable than confusion.

"You kidnapped me? I passed out and you brought me to New Orleans? You don't think anyone's going to notice I'm missing?" Colin was going to kill me when he realized I'd flouted every rule and precaution he'd set up. Even more annoying than my impending death was the fact he'd been *right*. "What day is it? How long have I been gone?"

He shook his head wearily. "Same day. 'Bout fifteen minutes since we left the park."

"You're crazy." Verity had been wrong to trust Luc. I could see that now. I thought he was trustworthy, but now that I knew she'd been mistaken . . . I started to drift toward the door, looking around for a weapon. There was a carved wooden statue of a bird that looked heavy enough to do some damage.

"Where you gonna go, Mouse? Strange city, no purse, bad ankle? Use some of that brain Verity was always braggin' on. I won't hurt you." He advanced on me, hands up to show he was harmless. "Sit down and eat your toast. You'll feel better."

"Right."

"I brought you here with magic. I'll take you back the same way, once we're done. But we had a deal."

"And I should believe you . . . why?"

"If I wanted to hurt you, I would've left you to the Darklings."

I edged away, shaking my head. It sounded logical, but everything about Luc defied logic.

"You want proof?"

"Proof would be good."

"Let me see your ankle." I braced myself against the wall, ready to bolt. He knelt at my feet and examined the wicked-looking cut. He pulled out a cloth and dabbed gently at the blood, his fingers light and warm. "Wonder you didn't kill yourself in these shoes. Not that I don't appreciate the effect."

"Are you supposed to be magically obnoxious? Because that I would believe."

He grinned. "Close your eyes," he said.

"Um, no." That was the sort of move you saw in slasher movies, right before the killer decapitates a C-list starlet. Instead, I focused on the fireplace, the sound of the logs crackling, the shadows the fire cast in the dimly lit room.

Luc spoke, the words like a flame licking at leaves, his fingers hovering over the stinging cut and the deeper throb of the sprain.

A sparkling warmth flowed over my foot, traveling up my calf along with Luc's fingers, and the pain receded to a pinprick before disappearing entirely.

He gave my leg a light squeeze, and I dragged my gaze away from the dancing fire.

The cut was gone.

My ankle was unmarked, as if there'd never been anything wrong at all. I reached down and touched the spot where the cut had been, the skin smooth and unbroken.

"You . . ."

He nodded, getting to his feet. "Try standing."

I did, taking his hand in case I started to collapse.

The room spun and he guided me back to the couch. I sat down with a thump, unable to even form the question. I looked up at him, speechless.

"Magic," he said, smug as always.

CHAPTER 12

I picked up the teacup again, needing something to do, and set it right back down when I couldn't keep it from rattling in the saucer. Cautiously, I probed at my ankle.

Luc settled in next to me, one arm stretched across the back of the couch, like he hadn't just turned the room on its end.

"Could you . . . you know . . . explain?"

"Not much to explain. There's magic in the world. Some people have a talent for it. Some don't."

"That doesn't make any sense." Magic didn't exist. Sure, it was a handy explanation for everything that had occurred lately, but it was *impossible*. I opened my mouth to say so, but Luc stopped me.

"You aren't going to tell me I'm wrong, are you? Been a long day, Mouse. Been a long couple of weeks. You really gotta argue somethin' you know you can't win? Everything you've seen tonight and you still don't believe me?"

"Magic? Actual, real, witches and spells and broomsticks magic?"

He mock-scowled. "Now you're just pokin' fun."

"Magic?"

He nodded.

"And your talent is first aid?"

"Among other things."

I couldn't stop touching my foot. "In the hospital. You healed me."

"Seemed like the least I could do."

A thought struck me. "Why didn't you help Verity? You could have fixed her! She'd still be—"

His voice was sharp, cutting off my words neatly. "I can heal people, Mouse, not raise the dead. Magic has limits, too."

I threw myself back against the couch. "Then what's the point?"

"What's the point of anything?" he shot back. "It's like any other gift—brains, or a nice jump shot, or bein' able to wiggle your ears. Something in my blood lets me tap into the magic."

"Verity had it, too?"

"Oh, yeah."

"Did she know? Do her parents?"

"She knew, but her parents had no idea. They're Flat, like you. No magic. There's usually someone in the family, though. . . ."

"Evangeline." It wasn't a question.

He tilted his head in acknowledgment. "She gave Vee some tips, started making more trips up to Chicago once she realized what was happening. But Verity needed more guidance. She was packing too much power to be running around unsupervised. So, we brought her down to New Orleans."

"She came home, though."

"Girl was stubborn. Said she wasn't missing her senior year, wasn't leavin' you. You ask me, she got spooked."

I traced a finger along the edge of a cushion. "She backed out of our New York plan. She was going to Tulane."

"Compromise. Evangeline let her come back for this year. After that, playtime was over. She had a job to do."

"But the Darklings . . ."

"Followed her home. We didn't expect that. Didn't know they were such a threat."

"I still don't get why they were after her. What was the special job?"

He rubbed a hand over his face. "More than a job. She had a destiny."

I threw my hands in the air, exasperated. "Oh, again with the fate thing? Really?"

"You asked," he snapped. "So shut up and listen, 'cause I don't feel like repeatin' myself. There's a prophecy—something magic folk, Arcs, have been hearing for as long as anyone remembers."

I bit my lip to keep from interrupting.

"The raw magic that all Arcs draw on ain't stable. It's powerful stuff—too dangerous to mess with directly. Like . . . a nuclear reactor. You mess around with nuclear energy at the source, you'd be dead. But if you convert it, you can power a whole town, right? Magic works the same way. There's lines—ley lines, Flats call 'em—all over the world. They connect to the raw magic, draw it out, convert it to somethin' safe for Arcs to use. You with me?"

Not really, but I nodded.

"Good girl. Each line matches up to one of the four elements—earth, air, fire, water. Most Arcs use only one type. The other lines just don't work for 'em, like the power's not switched on. If you want to do magic, you tap into your element's line."

"What's your element?"

The fire in the hearth blazed up with a whooshing sound, and he grinned. "Guess."

I rolled my eyes, gestured for him to continue.

"We rely on those lines. Not just to work spells, but for political stuff, physical safety, everything. Without the lines to balance the magic, our whole world would fall. But the prophecy, it says the lines will fail, bit by bit. And when they slip completely, there'd be one person who could fix it. Turned out to be Verity." He dragged in a breath, carefully watching my expression. "Do you believe me?"

"Um . . . no. Even if I did, it's not logical. If Verity was going to save your world, why would anyone want to stop her? That makes no sense." None of it made sense, but it seemed like my only hope was to treat what he was saying as fact.

He looked weary, his eyes shadowed. "There's a group, the Quartoren, in charge of things. They make the rules, ensure all the different factions get along, make sure everything's running smooth. If the prophecy's right, and the Torrent comes, it'll all crash down. Chaos, pure and simple. The raw magic will wipe out the weaker Arcs. Be the perfect time to come in and take charge . . . magic fluctuating, Arcs dead, Quartoren scrambling . . . It's a power play. Taking out Verity was their opening move."

"Okay, so someone sent the Darklings after her to stop the prophecy. Who?"

"Still working on that." He looked at me, brow furrowed. "But now they're coming after you. I'm thinkin' it's got something to do with your taste in jewelry."

Unbidden, my hand crept to my neck. "I've had the ring for a few days, though. Why would they come after me tonight?"

"When did you put it on?"

"Just before the party."

He nodded, though his frown deepened. "Anything happen when you did?"

"It kind of . . . got brighter, but I was standing under a porch light. It was probably just a reflection. Why?"

"The ring reacts with the magic in Verity's blood, ties her into the lines. It sends out a kind of signal, but only for Verity, not anyone else. If someone tuned in right, if they were lookin' for it, they'd know when she put it on. They could use it to find her."

"You were tuned in? And the Darklings?"

"The ring's a family heirloom, part of the prophecy. I've been lookin' for it since Vee came home," he replied. "Darklings feed off of magic, so when the ring switches on, they come runnin' like it's dinnertime. Probably only held off because you were in a house full of people."

Assuming he wasn't crazy, it made sense. Kind of. "If the ring only worked for Verity, why would it matter if I wore it?"

"Something about you set it off." He took my chin in his hand, turned my face from side to side, inspecting it. "You sure you ain't got magic?"

I pushed his hand away. "No, I don't have—do I *look* like someone who can do magic? Wouldn't I have used it tonight?"

"Didn't ask if you were good at it. Could be you're not full strength. Or too scared to try."

"I'm just me. Plain, ordinary me. There's nothing special, much less magical, about me." Which was exactly how I liked it.

He pointed one long, elegant finger at me. For a brief hysterical moment, I thought he was going to work some sort of spell and I'd end up as a frog or a coatrack or something. "Nothin' ordinary about you, Maura Fitzgerald, no matter how much you're wishing otherwise." He paused, eyebrows lifting. "How's your daddy doing in Terre Haute? Parole hearing coming up soon, right?"

"Don't talk about my father."

"How about your uncle, then? Charming Billy Grady, the only Irishman in the Chicago Mob, runs your neighborhood and a good stretch of Western Avenue? Talked the Outfit into letting him run the territory, 'cause he could share the profits and keep the peace?"

"That's just talk," I said dully.

He shrugged. "Whatever. But that ring shouldn't light up for anyone except Vee. Since it did, might be good for your longevity if we could figure out why. Tell me 'bout the alley."

My fingers knotted together in my lap. Luc covered them with his own. "I can make it easier to remember."

My laugh sounded hollow, even to my own ears. "There's not enough magic in the world for that."

He had the decency to look ashamed. "All I meant was, if you're blockin' something, there's spells that can help."

"And have you digging around in my head? No, thank you." I closed my eyes. "I was spending the night at Verity's house. We went out for ice cream. I was mad at her. She was following me home, through the alley, and all of a sudden, she just . . . stopped."

"Go home," Verity says, and at first I think she's angry, too, but there's a note in her voice, tremulous, and I glance back, searching for something scathing and awful and hurtful to say. She's ruined everything and I want her to suffer for it.

Her face is vividly white in the too-dark alley, and her voice carries perfectly in the sudden silence. It's as if someone has pressed the mute button, and my feet slow as something comes swooping down, and my ears fill with a roaring, shattering sound.

"Run, Mo! Just run, damn it!"

They're prowling toward her, saying something hoarse and guttural, horrifying even though I don't understand the words.

"Run!" she screams, her face stark and terrified. "Go!"

I do, knowing she'll be right behind me. But when I reach the end of the alley, banging into a Dumpster and grabbing a

door frame for support, Verity is twenty feet away, surrounded by the monsters. She's answering them, her voice
light and liquid, ringing out in the night like a crystal bell.
The things close in around her and it's like watching a candle
flame being snuffed, her voice changing from that urgent,
powerful music to a scream.

I go back.

I launch myself at the nearest monster. He's crouched,
arms reaching for Verity, but when I jump on his back he
bats me away like a mosquito, claws ripping open my hand
and forehead, and I land, bone-jarringly hard. Blood ob-
scures my vision instantly. I can hear her screaming still, so I
try again. In seconds, I am soaring across the alley, slamming
into the wall. The world goes dark.

When I wake up, they're gone. Verity lies nearby, her arms
and legs at strange angles. Her breathing is shallow and
much too fast, and when I look, her chest is the worst thing
I've ever seen, a jagged tear down the middle, making a sucking, rattling noise with every breath.

"Mo . . ." she gasps, faint as an echo. Her eyes are glassy
and distant, the pupils tiny pinpricks. "Sorry . . ."

"You're okay," I sob, trying to hold the wound closed, an
ocean of blood spreading around us, hers and mine together.
"Just . . . hang on, Vee, don't go, don't you go, don't leave
me. . . ." But there is too much blood, more than anyone can
survive, and she is so, so cold. Shock and blood loss, I think
dimly, remembering the first aid unit of health class. There's a
figure at the end of the alley and I fall toward it, still holding
Verity in my arms.

"And then I was in the hospital."

"I found you both in the alley," Luc said. "Somebody had
called 911. I patched you up the best I could before the cops
came. There wasn't anything I could do for Vee. Ten minutes
earlier, might have had a chance."

I didn't know I'd been crying until Luc brushed at the

wetness on my cheeks and laced his fingers with mine. "Mouse . . . Maura. I'm sorry."

"I tried to help her," I whispered. "It wasn't enough, but I tried."

" 'Course you did," he soothed. He turned my hand over to see the ugly raised line stretching across my skin. "I can make this go away, you know."

I pulled away, clasping my hands together. "I want it," I said, not willing to explain why, even to myself. "And I want the people who sent the Darklings."

He let out a shocked laugh. "I don't think so. The one tonight nearly killed you. They'll send more if you stay in this."

"I can help!"

"Not like that, you can't. Too dangerous, Mouse."

"These people . . . they have magic, right? They won't go to jail?"

"Little hard to lock up. There are other ways to stop them, though."

"Like killing them?"

He shifted. "Maybe."

"Then I'm going to help."

His eyes narrowed. "No, you ain't. Dangerous enough for an Arc. For a Flat, it's suicide."

"I don't care."

"Look, that ring should work only for Verity. For it to do what it did tonight . . . it must think you're her. We can use that, maybe even stop the prophecy. Do you have any idea what that means for my kind? But you go out and get yourself killed, lookin' for revenge, we lose everything."

"I don't care about your prophecy. I want justice."

His expression darkened for a second, then cleared, a crafty light entering his eyes, turning them a dazzling shade of green. Casually, he asked, "What if you could have both?"

"I don't need both."

"But you need me," he pointed out. "You try to do this alone, they'll drop you by lunchtime tomorrow."

Inside, I shuddered, but kept my face neutral. "And this matters to you because . . . ?"

"I've saved your life twice now," he said easily. "Be good to protect my investment. I'll make you a deal."

"You're a big one for cutting deals, aren't you?"

"Makes the world go 'round," he said.

"Charming."

"So I've heard. Like I said, seems like you can use Vee's ring, and that could be useful."

"Useful how?"

His tone was guarded. "Not exactly sure yet."

"But you have an idea."

He traced the chain with the tip of his index finger, and I shivered again. He kept his voice low. "I am chock-full of ideas. For right now, let's say that our association could be mutually beneficial. You help me, and I'll let you tag along, hmn?"

He'd saved my life (twice), healed my wounds, fed me tea and toast, explained more than anyone else had since Verity died and yet . . . I was missing something. There was more to this than what he was telling me. But even if he didn't have the answers I needed, he was the only one who could help me get them.

"I'm not tagging along. This might be your world, but I've got the ring. We're partners."

He looked up sharply, searching my face, and finally nodded. "Partners, Mouse. Should make for an interestin' ride."

CHAPTER 13

I spent the next few days waiting for someone—Colin, Luc, my uncle, a horde of Darklings—to jump out at me. It made for a rocky start to the school year.

Kowalski, however, was a surprise. He sat on one of the benches outside the front door of the school. The light still had that end-of-summer glow, even in September, and the leaves were barely edged with yellow, like they were only toying with the idea of changing. Kowalski had both arms thrown over the back of the bench, soaking up the sun and admiring the view. His tie, purple and orange plaid, was so hideous it nearly vibrated. He spotted me and raised a hand in greeting as I came down the steps. I cast a quick, panicked glance at the curb, where Colin was parked. He'd given the all-clear sign, but no way would he wait patiently on the sidelines while I chatted with the police.

Kowalski stood, and on cue, Colin climbed out. I frowned, trying to will him back, but even with Verity's ring hidden beneath my shirt, I didn't have any powers. He kept coming.

"Nice weather, isn't it?" Kowalski said, gesturing at the puffy clouds drifting above us. "Hard to believe it'll all be over soon. I tell you, Mo, winters here are getting to be too much for me and the missus. Soon as Jenny heads off to college, we're moving to Pensacola."

I didn't say a word, simply shifted my bag a little and forced myself not to touch the ring, safely out of sight.

Kowalski breathed deeply, gazing upward. "Yep, I'm gonna fish every day. Trout, maybe, or redfish. Worlds different from what we get up here." His eyes lowered to mine. "Can we chat for a minute?" He gestured to the bench where his sport coat lay in a heap.

I remained standing. "I'm not supposed to talk to you without my lawyer."

He nodded. "Sure, sure. I just figured you might want to talk, you know, off the record. It's not even about the case."

He turned and lifted the tired-looking sport coat a few inches off the bench. Underneath was my purse, the one I'd lost at the playground. I groaned without meaning to.

By the time Luc had brought me back to my room that night, the sky was turning pink and blue, the sun edging over the horizon. Exhausted from the entire night, and nauseated from going Between again, I barely managed to pull on an old T-shirt before falling into bed. When I'd realized the purse was gone, I'd figured it was a lost cause.

"You want to call Ms. Stratton now? Your phone's still in there."

I sank onto the bench, dropping my messenger bag with a thud. Colin was ten yards away, looking totally uninterested but listening to every word. I could deal with him later, though. The first thing to do was take care of Kowalski.

"Good choice," he said. "Some kid at the grade school over on Montvale found it at recess today, turned it in to the uniform at the school. And when he checked the ID, your name rang a bell."

He handed it to me. The damp, mud-stained leather squelched unpleasantly when I gripped it.

"Must've been caught in that rain we had Sunday morning. What I'm trying to figure out is, why wouldn't you have gone looking for it? I mean, there's money in there, and your keys and phone—didn't you miss it?"

"I figured whoever found it would keep it," I said. Colin was watching me openly now, his face thoughtful, like a hawk trying to decide the exact right moment to swoop in on a baby rabbit. "I'm surprised they turned it in."

"Oh, people can surprise you. All the time."

I smiled tightly and reached for my book bag. "Well, thanks for bringing it back."

"My pleasure." He slapped his hands on his knees, like he was about to stand, and then settled back. "What were you doing over there, anyway? Hard to believe you'd be running around the city at night."

"I was at a friend's house," I said stiffly. "We went for a walk, and I must have left it behind. I've been kind of distracted lately."

"Can't blame you there. I'm glad we were able to return it. Your uncle's tax dollars at work, huh?" He stood up and shrugged into the navy sport coat.

"Thanks again, sir."

Two steps, and he turned back. "The uniform said something else, too. The playground was pretty ripped up—big gashes in the dirt, a couple of spots even looked scorched. And they had one of those big metal climbers, looks like Epcot. You know the type?"

"I've seen one before."

"Well, a bunch of the bars were cut away—sliced through, like someone was taking apart a Tinkertoy. Damndest thing. I don't suppose you noticed anything like that on your walk?" He watched me closely, hands tucked in his pockets.

"Nope."

"Figured." He set off down the sidewalk, calling back over his shoulder, "You might want to watch yourself, Mo. Your friend over there doesn't seem to be doing such a bang-up job."

Colin's chin jerked up, and Kowalski strolled away without another glance. Colin was next to me in three strides.

"Don't be..." I began. Colin grabbed my elbow and hauled me across the street. "...mad."

"How was your *book?* The Shakespeare you needed to read?" he snarled, throwing open the passenger door and shoving me in. He tugged at the seat belt, leaned across me, and I slapped his hand away.

"Jeez! I can do it!"

"Really? You're not showing me you know fuck-all about taking care of yourself!"

Kids were coming out of school, a crowd of girls in blue plaid skirts and navy sweater vests. They clustered together, staring at the truck. I snapped the seat belt in place and sank down farther in my seat. "Keep your voice down!"

He slammed my door and stalked around to his side. I cringed as he slid in. "Right. Wouldn't want people to stare. I'm sure nobody noticed you talking to the good detective."

"They're used to the police by now. Reporters, too. You're different."

"I'm here every day." He slid into traffic, sped toward home.

"Yeah. Scowling. You're kind of hard to miss." Pointing out that my classmates were staring at more than just his face wouldn't help the situation. "I'm sorry," I said in a smaller voice.

"Where did you go?"

"A party." *Louisiana.*

I could actually see the vein in his temple pulsing. "You snuck out for a goddamn *party?*" His voice dripped with disgust.

"It was the biggest party of the year. Everybody went. I'm kind of the resident freak show right now. Excuse me for wanting to be normal for one night."

He shook his head. "Ask me to take you. Don't sneak out in the middle of the night. You could have been killed."

He had a point, although not the one he thought. "Normal girls don't take their bodyguards to high school parties. Normal girls don't even *have* bodyguards."

"You're not normal," he said gruffly, his eyes sliding over me. "This would be easier if you were."

I bit my lip. "Thanks a lot."

"That's not what I meant," he said, tone softening. He paused and shook his head, back to business. "Where else did you go? And don't tell me the party was at the playground, or some line like that."

I swallowed. The trick to telling a lie, I'd discovered, was to keep things as true as you could. "There was a guy at the party."

Colin's hands tightened on the wheel. "Did he hurt you?"

"No. *No.* He was saying stupid stuff, and I was trying to avoid him, and I ended up overhearing these girls—the one who threw the party, and all her bitchy little friends, and they were talking about Verity, and me. . . ." My eyes burned and my throat tightened, but I dragged in a breath and kept talking. "They were saying it should have been me. They said I was the target, not Verity. Because of Uncle Billy. Why would they say that?"

The hard, angry line of his mouth seemed to soften for a moment. "The playground, Mo."

The man was like a Rottweiler. "I left. I took my purse and walked around until I got to the playground. It seemed like a good place to sit and think."

"You'd been drinking?"

"How'd you know?"

"Because I'm not stupid. Even if you think otherwise."

"I don't think that!"

He slammed a fist into the dash. "Then quit lying! Kowalski said that playground was trashed! You're saying it's a co-incidence?"

I picked my words carefully. "I didn't do anything to the playground."

"How did you get home?"

I almost laughed. "A friend."

"And the purse?"

"I was a little buzzed. I forgot it."

Colin shook his head as he pulled into my driveway.

"I'm sorry, okay?" I touched the thin cotton of his sleeve for a moment, felt the muscle like granite underneath. "Honestly, I am. It was a stupid thing to do."

"Yeah, it was."

"Are you going to tell my uncle? Or my mom?"

"I'm supposed to protect you," Colin said. "I can't do that when you lie to me and pull a bunch of rebellious teen bullshit."

I was surprised by how much his words hurt. I reached for the door handle, trying to gather up a few shreds of dignity. "In case you've forgotten, I *am* a teenager. And I wouldn't have to pull rebellious bullshit if you would stop making such stupid rules."

Startled at my own boldness, I hopped out of the truck, bag in tow, and stomped toward the back porch.

He followed me, footsteps thudding on the driveway. Great. I was hoping my dramatic exit would have been enough to end the discussion. The cranky, silent Colin of old suddenly appealed a lot more.

Halfway in the door, I turned around to find him inches away from me, jaw working angrily. "You're not telling me everything."

"Neither are you." I was sick to death of people keeping secrets. Everyone knew more than I did. Besides, Colin wouldn't believe me if I explained about the magic. He'd tell my uncle to have me committed.

"I am trying to keep you safe." He bit off the words. "That's all you need to know."

"The hell it is! Was Jill right?"

He threw up his hands. "Who's Jill?"

"The girl at the party. She said Uncle Billy was in the Mob, and they were actually coming after me, but they got Verity instead."

"Inside," he said, nudging me through the door.

"Is it true?" I dropped my bag on the kitchen floor. I'd always clung to the notion that my father was the only criminal in the family tree, no matter what people had whispered at church or in the hallways. But if Jill was right, Uncle Billy and my mom had been lying all these years, letting my father take the blame and holding my uncle up as some kind of saint. Which didn't make me less angry at my dad. There was plenty of mad to go around.

Colin leaned against the countertop, folding his arms. "We don't know who killed your friend. Until we do, your uncle figures better safe than sorry."

That wasn't the denial I was hoping for. "Safe from what?"

"Your uncle has . . . competitors. If they're looking for leverage, you and your mom are easy targets—you're the only family he has."

"Which is where you come in."

"Pretty much."

I chose an apple from the fruit bowl, to keep my hands busy. "What if you're wrong? What if it had nothing to do with Uncle Billy?"

He took out a glass and went to the fridge for iced tea, as familiar as if he'd always been here. "Probably it didn't. If someone was trying to send a message to him, they would have gone after you, and they'd have gotten it right."

I started to respond, but he held up a hand. "Which does

not mean you get to sneak out to a party, or whatever it is you were up to Saturday night."

"You said Uncle Billy wasn't involved!"

"I told you my opinion. I could be wrong. It could be that somebody's worried about leaving a witness. It could be lots of things, or nothing at all. Regardless, it's your uncle's call."

"You do whatever he says?" I leaned back against the wall, eyeing him over the apple. It was hard to imagine Colin playing by anyone's rules but his own.

"Billy's been good to me," he said simply. "And he pays me well."

"Are you going to tell him?"

He looked at me sourly. "I should."

"But wouldn't you get in trouble, too? How hard can it be to keep track of one girl? Doesn't that sort of thing get you kicked out of the bodyguard union?"

He scowled and focused on his iced tea, probably so that he didn't throttle me. "I won't tell Billy. *This* time."

I sagged against the wall a bit, relief flooding through me.

"But if you pull a stunt like this again, I'll not only tell him and your mom, I will move in."

"Oh, please." I waved a hand dismissively.

He set the glass down with unnerving precision and stalked across the room toward me. I flattened myself farther against the wall as he placed one hand on either side of me, so close I could see the scars and calluses. Not wanting to seem intimidated, I met his gaze. Mistake. Up close, his eyes were dark, dark gray, the color of flint, and I had the feeling they saw more than either of us wanted to admit.

When he spoke, I felt it in the base of my spine. "Kid, I will sleep outside your bedroom door and carry your books to class. Whatever it is you're up to—and I know you're up to something, so don't give me the big eyes—now is not the time for it. From here on out, you need to be straight with me. Are we clear?"

I started to give him my most innocent smile, and thought better of it. "Crystal."

"Good." He stepped back, and the oddly tense moment passed. After snagging the apple from me, he took a bite, giving me another long, appraising look, this one all business. "The alarm system never showed you coming back in. How'd you manage it?"

Ah, well. He'd wanted me to be straight with him. "Magic," I said, waggling my fingers.

The doorbell rang, and the temperature in the room seemed to drop fifteen degrees. Every muscle in Colin's body tightened and he tossed me the apple. "You expecting somebody?"

I shook my head.

"Stay here." He moved toward the door, hand at the holster on his back.

I wanted to point out that if someone were coming to kill me, they'd hardly ring the doorbell first. Colin didn't look like he'd hear a word I said, though, so I finished the apple and waited.

I heard the front door, and Colin, gruff as ever, as he let someone in. I strained to catch the second voice, but all I could hear was Colin summoning me.

"Visitor," he said as I walked into the living room. There was no gun in sight. Standing next to one of the ivory wing chairs, looking poised and slightly amused, was Evangeline.

"How are you, Mo?"

I wiped my hands on my skirt. "Okay, I guess."

"I find myself at loose ends today, and thought I might go downtown to do a little shopping. One of my favorite shops just received a shipment from Paris. I thought it might be worth inspecting. Would you like to accompany me? It's something Verity and I always did when I visited."

That wasn't all she'd done. She'd used those visits to train Verity, to get a feel for her powers. She'd groomed her to fulfill some grand destiny, and what good had it done? Evangeline didn't want to go antique shopping with me. If Colin hadn't opened the door, she would have interrogated me on the front stoop, those ice blue eyes pinning me as sharply as they were now.

I looked at Colin, who stood near the staircase, and he shrugged. "Fine with me," he said. "Call if you need anything."

Great. The one time I had hoped for an overprotective streak, Colin went all trusting on me. Was Evangeline doing some sort of magic even now? She didn't look like it, but what did I know about spells? "I'll get my bag."

"Of course," she said. "It was a pleasure to meet you, Mr. . . ."

"Donnelly."

"Mr. Donnelly. We should be back in a few hours."

"Sounds good." Colin followed me back into the kitchen and bent his head toward mine. "We're not done chatting," he said, his voice a quiet rumbling I could feel along my spine. "Do me a favor and stay out of trouble for the next little while?"

"I'll try." I even made it sound sincere.

And then he was gone. I went back out to the living room to face Evangeline.

"It's best we get under way," she said, leading me to the silver BMW idling in front of the house. "There's much to discuss."

CHAPTER 14

"I've had several fascinating talks with Lucien recently," Evangeline said as we pulled away. "You've been busy."

I double-checked my seat belt, smoothed my skirt over my knees, pushed at my bag with my toes—anything to keep from touching the ring. Luc had implied he and Evangeline were working together, but did she know everything? More than I did, that was for sure. "Lucien? You mean Luc?"

Evangeline frowned, disapproval radiating from her like a cold front. "It's a pity, really. Lucien comes from a renowned family, one of the most important in our world. The House of DeFoudre wields a tremendous amount of political power along with considerable magic. His father holds a seat on the Quartoren. One would hope Lucien would acknowledge his position by leaving behind such a childish name. Then again, he's always been an intractable boy."

She glided onto the Dan Ryan, merging seamlessly. "Your Mr. Donnelly is intriguing. A friend of the family?"

"Kind of." A thought struck me. "We *are* going antique shopping, right? Because he'll know if we don't. He's crazy-good like that."

"Luc mentioned you were under his protection. Inconvenient, but not insurmountable." She looked in the rearview mirror. "Yes, there he is."

I twisted in my seat. Sure enough, the beat-up truck trailed us by a few cars.

"You're not going to cast some sort of spell, right? Some sort of magical woo-woo to keep him away?"

"Magical woo-woo?" She sounded insulted. "Hardly. We can certainly go look at the shipment, Mo, if it will put you and your keeper at ease."

"He's not my keeper."

"Oh? Have I misconstrued your relationship? Lucien was under the impression that his role was merely to safeguard you."

I forced myself not to glance back again. For the first time, Colin's presence made me feel safe instead of annoyed. Once he'd stopped yelling, he actually treated me like a human being, which was nice. But it didn't change anything. Like the fact Uncle Billy was paying him. Or the fact he was out of my league in every possible way. And there had to be a body-guard code of honor forbidding him from getting involved with the person being guarded, right?

"There's nothing going on," I said, staring out the window at the skyline.

"Well, that makes things easier." She braked lightly as the traffic grew heavier. "Do you have the ring with you?"

"Yes."

"May I see it?"

I drew the chain out from underneath my shirt, and the ring swung back and forth, like a pendulum. "What does it do, anyway?"

"A number of things. It serves as a marker, identifying the subject of the Torrent Prophecy. It has belonged to Lucien's House since time began. As the Heir, he was the one who pre-sented it to Verity."

"Oh." Luc's earlier words about being attuned to the ring made sense now. I let go of the necklace, feeling stupid.

"According to legend, it was the tool Verity would use to

repair the magic—it would let her interact directly with raw magic, which is far too dangerous otherwise."

"Luc said I shouldn't put it on."

Her eyes drank it in. She lifted a hand as if to touch it, but traffic started up again. "He's quite right. The Darklings and their masters will be looking for it. They'll respond much more quickly the next time. But you should be safe so long as you don't wear it."

"He said they'd come after me anyway." It was something I'd tried not to think too hard about, or else the fear paralyzed me. Daylight helped. Being around people helped. Obsessively checking the dead bolt and alarm helped, even if they wouldn't do much good.

"It's a possibility."

"That doesn't make me feel any better." The air-conditioning kicked up, and I rubbed at my arms.

"There are measures we can take. They won't conceal you when you're wearing the ring, but they'll be sufficient otherwise."

I tilted my head back against the seat. "A spell?"

"Yes. It will hide you, even if a Darkling is as close to you as I am right now."

"I don't ever want to be that close to a Darkling again."

"A wise approach." She pulled into a parking garage and accepted the ticket. "It's a bit of a walk from here, but I do enjoy the view of the river. I hope you don't mind."

She led the way out to the sidewalk, ivory leather heels ringing smartly on the concrete.

"So, you and Luc are working together? To find out who killed Verity?"

She didn't break stride. "We have similar goals. I am the Matriarch of my House, as Lucien's father is the Patriarch of his. As such, I also hold a seat on the Quartoren. For the Quartoren—and our society—to survive, we must stop the prophecy. The Torrent will destroy the Arcs. My foremost obligation is to find out if Verity's destiny might still be fulfilled." Her brows drew together and her voice sounded strained as she continued, "But on a personal level, I very much want to discover who was responsible for my niece's death."

"Luc kept talking about a prophecy. He said Verity was supposed to save the world."

"She was."

"From what?"

We stopped along the Riverwalk. Somewhere nearby, Colin was watching over me like a cranky guardian angel, but I didn't have to look. The breeze tugged wisps of hair from my ponytail, the curving glass of the offices on Wacker Drive reflected the sky, and the water taxis and tour boats cruised past us on the river below. It was all so normal, a sight Verity and I had witnessed a thousand times. It didn't seem possible the rest of the world didn't notice she was gone. They continued about their routine as if nothing had happened. At least the Arcs recognized the sheer wrongness of her death.

"I'm happy to answer your questions, Mo, but I'd prefer we establish the cloaking spell first."

"Will it hurt?"

"A bit, to set it. After that, you won't notice it's there." She took my hand in hers and, with a quick slash of one perfectly French-manicured nail, nicked the pale inner skin of my wrist.

"Ow!" I said, trying to jerk away. The strength of her grip was surprising.

"You would find a Darkling much more painful." She stretched her free hand out over the railing, palm down. Waving her fingers in a graceful summoning motion, she took a deep breath, about to speak.

The gesture reminded me of something. "It was you. At the cemetery."

Her hand stopped and she raised an eyebrow, her expression glacial.

"You had on a blue robe."

"That was a ceremony for our kind. You should not have witnessed it." Despite the even, measured tone of her words, a dark, fast current of anger ran underneath them.

"Luc made you all vanish. He did something to me."

"Not to you. He concealed the ritual, like drawing a curtain shut at the theatre. You cost him the chance to participate," she added. "By rights, he should have led us. May we continue?"

I didn't answer, stunned by her words. No wonder he thought I was always interfering—ruining Verity's funeral, taking her ring—surviving when she hadn't. Now I'd demanded a partnership. He was either incredibly forgiving or incredibly desperate. I had a sinking feeling I knew which.

Evangeline began speaking in the strange, fluid language I'd heard both Verity and Luc use. I stood mesmerized by the sound. It was a startling contrast to the harsh noises of the city—the cabs and buses jockeying for position, the street musician across the bridge, the commuters and tourists rushing past us—and even though Evangeline spoke softly, it filled my head and blotted everything else out.

Still murmuring, she curled her fingers along the cut she'd made. I winced at the pain but stayed silent. Her fingertips beat a strange tattoo against my pulse. Suddenly the air felt twice as heavy on my skin, and I staggered under the uncomfortable pressure. The sensation vanished, and Evangeline was quiet again. She let go of my hand.

"That should suffice," she said. "It will break if you wear the ring, but for everyday concealment, you should be protected."

"You're sure?" The more magic I witnessed, the more dangerous it seemed. For once, it would be nice to have it on my side.

She looked offended. "Of course. Now, let's continue on before your protector decides I'm not to be trusted."

We made our way over to the Mart, crossing under the "L" tracks and weaving past tourists wielding cameras like weapons. The last time I'd been here, Verity and I had gone to an art show. I'd found a necklace I liked—glass beads and hammered metal spheres strung on superfine wires—but after one look at the price tag, I'd kept my hands in my pockets and trailed after Vee, who charmed the sellers and negotiated prices that were almost, but not quite, affordable. Now I followed Evangeline across the tiled lobby to the long bank of elevators, trying to distract myself.

"Luc said every Arc uses one element. Is yours water?" I asked as the elevator doors closed.

"Yes. Chicago is a good city for me, as is New Orleans, but even in the desert, there are lines of every element. The amount of power varies—not all conduits are equally strong—but a trained practitioner can accomplish much with even a thready line."

"What was Verity's talent?"

"Ah, Verity. She was so special," Evangeline said, her voice catching, taking on that dreary, dusty tone adults always used when they were being nostalgic. She paused, adjusting the lapel of her jacket, and continued. "I didn't realize it at first—I'd assumed she had a talent for water, as I did. It was the first kind we'd tried, and she took to it so naturally. It's quite common for such things to run in families, you know."

"Sure." Genetics I could understand. Verity's family passed along magical abilities, mine carried the chromosome for crime and deception.

"I asked Verity to complete a transformation—to change the contents of a bowl from apples to pears. It's a simple-enough task—we can neither create matter nor destroy it, but we can transform it quite easily. Child's play, really, but she'd only been using magic consciously for a few weeks. I wanted to see how much energy she could draw from the closest ley line. The closest *water* line," she emphasized. "Instead, she tapped into a nearby earth line. I'd never paid it much attention before then. It served no purpose for me."

"And that was a big deal?"

"Most Arcs can use only one element. A rare few can use two, and it's considered a mark of great power. Three is unheard of, except in the prophecy." She sounded simultaneously awed and envious.

"And Verity had three." Somehow, this was not a surprise to me. Of course Verity had more powers than the other Arcs. She had more talent than the rest of the senior class combined. Why should magic be any different?

"Yes. I tested her thoroughly, to be certain. With virtually no practice, no training, she could use lines of water, earth, and air masterfully. I consulted with elders, with historians and archivists, with the heads of the other Houses. Verity demonstrated her abilities for them, and all were in agreement. She was the prophesied one. She was the Vessel."

CHAPTER 15

"The Vessel." My voice echoed in the marble-tiled elevator. Even with everything I'd heard and seen, this seemed like a stretch.

"It's an antiquated term," Evangeline agreed. "But this prophecy—the Torrent Prophecy, as it's known, is an ancient document, one of the earliest in our recorded history."

"And it says Verity is a vessel?"

"Not 'a vessel.' *The* Vessel."

"Well, that clears it all up. What is this prophecy, exactly?"

"Lucien didn't tell you? He indicated you had formed a partnership. I assumed he had already explained. . . ." She trailed off delicately, as if she didn't want to get him in trouble.

"He was a little fuzzy on the details."

"Yes, he does play his cards rather close to the chest, doesn't he?" She gave me a faintly sympathetic look, then drew a breath and began to speak in the same ponderous voice people used when reciting Psalms. "'The Vessel for Three Talents must be bound to the last of the Fire-Marked House. So joined, she shall forge the lines anew at the hour the Torrent comes, else it shall sweep through the worlds and make as dust all who are unprepared.'"

I was still gaping, trying to make sense of it, when the elevator doors opened and she ushered me through the hall to a lushly carpeted showroom. "Quite dire, you see. Without the Vessel, there is no hope of stopping it," she said as the man inside hurried to greet her.

They chattered in French for a few minutes, and she turned to me. "I need to examine a few pieces, but it won't take long. Why don't you look around for a bit? It never hurts to develop an eye for quality."

Everything in the store looked old, and expensive. After one careful stroll around the room, I decided it would be better to sit quietly in the corner until Evangeline was done. I chose a chair that looked like it wouldn't splinter into toothpicks, and settled in.

Evangeline circled the room, so intent I decided she'd forgotten me. The salesman, Fabian, trailed behind her, anxiously offering up nuggets of information. Evangeline would nod, never sparing him a glance. Finally they stopped. Fabian burst into rapid-fire French, clasping his hands and practically bouncing on his toes. Evangeline turned toward me.

"What do you think?" she asked, gesturing to a tall cabinet with elaborate carvings and faded flowers painted all over it.

"It's fine, I guess." It was rude, but musty old furniture wouldn't help me find Verity's killers. Still, years of training kicked in. "The flowers are pretty," I said dutifully.

Fabian made a tastefully disapproving sound and slanted Evangeline a dubious look. He was slight and oily, with a sharp little rodent face and a greedy light in his shrewd eyes. "This is an eighteenth-century Parisian bibliothèque desk. Its provenance is exquisite."

"Better still," Evangeline said, "this piece hides its greatest charms." She gently pressed one of the gilt-covered flowers along the back. With a faint click, the panels on either side of the rosette slid away, revealing two compartments, both filled with ribbon-wrapped stacks of yellowing paper.

"The letters," Fabian put in, "are the correspondence between the wife of a French officer and her lover, an English spy. The liaison provided England with valuable intelligence that turned the tide of the Napoleonic Wars."

"You see," Evangeline said, her ice blue eyes on mine, "even something that appears superfluous at first glance can reveal hidden depths. Treasure, if you will. I always find such things fascinating." She turned away again. "Ship it to the store, Fabian, along with the Limoges and the damasks."

Fabian nodded enthusiastically, and scurried to the back, quivering with glee.

"So, Verity's ring is like the desk? It has hidden powers?"

"I was referring to you."

"Me?" I placed a hand on the shiny black tabletop next to me. "I don't have powers. Any powers. At all."

"And yet, you can wear the ring, which suggests that there is . . . something . . . unique about you." She paused as Fabian returned with a sheaf of papers. Withdrawing a heavy, gold-tipped pen from her purse, she signed each of them without a glance.

"Aren't you going to read them?"

"Oh, Fabian knows better than to take advantage of me."

He drew himself up to his full five foot four. "We pride ourselves on our honesty."

"Just so," said Evangeline. She issued a few more directions in French, allowed Fabian to kiss her on both cheeks, and swept outside, with me trailing after.

"I told Luc before—I don't have any magic."

"Which was obvious when I invoked the concealment spell. Had you any power, it would have repelled or augmented my efforts. Nevertheless, the ring responds to you. As it did my niece. The implications are significant."

"Yeah. Darklings try to kill me every time I put it on."

She ignored me. "What's perplexing is *why* it responds. No magic, no talents, nothing extraordinary about you. You have no bloodlines to speak of. You're nothing like Verity."

The words stung, more than I'd expected. I'd long ago accepted Verity was the star. I had willingly, eagerly been the one on the sidelines. But I wasn't *worthless*. "I never said I was," I shot back.

Evangeline eyed me, frowning, and it was clear I didn't pass inspection. "Bloodlines," she murmured. "Let me see your hand."

I held it out wordlessly. The gash Luc had healed was a livid purple scar—a little less ugly every day, but it still pulled when I wiggled my fingers.

"You touched her with this hand?"

"I tried to stop the bleeding."

"Blood binds magic as few other things can, and a sacrifice carries great power. It would have been a simple matter for Verity to go Between when the Darklings attacked, but she chose to stay and protect you."

I swallowed, hard, as she continued. "It's possible, I suppose, that once Verity's blood mingled with yours, some small part of her essence could have transferred to you— enough to compel the ring to accept you in her stead."

"Except I don't have her magic." Wishing I had magic wasn't going to make it happen. Wishing never made anything happen.

"That is troublesome. However, since the ring recognizes you, there may still be hope." She didn't sound all that hopeful, though.

"Hope for what, exactly? You guys keep saying Verity was going to save the world, but how?"

"All magic flows through the ley lines," Evangeline said. "But they're fraying, more rapidly every day. We had hoped Verity could repair them and prevent the Torrent from coming to pass."

"Why are the lines failing?"

"Entropy is not exclusive to this world, I'm afraid. Magic, like anything else, can devolve into chaos unless it's properly tended."

"Verity was going to repair the lines?"

"More than repair. According to the prophecy, when the Torrent finally occurred and the raw magic was loosed, the Vessel would re-form the lines completely. It would be a staggering display of power. She would literally change the world."

"But Verity can't fulfill the prophecy. What happens to the magic?"

"It continues to destabilize. Soon it will begin to rupture at the weakest points. There are things skilled mages can do to delay the ruptures, but they are temporary fixes. Once the raw magic breaks through, it will kill Arcs with weak or unrevealed talents. Constance, for example, has not yet reached the age for her abilities to surface, should she possess them. When the Torrent comes, she will likely not survive. Naturally, any Flats in contact with a line at that time will be killed as well."

She said it dispassionately, but I felt sucker punched.

"How many?" I asked.

"Pardon me?"

"How many Flats in danger?"

"I hadn't really considered the issue. Perhaps . . . one percent of the population? Population centers tend to spring up near the most powerful lines, so the casualty rates would be higher here, lower in rural areas."

One percent. Even at St. Brigid's, that was fourteen girls. Girls I'd known for years. And Con, too? Hadn't Verity's family suffered enough? Surely the magic wouldn't be so cruel—not that it had shown any signs of mercy so far. "Why would someone want that?"

"Pardon me?"

"Why would someone want all that raw magic flying around if it's so dangerous?"

Evangeline pursed her lips. "There are a variety of reasons, most of them political. There are groups—alliances, if you will—that regulate different aspects of our society. One of them may feel that in the aftermath of the Torrent, they would emerge stronger than other alliances."

"And they'd let innocent people die?"

"Power is a seductive thing. It's the rare individual who doesn't yearn for more than their allotment."

"Yeah, but most people wouldn't destroy an entire society so they could be king of the mountain." Then again, maybe it depended on the size of the mountain.

"Most people wouldn't risk interfering with a prophecy of this magnitude, either. Fate is not something one should treat lightly. The fabric of the universe will almost always buckle in order to maintain the pattern, and the repercussions are unpredictable. Which may again explain why Verity's ring responds to you."

"I don't believe in fate."

"No? What about God's will?"

"People keep saying Verity's death was God's will," I said. "In fact, whenever something bad happens, they tell me that. Like that makes it okay, or something. It doesn't. And it doesn't prove anything about God or fate or whatever. All it proves is, life really sucks."

Evangeline drove in silence for a while, and I stared out the window as the view changed from the high rises of the Loop to funky lofts to slowly gentrifying brownstones, and finally my neighborhood. It was mostly blue collar and a little shabby, but the lawns were neat and the storefronts were all occupied. People strolled down the sidewalks instead of rushing, heads down, to get someplace better. It wasn't fancy—it was a quiet place where people tried to make a life for themselves. For me, it was the place where everyone knew my family's shame—my father in prison, my mother loyally waiting for his return, my uncle a man to flatter and fear. And I was the one they all shook their heads over, the one they pitied because they believed who I came from defined who I was.

It didn't.

"I'd like you to consider something," Evangeline said as we pulled up in front of my house.

"What?"

"You've made it plain your interest lies in seeking revenge for Verity's death." I stared at our front stoop, the crumbling lip of the steps and the flecks of rust on the cast-iron railing, as she continued. "Yet Lucien and I are far more likely to uncover the truth, and more suited to meting out retribution."

"I promised her."

"We want to honor that. Promises carry a great deal of weight in our world, Mo. The people who killed Verity prevented her from fulfilling her destiny. Right now, they are feeling fat with overconfidence, believing their work is done. By stepping into her destiny and completing the task set out for her, you could prove them wrong. Verity's sacrifice would not have been in vain. A more complete revenge, really."

"Wait. You want me to be the Vessel? Stop the Torrent?"

She didn't wait for a response. "Consider it," she said, as Colin's truck pulled up behind us. "We'll be in touch."

CHAPTER 16

"Tell me more about the guy," Lena said, bouncing slightly in her chair.

I used the mouse to nudge a column on the monitor an eighth of an inch. "What guy?"

"The one who took you home from the party. He's the same one who picks you up after school, right? Do you two have a thing going?"

I didn't even know where to start correcting her. Explaining Colin was hard enough, even to myself. If I said he was a bodyguard provided by my uncle, everyone would think Jill was right, that Verity's death had been meant for me. Calling him a friend of the family meant he was fair game for all of the girls in school, which seemed too cruel, especially since he'd kept quiet about Jill's party. Saying he was a friend of *mine* was not only laughable, but awkward.

Colin was a lot of things—solid and stubborn and gorgeous, to name a few, but friendly was not the word I would use to describe him.

"We don't have a *thing,* and Colin didn't pick me up from the party," I said, trying to focus on the newspaper layout in front of me. We were doing a special memorial insert for Verity, and Lena's desire to investigate my newly complicated social life was slowing us down.

Lena slanted me a skeptical look. "How'd you get home?"

"Just a friend. No one you've met." Luc had been strangely absent since the night of the party, and the quiet was unsettling. I hoped it was because he was tracking down leads or figuring out how to stop the Torrent, not because he had changed his mind.

"Are you going to invite your just-a-friend to Homecoming?"

I was saved from having to answer by the approach of Ms. Corelli, the newspaper advisor. She was a comfortable-looking woman, with a sensible, brown bob, who managed to get the newspaper out on time without making everyone freak out. It was a nice change of pace from home, where my mother was perpetually in panic mode.

"Nearly done, ladies? I would love to be finished with this in time to catch the late news."

"You know, Ms. C, they have this thing now? CNN? You can watch the news any time you want. Very cool." Lena grinned, her finger paused on the article she was editing.

"They have this thing called a grade book, too," Ms. Corelli returned with a smile. "And I can mess with it any time I want. Where are we at?"

"We're in the final pass," I said. "Tweaking a few layout things, and Lena's proofing one last time."

"And the memorial?" I could feel her checking for any sign of an imminent breakdown.

"I found a few more pictures to include, but it shouldn't be a problem." Except, of course, the Verity we were remembering hadn't really existed.

I'd always known the girl the rest of the world saw, the charming, beautiful, talented girl they loved and admired. But that was only a public face. When it was just the two of us, Verity was . . . more. Sharper, funnier, more outrageous. Less perfect, certainly, but more real, and more precious. Not everyone got to witness that part of her—only me, because we trusted each other. Now I knew the truth—even with me, she'd been acting. There were vast patches of her life she'd never shared with me, and I couldn't help wondering, how was I different from the rest of the world? Trying to put together a memorial for her seemed nearly impossible. Every photo and quote we'd collected felt fake.

"If you want to let Lena bat cleanup on this one, it's okay," Ms. Corelli said.

I shook my head. "I'm fine. Really."

She rested a hand on my shoulder for a moment. "Sister Donna also wanted me to let you know they've heard from the NYU rep. She'll be here earlier than usual this year."

My stomach pitched and my hand tightened on the mouse. I'd been so caught up with Luc and Evangeline, I'd nearly forgotten my *real* plans. "For interviews, or a meet and greet?"

"Interviews *disguised* as meet and greets," she said ruefully. "They like to sit down and visit with the serious candidates. If you're not up for it, Sister Donna could explain."

"No!" The last thing I wanted was some sort of special treatment. That was the whole point of going to NYU. I was tired of people tiptoeing around me, talking in low voices, giving me the sympathetic head tilt and gently understanding smile meant to convey they shared my pain. It was *my* pain, and it was what kept me going.

"I'm looking forward to it," I said. Not quite the truth, but not a bald-faced lie, either.

"I know you're really counting on NYU, Mo, but remember, they've historically taken only one St. Brigid's student from each senior class. They'd be lucky to have you, but I don't want you to be too disappointed if it doesn't pan out. You have safety schools, right?"

I swallowed and turned back to the monitor. "Of course."
Lena, perceptive as always, stretched in her chair and checked the clock. "We'd better get going. They're not going to hold the weather report for us."

Ms. Corelli gave my shoulder another squeeze and headed back to her desk. "Yell if you need me," she said.

Suddenly anxious to get away, I stood. "I'm going to grab a Coke. Lena, you want anything from the vending machine? Ms. C?"

"Oooh. Caffeine. Mountain Dew, please," said Lena. Ms. Corelli shook her head and gestured to her ever-present travel mug.

The school always had a strange smell this late at night, a mixture of antiseptic, musty paper, and the competing perfumes of fourteen hundred teenage girls. The hall lights were on, but the classrooms were dark, and the effect was echoing and lonely. I rubbed the spot where Evangeline had nicked me, walked a little faster. She'd said the spell would conceal me from Darklings, but she hadn't mentioned whether they were the only ones I should be worrying about.

I arrived at the vending machine and paid my dollar, pressing the button for a Diet Coke. A bottled water fell out, and I swore. This was the wrong time for our temperamental vending machines to act up. I needed caffeine. Natural arctic springs weren't going to help me finish the paper. I dug in my pocket for another dollar, fed it in, and before I could push the button again, another water appeared. I frowned, my hand hesitating over the correct button, and a third tumbled out.

I knelt down and tried peering into the machine, but all I could see was the black plastic chute. A chuckle sounded behind me, and I looked up to see Luc standing underneath an antidrug poster.

I straightened, dusting off my knees. "Very funny. I want my money back."

He rolled his eyes and waved a hand. A Diet Coke rattled down the chute. "Water's better for you," he pointed out. "Clean living, and all that jazz."

"I need a Mountain Dew, too."

"Buy it yourself. I ain't a short-order cook."

"The machine ate my money, thanks to you. Start wiggling your nose, or whatever."

He muttered something under his breath, and I collected the second bottle. "Took you long enough to figure it out," he said.

"It's a vending machine. When it doesn't work, I assume it's broken, not that magical forces are aligning against me."

He came closer, brushing a wisp of hair away from my cheek. "Considerin' recent events, you might want to change your perspective. Where's Cujo?"

"Around." Outside, waiting for me to finish. "Why? You want to meet him?"

"Didn't come here for him," Luc said. The narrow space between our bodies nearly hummed with energy. "You have a good chat with Evangeline?"

"She makes me nervous." So did he, but I wasn't about to give him the satisfaction of admitting it.

"Might be the first sensible thing you've said since I met you," he said. "Evangeline's a Matriarch—the head of the House of Marais, and they're one of four running the show right now. She's okay, though. If she gets ornery, it's 'cause she's got a lot at stake."

Evangeline seemed too sophisticated to be called ornery, but I got his point. Driven seemed a better word. "Verity was her niece. Of course she does."

He all but patted me on the head. "And you can't keep as-

suming everyone cared as much about Vee as you. For a lot
of people, she only mattered because of the prophecy."

"Are you one of them?"

Tension surfaced on his face, his gaze going far away. As
he refocused on me, the lines around his mouth slowly eased,
and he ran his fingers through the hair flopping into his eyes.
"Don't misunderstand, Mouse. I believe in the prophecy. I've
spent my whole damn life gettin' ready for it. But me and
Verity . . . it wasn't just the magic that made me care about
her."

I looked away. The pain in his voice was hard enough to
hear. Seeing it turn his whole expression bleak was more than
I could handle. Knowing someone else loved Verity should
have made me feel less alone. Instead, I felt a wash of jealousy—and shame. They made the perfect couple, leaving me
on the outside. Again. I wasn't sure, though, which I was
more jealous of—Luc, for knowing who Verity truly was, or
Verity, because she got to have Luc. He was smug and irritating and clearly not good for me in any sense, and still I felt
this strange little hiccup in my veins whenever he looked at
me. I couldn't shake the feeling that Luc, more than anyone
else, saw me. *Really* saw me, instead of the girl I let everyone
believe they knew.

It was not a comfortable feeling.

I edged toward the door, eager to return to Lena and Ms.
C's gentle prying, but he stepped closer and cupped my elbow
with his hand.

"C'mon." His voice was back to normal—the overconfident drawl that made me want to hit him with the nearest
blunt object while closing my eyes and sinking into its warmth.
"We got work to do."

He drew a line of flame in the air with one finger, muttering at the same time, and I jerked away. The flickering line

was quieter than it had been in the park, but seeing it in the middle of the student commons still jarred.

"I've got to go back upstairs. We're finishing the paper." I raised the two bottles of pop as evidence. "They're expecting me." I didn't mention what Colin would do if he found me gone.

Luc paused in his tracing, the doorway half-finished, suspended in midair in front of our trophy case. The magic made the green of his eyes more vivid; it was practically radiating off of him. I wondered if it could be measured, if it showed up somewhere on the infrared spectrum or a Geiger counter. Magic would be so much easier if there was some way to *explain* it.

"Thought you wanted in on this," he said scornfully. "Of course, if working on your school project is more important than findin' out who killed Verity, scurry on back, Mouse. I don't have time to waste."

He finished the top of the door and started down the last side. I glanced back at the staircase, certain he wouldn't offer again. Verity would appreciate justice a lot more than some memorial in the school paper.

"Wait." I set the pop bottles under the trophy case. "Is this safe?"

"Does it matter? Hold tight, and we'll be fine."

"Couldn't we just take a cab?"

"To New Orleans? No." He reached his hand out. I took it, feeling my breath quicken.

Luc drew me closer, circling both arms around my waist. I didn't know where to put my hands—on his chest, around his neck, left hanging at my sides—and he smirked. "This ain't the time to be shy," he said. "How about like we're dancing?"

I rested my hands on his shoulders, feeling as shy and

geeky as a kid at her first dance, and he tightened his grip. We were close enough that I could see the weave of his T-shirt, a silky-fine black cotton, and feel the heat coming off his skin.

"See? Not so bad." His voice was low, rustling my hair. "Try not to throw up this time, hmn?"

CHAPTER 17

When we came through, I stumbled against Luc, my nose smashing against his chest, and he tightened his hands on my waist to steady me.

"I've got you."

The ground under my feet tilted and wobbled, and I clung to him. It was embarrassing, but so was throwing up on his shoes.

"You okay?"

My face was still buried in his shirt, soft jersey against my cheek, my eyes squeezed tight. I nodded once, uncertainly. When my head stayed on, I let go, stepping back. We stood in a courtyard, the air damp and sweet, with white flowers glowing against shrubs that looked glossy black in the dusk.

"Is it always like this? Going Between?" I clenched my teeth and willed the nausea to recede.

"Don't know," he said. He guided me over a path of tiny seashells that crunched under our feet. "Never had to bring someone through before you."

"What, you don't spend a lot of time with Flats?" I meant to sound sarcastic, but it came out genuinely curious. "What about school?"

"Didn't go. Not to your kind, anyway."

"Verity did."

"Vee's parents were Flat. Kids who grow up in a house with magic do things differently."

"So you never hang out with Flats? Really?"

"Not usually." He said it so offhandedly I knew it must be the truth. I wavered, unsure if I felt special or freakish. He leaned down and with two fingers tapped the lock on a tall wrought-iron gate. It swung open noiselessly. "Goin' Between should get easier the more you do it."

"I'm not planning on making this a habit." The idea of going Between as often as I caught a CTA bus made my knees buckle. Luc looked at me strangely but didn't say anything. "You didn't use the sword this time."

He shook his head. "Didn't need it. Every Arc has a channel, something to use when you need a lot of magic all at once. But it lacks finesse, hmn?"

"And you prefer finesse?"

"Oh, Mouse. I am all about finesse." His thumb rubbed a slow circle on the small of my back, and I tripped.

To cover, I asked, "What are we doing, anyway? You never said."

"Nobody knows who put the order out on Verity, or if they do, they ain't talking. Person we're meeting tonight, though, has the why."

"You said it was to break the prophecy."

"Magic's a funny thing; so's fate. Once you mess around with what's been foretold, you can't predict the consequences, like what happened with you. We need to know why they wanted the prophecy broken, what they hoped to gain. We get that, we'll know who killed Vee."

"What do I do?"

He paused. "Follow my lead."

His nonanswer made me wary. My expression must have shown it, too, because he stopped again, exhaled slowly, and took my hand. "This meeting . . . you ain't gonna like it. But people see you taking offense, we won't get what we need. And truth is, I shouldn't be bringin' you along—this ain't really your kind of place."

"Then why did you bring me?"

He smiled, mockingly. "You said you wanted to be involved, Mouse. Just tryin' to honor our deal." His expression sobered. "Whatever happens, whatever is said, you need to bite your tongue and let it go. Can you do that?"

I'd been biting my tongue for most of my life. Nice girls do not argue with their mothers, their uncles, their teachers, their customers . . . they don't argue. So for seventeen years, I'd been holding back, except with Verity. With her, I could say exactly what I thought, and she welcomed it. "And people always say you're the nice one!" she'd laugh. But I wasn't—I was the *quiet* one. Since she'd died, I'd been biting my tongue less and less. She would have approved, especially with Luc. But for tonight, for her, I could stay quiet once again.

"You'll explain everything, later? The stuff I don't get?"

"Don't I always?" He started off again, keeping hold of my hand.

"Not really, no."

We walked in silence the rest of the way. It felt different from Chicago, the night air heavy and warm, no hint of autumn. It smelled like flowers and spice instead of concrete and the lake. Luc's fingers laced with mine were strong and real, the only part of this night remotely normal.

"Here," he said, coming to a stop.

It was a boarded-up, dilapidated storefront. Graffiti was scrawled across the plywood-covered windows, a grime-covered For Sale sign was nailed to the door. "This? You're meeting these people here? It's a tenement."

"Spells hide more than people." He pushed open the door, music and voices spilling out, and guided me inside.

The room we stepped into was no tenement—dimly lit, with lamps casting warm pools of light onto scarred wooden tables, and a couple of pool tables with games in progress. In the opposite corner, a grizzled old man played something bluesy on a battered guitar while a stunning woman, her hair a waterfall of tiny braids, swayed and sang about love and lies. Her dress glittered, casting rainbows on the floor and walls. When she spotted Luc, she canted her body toward him, her smile a lush, blatant invitation. He acknowledged her with a nod and a quick gleam of teeth, but his eyes stayed cool and unreadable.

Keeping my hand firmly in his, Luc surveyed the room. People seemed to know him—many of the people seated at the long, copper bar nodded in recognition. Some of the people at the tables stopped their conversation and openly gaped.

He leaned toward me. "Be helpful if you could look a little less like a deer in the headlights. Maybe even pretend you like me."

I tamped down my irritation and smiled at him—a slow, lazy smile like the ones he gave me sometimes, the ones that made me the slightest bit light-headed. He blinked and smiled back, a hint of the predator showing through. I hadn't felt like prey before, but I did now. "You should do that more often," he said, lips brushing my earlobe, and went back to studying the room.

Finally he focused on a deep booth in the far back corner. The small circle of light didn't illuminate the occupant. The nearby tables were empty. He tugged me forward. "Showtime."

We approached the table, Luc keeping me partly behind him.

"Ah, Luc," came a satiny voice from the shadowy recess of the booth. "I was starting to wonder if you'd show."

"Niobe. Always a pleasure. May we sit down?"

"We?" A woman with skin the color of nutmeg leaned forward into the lamplight. "A new companion? Already? People might talk."

Luc pulled me closer, running his hand up and down my arm, the gesture more possessive than affectionate. "Good to give them something to talk about," he said easily. "Verity's gone. The old rules don't apply."

Niobe inspected me closely, and the pressure of Luc's fingers against my arm kept me from wriggling under her gaze. Her expression turned vaguely distasteful. "My agreement was with you alone. The girl's not welcome."

"She won't say a word," he drawled, toying with the ends of my hair. "She'll just sit and look pretty."

I jerked my elbow, overcome with a sudden desire to ram him in the gut, and he tightened his grip.

"She doesn't belong here."

"She belongs to me," he said mildly.

To him? Only my promise to Verity kept me from telling Luc exactly where he could shove his stupid sword.

"She waits at the bar. I don't conduct business with Flats."

He scoffed. "Didn't know you had such delicate sensibilities."

"The bar, Luc, or our business is concluded. You can have playtime later."

"Do it," I whispered, curling my fingers around the back of his neck, doing my best to look like a vapid girlfriend. I'd practically grown up at Black Morgan's. Magic or not, this was an environment I understood. People got funny when it came to doing business in front of others. "I'll be fine."

He scowled, but walked me over to an empty stretch of the bar. The bartender, a giant of a man with an intricately tattooed skull and biceps as big around as Christmas hams, started over.

"Don't you move from this seat," Luc hissed. "Don't talk to anyone, don't make a fuss. Just wait here all quiet-like and we'll be through soon."

"Diet Coke?" I said to the bartender, not wanting to give Luc the satisfaction of a response. My drink appeared before me instantly, in a frosted mug. I turned back to Luc. "Go!"

"Stay here," he said, and headed back to the sleek, terrifying Niobe.

I had a perfect view of the room from where I sat, of the stage and the pool tables, the entrance and Niobe's booth. Colin would have approved, at least from a tactical standpoint. Of course, if he knew I was here, Darklings and other magical bad guys would be the least of my worries.

"Anything else?" asked the bartender, polishing a nonexistent spot on the counter.

"No, thanks." I was content to nurse my drink and people-watch, and he made his way back down the counter to the other paying customers. It wasn't much different from Morgan's—smokier, but the scent only made me nostalgic. There were games running at both pool tables. The staccato clack of the balls and the soft *thwock* as shots were made was a nice counterpoint to the music. The singer seemed to have forgotten about Luc. She was back to singing to the entire room. I felt her gaze drift toward me a few times before shying away.

I couldn't tell if the pool players were using magic to throw the game. Maybe it cancelled out—if both players were drawing on ley lines, neither had an advantage. I wondered how much magic Verity's killers had, how good they were. They'd sent Darklings instead of going after her themselves. Were they not strong enough, even before she'd fully refined her powers? Or did they want to be untraceable? Was the attack a sign of desperation or a show of strength?

Someone sat down next to me, a nondescript guy in a T-shirt and khaki shorts, probably a little older than Luc. He

looked like most of the University of Chicago grad students I
saw whenever I was in Hyde Park, down to the scruffy blond
beard and wire-rimmed glasses. He ordered a beer, and
turned to me. "You need a refill?"

I held up my mug, two-thirds full. "I'm good."

"Aw, c'mon. Just a top-off." The bartender dropped off a
second mug for the stranger, and waved his hand at mine. Instantly, it was refilled and iced over again. Considering the
number of coffee cups I topped off every day, *that* was a talent I could actually use.

"I haven't seen you here before," Glasses Guy said.

"First time."

"Hey, welcome to the Dauphine! How about a toast?"

Luc had said not to talk to anyone, but it seemed harmless.
Being rude would only draw more attention. It might be better to play along and not make a scene. My mother's mantra
was finally serving me well. I shifted in my seat and lifted my
drink.

"To trying new things," he said, and I echoed him. We
clinked mugs and drank. I felt uneasy, too light in my skin. I
wished Luc would hurry up. Glasses Guy kept sneaking
looks at me, a small smile playing over his face. He was kind
of homely, with small eyes behind the glasses, a weak chin,
and a faint, grasping air of desperation. I kept my eyes on
Luc's booth, reflected in the mirror behind the bar.

"It's funny," he said after a while. "You seem so familiar.
Have we met before?"

"I doubt it," I said politely. I didn't have a lot of experience with pickup lines, but now wasn't the time for practice.
"I'm not from around here."

"Chicago, right? You've got the accent." I flushed. I'd always noticed Luc's accent but never considered I might have
one of my own. This guy didn't seem to have one at all—he
had the precise, untraceable voice of a news anchor.

"Is it that obvious?"

"No," he said cheerfully. "You're a long way from home."

I nodded and glanced at Luc's booth again, then my watch. Still not too late. How long before Lena noticed I was gone? Before she told Ms. C? Before Colin decided to check in with me and noticed that a bar sounds nothing like a journalism classroom?

Glasses Guy drummed the countertop erratically. "You waiting for someone?" he asked.

"Kind of."

"Just wondered. You keep checking the booths. I'm not making you nervous, am I?"

"No." Not until now, anyway. But I'd been riding CTA buses for years. You never—*never*—let someone know they were getting to you.

He held his hands up to show he was harmless. "Sorry. I just can't believe someone would keep a girl like you waiting here, of all places."

A girl like me. There was that phrase again. Granted, it seemed a little less insulting when it was coming from a guy trying to pick me up.

"Thanks." Despite a prickle of unease at ignoring Luc's instructions, I smiled at the guy. "So, you're from New Orleans."

"No, no. That's the funny thing about the Dauphine, you know? It's a crossroads. You meet people from everywhere . . . I knew another girl from Chicago," he added, stopping the incessant drumming. "About your age, I think. Maybe you knew her."

I set the mug down carefully, trying to catch Luc's eye in the mirror. He'd moved farther back into the booth with Niobe, impossible to spot. If I was on the bus, I'd be looking for another seat to come open right about now. "Chicago's a big city."

"Sure," he said agreeably. "But something about you reminds me of her. She was a nice girl. I heard things didn't go so great for her once she got back to Chi-Town, though."

I fought the urge to roll my eyes. Only tourists and newspaper columnists call Chicago Chi-Town. I pressed my index finger against the condensation beading on my mug, willing my hand to stay steady. "Really? What happened?"

"Oh, you know how rumors are. Some people said she got in over her head with raw magic. Someone said she actually thought she was the girl from the Torrent Prophecy. Like anyone would believe her."

"The Torrent Prophecy," I said. "You don't think she was?"

"Well," he said, leaning so close I could smell the beer on his breath, yeasty and sour, "if she really was the Vessel, she wouldn't have been so damn easy to kill, would she?"

I froze. What the hell was taking Luc so long? Were he and Niobe discussing Oprah's latest book club selection?

I turned the mug in my hand, trying desperately for nonchalance instead of terror. Whatever Niobe knew, this guy knew *more*, and his presence here was no accident. I needed to keep him talking. "Did you know this girl well?"

"Not at all."

"Then how can I remind you of her?"

"She was overconfident. She thought she was the Vessel, thought she could save the world. She had a *mission*." He spat the word. "And look where that got her. Her life leaking out of her in an alley, a toy for Darklings, and the world won't remember her, except as a failure." His face was flushed now, and his mouth opened and closed, little strands of spittle collecting at the corners.

The anger blazed up, uncontrollable. "She wasn't a failure!"

He stood up, knocking his seat over. "Without the Vessel, you can't stop the Torrent. It will sweep through the world like a cleansing fire. You and yours will fall before it. The Seraphim will not be stopped."

"The *Seraphim?*" Hazy memories of religion class with Father Armando came to mind, but somehow I didn't think this guy was talking about Bible passages. "I don't know what you're talking about." I scrambled off the stool and began to back away. Everyone in the room—bartender, customers, singer—pointedly ignored me.

His eyes flashed malevolently as he lurched toward me. "You don't know anything. You're a deaf and dumb Flat. I don't know why they think you're special."

"Who's *they?*"

"They think you've got something worth knowing. Should we see what it is?"

Suddenly, he brought his hands up and pressed his palms against my temples, crushingly hard. My sight blurred. A feeling of pressure and . . . wrongness . . . bloomed in my head as he snarled incomprehensibly. The room receded around me, except for the stranger's furious face, and a keening noise blotted out all other sounds. Visions of the attack in the alley, of Verity's body in the hospital, of the ring flashing on my finger sprang up in front of me, overlaying everything else.

At the very edge of the visions, I saw Luc vault out of the booth. He was moving so slowly I knew he'd never make it, not in time to save me, and I figured he was probably tired of doing that anyway. In the last desperate seconds before I lost consciousness, my flailing hand knocked against the nearly full mug. I fumbled, wrapping my fingers around the handle, and swung it across the side of Glasses Guy's face. There was a dull cracking sound, and his hands fell away. My legs crumpled beneath me.

Luc snapped into focus, bursting in as if he'd suddenly been released from slow motion, catching me before I hit the ground. "Mouse! You okay? You there? Talk to me!"

"I'm here," I said, my head lolling back. The words sounded watery and garbled in my own ears. "That guy isn't right."

He shoved me behind him and whirled to face the stranger. I stumbled against a table, knocking over stools, sending a tray of glasses to the floor and me after it. I landed on my side, cheek slamming into the ground. The ringing in my ears wouldn't stop, and I shook my head to clear it, pushing up to my hands and knees with effort. The other people formed a ring around the three of us, jostling and murmuring.

"This is neutral ground, Luc," said the bartender. "There'll be no fighting here."

"He violated the truce," Luc shot back. "He was Rivening her damn mind. If that ain't cause . . ."

"She's a Flat," the guy wheezed, staggering upright. "Neutrality doesn't apply to outsiders."

"She's my companion, under the aegis of my House. She has the same rights here as anyone else." Luc's lips were white with fury. He prowled toward the other guy, all refined, deadly rage.

"She accepted my offering. Her protection ceased." The stranger's voice had a petulant, whiny note.

Luc's gaze slipped to me. "She didn't know."

"Men," Niobe said, shaking her head and helping me to my feet. Her voice was low and amused. "They're always convinced they should be the ones to settle things."

"What truce?" I asked. Luc lunged, rushing at the guy and slamming him into a table. Around us, the crowd jeered and shouted.

"Magic may not be used to harm another within these walls. It's an ancient decree, and a useful one. Men always find a way, though, don't they?" I watched Luc slam his fist into my attacker's gut, dodge a blow, land another punch to the jaw.

"That guy—he *was* using magic! And it hurt!"

She gave me a pitying look. "Rivening does, I've been told. He was invading your mind, taking control over you. It's absolutely forbidden among Arcs, but . . . you're Flat. You don't count."

Of course I didn't. "Luc left me there to be picked off?"

"No. You carried the protection of his House, until you accepted an offering—your drink, in this case—from the other one. In doing so, you stepped outside the wards Luc had placed around you."

"Wards?"

"Shields." She lifted a hand, and the air around me stirred. You carry some with you still . . . powerful ones, placed by another. But whatever spell Luc worked on you dissipated the moment you shared a toast with that one."

Luc put a spell on me? Without my permission? I'd kill him myself, once we got out of here. *If* we did.

Luc and Glasses Guy were grappling on the floor, everything was disintegrating in front of me, and I couldn't stand on the sidelines any longer.

"This truce—it applies only to magic people? Not to Flats?"

Niobe considered, turning the full force of her smile on me. "Any action you take here will not be held against either of them; you are entirely free. That's a unique situation among our kind. I would have thought you entirely at a disadvantage, but perhaps I was mistaken."

"Don't be so sure," I said. Luc lashed out with a kick to the side of the guy's knee, sending him into the crowd. Someone helped him to his feet and shoved him toward Luc. As the crowd pressed in, my line of sight was blocked.

"Why aren't they helping Luc? Everyone saw what that guy did to me! Shouldn't someone do something?"

"Your attacker violated no laws," Niobe said patiently. "And Luc won no friends by bringing you here. The Dauphine is considered a refuge from the Flat world. Most view your presence here as an insult."

Through the gaps, I spotted Luc as he fell backward. Glasses Guy tackled him, jamming his elbow into Luc's windpipe. I stopped thinking and pushed toward them, snatching up a beer bottle from a nearby table. Luc was struggling to get up, but the other guy punched him in the stomach, hard, his face twisted and blotchy with rage.

"She won't be enough," he snarled at Luc. "The prophecy's been broken, and no Flat girl can restore it. She'll die before she gets the chance. The Torrent will cleanse the world and then the Seraphim will ascend. We will restore our world to its place of power, purify the lines. She won't be—"

I slammed the bottle into the back of his head and it shattered, some of the glass flying back and catching my cheek. The impact knocked him off Luc and onto the floor, stunned. For a second, Luc gasped for air. Then he rolled to his feet and grabbed the neck of the bottle from my hand. As the stranger struggled up, Luc barreled into him. The crowd parted as Luc pinned him against the wall next to the stage, pressing the jagged glass against the guy's throat. A trickle of blood welled up and he froze, eyes rolling back in his head. The crowd quieted. Even the singer had stopped, her shimmering dress falling still.

Luc's voice was quiet and lethal. It carried across the hushed room.

"I would drop you here, *homme,* but instead, you get to play messenger boy. Go back to your people. Explain to them how you fucking failed tonight. Tell them the girl is off-limits. Tell them that I'm comin' for them. Tell them that when I do, I will turn their bones to ash. I will bring about the prophecy, and their cause will be over before it even starts. And when they kill you for your failure, which they will, remember they're bein' more merciful than I ever would."

He pressed harder on the bottle, the blood coming faster. He ordered over his shoulder, "Mouse. Get over here."

It seemed smart not to argue.

"Grab tight," he said.

I linked my arms around his waist, and his free arm went around me as he slashed a door next to us, wrenching us Between.

CHAPTER 18

We fell into Luc's apartment, our arrival clattering in the quiet darkness. His arm stayed firm around my waist, his hand tight on my arm, and he never broke stride, propelling me toward the couch as I stumbled over my feet, trying to catch up. He shoved me the last little distance, and I landed with an ungraceful thump and grunt. He ignored me and went to the sideboard, poured several fingers of bourbon into a glass, downed it, and poured again.

It was infuriating, his ability to go Between without a hitch. Bad enough I had to rely on him to ferry me through, but it was so damn easy for him, like dancing, while I flailed around like an idiot. Everything was easy for him. He knew the rules, he knew the players, he knew how all the magic worked. He'd been born to it, like he'd said, while I felt like I was watching a Japanese movie with Swedish subtitles.

I brushed at the wetness on my cheeks. My fingertips came away bloody.

Another sign of how far gone things were, that I could look at my crimson-streaked hand and feel annoyance instead of shrieking panic.

Luc came at me, glass in one hand, bottle loosely grasped in the other.

"That was stupid," he said. His voice was icy and his eyes were hot. I wanted to shrink back into the soft leather of the couch, but I was wobbly from the jump, and angry about the spell, and most of all, I was right, so I wiped my fingers on my jeans and sat up straighter.

"That was *useful*," I shot back. "You said we needed to find out which alliance gave the order to kill Verity. Now we know."

He slammed the glass down on the table so hard I thought it would crack. "There were better ways. *Quieter* ways."

"I'm tired of being quiet! You're the one who wants me to save your stupid world! You should be freaking thrilled I finally *did* something instead of waiting around." He was still standing, towering over me, and I shoved off the couch to stand toe-to-toe with him.

"Jesus, woman! You been ignorin' every damn thing I've said since the day we met, and tonight you decide to make some noise? I sat you down at the damn bar and I said, 'Don't move. Don't talk to anybody. Just wait here and don't make a fuss.' *That's* when you decide to play ball?" He shook his head disgustedly and took another drink.

"I'm not a golden retriever," I snapped. "You don't pat me on the head and tell me to stay, you asshole! Why did you bring me if I wasn't supposed to do anything? Why the hell did I blow off the newspaper? And sneak away from Colin? To sit at a stupid bar? Screw that! We're supposed to be partners!"

"That was your idea."

"You agreed! So treat me like one. Niobe said you did some sort of spell on me—and you just neglected to mention it?"

He folded his arms. "It's a small working. If you accept food or drink from someone, you're under their House's protection, like a guest. Not even a spell, really, just a custom. If you weren't in the habit of letting strangers buy you a drink, you would have been fine."

"Don't blame this on me! I can't follow the rules if you don't tell me what they are! If we're partners, you need to tell me things. And you don't get to shove me off to the side while you go after the people who did this." I paused, a sudden insight flashing through me. "That's why you're so mad. I got the information, not you. But *I got it*. The Seraphim, whoever they are. That's what we wanted tonight, right?"

His face darkened, a flush spreading across his cheeks like fever. "What I wanted was for you to stay out of trouble, not start riskin' your neck. You're lookin' for revenge, and that's fine. I'm all for it, Mouse. But let's be real clear—it ain't worth your life. I need you alive, even if you don't seem to care."

My stomach clenched—with anger, or shame, or some mixture of the two, and I stared at my hands, twisting them together. I sank back down on the couch, all the fight gone. Funny how I'd stopped missing Verity, just for a minute, when Luc set me off. Now it rushed back in.

"I wasn't . . . you don't . . . I promised her," I said finally, and now the dampness on my cheeks wasn't blood.

"I know." The harshness was gone from his voice, leaving behind sympathy and something else. "It won't bring her back, though. And you can't trade her life for yours. Vengeance doesn't work like that."

He handed me the glass of bourbon and I curled my fingers around it, feeling the warmth where his hands had been. I sipped cautiously, expecting the burn. Even so, I couldn't keep from coughing a little and wiping my eyes.

"Listen to me, Maura." He sat down next to me, and I froze at the sound of his voice saying my name, so different from anyone else. "You made a promise, and that's a good thing, a noble thing. It's got its own magic. But you can't risk yourself like that again. She wouldn't have wanted it."

I took another swallow of the bourbon, bigger this time, and let it sear me all the way down. Staring into the glass, I said, "I ran. In the alley that night. She stayed. I *ran.*"

I'd expected him to be angry, or disgusted. I could even have envisioned sympathy, if he was feeling generous. Instead, he was brusque and practical. "You'd have died. You couldn't help her then. Now you can. But you need to be smart. You need to trust me."

Being smart and trusting Luc weren't exactly synonymous. Everything he'd said and done, from the moment I met him, was only ever a half-truth. More than I'd gotten from anyone else, but still not super-reassuring. No, trusting Luc wasn't smart, but sitting on his couch, angry and bleeding and reckless from the bourbon, I did anyway. He smelled like saltwater and cinnamon, sharp and spicy, and his eyes were a clear bottomless green, and all I could do was nod, because suddenly I couldn't breathe.

He touched my cheek, where the flying glass had cut me. "Looks like you caught it pretty good. Close your eyes."

"Why?"

"So I can fix it. Can't take you home looking like you were in a bar fight. What's Cujo gonna say?"

I had a pretty good idea of what Colin would say—none of it good, all of it loud. "I meant, why do I have to close my eyes?"

He shifted. "Feels strange to have you looking at me, I guess."

"I like to," I said without thinking. "Besides, it's not fair. You're looking at me."

He held back a smirk, only partway successfully. "Suit yourself."

"I will."

He brushed his fingers over my cheekbone and whispered something, words I would never be able to make out, no matter how hard I listened, and the familiar sparkling current coursed over my skin. I wanted to lean into his warmth, let it melt the frozen place inside me, but I kept my focus on Luc's eyes, luminous green and gold now, as if they were lit from within. Even his skin seemed to take on the faintest sheen— of sweat, of magic, I didn't know which, and didn't care, because he was so beautiful. I brought my hand up and traced the planes of his face. Instead of pulling away, his palm curved along my jaw. His thumb brushed my lower lip, feather light.

I shivered, the rightness of his touch making everything hazy.

I stopped breathing, stopped moving, afraid it was only the magic making everything happen and I didn't want to disrupt it. He leaned toward me, sliding his hand behind my neck, pulling me in as inexorable as gravity, and kissed me. His lips were soft—softer than I expected, and even warmer than his skin, and he tasted like bourbon and burnt sugar and secrets, sweet and a touch of bitter, and completely Luc. He was gentle at first, slow, easy kisses, but I nipped at his lip, once, and then there was nothing slow or gentle, only his mouth crashing against mine, lips and tongue and teeth, one hand tangling in my hair, the other one bringing me closer, and I forgot there was any world at all outside of Luc, here with me.

He pushed my hair back, his lips tracing down my neck, and I wanted to laugh, but all I could do was gasp, because it was like fire, a line of heat wherever he touched, and his other hand was sliding down my throat, reaching for the buttons of my shirt. They practically melted away, and his fingers slowed, tangling in something. . . .

Verity's ring.

All the heat fled, like a flame doused with ice water, and we both stopped at the same time. Our breaths were deafening. He let go, and I missed him instantly, hating myself for it.

"I'm sorry," I whispered. "I'm so sorry." Was I apologizing to him or Verity? He was her *boyfriend.* She'd been dead less than a month, and I was jumping her boyfriend, because apparently my failures as a best friend weren't limited to leaving her to be slaughtered by Darklings, I needed to poach the boy who loved her, too. Luc looked poleaxed, motionless except for his hands, clenching and unclenching at his sides.

"Don't apologize." His voice was rough and dark. He reached for the bottle of bourbon, ignoring the glass, and took a swig, gripping the neck of the bottle so that his knuckles turned white.

"I can't do this," I said, not looking at him.

"It's not . . ." He scrubbed a hand through his hair, studied the label of the bottle as if it held answers. "It's not wrong, Mouse."

Mouse again. The distance was good, I told myself. We needed that distance. Bad things happened when he used my real name. I didn't miss the sound at all.

"I should go." I pushed up, only a little unsteady, and grabbed for the arm of the couch, curling my fingers around the soft black leather.

He stood up but didn't move toward me. I didn't know if I was grateful or disappointed. "Don't."

"Really, no. This was a mistake." My shirt gaped open, and I buttoned it up again, my fingers clumsy in their haste, knocking into the ring.

"Because of Verity?"

His hair had felt cool and glass smooth under my fingers when we kissed. I watched it fall into his eyes again, the urge to push it back somehow painful. Had Verity done that? I could picture them, heads together, hers shimmering fair and his so dark it seemed to absorb the light. Had they slept together? I shook my head to keep the image from coming into focus.

"We weren't like that," he said, breaking the silence. "Me and Vee."

Could he read minds now? Magic sucked. Even if they weren't sleeping together, there was no denying they had some kind of connection. It was written all over Verity's face in her New Orleans pictures; it rang out like a bell every time he spoke about her. Only an idiot would have missed it. Only a fool would try to compete. "You cared about her, though."

A slow, cautious nod. "I did."

"You miss her." It was like pressing on a bruise to see how much it hurt.

"I do." The answer: It hurt like a bitch.

"You said . . ." My throat closed up. "You said you needed her."

"Not the only one who said that."

He took a step closer, carefully, like I would bolt if he moved too quickly. Never let it be said Luc couldn't read women.

"You liked it. Kissing me."

I ducked my head. "That's not the point."

"The hell it isn't! You liked it, and so did I, and that's somethin'. That *matters*."

"Not enough," I whispered. Too much, and not enough, all at once, and the unfairness of it made my heart start to crack. I could feel it inside me, a new fresh ache crowding in with the old. He took my hand, laced our fingers together.

"So, we're gonna fight this? Christ, there's not enough trouble comin' our way? You want to make it harder?"

"It was a mistake," I repeated, shaky. "Please, Luc. Can't we just go back to the way it was before?"

"No. And I wouldn't want to, Mouse, even if we could.

Remember that, later." He looked, for a moment, regretful. "Kisses change things. No gettin' around that."

I tugged my hand away, and he nodded slowly. "I'll take you home. But don't think we're done. I keep telling you—no point in fighting fate."

"You're saying this is fate?"

He grinned at me, the way he always did when he knew more than me. "You're saying it's not? Let's get you home."

CHAPTER 19

When Luc brought me back to the school, he said nothing more than *"À bientôt."* Before I could respond, he brushed a light kiss over my cheeks, turned, and vanished.

I trudged back upstairs, fighting back tears. I needed to believe Luc about a lot of things—the Torrent, the Darklings, his ability to take me Between safely—and now all of them fell away. What I most needed to believe was that he and Verity weren't in love. I couldn't betray her by falling for him, and I couldn't trust his feelings for me otherwise. I hadn't decided yet if I'd take Verity's place in the prophecy, but I sure as hell wasn't interested in filling her place with Luc.

I'd been gone for an hour and a half, tops, but it felt like the entire night. Still, I dreaded explaining my absence to Ms. C. Lena, though, must have been keeping watch, because she came bounding out of the room the minute she spotted me.

"Where have you been? I went to look for you and—" She broke off. "Are you okay?"

I looked down, making a show of checking my watch. "I lost track of time," I said, frantically composing a story in my mind. "I went outside for some air and ran into the guy from the party. He's just a guy, not a boyfriend. He knew Verity."

She looked at me suspiciously. "From this summer? She was seeing someone before she left?"

"No. She met him down there. Don't say anything, though. I don't think a lot of people knew about him."

"But you do."

"He came up here after she died." I didn't trust myself to say more. "What did you tell Ms. C?"

"The only thing she'd buy. You were having a hard time putting together the memorial. I put your bag in my locker, by the way."

"Thanks. I owe you."

"Big-time."

We retrieved my bag, and I texted Colin to let him know I was ready. Lena waited with me by the doors. Colin's rule—even on a beautiful autumn night, stay inside until he gives the signal. Now that I knew what sorts of things came out at night, I didn't mind so much.

Lena tapped a foot on the tile floor, studying me. "You and Verity always seemed like such a tight unit. Self-contained, you know?"

"She had tons of friends," I said, surprised. "Everyone liked her."

"They like you, too. But Verity . . . she let people get close, or at least think they were. You don't do that."

I fiddled with the flap of my messenger bag, clicking and unclicking the latch. Maybe I didn't welcome people in the way Verity did, but it was common sense. I didn't want to have to explain my father, or listen to poorly disguised questions about Uncle Billy's business interests. Even when I was little, it didn't take long to figure out parents didn't want their kids playing with me. They were happy to rely on my uncle for help, for jobs, tracking down a wayward spouse or covering a debt, but setting up a playdate with the felon's daughter was a different matter.

"I'm just saying . . . it might not be the worst thing in the world, you know. To reach out. Or to let people reach out to you."

Outside the double doors, Colin honked, two short bursts. "Thanks again for covering."

"Anytime," Lena said, a little sadly.

"Hey, do you need a ride?" No way was I letting another friend go home alone in the dark.

She smiled. "No, I'm good. Ms. C is waiting on me to click 'send.' We'll walk out together."

"Okay. See you tomorrow." The temperature outside was at least fifteen degrees cooler than it had been in New Orleans, and the cold made me clumsy as I climbed in and fastened my seat belt.

"Home, Jeeves."

He turned the heater on, fighting a smile. "Don't call me Jeeves. You get the newspaper done?"

"Mmn-hmn." It should be alarming, how effortlessly I was lying these days. "I just want to go home and crash."

Colin humphed. "Naptime has to wait. Your uncle wants to see you."

"It's after eleven."

"It shouldn't take long."

Dread settled over me. "Am I in trouble? Did you tell him about . . ."

"The party? No. Relax."

Easy for him to say. I leaned my head against the cool glass of the window, trying to find a comfortable position. The adrenaline rush from the bar was gone, and my head felt heavy and stupid. Not the best state to see Uncle Billy in. "God, I'm tired."

Something in my voice must have worried Colin, because he reached over and ruffled my hair gently. "Hang in there a little longer, kid."

I closed my eyes, remembering our first meeting. "Don't call me kid," I said, too exhausted to put any real force into it. "What do you do when you're not here?"

"I've got some side projects."

"Bodyguard projects?"

"Woodworking."

"You're a carpenter," I said, breathing in the scent of pine shavings, remembering the nicks on his hands.

"Yeah. Nothing big right now, though. A coffee table, a mirror."

I touched the spot on my cheek where Luc had healed me. "It sounds nice."

The truck slowed, shuddered to a stop. "Ready?"

A moment later, he opened my door. The unexpected courtesy jolted me from my stupor, put me on alert. If Colin was being kind, something bad was about to happen.

We entered the bar, and I flashed back to the Dauphine, my heart pounding. Here, though, no one marked our arrival. The weeknight regulars weren't looking to socialize, and neither of us was unfamiliar here.

The two plasma TVs at either end of the bar were showing the highlights of the Sox game. Charlie grimaced at a replay of the Twins scoring yet again. "Won't be seeing much ball come October," he said.

There was a strained note to Colin's laugh. "Can we go back?"

"Sure. He's waiting."

"Mo," cried my uncle as I approached his booth, Colin at my back. "It's good to see you, darling girl! Colin says you've been busy. Poor thing, you look dead on your feet."

"Long day," I said, sitting down.

"Indeed. Your mother and I have been discussing your school plans."

Not surprising. My mother didn't want me to go to New York, and who better to help her in her quest to keep me home than Uncle Billy, who'd always promised to help with tuition?

"My college plans are the same as they've always been." I folded my hands on the table in front of me, met his eyes. If he'd called me here to push my mom's college agenda, I was going to shatter like the bottle I'd broken over Glasses Guy's head.

"We can discuss it later," he said affably. "In truth, Mo, I called you here for another reason. The police are closing in on some suspects in Verity's case."

"Suspects?" It had to be a mistake.

"Yes. And there's every chance you'll be called in to identify them. I wanted you to be prepared. Do you remember the description you gave the police?"

"I don't think it was very useful." That was putting it mildly—a Darkling wasn't going to show up in any book of mug shots.

Uncle Billy unfolded a piece of paper on the table. Elsa's strong, slanted handwriting was unmistakable, even upside down. "You described them as tall, with black sweatshirts or jackets covering their faces."

"I couldn't really see them."

"And you couldn't understand what they were saying?"

I shook my head.

"Could it have been Russian? You've not heard it spoken much, I'll wager."

"I don't think it was Russian." Unless the Darklings had arrived via Moscow, which seemed unlikely.

"But it could have been," he pressed. "It would make sense. If they brought out several big Russian fellows and asked you to identify them, it wouldn't be a stretch to say yes."

"Except I didn't really see them," I said again, stubborn for reasons I couldn't name. My instincts, which I'd never paid much attention to, hummed a warning. I could feel it from my spine to my fingertips. How much of my family's history was true? It all seemed suspect now, impossible to tell the solid parts from the illusions, just like my friendship with Verity. It was so disorienting, and exhausting, and without anything real to go on, the only thing left was my instincts. I touched the chain around my neck as Uncle Billy tapped his fingertips on the scarred tabletop.

"The men you'll be asked to identify are very dangerous individuals. They're exactly the sort that would have hunted down Verity."

"They didn't do it!"

He stilled for a moment, then wagged a finger at me. "If you didn't see them, you can't be sure."

"You want me to identify these people even if I don't recognize them? Accuse them of *murder?*"

He stared at me hard, the storm clouds gathering on his face, but his voice still held a cajoling note. "I want you to make allowance for the time of night, your state of mind, the good you could do by taking these men off the street."

"How would I do that?"

"One has a scar on his right forearm. The other has a flower tattooed on his chest. Easy to overlook at the time, but now you've had a chance to reflect. They might stand out a bit more."

I glanced up at Colin, who had developed a sudden interest in his shoes. He looked tense, the strong, square line of his jaw set, stubble glinting in the dim light of the bar.

"I have to go." I slipped out of the booth.

"You just got here!" There was no outrage in his voice, only shock, but that wouldn't last long.

"School night. You know how Mom gets." I strode toward the front, not bothering to see if Colin followed.

"Talk some sense into her," I heard my uncle growl.

Colin caught up to me at the truck.

"He wants me to lie. You know that, right?" I slammed the door so hard the window rattled.

"It was kind of hard to miss."

"Those guys? The Russians? They didn't kill Verity."

He started the engine and let it idle for a moment. "Probably not. Doesn't mean they haven't killed somebody else."

"And that makes it okay?"

"I didn't say that." He pulled into traffic.

"If I identify these guys, the police will stop looking for the real killers." Which wasn't terrible, actually. They'd never be able to arrest the Darklings or the people behind them. It would get Kowalski off my case. Another lie, though. Like there weren't enough already.

"Your uncle won't stop. You might like his results better." Colin's voice was emotionless, but I knew what he meant. The problem was, Uncle Billy was no more equipped to handle Darklings than the police department. Whatever brand of street justice he was prepared to mete out didn't involve magic.

A thought struck me. "What would happen to you? If I did ID these guys?"

"Are you trying to get rid of me?" He raised one eyebrow. "I'm here until Billy thinks you're safe."

"He said having these guys arrested would make the neighborhood safer."

"I think your uncle has a different standard for your safety than for the neighborhood as a whole. Sorry." He didn't sound very sorry.

"So I should expect Kowalski tomorrow?"

"You've got a little time."

"What would you do?"

"If I were you? I'd figure out what girls talk about when they all go to the bathroom together."

I shoved him, strangely grateful for the lame attempt at humor. "I'm serious!"

He considered. "It depends on what you want, Mo."

"Justice," I said instantly.

He jerked a shoulder. "After that."

"What do you mean?"

"The rest of your life can't be about grieving for your friend. However this plays out, you're going to reach a point where you have to live for yourself, not her. Billy's not kidding when he says it'd be better if these guys went away, for a lot of reasons. But you don't have to be the one to make it happen. It's a path. . . ." He paused. "It's a road that doesn't have a lot of off-ramps, you know? You choose it, or you let it choose you, and it might be hard to turn around later. It might be smart to keep your options open for a while."

"You don't believe in fate?" I dug my fingers into the door handle, waiting for his answer.

His mouth hardened. "People make their own fate."

I didn't say anything, and after a long moment, he continued. "Once you start choosing, you set things in motion a certain way. Things can settle in pretty firm, before you realize what's happened. It doesn't mean you shouldn't decide, but you have to see the consequences."

I wondered if that was how Colin had ended up working for Billy, and if he regretted it now. The question hung between us, full and tempting, and I nearly asked. Then it struck me that, from the beginning, Colin had always deferred to my uncle. He'd made it clear he was working for Uncle Billy, not me, and what I wanted took a backseat to my uncle's wishes.

Tonight was the first time he'd encouraged me to think about what I wanted instead of giving me orders. Grilling him about a past he'd never wanted to talk about seemed like a lousy way to repay him. Instead I leaned against him, feeling safer in the darkened cab of his truck than anywhere else. My eyelids grew heavy, and we rode in silence until he pulled up in front of my house.

"Get some rest," he said as I climbed out. "Worry about the ID tomorrow."

I considered telling him there was more than my uncle's demands worrying me, but I didn't. There were limits to what Colin could understand, no matter how much he'd surprised me in one evening.

CHAPTER 20

As it turned out, I didn't need to worry about the identification, at least not right away. Kowalski didn't contact me, and neither did Uncle Billy. When I asked Colin about the unexpected calm, he shrugged and said a little time helped when you had a decision to make.

Luc must have been operating on the same principle. I kept expecting him to pop out from a locker or drag me into a classroom for another trip Between, but I didn't see him for more than a week. He hadn't vanished completely—I opened my locker one afternoon before AP Chem and was caught in an avalanche of jasmine blossoms. As I finger-combed them out of my hair, trying not to grin like an idiot, Lena shook her head knowingly.

Guys had always gone for Verity, not me, and I had been fine with that. They'd bring along a friend, we'd all go out together a few times, and then lose touch. Pleasant, but not memorable. Nothing that really shook me. Certainly, none of them had been worth enduring my mother's endless lectures about What Boys Were After and What Nice Girls Didn't Do.

Luc, though, shook me plenty, and it wasn't only his magic. Every time I picked another waxy white petal out of my collar or notebook, I felt another wash of emotion. Nervousness, guilt, and lust tangled inside me.

Even if Luc was telling me the truth about him and Verity, it didn't change the fact that my focus should be finding her killers, not a boyfriend. Falling for him was like forgetting Verity, and that was the one thing I couldn't—wouldn't—do.

But forgetting the way he tasted, the feel of his hair under my fingertips, the warmth of his skin, seemed impossible.

I needed to prove I was still committed. To show Verity she was my priority. So in between Chem and Calc, I called the number on Evangeline's card.

"Mo," she said, "I'd been hoping to hear from you."

"You said if I wanted to . . . take over for Verity . . . there were things we had to do."

"Yes. There's a ritual you'll need to complete."

"A spell? Like before?"

"Not exactly. The concealment spell was passive—a spell applied to you. This time you'll be an active participant."

"Can I do that? Without magic?"

"If I thought otherwise, I wouldn't suggest it."

"Oh." Being an active participant sounded good. I was tired of sitting back and letting everyone else take the lead while I waited in the corner or at the bar—which hadn't turned out so great, anyway. But there was still so much I didn't understand. Magic seemed like a new, exotic kind of physics, where Newton and Einstein didn't apply. I knew there were rules, but I couldn't begin to make sense of them. Instead, I blundered around breaking them. In my experience, nothing good had ever come from breaking rules.

"I'll contact Lucien," Evangeline said over the faint hiss of the connection. "Unless you'd care to."

"No!" I said it too fast. "Go ahead."

"Can you dispense with your bodyguard for the evening? We don't want an audience."

I bit my lip. "I'll try. He's kind of stubborn sometimes."

"There are steps we can take, if necessary."

The coolness in her voice alarmed me. "I'll take care of him."

"Excellent. I'll need a day to prepare. Does seven-thirty to-morrow evening work?"

"Sure."

"Verity would approve," said Evangeline. "I'm absolutely certain."

Nice to hear somebody was.

"No way." Colin folded his arms and tipped back the kitchen chair. "You know the rules."

"This is different! It's Verity's great-aunt, for God's sake. How much trouble can I get into with an antiques dealer from New Orleans?"

A smile played around the corner of his mouth. "You? I'm guessing a hell of a lot. You could find trouble on your way to the mailbox."

"The mailbox is attached to the house," I pointed out.

"You'd manage."

I punched him lightly in the arm. "Seriously, Colin, I think she felt insulted last time. It's like you don't trust her."

"I don't trust anybody," he pointed out. "Even antiques dealers."

"Even me?"

"Your track record in the trust department isn't so hot."

"Please, Colin."

"You," he said, letting the chair thump to the floor, "were supposed to be an easy job. You know that? Your uncle asked me to keep an eye on you, and I thought. 'She's had a tough time, she seems like a nice, quiet girl, and I owe Billy, so . . . sure.' But every time I turn around, you're throwing me a curve. I am beginning to think you misrepresented yourself."

I sank into the chair opposite him, clasped my hands around one knee. The idea of being more than he'd expected was oddly pleasing, but it also made me wonder what he owed my uncle. It must be big. "I really am a quiet person. I used to be, anyway, but after Verity died, things changed. *I* changed. And I want to go back to the way things were, but there's stuff I need to do first."

"Your life was that good before?" He raised an eyebrow.

"It was okay. Not perfect, with all the stories about Uncle Billy. And my mom is . . . well, you know what she's like." I glanced away. "My dad's coming up for parole soon."

He nodded.

"I don't want to be here once he's home."

"So, New York, huh?"

"New York. It's easier."

"I can see why you want to get back to that life," he said dryly.

"Verity was *alive*. I was normal, kind of. It would be nice to go back to normal."

"And going off somewhere with this woman is going to help?" He didn't try to hide his skepticism.

"Yes. Maybe." The answer had to be yes. And we had to succeed, because I couldn't keep going if I failed Verity again.

"One condition."

I tried to meet his steady, dark gaze without flinching. "What?"

"You can go, just this once. But tomorrow, you and I are going to have a talk."

"A talk?"

"About this 'stuff' you need to do. I can't shake the feeling you are up to something you shouldn't be, Mo. Maybe it's for a good reason, but I still need to know about it. I'm getting used to you. It would suck if something happened because you didn't trust me."

"You'll really let me go tonight? No following us five cars back? Not that you'd catch me doing something wrong," I added hastily. "It's the principle."

"Once. Tonight. Text me when you get there and when you get back."

"That's a lot of checking in."

"You don't like it, stay home."

"You've got a deal."

CHAPTER 21

I waited for Evangeline on the front stoop. Colin sat next to me, long legs stretched out, the picture of ease. Disapproval radiated off him, but he didn't mention it. Around us, neighbors gossiped over fences, kids played tag and rode their scooters on the bumpy sidewalk. The scent of charcoal and grilled meat perfumed the air. I'd told my mother Evangeline wanted my help going through some of Verity's photos for her parents, and she'd agreed, especially once Colin signed off on the trip.

I'd switched out of my uniform into jeans and a T-shirt, with a hoodie on top against the chill they were predicting. There had been no Indian summer this year, only a steady decline in light and warmth. Dusk was already falling, shadows lengthening, and the steps hadn't held on to much of the day's heat.

Colin stood as Evangeline pulled up. "You have your phone? It's on?"

"You said you wouldn't track me," I reminded him, glancing nervously at the silver BMW.

"I want you to be prepared," he said.

"Can you please try to think positively?"

"I'm positive you should have your phone on."

I showed him the screen. "Satisfied?"

"Not really. Call me when you get there."

"And when I get home. I'll be fine. Evangeline won't let anything happen to me." That, at least, I was sure of. I touched his sleeve lightly. "Thank you."

He rested his hand on top of mine. The weight of his fingers, warm and strong, was reassuring. "Take care of yourself."

I drew away, reluctantly, and headed down the walk. I could feel his gaze on me the whole way. As we drove off, I looked back. Colin was standing on the steps, hands jammed into his pockets, the surest thing on the street, and something in my chest ached at the sight.

"My compliments," said Evangeline. "I wasn't sure you'd be able to persuade him."

"He trusts me." The words made me a little queasy. "I've been lying to him since we met, but he trusts me."

"Sometimes one must do distasteful things for the greater good," she said. "It's a lesson you should learn now, while the consequences are merely uncomfortable."

Right. "What happens tonight?"

"The Binding Ceremony. It's a ritual many Arcs go through, and it's mentioned specifically in the prophecy. If we succeed, it will confirm your ability to take Verity's place."

"And if we don't?"

"Then the Seraphim, whoever they are, have won."

"What does it do? The spell?"

"Binding allows the participants to draw on each other's magic, sharing the power of the lines. For example, if a Water Arc was bound to one who uses Earth, they could use the magic of an Earth line, thanks to the ceremony. It's taxing for both parties but can be useful."

"So it increases your power."

"Yes. It also provides a degree of protection—you're considered a ward of the house you're bound to. Had you and Luc been bound before your adventure at the Dauphine, your attacker could not have used magic against you. You'll be much safer after this."

Bound to Luc? My heart began to race. Luc could protect me from Darklings and crazy Arcs, sure, but the idea that I would be bound to him—by magic or anything else—didn't seem safer. Not by a long shot.

We drove to Lake Michigan and picked our way over the rocks to the shoreline. We watched as the fiery curve of the sun sank below the watery horizon, and she turned to me, offering her elbow. "Shall we?"

She brought me Between and I opened my eyes in a high-ceilinged stone room. A fire flickered at one end.

"Do you need a moment to recover?"

I checked myself—the room wasn't spinning and my mouth didn't have the usual about-to-barf bitterness—and shook my head. "It was easier this time."

"I've had considerably more practice than Lucien," she said. "He'll meet us here shortly."

I toyed with the drawstring of my hood and said nothing. How was I supposed to act around him now? What would Verity have done? With any other guy, she would have been just frosty enough to keep him at bay, but Luc wasn't any other guy—he was Luc, and there'd been something between them. For the eighteen zillionth time, I wondered if she'd loved him, if he loved her, if he'd only kissed me because I was as close as he could get to Verity. I'd hoped by now the idea wouldn't hurt as much.

I was wrong.

I wandered over to the fireplace. The low flames licked at the neatly laid logs, giving the room a soft glow and comforting crackle. "Each night, a lump of charcoal is removed. The priest or priestess tends it until dawn, using their breath as bellows, and to rekindle the fire the next morning. Fire and air, you see," she said.

She gestured to the floor beneath us. Polished stones, each

no bigger than an egg, were fitted together in a shifting, swirling pattern. "River stones. Earth, shaped by water. Everything here represents the links between one type of magic and another."

"How old is this place?" Everything had a patina of well-tended age, rough edges worn smooth through years of use.

"As old as memory. This is where our kind comes in order to be bound together—the Binding Temple."

In the center of the oval room, four stone columns stood like compass points, one in each direction. Emblazoned on each was a series of intricate drawings. Up close, I realized they weren't drawings, but meticulous carvings, and I lifted a hand to touch them.

"Don't touch them," she said sharply. "Few of our kind can withstand them; you would be killed before you recognized what was happening."

I took a hasty step back. "What are they?"

"Direct portals to the raw magic."

"Who carved them? I mean, if you can't touch them . . ."

"The original Matriarchs and Patriarchs. Those who led our Houses at the dawn of our world. Much has changed since then, and our powers are not what they once were."

"But wasn't Verity superpowerful already? Why would she need to be bound to anyone?"

"In order to repair the magic, Verity needed access to all four elements. And Lucien is a DeFoudre, Heir to his House. Their binding ensured the magic would be evenly balanced among the four Houses."

"So this is some sort of arranged marriage? Because I'm not . . . with Luc. . . ." My entire body blushed. "Maybe this isn't such a good idea."

"It's not a marriage, but binding does forge an unbreakable link. It should never be undertaken lightly."

Panic started to build, closing my throat. "I don't want to be tied to Luc forever."

She touched my shoulder, solemn. "There is no halfway when it comes to such things, Mo. Binding the Vessel and the Heir is part of the prophecy."

"What if it doesn't work?"

"If we fail tonight, the Torrent will proceed unchecked. Our world will be irretrievably broken, yours imperiled."

I was here for Verity, but the reminder that there was more at stake tugged at me. "Is it dangerous? The Binding?"

"Not in the ceremony, per se. To be bound makes an individual uniquely vulnerable, because you give away a piece of your self—your strength. But you gain strength as well."

"And it has to be Luc?"

"Lucien is the last of the DeFoudres."

"What, no cute brothers?"

Her mouth turned down. "There was. He died when Lucien was still quite young. Lucien's role in the prophecy was sealed before his talents surfaced."

I closed my eyes, swamped with pity and a sudden understanding. Luc believed in the prophecy because he'd been raised to play his part in it, because it made sense of his brother's death. Like me, he'd been the one left behind, but he'd never even had a choice. "I didn't know."

"No. He wouldn't speak of it to you."

Of course not. I wasn't the chosen one, just the stand-in. I wasn't the girl he wanted, just the one he could have. And if we went through with this, we'd be stuck with each other for the rest of our lives.

"I'm not sure . . ."

She gave a small, regretful shrug. "There is no other way, Mo. Consider it one of the terms of your employment."

My jaw dropped, irritation crowding out nervousness. "My employment? I'm doing you a *favor*, Evangeline. If I can help you out, great, but that's not why I'm here."

Her chin came up, eyes narrowing. "You're here to play a

part. Do it well, and you can have the justice you keep clamoring for. If not, you're of little use."

Her meaning was clear. If I couldn't pull this off, she wouldn't help me find out who'd killed Verity. It struck me that Evangeline and Uncle Billy would probably get along quite well—both of them knew how to manipulate you so deftly that by the time you realized you were being handled, there was no way out. Evangeline might do it with cool elegance, and Billy with folksy charm, but underneath, they were both weaving webs.

I'd taken too long to recognize it, but now that I had, I wasn't going to play the fly.

I jammed my fists into the pocket of my sweatshirt. "And Luc's okay with the change?"

"Lucien understands the responsibilities of his calling."

A responsibility. That's what I was to Luc—an obligation, nothing more. Something prickled behind my eyelids.

In all the years we'd been friends, I'd never wanted to be Verity. I'd wished for a family like hers. I'd admired the way that she made friends, how easily she moved through the treacherous waters of junior high and high school, like it was all one amusing adventure. But I'd never tried to *be* her. Until now.

God, it sucked.

It sucked because I *liked* being on the sidelines, not in the spotlight. It sucked because I couldn't do magic, or read people, or be brave, and she could. Most of all, it sucked because I wanted Luc on my own terms, and if I went through with the binding, the terms would be Verity's. I wouldn't really have him at all.

I could keep my word to my best friend or I could ask Luc to ignore the prophecy and be with me, but I couldn't do both. And you're never supposed to choose a guy over your friends, right?

"How long will it take?" I said, trying to ignore the hollow feeling in my chest.

Evangeline smiled, her eyes gleaming like a cat's. "Not as long as you'd expect." She pointed to an opening cut into the wall. "There's a small pool through there; bathe, change into the clothing that's been left for you. I'll summon Lucien. When you're ready, we'll begin."

I walked slowly through the narrow passageway, trailing my fingers over rough stone walls. It opened suddenly to a room with a perfectly circular pool in the center. Stone steps led down into the water, and light from a dozen small torches made the surface flicker and glow.

I edged around the pool to a wooden bench and toed off my shoes, looking around uneasily. Anyone could come in and see me. Before I lost my nerve, I shimmied out of my clothes and slipped into the water.

It was warm as a Jacuzzi, the water coming to my shoulders. I drifted for a few minutes, letting the heat penetrate to my bones, hoping it would soothe my jangling nerves. My hair grew heavy as it soaked up the water, and I let myself sink below the surface. It was tempting to stay like that, cocooned in the warmth, the only sound my own heartbeat, my entire body weightless. Eventually, though, I had to come up for air.

I could do this. We would stop the Torrent and I would walk away. Whatever linked me to Luc would have to unlink. Verity's world wasn't mine. If I'd learned anything in the past few weeks, it was that—and there was no reason for me to stay any longer than I had to. My own life might be a disaster, but I understood the rules, or most of them, anyway. I would never understand how the magical world worked, or the people in it. Why bother trying?

I'd treat this as a job, the way Colin treated me. Something to avoid being tangled up in. My mind flashed to the image of my hand on his sleeve, his fingers closing over mine. I couldn't imagine what I'd tell him tomorrow, but it wouldn't be the truth, and I felt bad about it.

I ducked my head under the water one final time and climbed out of the pool. Folded on the bench was a thick white towel, and I wrapped it around myself. After the warmth of the pool, the cool air of the room gave me goose bumps, and I snuggled into the fluffy cotton, squeezing my hair dry as best I could. The change of clothes Evangeline had mentioned was hanging from an iron hook in the wall.

It was a dress—dark blue silk shot through with silvery threads like stars. I slipped it over my head and hugged my bare arms as the hem settled around my ankles. My hands were shaking as I dragged my fingers through my hair.

There was nothing left to do but go back. As I padded through the hall, I wondered if Verity had resented the prophecy. Had she felt that it was taking away her freedom? Or had she believed it so much that there was no room for resentment, the way Luc seemed to?

The walk back to the main chamber seemed shorter, no matter how slowly I moved. Luc had arrived, and he was speaking to Evangeline, too low for me to hear. He was wearing loose pants, the same fabric as my dress, and no shirt. I pressed my lips together.

"Thought you might be trying to find a back door," he said, catching sight of me. His voice was light, but his expression was clouded, eyes roving over my face.

"No such luck," I said.

"You ready?" He held out a hand, beckoning.

I couldn't speak. My mouth felt cottony and my skin felt feverish, and I stared at him, the shape of his mouth so soft against the planes of his face, the firelight throwing glints of gold into his hair. My fingers curled into the fabric of my dress, crushing the delicate silk, reminding me of his skin when we'd kissed. I wanted that again, the swooping feeling, the heat, the sheer glorious recklessness of it. To go through with the binding meant giving all of that up. I'd be accepting that I was only second best, second choice, the consolation prize.

He stepped closer. "We need a little time," he said to Evangeline.

She shook her head. "We don't have it. It's imperative to find out if she'll suit."

"She will," he said quietly, keeping his eyes on mine. "But we do it right, or not at all." I flinched at the threat in his voice. There was none of the charming persuasion I was used to, the easy command. This was bluntly menacing, and I tried to pull back. He tightened his hold on my hands and turned to Evangeline. "Go. Now."

Her mouth pursed, like she'd bitten into a plum and discovered a lemon underneath. Then the look smoothed out and she inclined her head. "Five minutes." With a sweep of her hand, she opened a door to Between and vanished.

Luc looked at me as if he'd never seen me before. "You have curly hair," he said, threading his fingers through it.

It was such a strange thing to notice, I couldn't help relaxing. "I . . . do. I wear it straight, mostly." I'd always hated the wild, frizzing springiness of my hair. Bits were always escaping from whatever clip or scrunchie I'd put in, wisps flying everywhere. It was easier to blow-dry it straight and rely on an arsenal of styling products.

"I like it," he said. "Like the way the light catches."

"Thank you," I said automatically, tensing up again. "You don't have to be nice. We can just get this over with."

"Mouse, you know I never do anything just to be nice. Well, almost never," he amended. Out of thin air, he produced a small, carefully folded piece of violet silk and held it out to me.

"My scarf!"

"You forgot it at my place. I thought you might be missin'

it." He wrapped it around my neck, his fingers gentle and warm through the thin fabric.

"Thank you," I said. This time, the words were genuine.

"You're welcome. Still nervous?"

"Aren't you?"

"It doesn't signify." He laced his fingers through mine. "I'm sorry it's all shaking out like this. If there was another way, I'd take it, I swear."

Meaning being bound to me, fate or no fate, was the last thing he wanted. I looked away.

"Breathe for me, Mouse. C'mon."

I blew out a shaky breath, and he tugged me closer, brought my two hands to his lips. "It won't be so bad."

"Is it going to hurt? Magic always hurts."

He cocked his head. "What do you mean?"

"Going Between. Evangeline's concealment spell. The guy at the bar. Every time I get near magic, it hurts."

"All magic has a cost," he said, sounding apologetic. "You've been taking the worst of it, bein' Flat. Does it hurt when I heal you?"

The sparkling warmth whenever he touched me was unsettling, but it didn't hurt—not the way he meant, anyway. "No. You?"

He shrugged. "Nothing I can't handle. Tonight's different. It'll hurt a little, but you'll feel a rush at the same time."

"You did this with Verity? The spell?"

His grip loosened. "No. She wasn't ready. I gave her the ring right before she came back. We figured there was still time."

I considered that. Verity was not a patient person. She didn't know the meaning of delayed gratification. If she wanted Luc, she'd have gone through with the ceremony before she came home. Maybe he'd been telling me the truth. Maybe they hadn't been together, not really. If so, I'd have a part of him Verity hadn't.

The guilt that had been dragging at me like an anchor lessened slightly.

"What happens . . . after?"

"That's up to us. Binding doesn't force you to care about someone. It deepens what's already there."

Oh, hell. My feelings for Luc, awkward and terrifying as they were, would be more intense, and he . . . would still want Verity. But Evangeline had said that I could go back to my normal life. Maybe I'd be like the soldiers on the History Channel, the ones whose war wounds acted up whenever it was going to rain. Maybe I'd carry the connection with me but miss him only when there was a drop in the barometric pressure. In which case, I could move to the desert and I wouldn't think about him anymore.

He let go of my fingers and cupped my face. "It's okay to be scared. But it won't work if you're not willing, if your heart's not in it."

The sheer beauty of him in the firelight overwhelmed me, his skin like amber, the absolute rightness of his fingers curving along my face. I could feel my pulse kicking up, my breath coming faster.

"Your heart in it?"

My heart—the eight million pieces it had cracked into since that night in the alley—couldn't say no. I nodded. The fall might kill me, but I couldn't help jumping.

It was possible this wouldn't be a complete disaster. It wasn't *completely* unthinkable that I could step into the prophecy, prevent the Torrent, find the people who had ordered Verity's death, make Luc love me, and survive. Unlikely, but not impossible.

Of course, when Evangeline appeared, looking even more annoyed and superior than usual, "unlikely" seemed too generous a word.

"Are we all feeling better now?" she asked, brushing at the perfectly smooth linen tunic she wore.

Luc raised an eyebrow. "Awful easy for you to be flip, since you ain't the one going through the ceremony."

"Indeed. But I seem to be the only one of us mindful of how dire this situation is."

"That's crap," Luc said in a low, furious voice. "You think you got a better grip on this because you're a Matriarch? Mouse and I, we both paid a price to be here, and we know what's at stake."

"I'm ready now," I said, hoping my voice sounded stronger than I felt.

"Shall we, then?"

Luc reached for my hand, gave one encouraging squeeze, and led me to the stone columns at the center of the room. The tops tapered into arches, joined in the middle to form a dome. Evangeline stood just outside the intricately carved columns while Luc guided me underneath, careful to keep either of us from touching the stone structure. The hum of their power made the nape of my neck tingle. I edged away.

"You have it?" he said to Evangeline.

In response, she spread her hands apart, and a fine platinum chain appeared. Pooling the ends in her hands, she spoke, her voice taking on a formal, almost singsong cadence. "In the beginning, there were only the elements: earth, air, fire, water. Utterly separate, they raged against each other, blunting their power. As Arcs learned to pull strength and magic from the elements, they, too, waged battles.

"At the height of war, the unthinkable occurred—a daughter of Fire fell in love with a son of Earth, and he with her. They hid their love, knowing such a secret would devastate their Houses. Miserable apart, they chose to steal away, but were caught. The girl's Patriarch challenged the boy to a fight. Before he could strike the boy down, the girl interceded, swearing by her breath, and blood, and magic, that she and her beloved were as one, and to injure the son of Earth would do harm to her as well.

"The daughter called on her lines to defend them, and her love did the same. Their lines—fire and earth—met and tangled, but instead of battling formed a greater protection against the magic of the Patriarch. The power of the lines marked them forever, binding them eternally, strengthening them beyond their individual talents. That was the first binding.

"Today, we call on the lines to unite Lucien and Maura, to bind them together according to the ancient tributes. Their sacrifice shall bring them increase, as it has been since the first. They shall become each other's refuge and strength, and stand for each other before the world."

I started to hyperventilate, the room growing fuzzy around the edges. Luc squeezed my hand.

Evangeline continued. "You must come here with an open and willing heart. Lucien, Heir to the House of DeFoudre, do you come thusly?"

"I stand beneath the First Arch, heart open and willing, ever thus." He gave me a crooked smile, encouraging.

"Maura, daughter of—" Evangeline hesitated, as if she was just realizing what a poor substitute I actually was. "Maura, daughter of the house of Fitzgerald, do you come thusly?"

I nodded, and Evangeline waited for more, but I couldn't remember the words. Finally, she sighed, the formal speech crisp with impatience. "I stand beneath the First Arch . . ."

"I stand beneath the First Arch . . ."

"Heart open and willing, ever thus."

"Heart open and willing, ever thus." I *was* willing. It had to be done. Painful as it was, Luc had laid my heart wide open the first time he kissed me. Whether I did it for Verity, or me, or both, I was stuck. Going back would be the actual end of the world.

The tension in Luc's shoulders seemed to ease a little.

Evangeline spoke again. "At the first binding, our ancestors were thrice-bound. So, too, shall you be. This chain represents the lines of your magic."

Luc held up his arm, and deftly, Evangeline wrapped one end of the chain around his wrist. "Breath, blood, and magic," she said, looping the silvery length around his wrist with each word.

He copied her, so quietly I saw more than heard it.

She repeated the whole wrist-wrapping thing with me, and I responded as Luc had. Was this it? The only pain I felt was a deep ache in my lungs, and I didn't think that's what he'd meant.

Luc laced his fingers with mine, then rested his other hand on my waist, pulling us together. He nodded encouragingly, and turned to Evangeline.

She looked wary, but said something in the liquid language I'd heard both her and Luc use. The same language Verity had spoken in the alley. Luc repeated the word back, slowly and clearly, and his fingers tightened on my hip. Evangeline shifted to me. I was supposed to repeat it, too, but I didn't know how. I wanted to ask Evangeline to say it again, but something in her face, graven and forbidding, prevented me. So I sighed and gave it my best shot, praying that the magic was listening to my intention, not my pronunciation.

Luc smiled, a slight curve of his lips, and bent his head to mine.

It started like a decorous, Evangeline-is-three-feet-away kind of kiss, and then his hand slid up my back, and he tilted his head, changing the angle, deepening the kiss, and I forgot all about Evangeline and my inadequacies in foreign languages. I leaned in, ignoring the doubts and concentrating instead on the need crashing through me, the satiny feel of his skin under my hands, and the taste of him, dangerous and sweet twined together.

Finally, he broke away, his expression a little bit stunned. It would have been an ego boost, but I was pretty sure I looked equally blown away.

Evangeline cleared her throat. Luc let go of my hand, turning it palm-up and placing his next to mine. The scar across it had faded a little more, and he brushed his finger over it gently. She spoke, and Luc repeated the words, his eyes never leaving mine, exaggerating every syllable. I copied him as best I could, encouraged.

Evangeline produced a glittering black rock, and quick as a snake, sliced across our palms. I shrieked, trying to pull away as a needle-thin line of blood welled up. Luc held me fast, pressing our hands together.

I was getting it now—breath, and blood, which I would have appreciated some warning about. Magic was the last one. How were they planning to get around the fact I didn't have any powers of my own?

Evangeline waited until she had my full attention, and said one last word. Luc echoed her, letting go of my hip to wrap his fingers around my wrist, where the chain was. I mirrored him and blundered through my part. What if I got it wrong? What if I was casting some sort of spell that turned us all into badgers, or stone, or caused an earthquake? What if I ruined it?

I winced as Luc's fingers clamped down. But it wasn't Luc—it was the chain itself, brightening in the dim light, changing from silver to platinum to supernova white. As I watched, the chain seemed to grow finer, sinking through my skin as it tightened. And it *hurt*. It was as if the line were actually cutting through me, burning through layers of skin and muscle and bone, and I trembled with the effort not to cry out. Luc felt it, too, the skin drawn tightly over his face, sweat beading on his forehead and over his lip, but his hand stayed pressed against mine. The pain radiated outward, and just as I was about to wrench myself away from Luc, unable to take another moment, warmth flashed through me, chasing away the pain. It was like lying next to a fire after you'd been in the snow too long—the relief was tremendous, but startling. Luc steadied me as the feeling faded, drawing me toward him. "As it was before, it is now. You are bound to one another, breath, blood, and magic, henceforth." Evangeline placed her hands on our heads. I was so weak I could barely stand against the slight pressure. "May you each strengthen the other as you walk the path fate has laid."

She released us, and the imposing mask she'd worn through the ceremony dropped. Her pale blue eyes were wide, her face almost slack. "It worked. I never imagined . . . See her home," she commanded Luc. "We'll reconvene after the mages and I have studied the implications."

With a sudden gust of magic, she was gone.

Luc tightened his arms around me. "See? That wasn't so bad, was it?"

CHAPTER 22

Luc brought me Between at the side of my house, away from the streetlights, and walked me to the front steps. The trip was easier than usual, but he kept a firm grip on me anyway.

"How you feelin'?"

"Okay, I guess. I thought the ceremony would be more complicated."

"Just 'cause something's simple doesn't mean it's easy. You did good."

I looked down at my wrist, at the rapidly fading welt where the chain had sunk in and vanished. "Is it inside of me?"

"In a way. It's joined to the lines, so it's not really part of this world anymore. It's still there, but you can't see it."

"How much room do we have?"

He cocked his head. "What do you mean?"

"Well, it was a pretty short chain. Are we going to be Siamese twins?" I could imagine the look on my mom's face when I showed up with Luc in tow, unable to move more than eight inches from him. God, I was stupid. I hadn't even asked what the consequences of binding would be, or how it was going to disrupt my life. I should have planned it out more, looked at all the angles. Instead, I'd only seen Luc.

Luc, who was struggling not to laugh, and failing miserably. "You got as much running room as you need, Mouse. It ain't that kind of chain. You can go anywhere in the world you want. We'll still be bound."

I couldn't decide whether that was reassuring or not. "What's next?"

He trailed a finger along my collarbone. "Depends what you want. We can go somewhere else. Back to New Orleans, or any place you like. Privacy would be nice, hmn?" He angled his head and leaned in for another kiss. The press of his lips against mine was different from before—less tentative, more possessive. It should have been irritating, an echo of his act at the Dauphine, but it wasn't. It was exciting, and my skin felt as if it were on fire, and I kissed him back just as hard, opening my mouth to his, for the first time meeting him as an equal.

"Name it, Mouse. Anywhere in the world, and we'll go right now." He nipped a line of kisses down my neck, and I let my head fall back, feeling more powerful than I ever had in my life. Even knowing what we were up against, knowing I should be focused on stopping the prophecy, I couldn't make myself turn away from him. It was like a drug, this recklessness, leaving my whole body alive with sensation. Luc's eyes glittered in the porch light, and the sharp planes of his face were shadowed and tempting. I wanted to trace them, burn them into my memory through touch alone. I wanted to see his face change and know it was because of me.

Except it wasn't me, I realized, even as Luc's arm slid around me. The knowledge seeped into me gradually, chilling me from the inside out. It was the binding. He'd said as much before the ceremony, and I'd accepted it. I had known the cost. I just didn't realize I'd have to pay so soon.

"Inside," I said, feeling regret and resolve and sheer longing trip over each other within me. I stepped back. "I need to get inside. My mom's in there."

"She won't notice." Luc tucked a wayward lock of my hair behind my ear, his fingers trailing along my neck. I felt the current of magic between us flare up.

"What are you doing? I mean, what spell?"

He looked sheepish. "You can feel it? Wasn't sure you'd be able to."

"What is it?"

"A kind of concealment. It keeps Flats from noticing anyone connected to the spell."

"Connected."

"By touch." He brushed a thumb over my nape, and I shivered. "It's a low-level thing. You start screaming or breakin' windows, people would mark it. But it's handy when you want to get around without a lot of questions."

"The hospital. That's how you were able to get into my room. And to see Verity."

"Like I said, it comes in handy."

"But what do people see?"

"What they expect to. Not so different from real life, I guess."

I pulled away, studying him. He leaned against the doorjamb and stared back. His gaze was slower and more thorough. More . . . intent. I tried to ignore the heat licking along my skin. "I can still see you."

He shrugged. "We're bound. Makes a difference. Besides, you're expectin' to see me."

"Could you hide now? Even though I know you're here?"

He grinned, slow and lazy, and then, as if I'd blinked for too long, he vanished. I turned slowly, searching for any sign of him—a ripple in the air, the sound of his breathing, anything. I could feel just the faintest hint of something against my wrist, where the chain had been, an odd tension.

"Okay," I called, feeling foolish. "You can come out now."
Nothing.

"Luc? Come on."

Just the regular traffic and late-night neighborhood noises. Someone wheeled their garbage can to the curb. A few houses away, a car started up and drove off.

I sighed. "It's very impressive, okay? I am in awe of your magical hide-and-seek abilities."

I jumped at the feeling of his hands on my waist and stifled a shriek. The same unseen hands crept under the hem of my T-shirt, grazing the skin, brushing along the lower edge of my rib cage, feather light, and I was nearly dizzy with wanting him again.

His breath was hot against my shoulder, and it seemed impossible that he could make me so crazy when I couldn't see him. I turned toward him, and he backed me up against the door frame, his mouth on mine, my body turning to liquid, my brain not far behind.

He reappeared, his expression wolfish. "You sure you want to go inside?"

I blinked at the smug note in his voice. It wasn't fair. He had magic and confidence and he was gorgeous, and I was . . . just me. I pushed my hair back and then straightened my shirt, pleased my hands were steady. "I do. Colin's waiting for me to call."

Luc scowled, face darkening. "What's the deal with him?"

"With Colin? My uncle asked him to keep an eye on me."

"Ain't necessary. You know that."

"My uncle doesn't. Even if I could tell him the truth, he wouldn't believe it. It's like you said—he expects to see the danger coming from something he already knows, so that's where he sees it. Colin's not so bad."

"He's in the way."

I cocked my head to one side and gave him my most saccharine smile. "Jealous much?"

He scoffed. "No reason to be. Cujo's not the one you're bound to."

"Evangeline said binding isn't about that. It isn't romantic."

"Doesn't have to be, if you want to get all technical 'bout it. Seems silly to fight it, though." He curled a lock of my hair around his finger, seemingly fascinated. "Look, Mouse. I ain't thrilled the man's hangin' around all the time, but he's low on my list right now. We got work to do."

Right. Work. Because this was a job. I moved back, and he let go of my hair. "What's next?"

"We need to find the rift where the Torrent will start. Figure out how to stop it. Then . . ." He shrugged. "Then we stop it."

CHAPTER 23

I thought I was prepared to face Colin the next morning, but the swell of nerves and guilt when I heard his knock proved otherwise.

I checked the mirror one last time, half-expecting the events of the night before to be written across my face like on a billboard. Surely the binding would leave some visible trace, would let some of the sparkling feeling still thrumming beneath my skin reach the surface. As usual, I was wrong. The same old Mo peered out, more tired than usual, but otherwise nothing special.

"Mo!" Colin called. I heard the beep as he deactivated the alarm. "Come on!" There was a clear note of warning in his voice, and it wasn't because he was worried I'd be marked tardy.

I headed downstairs, hitching my bag over my shoulder and trying to look natural. "Almost ready."

"Late night," he commented, looking me over as I slipped on my Birks.

"I guess. Can I stay home?" *And avoid this conversation, maybe?* I'd spent most of the night wide-awake, worrying about what to tell Colin, and thinking—okay, obsessing—about Luc. Unfortunately, none of my tossing and turning had brought me closer to a plan. *If Verity were alive, she would know what to do. And I wouldn't have to deal with any of it.* I felt disloyal even thinking it, pushed the traitorous thought away.

Colin closed a hand on my shoulder and turned me to face him fully. Unnerved by his scrutiny, I brushed at my skirt. "What?"

He shrugged, letting go. "You look . . . I don't know. Something."

I pulled my uniform blazer out of the coat closet. "Good something or bad something?"

"Different something."

Alarm and curiosity bloomed inside me. "Still plain old me," I said, hoping it sounded convincing.

He chuckled and held open the door. "Someday, you're going to see yourself, Mo. Really see yourself. And you'll give new meaning to the phrase 'holy terror.'"

I rolled my eyes, somehow flustered and pleased all at once. "Whatever."

"I'm not sure I want to be around when that happens." He laughed again and gestured to the truck, not waiting for a response. "Coffee's getting cold."

If anyone was different this morning, it was Colin. He'd never been in such a good mood, so willing to joke and chat. I was about to ask why when it hit me with such force I rubbed at my forehead: He was cheerful because of our deal, and my promise to tell him the truth. Which I couldn't do, especially now.

So I sipped at my coffee and racked my brain for a way to tell him what he wanted to know without saying anything at all.

"Well?" he said expectantly.

"We'll be at school in fifteen minutes. It's not really enough time to explain."

"It's enough for a start," he said firmly, glancing over. "This is not the day to jerk me around."

Like there was ever a good day for that. I shifted in my seat and studied the storefronts and two-flats slipping by.

"I don't . . ." I shrugged, turning my hands over, palms up, unable to find the words. "I don't know how to start."

"The beginning would be nice. Or we can start with what happened last night. I'll take either one."

"I told you. I had coffee with Evangeline. We talked."

"About what?"

I took a deep breath. Colin deserved the truth, but he wouldn't believe it. And on the off chance he did believe me, there was no way he'd let me carry on. All I could do was give him half-truths and hope it was better than an outright lie.

"Verity." Funny, how little we had spoken of her. I wondered what he would have thought of Verity. She would have made him nuts, probably. She was so charming, and everyone loved her, but Colin was immune to charm.

He made a "get on with it" gesture but didn't say anything.

I laced my fingers together tightly. "You guys think I was the target of the hit, but I wasn't. Verity was."

"Mo, it's been looked into. Nobody put a contract out on her." His voice was the gentlest it had ever been.

"Nobody you *know*. I bet you haven't found anything about a contract on me, either, have you?" I didn't wait for a reply. "The whole thing was about her, not me."

"It's about Billy," he said, and he had that tone, that weary, long-suffering tone adults had been using with me since forever, the one designed to make me feel like a child. I loathed it, especially from him. I wasn't a child any longer.

"The ID is about Uncle Billy," I corrected him. "It's got nothing to do with the truth. Which is what I'm after. If you aren't going to listen, there's no point to this conversation."

He shook his head, almost amused. "You're trying to find out who killed your friend? And you think this Evangeline woman is going to be useful? Go to Billy if you want results. He's got contacts."

"Not in Louisiana. I need Evangeline if I'm going to go after who ordered it." It was the most I could tell him without hurting everyone.

He squinted at me, as if he couldn't quite understand what I'd said. "Who ordered it? Who *ordered it*? Are you fucking *kidding* me?"

My phone rang, and I snatched at it, desperate for a diversion. "Lena! What's up?"

"Just checking if you're ready for the Chem test today."

"The . . . oh, *crap*."

"Do not even tell me you forgot about it. That test is, like, twenty-five percent of our grade."

"Hang up," snarled Colin. I waved him away.

"I can't believe I forgot."

Lena snorted. "No kidding. Look, I'm in the caf. If you blow off chapel, we can cram a little more. Or maybe you should go to chapel after all. It might be the only thing to help you."

"Very funny."

"Hang up. Now," Colin ordered.

"Grab me a Diet Coke," I said to Lena. "I'll be there in ten."

I hung up and he reached for my cell, eyes still on the road. "No more interruptions. We are going to settle this."

"I have a test," I said pointedly, holding on to the phone. "A big test. I need to study."

"I don't give a rat's ass about your test, Mo. Are you actually saying you and Verity's aunt are planning on going after a killer? A group of killers? Because even if you're right about this—and you're *not*—what makes you think that you and a lady who sells Louis Quatorze dining sets can possibly handle this?"

"Because I have to. Haven't you ever done something, just

because it was the right thing to do? Ever? Or do you only care if you get paid?"

He grabbed my arm, hard, and let go just as suddenly. My phone beeped.

Colin made a dangerous noise, and I scowled back. "It's only a text."

A picture, actually. Of Lena, in the cafeteria at school, notes scattered around her and two cans of pop nearby. "That's weird," I said, checking the number. "Blocked."

The phone beeped again. Blocked. Again.

It was a picture of The Slice, my mom behind the register. I could see her nametag clearly and the rickrack trim on her apron. Whoever had taken it couldn't have been more than a few feet away.

Another beep.

"Jesus," Colin said. "Does that girl ever stop?"

"It's not Lena."

This time, it was a shot of Colin leaning against the truck, wearing the same gray T-shirt and brown jacket he had on right now. My house was visible in the background. This one was taken from farther away, maybe halfway down the block.

"There was no one hanging out this morning, was there? Outside the house?" Of course not. Colin would have spotted them. The angle, the distance . . . whoever took it had been inside a house. Inside a neighbor's, maybe.

"No. Why?"

He grabbed the phone as another message came through. I leaned over and looked. My bedroom, so close you could see the unmade bed through the window. I'd been raised to make my bed every morning, first thing. You didn't even head to the bathroom to pee until the covers were straightened and the pillows fluffed. Along with no meat on Fridays and attending holy days of obligation, it was one of the foundations of my mother's faith. This morning, I'd been exhausted, and running late, so I hadn't bothered, for maybe the third time in my whole life. The picture had been taken this morning, since Colin had picked me up.

Colin pulled over with a screech of tires, prompting a lot of angry honking and middle fingers from the other cars.

"What were the others?" He started thumbing through the message log.

Another one came through, and somehow I knew, even before he opened it, what this picture would be. Luc, kissing me under the yellow glow of the porch light.

Colin's jaw clenched, his eyes narrowing to slits. "Coffee, huh?" The bite in his voice was painful.

"It's not what you think," I said, knowing how completely lame I sounded. "Really. He knows Evangeline."

His voice was acid as he studied the picture. "I'm going to guess you didn't notice anyone?"

I shook my head. "The numbers are all blocked," I pointed out, trying to change the subject. "And that first one, of Lena? They *just* took that. She was getting me a pop when we hung up."

The phone rang, and Colin hit the speakerphone button, gesturing for me to respond.

"Hello?"

"Hello, Mo." A man's voice, but no one I knew. A glance at Colin showed he didn't recognize it, either.

"Who is this?"

"A friend. With some advice."

I swallowed. "Oh?"

"See how easy it is to pick people out of a crowd? Make sure you do it right when it's your turn, huh?"

"What do you—"

The call ended and Colin swore, slamming his fist into the dash and wrenching the truck back into traffic. He stared straight ahead for a moment, clenching the wheel, the pulse in his throat visible. He was so different from the cheerful, laughing guy who'd stood in my living room this morning, I barely recognized him.

He cut across town, speeding away from the school, checking his mirrors more than usual.

I waited until I could speak without my voice shaking. "What's he talking about?"

"The ID. Kowalski's coming by the school this afternoon. They made the arrests, and you're supposed to go down to the station."

"So who was that? Uncle Billy's secretary?"

"Not Billy. Somebody higher up."

I forced myself to ask, the words coming out small. "In the Mob?"

Colin didn't say anything, but his face had a hard, grim look to it.

"Why is the Mob taking pictures of my friends? My bedroom?"

He checked the mirrors, made a right, looked again. "To show how vulnerable you are."

"But . . . I have you."

A muscle in his jaw jumped. "Not all the time. And I'm not watching your friends, or your mom. My job is to keep you safe, Mo. Nobody else."

"What about my mom? Is she—"

"She's fine. Billy's had people watching her for a while. They're just less visible. And to be honest, your mom's a lot less trouble."

My stomach clenched. Who else could they go after? Without Verity, I was a pariah at school. The only one who even gave me the time of day lately was . . .

"Give me back my phone."

"What?"

"The phone, Colin. *Now.*"

He handed it over silently, watching me out of the corner of his eye as we sped through the city.

I dialed frantically, counting the rings until Lena picked up. "Lena? Is everything okay?"

"Fine, but chapel starts in a few minutes. If we're going to skip, now's the time."

I wanted to warn her. I wanted to tell her to run away, to go to the office, or at the very least to stick near a group, preferably away from windows. The thought of someone going after Lena because of me made my stomach pitch and my breath go panicky. But telling her the truth about my uncle would mean the rumors weren't idle gossip anymore. They would be facts, and a whole new set of problems to deal with.

"Traffic's terrible," I said, trying to sound aggravated instead of hysterical. "I'm not going to make it. Go ahead to chapel and I'll see you in class."

"You want me to light a candle for you?" she teased.

"Probably not a bad idea," I muttered, as Colin parked in front of a dingy warehouse.

He stayed close as we crossed the cracked, weed-choked sidewalk, yanked open the sliding door, and pushed me inside.

"I have a test," I reminded him as he punched a code into an alarm box.

"Forget about the damn test, Mo."

Dusty light shone through the windows high above us. Instead of the pallets, crates, and boxes I'd expected, it was a workshop. A carpentry workshop, with big electric saws scattered around and one wall made of Peg-Board with hand tools lined up at precise intervals. The air smelled like wood shavings and varnish, a clean, pungent scent that made my nose twitch, but not in a bad way.

His hand still on my back, Colin pushed me across the workshop and through an industrial-looking metal door, yanking it shut behind us and fiddling with another alarm panel. The lights came on, and if the workshop out front had surprised me, it was nothing compared to this room. My breath caught for a moment, and I turned to him.

"You live here?" It was stark and beautiful at the same time. Plain white walls, scarred cement floors, the same high-up windows as the workshop in front. But the furniture was beautiful, polished wood glowing quietly in the morning light. It smelled like lemon oil, bright and homey. A few rugs were scattered around, and there was a threadbare, dark blue velvet sofa and an ancient leather recliner near a pot-bellied stove. There was nothing lying around, no clutter or mess, but it didn't seem stiff, just spacious, like there was all the room in the world you might need to breathe and all the time you needed to take it in. "It's amazing."

He shrugged, his expression uncomfortable, and he pointed to a pair of doors opposite us. "Bathroom. Bedroom."

"You really live here?"

"Where did you think I lived?"

"I don't know. The truck, maybe? The Batcave? This is supernice." Nicer than I would have guessed, considering the state of Colin's truck. I'd always assumed he was barely scraping by, but I was wrong. Why was he hiding it, then? What else was he hiding?

"Glad you like it. I'll be back in a little while. Stay put."

"You're leaving?"

"I need to talk to your uncle."

"Take me with you!"

"If I knew who I could trust, I would. This is the safest place to keep you. Only a few people know about it, and I trust them."

"Uncle Billy?"

He paused. "Yeah."

Uncle Billy didn't seem particularly trustworthy to me right now, but I was willing to take Colin's word. Fear, I was discovering, had a way of crystallizing things. It might not make your decisions easier, but it made them sharper. And faster.

"Help yourself to the food. Study for your test. Watch TV if you want," he added, jerking a thumb at a black lacquered cabinet. "Mo, for once in your life, do what I tell you. You are in eighteen different kinds of shit right now, and that doesn't even count you playing Nancy Drew. Which I haven't forgotten about, by the way."

If he'd told me to stay out of anger, I would have pushed him more. But there was none of that in his face, only gravity and concern, so I sat down on the couch, folding my shaking legs underneath me and tucking my skirt around my knees. "You're worried."

"I didn't expect them to go around Billy," he said. "I thought they'd let him handle you."

"Well, he thought you'd handle me. Look at how that's turned out."

"You have a point. Now, stay put."

And so I stayed. There was nothing on TV, I wasn't hungry, and there was no way I could focus on atomic masses and isotopes. Instead, I wore a path into the faded navy and maroon rug, turning over the ring in my hand, wondering how much danger Colin was in because of me. The thought only made me walk faster.

When my phone rang, I dove over the back of the couch to reach it.

"Congratulations on the binding," Evangeline said, her voice a few degrees warmer than usual. "You did quite nicely."

"You seemed surprised that it worked."

"Wishing for something and seeing that wish actualized are decidedly different things," she replied. "I'm intrigued by the possibilities."

I rolled my eyes, then stopped. What if she could see me? I

was tired of not understanding how things worked—in magic and in life. "This is kind of a bad time, Evangeline. Can I call you later?"

Her voice frosted over again. "I'm sorry to be such an inconvenience, Mo. But I thought you'd be interested in what I've learned about our next step."

I pressed my fingers against my eyelids. "Okay."

"Do you have the ring with you?"

"Of course. Always."

"Excellent. We've located a group of lines that have grown unstable. We believe the ring will allow you, with Lucien's help, to reinforce them."

"That's a good thing, right?"

Her voice was more enthusiastic than I'd ever heard. "If you can do this, we may be able to circumvent the Torrent completely."

"Like preventative maintenance?" It sounded almost too easy, but with everything crashing down at once, easy held an undeniable appeal.

"Exactly. Lucien will come for you this evening. The sooner we can attempt this, the better."

CHAPTER 24

Colin came back two hours later, slamming into the room with poorly contained rage. He set the alarm, his movements furious and precise, and stowed his gun in a locked metal cabinet. Thumping down in the cracked leather recliner, he eyed me warily.

"What happened?" I closed the copy of Hemingway stories I'd found on the bookshelves. "Did you talk to Uncle Billy? Is my mom okay?"

"Your mom's fine." He drummed his fingers on the armrest, then leaned forward, like he'd suddenly decided something. "How much do you know about your uncle's business?"

I lifted a shoulder, an icy blackness welling up inside me. "I've heard the rumors. Until Verity died, I assumed that's all they were. God forbid someone in my family actually tell me the truth."

"They're trying to protect you."

I recalled Luc's words after the Darkling attack. "He runs the neighborhood for the Outfit, right? All the protection and the money, they go through him. He keeps the peace and makes a profit."

He looked down at the floor. "Close enough."

"You work for him," I said, fitting it together, feeling slow and stupid when the pieces finally clicked. "You work for the Mob."

"Right now, I work for Billy, watching you. That's it." His voice was tired, but I was too angry to feel sorry for him.

"What about the carpentry?"

"You could say I have a versatile skill set."

I shoved my fists into the pockets of my blazer. "Absolutely! Handy with a gun *and* a belt sander. You're a regular Renaissance man, aren't you?" I was mortified by my own naiveté, at how willingly I believed the stories everyone had fed me. "You're as big a liar as he is."

He scrubbed a hand over his hair. "Don't start, kid. You want to judge me, wait until you've got all the facts."

I ground my teeth together. "I don't *have* any facts. Because no one will *tell* me anything. Do you know how frustrating that is?"

"I've got a pretty good idea. How's the boyfriend, Mo? You know, the one you don't have?" The anger in his voice was like knives. "You're keeping as many dirty little secrets as anyone, so knock it off with the righteous outrage crap."

He had a better point than he realized. I sat back, chastened. He pinned me with a glare and went on. "Yes, Billy works for the Outfit. He's survived as long as he has because he's smart—he doesn't get greedy, he doesn't overreach. It's worked out pretty well, but now there are new players on the scene."

"The Russians."

He pushed out of the chair and headed toward the kitchen. "They're not just coming after Billy. They're coming after the entire organization, and they're bad, bad news. They make the Mob look like a bunch of little old ladies on Bingo night. They're looking to get a foothold here, in Billy's territory."

I trailed after him. "If I identify them as the guys who killed Verity . . ."

"It helps Billy and his people keep hold of the power."

It always came down to who had the power, didn't it?

"Tell me about my dad."

He turned away, opening and closing cabinets at random. "I wasn't around then."

"But you know. I *know* you know." I stepped in front of him, needing to see the truth.

He crossed his arms, mouth tight.

"It was my uncle, wasn't it? My dad was innocent. Uncle Billy set him up." I exhaled, a sudden lightness seeping through the dark and rage, and a sense that maybe I could be free.

And then I caught sight of Colin's expression, pitying, so regretful.

"It wasn't a setup," he said. He pushed away from the counter, pacing again, worry and frustration swirling darkly around him.

"But . . ."

He paused and met my eyes. Whatever lies I'd been told, Colin was being straight with me. "Your dad knew what he was doing."

I started to demand more details, but he held up a hand. "No. It's not my place. This is between you and your folks and Billy. I've already said more than I should."

"But—"

"I don't want this between us," he said. "And you have bigger problems than your family history right now, Mo. You need to make a decision about the ID."

Like I cared about the ID, after everything he'd just said. But if Colin thought it was a problem, it was. I dropped into the kitchen chair. "Do you think I should do it?"

"No way I'm answering that," he said grimly. "Whatever you decide, I'll back you up. But we can't put it off any longer."

Hearing him say "we" was a comfort, and I was suddenly ashamed of my behavior. He'd done nothing but try to protect me, from my uncle as much as anyone else, and all I'd done was lie. I caught his sleeve. "What I said before . . . I'm sorry. It doesn't matter who you work for. You're a good person. You're probably the best person I know."

He ran a hand roughly over my hair. "You need to meet more people, kid."

Elsa the Lawyer was at the station when we arrived, conferring with Billy. Kowalski glowered at the two of them and transferred the frown to Colin and me.

"Aren't you supposed to be in school?"

Elsa stepped in. "You asked us to produce her for the lineup, Detective. We arrived early, as a courtesy. Now you're complaining she's here?"

"As much money as that school sets you back, I'd think you'd want her in class, that's all," he grumbled, hauling open a metal door. The eye-level window was covered with a piece of cardboard. "In here, Mo. It won't take long."

Colin and Billy both moved to follow me, but Kowalski held up a hand. "Just the lawyer, boys," he said. "You can wait out here."

"A word with my niece, Detective." Uncle Billy drew me aside, patting my hand. "Now, Mo, I am sorry about what happened earlier. It was inexcusable, my associates frightening you that way, but it just goes to show how important this is."

He'd done this to me a thousand times before, laying on the charm and understanding, right before he laid down the law. It had always worked, too, so who could blame him for going with the same old tactics? But I wasn't that quiet, biddable girl anymore. I had seen too much, and now I could see him for what he was—no longer my affable Uncle Billy, but a liar and a criminal and the root of my family's shame. My hands curled into fists.

He continued on blithely. "There's two men in there, with the markings we discussed earlier. Kowalski will ask if any of them were in the alley, and you will tell him about those two men."

"Lie, you mean." My voice was thin and nasty.

His grip tightened on my arm for a split second. "The alley was black as pitch. Who's to say it wasn't them?"

"I am."

Kowalski ushered me into the room, Elsa close behind. I could feel Colin's eyes on me as he leaned against the wall, his arms folded over his chest.

Kowalski shut the door with a tug and a thud, Billy's outraged face disappearing behind an inch and a half of steel. The room was tiny, just big enough to fit a countertop with a phone and three scarred plastic chairs. Above the countertop was a window the width of the room. Kowalski waved at the chairs and laid a thick file folder on the counter. "Take a seat, if you want. It's pretty simple, Mo. Six guys, in a line. You see if you recognize anybody. I can make them talk, if you need to hear their voices, or make them come up to the window, if you want a closer look. Take your time, look at all the faces. There's no rush."

He sat and made some notations on a piece of paper. "Just gimme a minute," he muttered. "Damn paperwork's gonna be the death of me."

Elsa murmured, "Is there anything I should know about? Has anything changed?"

Only everything. "No. Just nervous," I said. She smiled encouragingly.

"They can't see you," Kowalski said, overhearing me. He picked up the phone. "Send 'em in." They walked in, all six men with blunt faces and cold eyes. I spotted the two my uncle was after almost immediately. They stuck out from the others even without the advance warning. Their eyes weren't merely cold, but dead. I shuddered involuntarily. Maybe Billy had a point.

"Step forward," Kowalski said into the phone. "Anybody look familiar, Mo?"

You didn't need magic to sense the evil coming off of these two. Billy had betrayed me, but I had to wonder, would it be so bad to get them off the street? It was my neighborhood they were moving in on. Houses I'd trick-or-treated at, customers I'd been waiting on at The Slice since I could see over the counter. They wanted to come in and rip through the fabric of my everyday life, when Verity's death had already left it in tatters. I could still go after the Seraphim. What was the harm in protecting the people around me?

"Can you make number two show me his tattoo? The one on his chest?"

"You didn't mention a tattoo in your description," he said, squinting at me and back at the pile of papers.

"It's possible seeing the perpetrators has triggered her memory," Elsa cut in smoothly, and Kowalski muttered into the phone again. A moment later, without a hint of surprise or emotion, Guy Number Two shucked off his grease-streaked shirt to reveal a badly inked blue rose.

"Does that help?"

I made a noncommittal noise, and Kowalski eyed me suspiciously.

"What about number five?" I asked.

"You want him to take off his shirt, too?"

"He can just roll up his sleeve."

The burn scar was the size of an apricot, shiny and pink, long-healed. My own scar throbbed at the sight of it, and I pressed my hands against my thighs.

It would solve a whole bunch of problems. Kowalski would close the case and leave me alone. Two sociopaths would stay out of my neighborhood. Billy might even take Colin off babysitting duty, freeing me up to deal with the Torrent and find Verity's killer. It was one lie, and so much good would come of it. . . .

But Colin's words came back to me. *You have to see the consequences.* And tucked among all those good things was one undeniable consequence—I'd be more like my uncle than I'd ever wanted.

"Mo? Do any of them look familiar? Did you see any of these guys in the alley that night?"

My words came from far away. "I don't recognize any of them. I don't think any of these guys were there."

"Are you sure?" Elsa's voice held the faintest edge. "None of them?"

"No. I'm sorry." I didn't know who I was apologizing to.

Kowalski closed the folder and stood up. When he spoke, his voice was weary. "It's okay. The ID would have helped, but we've got other evidence, too. I appreciate you trying."

He walked us out to the lobby area, where my uncle and Colin were waiting. No one said much of anything until we reached the parking lot. "Well?" Billy demanded.

Finally Elsa answered. "Mo was unable to identify either suspect."

Billy swore. "You ungrateful little brat! Do you know what you've done?" He grabbed my arm and shook me once, hard. Instantly, Colin was beside me.

"I told the truth," I snapped, wrenching my arm away. "You should try it sometime."

"Don't you take that tone with me. Those men are danger-ous."

"Why? Because they're criminals? That's a little pot-meet-kettle, isn't it?"

He went still as the storm built, and he stepped so close I could see my reflection in his pupils. "They are nothing like me! Don't presume to understand the pressures of my posi-tion. You are a *child*."

"Oh, yeah? That's who you send to do your dirty work? If those two were so bad, so important, go after them your-self!"

Colin stepped between us, and Uncle Billy turned on him.

"You were supposed to talk to her! What in the hell am I paying you for?"

He set his jaw, and his words were careful and even. "You said to keep her safe. Is that still the job?"

You could see Billy clamp down on the anger, fingers twitching as if he was fighting the urge to throttle me. "Yes. She's making it harder for both of you."

"I like a challenge," Colin said, and led me away.

When we were far enough down the sidewalk, he sighed. "That could have gone better."

"Do you think I should have done it?"

"Not really. I wish you hadn't gone toe-to-toe with your uncle in the parking lot, though. All it did was piss him off and make him look bad. I'm trying to keep you off people's radar, Mo. You're not exactly cooperating."

"Sorry." I kicked a crumbling chunk of pavement away.

"You were honest. Most of the time, it's a good thing." He looked over at the truck. "Times like now, for instance."

I looked up to see Luc leaning against the truck, a fedora pulled low over his eyes. His smile glittered and I felt my heart catch in my throat even as disaster loomed. I kicked a pebble, harder than strictly necessary, into the gutter.

"Afternoon," he called, tipping the hat up, eyes full of mischief. We crossed the street, Colin seething next to me, and Luc brushed a kiss over my cheek. Then, snaking one arm around my waist, he stuck out the other hand for Colin to shake. "Figured it might be time to introduce myself."

CHAPTER 25

"What were you thinking?" I grumbled, hours later, as Luc dragged me down a darkened corridor.

"Told you—seemed like time I met Cujo face-to-face. The man was gettin' suspicious."

"That's what he does—he suspects. *Everyone*. It's his job. And he's crazy-good at it."

"Relax, Mouse. Now we've met, he won't worry so much. I showed him I'm harmless."

Right. Harmless. Kittens stalking yarn balls were harmless. Luc was a lot more panther than kitten. He'd put on a show for Colin and then left, but when he'd arrived in my room after midnight, he'd barely said hello. Instead, he'd brought me Between, to here.

"So you're actually telling me that the Water Tower is some sort of woo-woo holy place? Seriously?" I didn't bother to hide my skepticism. "It's a stop on a bus tour, not a shrine."

Evangeline clipped ahead of us through the dark and echoing corridors, calling back, "Correct me if I'm wrong, but this building is a significant part of the city's history, yes?"

I pulled out of Luc's grasp. "It's one of the only buildings that survived the Great Fire, back in the eighteen hundreds. But that was engineering, not magic. Stone doesn't burn."

"Please don't be so literal, Mo. It is the mark of an inferior mind. This building is rich with history—the walls practically hum with that energy. And to be so intimately tied to three of the four elements magnifies its power."

"Water, fire, stone," I murmured, passing a picture of the crenellated tower standing proud amid the rubble of the Fire. "Wouldn't it be better if it tied into air, too?"

Luc gave me a tense smile. "No need to get greedy. It's like talents—the more you have, the rarer it is. Only place we know with all four elements in one place is the Binding Temple."

"Oh." *That* seemed like a topic better avoided, so I tried another. "Why are we here?"

Unerringly, Evangeline led us toward the center of the building, to the base of the tall limestone tower, and we stopped underneath it, staring up into the vast empty chamber. Faint moonlight shone in from the windows at the very top, leaving us in a weak pool of light.

"The fact that you and Lucien were able to complete the Binding Ceremony was a surprise to me," she admitted. "It struck me that perhaps the prophecy was more flexible than we had previously imagined. I began to look at our scholars' findings with a fresh eye."

"You're telling me there's another way? The prophecy might be wrong?" Luc asked harshly.

"There's *wiggle room?*" My entire body went rigid. Verity had died, Luc was stuck with me, I was playing second-string savior, and none of it had been necessary?

Evangeline held up a hand. "Calm yourselves, children. The prophecy stands as it always has. But if my niece's death has proved anything, it is that the fabric of our destiny is not as tightly woven as we thought. To be frank, Verity stood a much better chance of survival than you do, Mo, but even she had no guarantees."

Luc looked up from the window, where he was tracing an

ornate stone lion's head, and shot her an accusatory glance. "You promised the binding would protect Mo."

"I believe it will. If the prophecy will bend to allow Mo to take Verity's place, perhaps the timing might also be adjusted. We've always assumed the Vessel can face the Torrent only at the very moment it begins—that the repairs must be made after the lines have failed. Now, our hope is that you might reverse some of the most decayed sites before the Torrent reaches its peak. A more gradual approach would be safer, and if Mo can shore up sufficient lines and junctures, we may stave off the Torrent altogether."

"Maybe," said Luc. "If she was ready. She needs more time to figure out how it works, what she can do. Why are you rushin' this?"

"How will she figure it out without experiencing the lines, Lucien? You're losing sight of the larger picture. Perhaps the binding has clouded your judgment."

His face darkened. "It's nothing to do with that."

"Excellent. Then you should have no trouble remembering your loyalty lies with our world's future."

She addressed me over Luc's shoulder. "The Binding Ceremony proved the ring accepts you in Verity's place. You'll use it now."

"How?"

"It will let you tap into the lines while providing a buffer against the raw magic. Between Lucien's magic and the ring, there should be protection enough."

"How dangerous is it?" I asked. Did it matter? I'd sworn to get justice for Verity, no matter what the consequences.

Evangeline looked straight at me. "We've told you all along. Raw magic is deadly to Flats."

"So if Luc can't protect me . . ."

"I will," he said, but Evangeline cut him off.

"Then the Torrent will come. If you're in contact with a

line when the magic ruptures, you'll be killed instantly, just
as any other Flat would."

I swallowed. "And the lines . . . there's a lot of them?"

"You're standing in one right now. There's another three
inches from your left ear. They aren't rare, Mo, just invisible."

"It's too risky," Luc said. He moved to me, taking my
hand. "You're not ready."

My shoulders slumped at his words. But I forced myself to
ignore the hurt, addressing Evangeline instead. "What do I
do once we start?"

Her glance slid away. "We think there will be a tangible
component to the magic, something you can manipulate, but
we can't be certain until you've actually begun the work. It's
a question of faith, I suppose."

"Faith," I echoed. Twelve years of actual written tests on
the subject of faith, and this particular situation had never
been on the syllabus.

"The ring will bring the Darklings, though."

"There are spells we can set—wards of protection that will
shield you. You may not have seen me fight as Lucien has,
but I assure you I'm up to the task."

"We should wait," Luc said again, charm slipping into
something more urgent. "Bring in the others. More help we
have, the better."

"There are others?" I asked. Evangeline waved a dismissive hand.

"I've spoken with them. Convening the Quartoren will
take too long. They feel it's best to proceed immediately.
Even your father agrees, Lucien."

He frowned, shaking his head slightly, and grabbed my
other hand. "You can say no. We can put it off a little longer.
This ain't right."

Evangeline shook her head, as if puzzled. "What is it

about her that you question, Lucien? Her abilities, or her courage? Or her commitment to our cause?" She brushed him aside and rested her hands on my shoulders, giving me an encouraging smile. "I no longer doubt any of those things about you, Mo. Verity didn't, either. Will you do this for her?"

Slowly, I pulled the ring out from beneath my shirt. Luc fumed only steps away. "She saved me," I said, trying to make him understand. "I need to make it up to her."

"And you shall," Evangeline said, shooting Luc a triumphant look. "We'll take care of the Darklings. Lucien, begin setting the wards."

His face was hard, the planes and angles less forgiving than they'd ever been before. Wordlessly, he reached behind himself and drew the same sword he'd had the first night the Darklings had attacked. The gleaming blade traced patterns in the floor and air around us. Dark red flames shimmered, brightest where his sword touched them. Soon the air was alive with the shifting lights.

Evangeline regarded him critically. "You've been practicing."

He barely glanced up. "She's going to need all the help she can get."

He thought I'd fail. The realization cut into me more deeply than any magic could. I knew he would protect me— he'd told me enough times that I was their last chance—but I had hoped he'd believe in me, too.

"What do I do?" It felt as if the world was picking up speed around me while I stayed still.

"Trust your instincts," Luc said, not pausing in his spellwork.

Oh, God. We really were screwed.

Evangeline joined him, adding wavering lines of crystalline blue. "Once you've accessed the magic, work as quickly as you can. Don't allow it to pull you in too deeply. Lucien will remain with you. I must stay on the other side of the wards. Should there be too many Darklings, we'll retreat."

Luc stopped casting spells and came to stand next to me, more anxious than I'd ever seen him. "This will hold," he said quietly, tapping my wrist. A small burst of magic pulsed along the binding, a jolt of heat under my skin. "I'll keep you safe. Trust me."

With shaking hands, I slipped the ring off the chain, held it cupped in my palm. The blue stone shone dully in the moonlight, the four diamonds surrounding it like stars. "The way you trust me? You don't even think I can do it. Let's finish this, please."

He took the ring from me, not meeting my eyes.

"Begin," called Evangeline from the edge of the circle.

Luc turned slowly, inspecting the lattice of glowing magic that surrounded us. Dragging in a breath, sorrow plain on his face, he slid the ring onto my finger. It nestled snugly against my hand, and we both stared at it, the tips of my fingers still caught in his.

The strange starburst chased across the surface of the stone, exactly as it had the first time I'd put it on. The golden band got hot as the starburst intensified and spread, spinning rapidly outward. All four diamonds glowed bluish white, the intensity startling in the dim room.

"It didn't do this last time," I said. "In the park."

"More magic here," he replied.

Tracings of light began to crisscross the floor with a shattering sound, like ice on Lake Michigan just before it thaws. I pulled back, but Luc kept my hand in his.

"Lines are respondin' to the ring." His voice was a whisper. "Hold on, Mouse."

I didn't need to be told. The lines pulsed around me, in time with my heartbeat. Was this how Arcs lived? The lines overlaying everything, magic pulling on them all the time? Was this how Verity had felt? I shook off Luc's hold, moving

toward the lines in front of me as if weightless, my eyes drifting shut. I didn't need to see—I could feel the distinctive
brushstroke of each one—fire was warm and silky, reminding
me of Luc, and air was glittering and needle-fine, water cool
and slick, earth rough and substantial. The intersecting lines
called to me more insistently. I reached out for the strongest
one, remembering Evangeline's instructions not to be drawn
in too deeply. But the pull was irresistible, and my hand
stretched out of its own accord, about to plunge into the
stream of energy.

Behind me, something came Between with a ripping sound.
My eyes snapped open and I saw a horde of Darklings massing
around the framework Luc and Evangeline had constructed.

With a cry, Evangeline stepped forward, a long, forked
staff appearing in her hands. She began to turn it slowly,
gradually increasing speed as the Darklings approached her.
Light streamed out of the staff, crackling like lightning, and
the smell of ozone filled the air.

Next to me, Luc cast more wards, building up an ever-
brighter wall of magic around us.

One of the Darklings sprang toward Evangeline, and she
moved to meet him, spearing him with the twin prongs on
the end, shouting spells nonstop. The leathery black shape
simply disintegrated, and the other creatures screeched in
outrage as the staff picked up even more speed, the ends blur-
ring as she whirled it around.

"Keep going," Luc shouted over the noise. He turned so
that our backs touched, him facing the Darklings and me
looking straight at the tangle of glowing lines. I could hear
him chanting. The ruby wards shivered in time to the rhythm
of his words, and I reached into the storm.

The first touch was like a blow. My head snapped back as
it rushed over me, all four types of magic scrambling together
and crashing around me in a maelstrom of noise and sensation. The link to Luc surged, steadying me as much as the

pressure of his back against mine. I saw one of the Darklings fall and vanish, and the familiar stench rose up.

The floor splintered around me, the noise deafening. I closed my eyes again, trying to hold on to the lines. They felt like thick, smooth rope, the power throbbing just beneath the surface. In places, they were rotting, pits of nothingness spreading rapidly under my fingers. The dark places crumbled, and a more destructive power flowed out, coating my hands with something oily and corrosive. This was the rupture they'd warned me about.

How to fix it? Some part of me clung to my connection to Luc, and I tried to draw on it. Even with my eyes shut, I was hyperaware of him, where he stood, the spells he cast, his strength fueling me. I smoothed away the dark places and watched the line form true again, but it wasn't enough. As fast as I repaired one line, another rotted away. I couldn't keep up. I needed more power than even Luc could give me.

The ring. Powerful enough to attract Darklings, to raise the lines, Evangeline had said it was a tool to repair the magic. It blazed against my hand and I opened myself up to the whirling energy skittering sun-bright across the blue stone.

For a few seconds, it worked. The power contained within the gem careened through my body and ricocheted out into the lines. Triumph surged through me.

And then the darkness turned.

It fed on the magic, growing larger and faster, hungrier as it raced back along the lines, trying to enter me. The line I was repairing slipped away. Everything was slipping away.

"I can't hold it!" I cried.

Behind me Luc swore. The remaining three Darklings were beating against the wards, sending up sparks. The shimmering spells were burning out under the attack, but Luc was putting up new ones as they fell. His breath came faster now; I could feel it matching my own in a strange synchronicity. I gathered myself to try again, dipping my hands back into the ever-widening tumult, bracing myself against the pull of the raw magic.

Evangeline screamed, and I looked up to see a Darkling knock her across the room. She landed with a crack against the massive stone window frame. The sparkling blue lights of her wards dimmed, some going out entirely, and she lay immobile on the floor. Luc pulled a set of palm-sized knives from his waist. He whipped them, one after another, at the Darkling, nearly severing the head. It fell next to Evangeline.

"It was working!" he shouted. "What happened?!?"

"I don't know!" Every breath was an effort to keep myself from being sucked farther into the magic. The ruptures scalded me, but the healthy lines felt like a balm against my skin. If I could hold on to one long enough, maybe I could gather the strength to fight off the blackness. "I used the ring, but it's getting worse!"

Luc stumbled as the wards started to fail. "It's feeding the rupture!"

A crash sounded down the hallway—the sound of breaking glass adding to the chaos.

"Trouble's comin'," Luc called.

A moment later, Kowalski and Colin burst into the room at a dead run, guns drawn, skidding to a stop on the marble floor. Sweat soaked Kowalski's white oxford, and his face was mottled red and gray, his breath coming in pained gasps. "What in the hell is going on here?"

"Mo!" Colin took another step and Luc threw out his hand. A line of reddish flame soared up from the floor, forcing the men back. "You okay?"

"Colin, you have to go! It's not safe!"

"What are these things?" Kowalski demanded, training his gun on the Darkling nearest him.

Neither of the two creatures paid Kowalski and Colin any attention—as Luc had told me before, they were drawn to magic, not Flats. As long as Kowalski and Colin didn't get between the Darklings and me, there was a chance—a small, spindly chance—the creatures might not attack them.

The magic was a bigger threat. The rupture was yawning now, slipping out of my control. I tightened my fingers on the lines but they only crumbled faster, the rawness burning through.

"Mo, come on," Colin called. He fired at the Darkling closest to me. It cocked its head, its bone white talon still scrabbling at Luc's wards.

"Get out!" Luc roared. It was all the attention he could spare. He was calling fresh spells continuously, his voice ragged, as though the words themselves were inflicting pain on him.

Kowalski fumbled for his radio, but it exploded in a shower of blue sparks.

"It's going," I wailed as Evangeline's wards failed completely, the lights disintegrating to nothingness. "Luc!"

"We have to leave," Evangeline rasped, slowly rising to her knees. She clung to the stone windowsill, blood vivid at the corner of her mouth. "We've failed."

"No! I can do it!" But I couldn't. It was all breaking down too fast, all my worlds crashing together while the magic ruptured, the wards falling around me and the Darklings entering the circle. I couldn't hold the center, and now everyone was in danger.

"We stop now and it all goes," Luc shouted. "We've got to finish it!"

Kowalski eyed me across the wall of deep red flame. "I'm coming to get you, Mo," he said, signaling to Colin. Colin gave a thumbs-up and pulled a second gun from his back, and trained both of them on the Darkling closest to me. Kowalski was eerily calm, moving purposefully toward us while Colin squeezed off shot after shot.

"Give me the ring," Evangeline insisted. "It's all the Darklings care about. They'll follow it, not you."

"I can't get to the magic without it! I won't be able to fix it!"

"The lines have ruptured. They're beyond fixing now. Throw me the ring!"

"The ring *caused* the rupture! Don't give it to her!" Luc shouted. He'd stepped away to fight one of the Darklings, and I could hear the whooshing sound of the sword slicing through air and connecting with rotten flesh. The familiar stench filled the air. Kowalski kept advancing toward me, nodding encouragement even as his eyes darted wildly around the room.

Evangeline's voice was soft, reassuring under the chaos. "We can hide you again, Mo. We can reestablish the cloaking spell."

I turned toward her, desperate for refuge. Not just for me, but for all of us.

Kowalski paused as Colin reloaded, waiting for his sign before starting forward again. All at once, the Darkling bounded across the room, the floor erupted beneath me, and Luc yanked with all his might on the invisible chain connecting us.

I cleared the explosion by a thread, landing sprawled at Luc's feet.

Kowalski wasn't so lucky. The geyser of raw magic caught him full in the chest and swarmed over his skin, *into* his skin, lighting him with a horrible brilliance, and then he was a limp blackened mass on the floor.

I screamed, and Colin raced toward me. The Darkling lit on him with a screech and Luc knocked it back with a pulse of coppery light.

"More Darklings will come," Evangeline said, gasping. "The rupture will draw them. Even if they don't kill us, your friend can't survive here. Give me the ring."

Colin scrambled away from the Darkling, still angling for me. Luc continued to fight. "Mouse! Don't! Trust me!"

"Are you crazy?" The Darkling slashed against Colin's arm and blood poured out. His cry of pain made the decision for me. "We have to get out!"

I pulled the ring from my finger and tossed it to Evangeline in a high arc. The light from the stone was brilliant, even against the magic streaming everywhere. She plucked it out of the air deftly.

"Good girl," she said with a wintry smile.

With a grunt, Luc beheaded his Darkling and sent another bolt toward Colin, just missing him but knocking the other creature back through the window.

Luc shoved me at Colin and whirled away. He sent a stream of red-orange flame down the length of the sword, dead center at Evangeline.

I shrieked.

She deflected the bolt with a casual flick of her staff.

"Bitch! You set us up," he hissed, dragging his sleeve across his brow. "You didn't want to stop the Torrent. You wanted to start it."

"What?" I scrambled to my feet. Colin gripped my waist and tried to drag me away, but I fought him, planting my feet and swinging wildly. Without the ring, I could no longer see or feel the lines whipping around the room. I knew they were there, ready to take us both out like downed wires in a storm. If they touched us, we'd be dead. We couldn't move, and we couldn't stay. "She's on our side, Luc!"

He gave me a pitying glance, aiming the sword at her again. Dark red flames pulsed along the blade, barely restrained. "She lied to us. From the start. She's part of the Seraphim, Mouse. Hell, maybe she's the leader."

Evangeline tilted her head, admiring the ring held delicately between her index finger and thumb. "Not the leader,

Lucien. Nothing so grand. Any service to the cause is a glory and a privilege. How did you know?"

"You shouldn't have said my old man was on board. He would never try to do an end-run around the prophecy."

"Yes, Dominic cleaves to the old ways, doesn't he? It's certainly cost him enough, yet he follows the prophecy as slavishly as any. Still, the Quartoren could have overruled him."

He snorted. "Like that would ever happen. You lied about the Quartoren. You played Mouse like a fuckin' Stradivarius, with all your talk about what Verity would have done. You knew she'd do anything if you dressed it up like that. You told her to open up the most powerful group of lines you could find and asked her to do a patch job.

"Got that, Mouse? She asked you to do open-heart surgery with a Band-Aid and a butter knife. Now it's in motion, right? Just like you wanted."

"We thought removing Verity would ensure the Torrent would occur unchecked. But when the ring responded to Mo, we knew we hadn't been entirely successful." She gave me a contemptuous glance. "You were so weak. Pathetic, really, with all your noisome talk of justice and grief. We didn't think you were truly a threat. Why reveal ourselves when we could simply allow you to fail?

"When you completed the binding, we realized we'd looked at it from the wrong perspective. The Torrent *needed* the Vessel in order to begin, so we turned you to our own ends. Here you are, present at the hour the Torrent has begun, the one that made it possible. And without the ring, you have no way to reach the magic again. You've done us quite a service, Mo."

"You killed Verity." My stomach heaved and I staggered, feeling Colin's arms around me. His voice sounded like a dream, urging me away.

"I tried to talk my betters out of it. I believed she could be swayed to our position, but I was unsuccessful. She asked for time to think, and insisted she return home. As if she could run from us. My superiors suspected she was planning to inform the Quartoren, and we couldn't allow that. As I told you once, sometimes one must do unpleasant things for the greater good." She turned those awful, pale eyes on me. "Lucien, for example, bound himself to a poor substitute for the girl he was meant to have. Ultimately useless, I grant you, but honorable in its way."

The flames on Luc's sword blazed brighter. "Give the ring back."

She laughed. "I don't believe I shall. You're welcome to try to take it, Lucien, but your Flats won't last much longer here."

He paused, glancing uncertainly at the floor around me. I couldn't see the lines, but I knew they must be inching closer, sliding out of control.

"Oh, Lucien. You do struggle, don't you, when you must act for yourself instead of the prophecy? It's quite sad." She shook her head, palming the ring. "The Torrent has begun. More Darklings are coming. Feel free to give chase—all it will cost you is Mo."

And then she vanished.

A roar I knew too well was building, Darklings coming Between in waves. Luc stood in the ruined center of the circle, looking utterly defeated. Colin pulled me toward him, and I'd run out of strength to fight. Blood soaked his shirt, dripping onto the floor, and his face was white with shock. "We have to get you out, Mo. The police are coming."

"Luc?" I said, taking a step toward him, not caring about the lines.

He stared at the place Evangeline had stood, sword held loosely in his hand, his expression ravaged. "We lost."

"We can't fight them," I said, tugging on his hand. "We have to go."

High above us, the Darklings battered the tower. I reached

for him as bricks and mortar began to shower down. "Luc, please!"

He slung his sword over his back and stepped toward me and Colin, taking us Between and away from the swarm of Darklings.

We landed on a nearby roof. The sand-colored limestone of the Water Tower was covered with hordes of Darklings, more than I could have imagined in this or any other world.

"Kowalski," I said softly. "He's still inside."

"The cops will be here soon," Colin said. "They can't find us here."

"What do we do?" Blood was still pouring from Colin's arm. I stripped off my sweater and pressed it against the bloody gash, trembling violently.

Luc stared at the tower. "How do we stop them?" I asked, over the howling wind.

"We bury it," he said.

He raised his hands and closed his eyes, and the now-familiar language of spells poured forth, stronger and angrier and harsher than I'd ever heard before.

With a giant whooshing sound, an explosion rocketed up beneath the Water Tower. The entire structure trembled and collapsed into rubble. Flames licked at the base, like an echo of the fire it had survived over a century ago.

"My God," I breathed. "Why . . ."

"They'd feed on the magic," he said furiously. "They'd get stronger and devour everyone in their way. I sealed it as best I could. My father and his people can finish the job. Not that it matters now. We're only gonna have a few days before it all goes." He rounded on me. "Why did you give her the ring?"

"She said it was the only way to save us!"

"And I said I'd protect you!"

"From the minute we walked in there, you were saying I wasn't strong enough. You didn't even want me to try!"

"You weren't ready! But there you go, throwing yourself in 'cause Evangeline says that's what Verity would do. You don't know what she would've done. Nobody does!"

"So I shouldn't even try, right? Everybody knows I can't really take her place. I wasn't ever going to be enough. You even told me that, but I was too stupid and crazy about you to listen!" To my horror, hot tears sprang up and my voice cracked. I pressed the sweater more firmly against Colin's arm, trying to get myself under control.

Luc gaped at me. "Christ, Mouse! This isn't about Verity anymore! I didn't want her, and I didn't want you to be her. I *never* wanted you to be her, and hell if I didn't knock myself out tryin' to make you see that. We weren't ready, but you listened to Evangeline instead of me. I knew once we started, we couldn't pull out, but you wouldn't listen to me *again*. And then you gave her the ring? If you had listened to me— trusted me—we would have had a shot."

He shook his head in disgust. "You want to know what Verity would have done? She would have honored her damn promise. She would have held on to the ring and trusted her partner, not some shriveled-up old bat who promised an easy out. She would have been the person she was supposed to be, not run away from it 'cause it was hard. Too much to ask from you, I guess. And now everything's ruined, sure as that building over there."

His words knocked me back as hard as any blow from Evangeline, but my anger gave me the strength to lash back. "Welcome to the club! You and your stupid destiny have been ruining my life since before I even met you!" I shouted, wanting to hurt him as badly as he'd hurt me. "You've taken my best friend and my future, you're burning down my city, and I've nearly died more times than I can count! I went in there tonight knowing the magic could kill me, and I *went anyway*. And you *let me*. You've been manipulating me since day one, Luc. Why would I trust you?"

"Because we are *bound*, Maura Fitzgerald. Doesn't matter what you think of it, who you love, what you're scared of—anybody in the world you can trust, it's the one you're bound to. Hell, yes, you're supposed to trust me." He stopped, stared at the remains of the Water Tower, and turned to me again, naked desperation in his voice. "Maybe it's not too late. We could try again. . . ."

The thought of opening myself up to the acid burn of raw magic again, letting it eat away at me, made me nearly retch. I'd seen it kill Kowalski, had felt it reaching for me before Luc yanked me back. Trying again would mean my life. And for what? He'd just admitted I wasn't enough.

Colin's face was gray with pain and shock. Suddenly he sagged against me, his weight nearly toppling us both. I staggered, trying to keep upright. We needed to leave.

"I tried, Luc. I really did. But I'm not the one you need." He looked stricken, lost, and my heart broke for him a little bit, in spite of everything. "I'm so sorry. But . . . I can't. I just can't."

CHAPTER 26

I helped Colin to his kitchen table, easing him down to the chair. "We should get you to a doctor," I said. "You're going to need stitches."

He shook his head, ashen-faced. "Where's Luc?"

"Gone. Don't worry about him now." Colin had refused to go to the hospital, so Luc had returned us to the truck, then disappeared.

"You're a terrible driver," he said through clenched teeth. "No wonder you don't have a license."

"Got us home, didn't I? You can teach me sometime." I tried to sound nonchalant, but when I pulled my wadded-up sweater away from his arm, the room spun on its axis. "Oh, God. I'm not good with blood."

He grunted and pressed the sweater back down. "Under the sink. First-aid kit."

I nearly knocked over the chair in my hurry to get it. "A Band-Aid isn't going to do the trick."

He pointed to a cabinet. "Bring me the Jameson's," he said, his voice rusty and almost unrecognizable. I pulled out the bottle and a short, heavy tumbler, poured him a generous three fingers, and passed it over.

He closed his eyes and downed it in one long swallow, dropping it back to the table with a sharp thunk.

"Again."

I poured again, he drank again.

"There's superglue in there," he said, opening his eyes and gesturing to the shoebox full of supplies. "Peroxide, too. Clean it out, smear a bunch of glue on, hold it shut till it dries. Good enough, for now."

As I dabbed the glue onto his arm, careful not to permanently stick my fingers to his bicep, he stared at the bottle on the table. His breathing was slower now, and his color better, though he still looked haggard.

"How did you find me tonight?" I asked. It wasn't the question I'd meant to ask.

"GPS on your phone."

"And Kowalski?"

"Had been tailing me since we left the police station."

"Oh." It seemed impossible that had been only this afternoon. I felt I'd aged a century. My entire body was stiff and battered, my throat raw from screaming. My hands were cramped and trembling, even now. I blew gently on the glue to speed the drying and then wrapped a layer of gauze around his arm. Taping the bandage in place, I looked up at him. "Please say something."

"Pour."

"Something other than that." I poured anyway. "Do I get some?"

"No."

I'd figured.

He rubbed a hand across his face. "I don't even know where to start. Jesus, Mo. You're all right?"

"I think so."

"Good. That's good." He shifted in the chair and set his gun on the table between us, looking weary. "Is any of it going to make sense to me? I mean, you are clearly involved in a bunch of really weird shit that doesn't have a thing to do with Billy and the Outfit, but will it make sense to me at all?"

I gave a small shrug and chewed on my lip.

"Time to start talking, kid."

So I did. I told him everything, from the beginning, from the first night in the alley to Evangeline's betrayal. I told him about the prophecy, and Luc, although I skimped on the details there. I spilled it all out in front of him, feeling the impact of how completely I'd failed all over again. When I was done, my eyes were gritty from crying and my abused throat could barely manage a whisper.

"You're sure you're okay?"

"Mostly." I hugged myself. My sweater was ruined, and now, clad just in a tank top, I couldn't get warm.

"I don't know how to protect you from this," he said. "Can we move you? Start you over somewhere else? Billy has a lot of contacts in Boston. Portland, maybe? Portland's good."

"I'm not moving to Portland," I said. "Besides, I'm out of it now."

"You could have died tonight, Mo. I came in that room and saw you looking like a goddamn Roman candle, you were so lit up. I could see your *bones*. And all those lights, bouncing around, and those things. . . ."

"Darklings."

"Right. They were headed straight for you, and all I could think was that they were going to cut you down before I could get there."

"I'm sorry," I whispered, and began to tremble, teeth chattering.

He stood and grabbed a thick, cream-colored blanket from the back of the couch. "Here."

I wrapped it around my shoulders, grateful for the

warmth, and propped my chin in my hands. He sat down again, scrutinizing me, but I couldn't meet his eyes.

"Kowalski's dead," I said, unable to keep the wobble from my voice.

"Yeah."

Water. A glass of water would soothe my throat and keep me from having to see the expression on Colin's face. I walked over to the sink and ran the tap, still clutching the blanket around me. "He has a daughter my age. Did you know that?"

"I did not."

I tried to remember what Kowalski had told me about her. "Jenny," I said eventually. "Her name is Jenny."

He didn't say anything for a minute. "It counts for something, Mo, that he was trying to protect you. There's honor in that."

Cold comfort for Jenny. I boosted myself up on the granite counter and rested my head on the cabinet behind me. "Maybe. Mostly, when people say they're trying to protect me, they're really trying to find a way to feel better about lying. Like my family. Or Luc. Verity, even. Have you noticed that?"

He spoke carefully. "It's possible your family has more to lie about than most."

"Bad things happen when people try to protect me. Verity tried, and it got her killed. Kowalski tried, and it got *him* killed. The Darklings almost got you, too." I thought of Luc, yanking me back from the raw magic before it could consume me. "Bad things," I repeated, shifting my gaze from the ceiling to his face. "And it's your *job*. You're fired."

He smiled for the first time that night, standing and crossing the room to me. "We've been over this. You can't fire me."

"I just did."

"Billy—"

"Billy doesn't get to decide for me anymore. There was never a hit on me. I'm no longer any use to Evangeline, so there's no threat from her."

"I wouldn't be so sure about that," he said, frowning.

I brushed his words away. "You shouldn't be around me."

He placed his hands on the countertop, boxing me in. "I like being around you, so knock it off. I'm not going anywhere."

The quiet settled over us. My head felt floaty and disconnected. Colin didn't complain when I leaned forward and rested my head on his shoulder, just put one warm, strong arm around me. He smelled like soap and cedar and wool blanket. It would have been peaceful, if the images of the night hadn't kept crowding into my head.

"So, when this Luc guy talks about the end of the world, does he mean the actual end of the world?"

"As in, is this our last night on earth?"

"Something like that."

I straightened. "That is . . . unclear. The prophecy says that if the Torrent isn't stopped, anyone unprepared will be swept away like dust."

He raised an eyebrow. "Sounds pretty end-of-days."

"I know. For people like us . . . it depends on how close we are to the lines, I guess. For Luc's people . . . it'll be bad, no matter where they are." My stomach clenched at the thought.

"And you're supposed to stop this?"

"No. Verity was. I was just the substitute."

His voice sharpened. "You're not a substitute."

"I didn't mean it like that."

He stepped toward me, anger making his eyes go darker. "Sure you did. You told Luc you were willing to die tonight. I heard you say it."

"I meant—"

"I know exactly what you meant. And I know how close you came." He grabbed my arms and gave me one sharp shake. "Don't you ever do that again, or I will kill you myself. You think Verity wanted you to die for her?"

Mo, run! "No." My voice sounded pitifully small.

"You think Luc wanted you to? He saved your ass, Mo. I don't trust him, and I will not be destroyed if this Torrent you keep talking about fries him like a piece of KFC, but when he had the choice to save you or go after Evangeline and the ring, he chose you."

"He doesn't even see me," I said softly. "Not really."

Colin pursed his lips, very deliberately let go. "Maybe. Maybe not. If so, it's his loss. I know what I see when I look at you."

"What?"

"Someone extraordinary."

I shook my head, and he laughed a little. "I understand wanting a quiet life. I've been looking for it since I was eleven, and this—" He gestured to the rest of the house. "Right here, this is the closest I've gotten. So I understand, more than you know. But sometimes, Mo . . . sometimes you just shine, and it doesn't have anything to do with magic or prophecies. It's just you. I wish you could see it."

I pressed my fingers to my eyes, and his voice turned incredulous. "Are you crying?"

"No." I pressed harder. No use.

"Come on, kid. After everything that's happened, now you cry?"

"I'm not *crying*," I said, but he tugged my hands away from my face. "And stop calling me kid. I *hate* when you do that."

"Yeah," he said softly. "I should really stop."

Gently, he swept a thumb under my lashes, catching the tears before they fell, rubbing slowly along my jaw.

I put my hand, palm out, square against his chest. The warmth of his skin through his cotton T-shirt was shocking, and I could feel his heart beating, the seconds stretching out unbearably. The blanket slithered to the floor, and he closed his eyes for a long moment.

"Mo?" His hand dropped, closing on my shoulder, one finger sliding under the strap of my tank. "This is not a good idea."

The world might have been ending, but Colin was solid and safe and alive mere inches away from me, and I was alive, and suddenly it seemed like the very best idea ever.

"Does it hurt?" I whispered, touching the gauze on his arm.

"No." His other hand closed around my hip, anchoring me on the counter.

"That's good." I leaned toward him, the tiniest bit, and he inhaled sharply, wrapping his fingers in the strap of my tank, pulling it tighter, bringing me closer.

"Mo," he repeated, warningly.

"Then tell me to stop."

He shook his head, one short negative movement, and it was the easiest thing in the world to kiss him, pressing my lips lightly against his. He stayed very still. I drew back slightly to see his eyes, dark and glinting like the lake at night, scanning my face for something unknown.

"Tell me to *stop*," I said again, and this time when I leaned in, he did, too, his hand sliding around to my back.

It was different from kissing Luc. Steadier, somehow, and easier. Colin tasted clean and sharp, and I could feel myself slipping into the want washing over me. He stepped between my legs and hauled me closer against the solid expanse of his chest, the heat of his skin nearly scorching me through our shirts. I tugged at the hem of his T-shirt and he stopped kissing me long enough to shuck it off and throw it toward the coffee table. He paused, looking down at me, and slipped the strap of my camisole off, baring one shoulder completely, brushing his fingertips down my neck in a slow sweep. I leaned in to kiss him again, hardly breathing for all the hunger building in my blood.

His hair was softer than it looked—he wore it so short I expected it would feel coarse and bristly, but it was down soft and I raked my fingers through it, then down the broad planes of his back, startled to encounter scars there.

His teeth scraped against my collarbone, and I whimpered, pulling his mouth back to mine, drinking in the taste of him like the end of summer, all light and heat and slow burn. My fingertips curled around his belt loops, and he pushed up suddenly, his hands caging me in, his breath fast and heavy.

"What?"

He leaned his forehead against mine, closed his eyes. "We need to stop."

"What? Why? Because I didn't mean it, before."

"I know. But we need to." He tugged the straps of my camisole up, smoothed my hair.

"Why?" I wished for the blanket back, wanting to hide from whatever he was about to say.

"Look, falling into bed would be nice, but it won't make everything go away."

Everything like Luc, he meant. Amazing how that guy could ruin things without even being in the room. "You're saying no."

"It's too complicated. Everything about you is complicated. Your age and your uncle, you and Verity and Luc and the magic. I'm not sure there's a way to get clear of it all."

I would not cry. I would *not* cry. Instead, I bit my tongue so hard the blood tasted like pennies. "Way to take the easy way out, Colin. Those are lousy reasons."

He nodded tiredly. "Maybe. But take them away, and I'd still say no."

I wrenched away. "Wow. Thanks for letting me down gently."

He stepped toward me again, clamped his hands on my wrists, and held me in place. I stared at the granite beneath me, trying like crazy to be angry instead of humiliated. He leaned in, his voice rasping over my skin. "I told you. You are complicated. I don't like complicated, Mo. I don't like relationships. I like simple, and no strings attached, and you come with more strings than the goddamn symphony. And the hell of it is, I'm okay with that."

"So, what is the problem?"

"Look at me."

It took forever. It felt like stars burned out and were born again before I could gather up the strength. When I finally managed to turn my head, his mouth was curving inches from mine, his eyes obsidian-dark, our breath mingling as he said, each word slow and distinct and like a promise, "I will not be your rebound."

I started to protest, but he cut me off. "You should get that better than anyone. Settle whatever is between you and Luc. Decide what you want, not just from me, but from your life. Once you do—and not until then—we can figure the rest out." He let go of my hands and stepped back. "Got it?"

I nodded, not trusting myself to speak.

"We okay?"

I nodded again. Maybe if I acted like it was true, it would be. Eventually.

"Good. 'Tell me to stop,'" he mimicked, and winced as he pulled his shirt back on. "Jesus. I knew you'd be a terror."

I waited until he'd crossed the room, giving me space to collect my thoughts. "What now?"

"Now I take you home."

"No! Please, Colin. I can't, not after everything with Billy, and then Kowalski. . . . I can't pull off normal. Not tonight."

He sighed, looking at me expectantly.

I whooshed out a breath. "Can I stay here? Just for tonight? I'll sleep on the couch, you won't even notice me."

"Just for tonight," he said, smiling wryly. "And I'm taking the couch."

CHAPTER 27

Ilay alone in the middle of Colin's four-poster bed, aching from exhaustion and memory. Every time my eyes started to close, I pitched into the yawning pool of raw magic, saw Kowalski thrown into the air, the Darklings swarm over the Water Tower, and the terrible emptiness of Luc's face as we watched it all burn. As the dawn crept pink-edged across the high bedroom windows, I slipped back into the living room.

Colin was awake, staring at the fading orange embers in the woodstove, looking like his dreams had been equally unpleasant.

"I called Billy," he said, straightening. "Your mom's freaking out, but he's handling her."

"What did you tell him?"

He looked slightly ashamed. "I said you were pulling rebellious teenage bullshit and it was better to let it run its course."

I started to protest and he shrugged. "We can't tell him the truth. He doesn't like this, but he gets it. He'll smooth things over with your mom. It's the best we can do for now."

I didn't know what to say to that.

"C'mere," he said. I curled up next to him on the couch, drifting off to the sensation of his hand running over my hair.

It was full daylight when I woke again, Colin's arm still snug around me. I sat up and he jerked awake, one hand closing over my wrist as he scanned the room.

"I've got to get to school," I said, trying to sound as if everything was normal.

He studied me. "You feel up for it?"

Not at all. "What else am I going to do?"

"You need to run home first? Get your stuff?"

"Um . . . sure." The silence grew oppressive, until finally he bumped his shoulder against mine.

"We okay?"

"Sure." Like I'd said, what else was I going to do?

We didn't say anything, the awkward quiet lasting all the way to my house, where I changed into a fresh uniform and gathered my books. Periodically, one of us would start to talk, then lapse back into silence. There was no safe conversational ground, and neither of us had the energy to discuss all the stuff we really needed to.

A block away from school, Colin finally spoke. "You're not going to vanish on me, are you?" he asked. "Get all weirded out and bolt?"

"No vanishing," I said.

He parked the truck and came around to open my door. "Thanks," I said as he helped me down.

"Mo." I tried to pull away, not wanting to hear his reasons or his regrets, but he wouldn't let go of me. "We'll figure this out. I promise."

If I opened my mouth, something stupid would tumble out, so I said nothing. He brushed a kiss over my forehead, so light I feared it was a dream.

I stepped back, and he gave me a rueful smile. "That didn't happen. Get to class."

Hitching up my bag, I started inside, trying to sort out the emotions tumbling through me. Grief and guilt for Kowal-

ski's death and my failure to hold the lines. Rage at Evangeline, for betraying all of us. I'd never gotten the justice I'd
sworn for Verity, and that burned, deep in the pit of my
stomach. A gaping hurt over Luc, but I pushed that away. I
touched my fingers to my lips just as the invisible line beneath my skin flared.

I stumbled, but managed to catch myself on the iron
handrail.

Twenty feet away, leaning against one of the front doors,
was Luc.

It took every last shred of pride I had not to cut and run—
back to Colin, or into school, or to the ends of the earth. The
temptation was dizzying. Instead, I squared my shoulders
and continued up the wide stone steps past him.

"That was cozy," he said, his voice like a lash. "Didn't
take you hardly any time at all to find a replacement, hmn?"

I flinched. "Go away, Luc. We're done."

He tapped my forearm. "This says otherwise."

I snatched my wrist away like it burned, and he rubbed the
spot on his own arm where the chain had bound us.

"The Torrent's started," he said. "It's slow, just pockets so
far, here and there, but it's picking up speed."

He looked as haunted as he had the first night, in the hospital, when he'd taken me to find Verity. I understood now—
failing to stop the Torrent meant more than one friend's
death for him. It meant his entire world, smashed beyond
recognition, the whole purpose of his life come to nothing.
He would probably survive, but I wasn't sure he'd actually
live.

"I'm sorry." It was all I could offer him, and not nearly
enough. "For all of it. But I can't help you."

"You're still the Vessel," he said. "Like it or not, you're
the chosen one now. We could try . . ."

"I can't keep trying to be her," I said. "It will kill me, Luc, as sure as the magic would."

He started to speak, but Lena raced up to us, halting inches away. She gave him a frankly appreciative nod. "Hey! It's the secret guy! All becomes clear."

"He's not—"

"Whatever. Can I talk to you?"

It was easier to let Lena pull me away than say good-bye, and when I looked back, Luc was gone.

"What?" I asked as she sped down the hallway like an F5 tornado. "Lena, chill out!"

"Are you kidding me? Do you have any idea what you're missing?"

"Not really."

"It's your destiny, Mo. Ready and waiting to meet you."

"What?" I dropped my bag, and she handed it back to me, then resumed towing me down the hallway.

"Hello? The NYU rep? She's just walked in, and you, once again, are nowhere to be found. The guy is hot, but get with the program." She scowled, and her meaning finally penetrated my brain.

"It's Visitation Day."

"What is *with* you?" she whispered fiercely. "I'm outside the counseling office, and Jill McAllister strolls in, all ready to chit-chat with the rep. She is in there *making an impression*, Mo, and you look like someone who can't be bothered! She is stealing your spot!"

"How do I look?" We stopped around the corner from the counseling office. I brushed ineffectually at my hair and wished I was wearing nice shoes instead of my usual ratty Birks.

Lena pursed her lips. "Honestly? Drop in a real casual line about how you've been up late working on the paper. You'll still look like crap, but it'll be for a good cause."

"How does Jill look?"

"Like a recruiting poster."

"Oh, excellent." I took a deep breath. In the last twenty-four hours, I'd faced down the Mob and Darklings. I'd plunged my hands into magic and lived. I'd thrown myself at Colin and survived that, too. I'd walked away from Luc and the Torrent. Surely, I could handle a college admissions officer.

Sister Donna handed out delicate bone china cups filled with steaming Earl Grey. Jill was already perched on a chair, looking as perky and wholesome as Lena had predicted, glowing with good health and a strong work ethic and valuable societal contributions, while I looked like a cross between Morticia Addams and Lucille Ball, only less with-it.

"Tell me about your summer, Mo," the NYU rep said.

Sister Donna bobbled the teapot and Jill smiled behind her cup.

"We've all had a difficult few months," Sister Donna cut in. "We lost a member of our St. Brigid's family, a dear friend of Mo's . . ."

Too worn-out to talk around it, I said, "She was murdered."

The rep's hand fluttered helplessly. "I'm so sorry! What a terrible loss."

Jill shook her head, the picture of composed grief. "Verity was a wonderful person. We've all struggled with this tragedy, but I think we've found her to be an inspiration, too. Losing her taught us not to take a single day for granted, to rise above petty concerns and strive to reach our potential. Don't you agree, Mo?"

Such a shame there were no magical ruptures under Jill to swallow her up. Painfully. "Absolutely," I mumbled, and took another sip of tea.

The rep, to her credit, tried again. "As you both know, applying early decision indicates NYU is your top choice. What is it that appeals to you about our institution?"

Jill jumped right in. "Well, your reputation for academic excellence, of course, and your commitment to diversity is very appealing. Having grown up in an urban area, that's *so* important to me. I also believe that you offer a great balance between the resources a large school can offer and the close, personal experience of small class sizes."

Did she have a brochure hidden in her sleeve? Had she gotten the list of questions beforehand? There was no way for me to compete with Jill and her complete co-ed package. What could I say? I wanted to go as far away from my family as possible? And when I got there, I wanted to be able to disappear?

"Gosh, Jill," I said, injecting my voice with as much fake cheer as I could, "you've hit the nail right on the head. Quality education, great setting . . . who could ask for anything more?"

"Jill mentioned she plans to study medicine. I understand you're interested in the sciences as well, Mo?"

At last, a question I could answer, land mine free. "Biochemistry, probably. I enjoy lab work, and I know you just opened a new facility. It would be a real privilege to study there," I said, trying to sound like the lab equivalent of Lassie—dependable, hard-working, capable of retrieving any graduate students that might have tumbled down the well.

"Well, we appreciate your enthusiasm. Do you come from a family of scientists?"

"No, I'd be the first." I hoped she didn't notice my gritted teeth or Jill's smirk.

"I've always found the nature or nurture discussion to be fascinating," she said. "Where do you two girls come down on that debate? Is there something you inherited from your

family that really...you know...makes you who you
are?"

Sister Donna looked slightly green.

"Oh, you take this one, Mo," said Jill. "I don't want to
hog the conversation."

"Wow, Jill. Thanks. You're so thoughtful." I set my teacup
down. "I've inherited lots of things from my family. I look
like my dad, I'm shy like my mom. Some of that stuff is ge-
netic, some is environmental." And some things defied explanation—like why Verity had been chosen as the Vessel, or
how she'd managed to pass it along to me.

"In the end, though, it doesn't really matter. I think the key
is to accept who you are, however you got that way. To em-
brace it, without reservations or hesitations. Because once
you own who you are, it's not a limitation anymore. It's a
source of strength."

Hearing my own words delivered in an admissions essay
tone made me understand them better. Fighting against my
family and the Torrent was only making it worse. If I could
just accept my role—in my family and in the prophecy—
maybe the chaos would pass through, and I could finally
have the chance to make a life I was happy with.

"I have to go." I stood, suddenly frantic to get away. "It
was so nice to meet you." I was babbling, knocking over my
chair as I shook the rep's hand and backed toward the door.
"NYU is a great school—it's my dream school, it has been
forever, and I think I'd be a tremendous asset to the student
body. Thanks so much for taking the time to meet with me."

She leaned backward, startled. Probably not a lot of
prospective applicants bolted mid-interview. "Mo, the early
decision committee meets in just a few weeks. I won't be visiting St. Brigid's again this year. Are you sure you want to
leave now?"

Her meaning was clear. If I took off, I'd be giving up my

shot at early decision, and maybe even NYU entirely. But if I broke my promise to Verity, I'd never be able to go to New York, even if I got in. "Believe me, I would love to stay. But there's something I have to do, and it can't wait. Thanks again!"

"Mo," said Sister Donna, trailing after me. "In Heaven's name, child, what are you doing?"

Jill smiled and waggled her fingertips. "See you around, Mo. It's been fun!"

The chapel at St. Brigid's was a separate building, a small stone church a half block from the main school. It was quiet and cool and mostly deserted, reserved for special Masses, the perfect place to hide. I ran for it, digging my phone out of my bag, wishing I could put more distance between me and the school. It was only a matter of time before they called my mom, and my mom called Colin.

Inside, the smell of beeswax and incense mingled comfortingly, and I dropped into the front pew.

It had been a long time since I'd prayed for anything bigger than a grade on a test, longer still since the prayers had been answered, and so I didn't form any actual words—just sat in the pew, with the wood worn smooth under my hands, and begged for time, and hope, and a hefty dose of miracles.

I pulled out my phone and dialed Luc. "You can find me because of the binding, right?"

" 'Course," he said. "Anywhere."

"Then find me."

I settled back to wait, hands twisting in my lap, eyes on the linen-covered altar. A moment later, footsteps sounded behind me.

"I should have guessed," said Colin. I spun around, banging my elbow on the pew back. "Have you *ever* done what I asked you? Even once?"

"How . . ."

"Did you think I was just going to drop you off and *leave?* After everything that's happened? Magic aside, things aren't over with the Outfit, not by a long shot." He glanced around the church, thumbs hooked in his belt loops, deliberately casual in the little jewel box of a church. "Looking for a miracle, Mo?"

"Maybe." I stood and walked to a small iron stand filled with red glass votives. "I have to go back. To finish it."

He followed, his hand closing over mine as I lit the long wooden match and guided it to an unlit candle. "What changed?" he asked, as the flame caught and straightened.

"Me. It's not about Verity. Or Luc, even. It's the right thing to do."

"For them."

"For me." I turned away from the flickering lights, and he kept my hand tight in his. "It's like you said before, about power. Who has it and who wants it and who's losing their grip. Billy and my dad, they ruined us to keep hold of all that power. Now it's starting again. He'll sacrifice me, just to move up and make his piece a little bit bigger."

He scowled. I could tell he wanted to disagree, but couldn't. "So this is about Billy?"

"It's about balance. The Seraphim think that if the Torrent comes, they'll be able to grab hold of the power in all the chaos, and who knows what they'll do with it. But it can't be good. It's never good when one person has all the power. It'll be devastating. I can't sit by and let it happen."

"It's too dangerous."

"I'll be stronger this time. I'll be better. You can't stop me, Colin."

His face took on a set, stubborn look. "Fine. I'm coming with."

Luc arrived with a sound like tearing cloth. Coolly, his

eyes flickered over Colin, whose hand was still twined with mine.

"Little busy, Mouse," he said, and I could see the lines worry and exhaustion had etched deeply into his face. "Didn't you say your piece already?"

"Take me back to the Binding Temple," I said. "Right now."

His eyes narrowed and his mouth thinned. "Not gonna happen. Temple's too unstable. Won't stand much longer."

"That's why I need to go there."

"It's too late. Evangeline's right, you can't stop the Torrent now."

"Then why did she take the ring?" His brows snapped together, his attention caught, and I rushed on. "If it was really too late, she wouldn't have cared about the ring, because it wouldn't matter if I could get to the lines. But she made sure I couldn't, didn't she?"

"Exactly. You can't get to the magic. There's nothing you can do."

"The temple has raw magic running through it. In the columns. I can do it there."

"Mouse, it'll kill you." I could see the struggle within him as he realized that I could be right, and the cost if I was. Watching him fight it only strengthened my resolve.

"It won't," I said, with a confidence I didn't quite feel. Yet. "And you'll protect me. We're still bound, right? Losing the ring didn't change that. I trust you."

"I don't," said Colin, stepping between us. "You take her in there, you take me, too."

Luc shot him a glance of utter scorn. "And what are you gonna do, Cujo? Shoot the magic? Frown at it real hard?"

"I don't give a rat's ass about your world and all its magic. I care about Mo. She thinks she needs to do this, fine. We do it. But I go, too, or she stays home."

Luc jerked a shoulder. "Long as you keep out of the way. I won't have time to babysit."

"Excellent," I said, feeling suffocated by all the testosterone in the room, and wanting only to get my plan into motion. "Let's go."

CHAPTER 28

The polished stone floor of the Binding Temple was cracked and smashed, the mortar in the walls turning to sand and pouring down in small rivulets. The air itself seemed to thrum with magic, pushing against me as if it was angry. For a brief moment, it seemed nearly sentient. But when I saw the First Arch, light streaming through the carvings, blindingly bright, I forgot all about magical theory. I'd thought I needed to know the rules about magic, but it turned out I needed to feel my way all along.

"I don't know how much time we have," Luc said, pitching his voice to be heard through the din. Each time another rupture emerged, there was a noise like a zip line, a whipping, snarling, high-pitched whine, and some other part of the temple crashed down in a cloud of grit.

He gestured to an ever-widening crack in the floor. It reached out to all four pillars of the archway. Every few seconds, a portion of the side sheared away and disintegrated. "You sure you're ready? You don't have to do this."

"I do," I said, walking past him.

"Mo," Colin said beside me, so soft I could barely hear him. "Please. Don't."

"I am choosing this. You have to let me," I told him. He

scowled, but nodded his understanding. I bit my lip in concentration and sank to my knees, reaching into the gap.

Immediately, the magic slammed into me, knocking me backward into the wall. I pushed up to my hands and knees again, wiping a trickle of blood from my nose. Colin rushed forward, helping me to my feet. Luc was right—having all four elements together was exponentially more powerful. It sounded in my head like a bell, deeply resonant, and I tried again, feeling carefully along the disintegrating pathways. I drew on Luc's magic as I searched for the weakest sections, trying to reinforce them with my Flat, useless fingers.

Luc motioned Colin away. "Too hot for you here," he said tersely, and laid one hand lightly on my shoulder.

A crash sounded behind us, and I faltered at a new voice.

"Oh, honestly, Lucien!"

"Evangeline. Shouldn't you be off polishing your broom?" He curled his fingers around the back of my neck. The magic flowed strong and true through our connection, heavy and golden in my veins.

"It's a new world. I wanted to bear witness when this room crumbled away." She looked around the ruined temple, her lip curling with disgust. "Bindings. The very notion one should sully one's power with another line's. It led to the decline of our people. The houses should have remained distinct, relations with Flats forbidden. It's what cost us our power . . . talents skipping generations, appearing randomly, like mutts from the pound. And who is your champion, Lucien? Pitiful. An insult to our world's legacy. It will be a pleasure to watch you fail."

I worked frantically as she rambled, eyes fever-bright, color high in her crepe white cheeks.

"Gloating makes you look old," he told her offhandedly.

She goggled at him, and then her eyes went icy blue as she recovered.

"I'm not surprised you're willing to risk the girl's life," she said sweetly. "You've always cared more for the prophecy than anything or anyone, just like your father. There's no reason to think a mere Flat would be any different. How on earth did you convince her to come back? She must be out of her mind."

"*She* is right here," I said. "Quit acting like I'm invisible."

"But you're so good at it." Before I could react, she whipped out her staff, slamming it against my sternum. I landed at the base of the arch, inches away from the crack in the floor.

"Mo!" Colin scrambled toward me, jumping over fissures while Luc pulled his sword and sent a bolt of magic toward Evangeline. "You tried. Let's go."

"I'm okay," I slurred, staring up at the glowing columns. "I'm so close, Colin. I can do it."

He helped me to my feet. "It's not worth it."

I touched his face, burning the feel of his stubble-covered cheek into my memory. "It is. I promised. Should I let everyone else suffer so that I can stay safe?"

He wove his fingers through my hair, tipping my face up and kissing me like I was made of glass. I memorized that, too, wanting to hold on to it forever. It was over so quickly, though, and he glanced around us, assessing everything.

"You need Luc?" Colin asked. Behind him, Luc and Evangeline battled ferociously, the magic from their weapons filling the air, mingling with the sparks from the rupture.

"What?"

"To do this—you need him, right?"

I shook my head, but Colin wasn't looking. Instead, he drew his gun and shot Evangeline, the bullet hitting her stomach.

She shrieked, turning the staff on Colin, the blue-black magic knocking him away from me with a sickening crack.

I screamed and struggled toward Colin, shaking off the pull of the magic coming from the rupture, the effort squeezing my lungs. "No!"

Blood was soaking Evangeline's front, and she pressed one hand to the wound, a blue glow spreading as fast as the bright red stain, healing herself. With the other hand, she leveled the staff at my throat.

"That's enough, Lucien, or I'll kill her this instant."

Luc froze midstride, the ruby lights on his sword flickering but contained.

"Your arrogance is staggering, Mo. You're a *Flat*. You're nothing but a shadow of Verity, and yet you presume to interfere here? You'll never be her. You'll never have Lucien, not truly, and you have nothing to fight with. You're powerless."

Colin made a weak noise and fell still. It took everything I had not to go to him. Tears streamed down my face, but I couldn't afford to be distracted now.

"You're right." I eased back toward the arch and its gaping chasm, my steps small and tentative, almost reluctant. "I've got nothing at all, except for what Verity gave me in the alley. I didn't even *want* that. But there's power in a sacrifice, isn't there? You said that once."

Luc's eyes shifted to mine, his sword still pointed at Evangeline. "Sorry," I mouthed, and I saw from the dread on his face the instant he understood.

"Whatever she gave you won't be enough," Evangeline countered, picking her way over the broken ground as it heaved beneath her. I used the distraction to take another step back, almost directly under the arch. The four columns pulsed with magic, the carvings standing out white hot, a keening, whirling nebula forming between them. The sound nearly blotted out her words. "The Torrent is upon us now. There's nothing you can do to stop it."

"Good." The magic geysered up between us and she stared at me, eyes rounding as realization dawned. "Because I don't want to stop the Torrent, Evangeline. I want to become it."

All around me, the archway was crumbling. I stepped into the center of the four carved pillars, stretched out my hands, and let the nebula consume me.

CHAPTER 29

The temple disappeared.

Everything disappeared, the entire world blotted out by a white so brilliant I closed my eyes to no effect. There was an instant—the space between a heartbeat, when there was nothing but white, and utter silence, and then, like a heart starting up again, the world rushed back in, and I watched it all re-form.

This must be what God feels like, I thought dizzily. I was everywhere, all at once, and I knew everything. I could see the temple, as if from a distance, Luc and Evangeline and Colin all frozen as the magic blazed around them. I saw my mother, scrubbing down the counter at the diner, and I could feel her joy in setting things right and orderly again, stained by her worry over me. I saw Billy in his booth at Black Morgan's, dispensing advice and whiskey, always with an eye toward maintaining his own place at the table. I saw Lena at school, currents of power and insecurity eddying about her as she sat in class, and the thready undercurrent of loneliness trailing after her.

I looked for Verity. An infinity of worlds were spread out before me, multitudes of lives and lines crisscrossing, staggering in their variety and their beauty. Her spirit should have been there, too. I wanted to see her, one last time, to say a

proper good-bye. But even as I drifted through, my height-
ened senses tracing out along the lines to search for her, I
couldn't find her. At the edge of the lines was a soft, dense
blackness, like velvet, and I tried to reach through it, convinced she was on the other side. It was impenetrable,
though. The magic wouldn't take me there.

As the magic surged inside me, panic did, too. The nebula
consumed me, turning me inside out, more painful than I
could have imagined. I was burning away. I forced myself to
breathe through the agony, and took the power in without
reservation. Cell by cell, I came back, filled with the knowledge of everything I could see, and suddenly the pain
dropped away. I wanted to stay forever, tied into everything,
at one with the lines and the magic. I could, too. All I needed
to do was follow the magic back to the source, like bread-
crumbs, and I could watch the entire world, the endless flow
of lives, forever.

I felt a sharp tug, but I ignored it to savor the power coursing through me. The tug came again, more insistent this time.

It was Luc, pulling me back. The magic was so seductive,
so welcoming, I'd nearly forgotten him and the world I'd left
behind, the job I'd set out to do. But our connection dragged
at me, and I remembered my promise to Verity. It was time
to go.

I gathered myself, pulling back from the source and bringing the magic with me. I took the pain along with the magic,
without trying to resist or fight, just channeling all that
power until it flowed out, whole again, made new again. The
lines took it over, the source pumping magic through them
like a heart. My work was done. I contracted as the nebula
dispersed, coming back into my body, landing hard on the
ruined floor of the Binding Temple.

I opened my eyes to see Evangeline standing over me, the
forked end of her staff still pointing at my throat. The last,
lingering shred of raw magic flowed out of me, and I flung it

at her with all of my might. It arrowed toward her like flame, too fast and powerful to block. She flopped back like a marionette whose strings had been cut, the staff clattering next to her. I slumped to the floor.

Luc came for me, his face streaked with dust and tears and blood, and gathered me up. "Mouse? What did you *do*?"

I tried to keep my eyes open, but they were so heavy, way too much effort. All the knowledge, all the magic was gone. I was empty, hollow, afraid I'd cave in on myself. The temple was crashing down around us, and the wild sound of Luc's heartbeat filled my ears as he shook me, gently at first, then harder. "Mouse? C'mon, now. Come on. Maura!"

I looked up finally, and his features swam into focus. A few feet away, Colin was sprawled motionless on the ground, his shirtfront charred. I stretched out a hand, grazing the bottom of his jeans. "No!" A familiar ache rose up in me, and I wailed, crawling across the floor to him. "Luc. Please, *please*. Fix him!"

The arch glowed brighter and brighter, emitting a shriek, and Luc grabbed for my hand.

"Keep hold of him," he grunted, and we jumped Between as the arch exploded and everything went black.

CHAPTER 30

To say that my uncle was unhappy to find me in the emergency room again would be kind of like saying the Chicago Cubs have had a stretch of bad luck, Series-wise.

And his relief at discovering it was Colin, not me, who had been admitted was short-lived.

He stood in the doorway, all outraged bluster, the familiar twinkling charm long gone. "This is because of you! If you'd done what you were told—" He broke off. Behind him, two guys I didn't know stood keeping an eye on the hallway and carefully not listening to every word we said. "I warned you there would be problems."

"I'm fine," I said, sitting up. I'd dragged a chair next to Colin's bed and fallen asleep, my head next to his shoulder, my hand covering his. "Thanks for asking."

"Tell me what happened."

His voice boomed in the tiny room, and I searched Colin's face for any sign he was waking up. He slept on, courtesy of the pain meds they'd given him. The muscles in my neck and back protested as I stretched and stood, unwilling to face down Billy while perched on an uncomfortable plastic chair.

"It doesn't concern you," I said steadily, no longer intimidated. It felt strange to be holding my own with Billy. I wasn't afraid—of him, or our family's secrets. Once I'd lost the fear, I found my voice. Now I intended to use it.

"Nonsense," Billy said. "You're my niece."

"This was never about me," I shot back, "which I told you when Verity died, but you wouldn't listen. Anyway, it's over."

"The hell it is! You've one of my best men lying there, and I'll know why."

"He's fine, too, by the way." Luc had repaired the worst of Colin's injuries before bringing us here. Time and Flat medicine would take care of the rest. "I'm sure he'll be touched by your concern."

I smoothed the blankets and stroked the back of his hand, avoiding where the IV went in. Then I stepped through the curtains into the hallway and Billy followed, seething.

"Donnelly's like a cat," he said. "He's come out of worse before and landed on his feet. Joseph Kowalski is dead."

I stared at my nails. They were broken and filthy, but my hand was perfectly steady. "That must make you very happy."

Billy jerked his chin at the doorway, and the two thugs slunk farther down the hallway. "No accusations, Mo? No lip? Yesterday you thought I was the root of all evil."

Not *all* evil. There was plenty to go around. "You weren't responsible," I said, feeling the weight of everything that had happened deep in my bones. "I'm not saying you aren't capable of it. But you didn't do this."

He cocked his head. "You don't seem surprised by the news."

"Not much surprises me these days." I folded my arms across my chest and met his eyes.

"I can see that." He leaned against the counter, smiled affably at a passing nurse, reverting back to his kindly uncle persona. "Ah, Mo. You're changing. The *world's* changing. It's hard for an old man like myself to keep up."

"Bummer for you, I guess."

"Watch yourself," he said, and there was steel in his voice again. "You might not like the choices I've made, but they've served you well enough. A good school for you, security for your mother. It's nothing to turn your nose up at."

"And all it cost me was my dad."

"Another man who made his choices." He clasped his hands behind his back. "We have a problem, Mo. Your display at the police station yesterday reflects on me. Badly."

I shrugged. My family had reflected badly on me my whole life.

"Believe it or not, there are people I answer to. People who are wondering why a slip of a girl thinks she can defy me without consequences. It sends an unwelcome message."

It was the opening I needed, the chance to put in play what I'd been working out during the long night at Colin's bedside. "Tell your bosses I'm a pain in the ass. Tell them you're shipping me to New York just as soon as school's out. You'd do it now, to teach me a lesson, but you have a soft spot for my mom. You'll save face and I get to go to New York. Everybody wins."

I took a kind of grim pleasure in using my family's desire to keep things quiet as a way to escape them.

He seemed to think about it for a minute. Then, "Why do you care about helping me save face?"

"Because you're the devil I know," I said quietly. "All that power has to go somewhere, right? Better to run it through you than leave it up for grabs."

"That it is," he said. "It strikes me, Mo, I may have underestimated you."

"You wouldn't be the first." I peered into the room again, saw Colin's hand shift restlessly on the blanket. "I don't want anything to do with your business. It ends now."

He kissed my cheek. "Sometimes, darling girl, you remind me of your father. Tell Donnelly he's still on the job."

With a wave of his hand, Billy gathered his minions from the end of the hallway and strolled out.

I watched until he was out of sight before letting out a shaky breath. My legs didn't quite want to hold me, but I made it back to Colin's bed just as his eyes drifted open.

"Hey," he said, giving me a weak smile. "You're alive."

"I had a really great bodyguard. Do you need anything?"

He shook his head. I curled up in the chair again, content to watch the rise and fall of his chest.

"What happened?" he asked after a minute.

"I'm not sure. The magic . . . it's different. But it should hold, for now." I didn't mention Evangeline. Later, maybe.

"You did good?"

"I think so." My eyes welled up and I reached for his hand. "You scared me."

He grimaced. "Now you know how it feels. You want to think about that the next time you decide to run off and save the world?"

I let out a shaky laugh. "I will."

"What about Luc?" There was more than idle curiosity in his voice, and I didn't know what it meant.

"He healed you and brought us here. Then he had stuff to do."

"Did you settle things with him?"

I touched my wrist. Luc had left without saying good-bye, which seemed pretty well settled in my mind. "Mmn-hmn."

Colin must have known I didn't want to talk about it, because he changed the subject. "Billy?"

I grimaced. "He's mad, but he'll get over it. He may have suggested I join the family business."

He brought my hand to his lips. "I'll talk to him."

"I can handle Billy."

Colin's eyes drifted shut again. "Question is, can he handle you?"

"Ha-ha." I watched him, studying the square line of his

jaw and the sweep of his lashes, the stubble on his cheeks and the calluses on his hands.

"I'm fine," he said a little later, eyes still closed. "Practically good as new."

I bit my lip. "I am really, really glad you're not dead."

"Me too." He shifted to the side of the narrow bed and patted the mattress. "C'mere," he said.

I crawled up next to him, nestling against his shoulder. "You said it was too complicated."

"It was."

"And now?"

His voice was fading, with the careful enunciation of a person trying to fend off sleep. "Now I don't know." His hand fitted against my hip. "That's a start, right?"

"It's a very good start."

CHAPTER 31

"I should have brought flowers," I said. "I meant to, but I forgot. It's been a little busy. You probably know that."

Memorial bouquets still crowded Verity's grave, though the petals were drooping and edged with brown. If I'd had magic, I would have fixed them. Instead, I knelt and placed them to the side, brushing away wilted blossoms and bits of dried leaves. The granite headstone sparkled in the late-afternoon sunlight.

In another section of the cemetery, a sea of navy dress uniforms gathered around Kowalski's family as the honor guard fired a salute. The noise cracked and hung in the air. I watched for a moment, then turned back.

"I keep thinking you'll call, or I'll see you in class." I remembered the velvety blackness I'd touched in the nebula. "Stupid, huh? Luc said even magic has limits, and he was right. He was right about a lot of things. I would tell him so, but he's gone. Who knows? I may never see him again."

The thought gave me a strange ache, and I closed my eyes briefly, willing it away.

When I opened them, Luc was crouched on the other side of the grave. "She talked about you all the time," he said, placing a bouquet of delphiniums, a pure, deep indigo, in the space I'd cleared off. "It was like I knew you before we ever met."

"Have you been waiting for me?"

The corner of his mouth turned up. "Only my whole life."

"Don't." My voice was sharper than I intended.

"I'm sorry." He looked genuinely contrite, and he straightened, holding out a hand to help me up. "How are you?"

"Fine."

"How's Cujo?"

"He's good. Thank you for saving him." Colin had come home from the hospital the day before, no one happier about his release than the hospital staff.

"You asked," he said with a shrug.

I twisted my fingers together, waiting. "It worked, right? We stopped the Torrent? Everything's okay?"

"For now. The magic's shifting. You did somethin' . . . we're still figuring it out."

"I was wondering what you'd do, after. This should keep you busy." He'd lived his entire life with the Torrent as his end point. How did he feel, having the rest of his life returned to him, free from destiny?

"You got plenty on your plate, too," he said, even as I shook my head.

"Can't argue with the fact you're the Vessel," he said. "There's work to do. Besides, the Seraphim aren't gone just because Evangeline is."

"She's really dead?"

"The Temple's destroyed. Hard to see how she could have survived that, even if the magic didn't get her." The magic I'd hit her with, he meant, the killing blow I'd delivered, the justice I'd wanted all along. I checked to see how I felt about it. Answer: Absolutely fine, thanks for asking.

He shifted. "We're still bound. Can you feel it?"

I concentrated, and there, light as a silk thread, was the familiar connection. "I hadn't felt it, since the Temple. I thought maybe it was broken."

"Not broken. Just quiet. Figured you might want some of that running room we talked about."

"I'm not running," I said. "Especially not from you."

He took a step toward me and closed his hand over my wrist. The connection flared up again, bright as ever, pulling me toward him. I jerked at the sensation but stood firm.

"See? I'm not hiding, but this isn't enough. You know I'm right." I drew away.

"You never let me explain," he said. "About Verity."

"It's okay," I said, despite the pain that came, fresh as ever. "You don't have to."

"I grew up believin' I was meant to be with the Vessel, Mouse. From the day my brother died, it was drilled into me the way you learned the Our Father. And I have to say, that was fine when Verity was alive. I was seventeen when her powers came through, and she was so beautiful, it didn't seem like a chore. Then she was gone, and you came blunderin' in, askin' your questions and mouthin' off all the time, never doin' what you were supposed to, and you were . . ."

"A *chore*?" It was a good thing I didn't have magic. I'd have dropped him where he stood.

"No! See, that's the thing—you were the one I would have chosen, even if there were no fate."

I took that in, testing the truth of it against everything we'd lived through. Regret welled up, tasting bitter and hard. "That's just . . . that's crazy."

He took my hand again, his voice urgent and hopeful. "I wanted you, even when I wasn't supposed to be with you. This makes it easier. Why does it have to be such a fight if we already know how it ends?"

My heart stuttered at his words, but I kept my voice even. "Because I *don't* know how it ends. Maybe I do have a destiny—in your world, or mine, or both—but for now, I want to make my own fate. I have to at least *try*."

His hair was falling into his face again, and I brushed it out of the way, remembering the first time he'd kissed me, back when I believed my only worth was as Verity's substitute. The mid-October light seemed to touch him with fire, and my throat ached at the sight. He turned my hand over and ran his thumb over the scar crossing my palm.

"Just because the Torrent's over doesn't mean we are. There's still a lot to be done. Think maybe you could make it part of your fate to lend a hand?"

I looked down at Verity's grave. For an instant, I wondered what she would have done, and then it struck me that it didn't matter. She was gone, and the prophecy was over, and my decision was entirely mine. The ties that bound me to Luc and the magic were ones I had created myself, of my own free will. And because I could say no, I told him yes.

Then I turned, in the fading light of the afternoon, and walked out of the graveyard into a world of my own choosing.

Food for Thought

1. At the beginning of the novel, everyone considers Mo a "good girl" because she is quiet and does what's expected of her. How does this perception help when she begins investigating Verity's death and her family's Mob connections? How does it hinder her? Does pressure to be "nice" cause problems for young women today?

2. Mo places a high value on the truth, but as she is drawn more deeply into both her uncle's world and the magic one, she relies on deceitfulness to accomplish her goals. Does her dishonesty serve a greater good, or make her hypocritical? Could she have solved Verity's murder and gotten justice without lying? How do her lies and secrets differ from her family's?

3. Luc believes fate determines who a person is, while Colin believes a person's life is a result of their choices. With whom do you agree? How can either philosophy alter a person's behavior? Is Mo now fated to live Verity's life, or can she successfully balance her own future with the role she has stepped into?

4. Everyone in the book keeps secrets from the people they care about—Verity kept the Arcs a secret from Mo; Mo does the same with Lena. Luc consistently holds back information about the Arcs, and Colin refuses to tell what he knows about Mo's father. Mo's entire family conceals the truth about their Mob connections. Is it ever okay to keep secrets in a relationship—whether family, friends, or

romantic? Have you ever kept a secret from someone for their own good? How did it change things? Can Mo and Lena have a genuine friendship while Mo is concealing so much of her life?

5. To stop the Torrent, Mo had to be willing to sacrifice her life. At what point does the well-being of the group become more important than the life of the individual?

6. At one point, Mo says that the eleventh commandment of the Fitzgeralds is "Thou shall not make a scene." How do Mo's own feelings about "making a scene" change throughout the book? How does her family's insistence on this rule impact her relationship with them?

7. Luc and Colin bring out very different sides of Mo—and she brings out very different sides of them. What are these differences, and why does each guy appeal to her? How does each character become a stronger or better person when they begin to change? Are any of the changes negative? In any relationship—platonic or romantic—is it better to be with someone who challenges you, or accepts you?

8. Mo has a hard time admitting her attraction to Luc, because she believes he was in a relationship with Verity. Why does that belief affect Mo's feelings—even after Luc tries to reassure her? If Verity had told Mo about Luc before she died do you think that Mo would act differently?

9. In *Torn*, Mo is introduced to a world of magic, yet she herself is "Flat," without any magical power. Why do you think the author made Mo a Flat rather than an Arc like Verity and Luc? Does being Flat give Mo any advantage when dealing with Luc and the Arcs? Are there situations you've been in where what is perceived as a weakness is actually a strength? What, if anything, is the benefit of being an outsider?

10. Mo is repeatedly forced to choose between her obliga-
    tions in the Flats' world and her promises to Verity and
    the Arcs. For example, she jeopardizes her chance to get
    into her dream school to stop the Torrent. What are
    some of the competing pressures facing teens today?
    When you have to choose between them, how do you
    make your decision?

If you enjoyed *Torn,* you'll want to check out
Touch of Frost, by Jennifer Estep,
coming next month from K Teen. . . .

My name is Gwen Frost, and I go to Mythos Academy—a
school of myths, magic, and warrior whiz kids, where even
the lowliest geek knows how to chop off somebody's head
with a sword and Logan Quinn, the hottest Spartan guy in
school, also happens to be the deadliest.

But lately, things have been weird, even for Mythos. First,
mean girl Jasmine Ashton was murdered in the Library of
Antiquities. Then, someone stole the Bowl of Tears, a magical artifact that can be used to bring about the second Chaos
War. You know, death, destruction, and lots of other bad,
bad things. Freaky stuff like this goes on all the time at
Mythos, but I'm determined to find out who killed Jasmine,
and why—especially since I should have been the one who
died. . . .

Chapter 1

"**I** know your secret."

Daphne Cruz leaned closer to the mirror over the sink and put another coat of pale pink gloss onto her lips, pointedly ignoring me the way all the pretty, popular girls did.

The way everyone did at Mythos Academy.

"I know your secret," I repeated in a louder voice.

I pushed away from the statue of a sea nymph that I'd been leaning against, strolled over to the door that led out of the girls' bathroom, and locked it. I might not care who knew Daphne's dirty little secret, but I was willing to bet that she would before we were through. That's why I'd made sure that all of the white marble stalls were empty and had waited for the rest of Daphne's friends to leave their spots on the cushioned settee in the corner before I'd approached her.

Once Daphne was satisfied that her lips were glossed to a high sheen, she dropped the tube into the depths of her oversize pink Dooney & Bourke purse. Next, she drew out a hairbrush and went to work on her smooth, golden locks. Still ignoring me.

I crossed my arms over my chest, leaned against the door, and waited. The intricate, raised figures of warriors and monsters carved into the heavy wooden door pressed against my back, but I ignored the odd lumps and bumps. The two hundred bucks I was getting for this job meant that I could afford to be patient.

After another two minutes, when her hair had been brushed a dozen times and she realized that I wasn't actually, you know, *leaving*, Daphne finally deigned to turn and look at me. Her black eyes flicked over my jeans, graphic T-shirt, and purple zip-up hoodie, and she let out a little snort of disgust, obviously offended that I wasn't wearing the latest designer threads like she was. That I didn't have the matchy-match look down pat that she and her friends had going on.

Apparently, today's theme had been argyle, because the pattern was on everything that Daphne wore, from her pink cashmere sweater to her black pleated skirt to the printed black-and-pink tights that showed off her legs. The contrast of light and dark colors made her perfect, amber skin look that much more luminous. So did the shiny lip gloss.

"You know my secret?" Daphne repeated, a sneer creeping into her voice. "And what secret would that be?"

So the Valkyrie wanted to be snotty. Not a problem.

I smiled. "I know you took the charm bracelet. The one that Carson Callahan was going to give to Leta Gaston as a *will-you-go-to-the-homecoming-dance-with-me* present. You snatched it off the desk in his dorm room yesterday when he was helping you with your English lit paper."

For the first time, doubt flickered in Daphne's eyes, and disbelief filled her pretty face before she was able to hide it. Now, she was looking at me—*really* looking at me—trying to figure out who I was and what I wanted. After a moment, her eyes narrowed.

"You're that Gypsy girl," Daphne muttered. "The one who sees things."

That Gypsy girl. That's what everyone at Mythos Academy called me. Mainly because I was the only Gypsy trapped here in this school for magical warrior freaks. The middle-class girl whose strange ability had landed her here among the rich, popular, and undeniably powerful. Like Daphne Cruz, a spoiled, pampered wannabe princess who also happened to be a Valkyrie.

"What's your name?" Daphne asked. "Gail? Gretchen?"

Wow. I was impressed that she even knew it started with a G.

"Gwen," I told her. "Gwen Frost."

"Well, Gwen Frost," Daphne said, turning her attention back to her purse. "I have no idea what you're talking about."

Her voice and face were both just as smooth as the gilded silver mirror in front of her. I might have even believed her, if her hands hadn't clenched the tiniest bit as she put her hairbrush back into her purse. If I hadn't known just how good girls like her could lie.

Just how good everyone could lie.

I reached into my gray messenger bag and drew out a clear plastic bag. A small silver charm shaped like a rose glinted inside. I might as well have shown her a bag full of pot, from the way Daphne visibly recoiled.

"Where—where did you get that?" she whispered.

"Carson hadn't finished putting all the charms on Leta's bracelet when he showed it to you during your tutoring session yesterday afternoon," I said. "I found this one way, way back behind his desk in his dorm room. It fell down there when you grabbed the bracelet and stuffed it into your purse."

Daphne let out a laugh, still keeping up the act. "And why would I do something like that?"

"Because you're crazy about Carson. You don't want him to ask Leta out. You want him for yourself."

Daphne slumped over, her hands dropping to one of the sinks that lined the wall below the mirror. Her fingers curled around the silver faucets, which were shaped like Hydra heads, before sliding down to the basin. Her French-manicured nails scraped across the white marble, and pale pink sparks of magic shot out of her fingertips. Daphne might only be seventeen like me, but Valkyries were incredibly strong. I knew that if she wanted to, Daphne Cruz could rip that sink out of the wall easier than the Hulk could.

Maybe I should have been scared of the Valkyrie, of the weird princess pink sparks, and especially of her strength and what she could do to me with it. But I wasn't. I'd already lost one of the people I cared about most. Everything else dulled in comparison to that.

"How do you know all that?" Daphne asked, her voice barely above a whisper.

I shrugged. "Because, as you put it, I see things. And as soon as I found this charm, I knew that you were the one who took the bracelet."

I didn't tell Daphne anything else about my Gypsy gift, about my ability to know an object's history just by touching it, and she didn't ask.

Instead, the Valkyrie kept staring at me with her black eyes. After about thirty seconds of silence, she came to some sort of decision. Daphne straightened, reached into her bag once more, and drew out her wallet. It matched her designer purse.

"All right," she said. "How much will it take for you to give me that charm and forget about this whole thing? A hundred dollars? Two?"

This time, my hands were the ones that clenched into fists. She was trying to buy me off. I'd expected nothing less, but the gesture still made me angry. Like everyone else at Mythos Academy, Daphne Cruz could afford the very best of everything. A few hundred dollars was nothing to her. She'd spent that much on her freaking *purse*.

But a few hundred dollars wasn't nothing to me. It was clothes and comic books and a cell phone and a dozen other things that girls like Daphne never had to worry about.

"Carson's already paid me," I said.

"So?" she said. "I'll pay you more. However much you want."

"Sorry. Once I give my word to somebody, I keep it. And I told Carson that I would find the charm bracelet for him."

Daphne tilted her head to the side like I was some strange creature that she'd never seen before, some mythological monster masquerading as a teenage girl. Maybe it was stupid of me, not taking her up on the cash that she was so willing to give me. But my mom wouldn't have taken Daphne's money, not if she'd already made a promise to someone else. My mom, Grace, had been a Gypsy, just like me. With a gift, just like me.

For a moment, my heart ached with guilt and longing. My mom was gone, and I missed her *so much*. I shook my head, more to push the pain aside than anything else.

"Look, just give me the bracelet. That's all I want. That's all Carson wants."

Daphne's lips tightened. "He—he knows? That I took the bracelet? And why?"

"Not yet. But he's going to if you don't give it to me. Right *now*."

I opened the top of the plastic bag and held it out to her. Daphne stared at the rose charm glinting inside. She bit her pink lip, smearing her gloss on her teeth, and looked away.

"Fine," she muttered. "I don't know why I even took it in the first place."

I did, because I'd flashed on Daphne when I'd touched the charm. As soon as my fingers had brushed the silver rose, an image of the blond Valkyrie had popped into my head. I'd seen Daphne sitting at Carson's desk, staring at the bracelet, her fingers tightening around the metal links like she wanted to rip them in two.

And I'd felt the other girl's emotions, too, the way that I always did whenever I touched an object or even another person. I'd felt Daphne's hot, pulsing jealousy that Carson was thinking about asking out Leta. The warm, soft, fizzy crush that Daphne had on Carson herself, despite the fact that he was a total band geek and she was part of the popular crowd. Her cold, aching despair that she didn't like someone the rest of her snobby friends would approve of.

But I didn't tell Daphne any of that. The less people knew about my gift and the things I saw and felt, the better.

Daphne yanked the bracelet out of her bag. Carson Callahan might be a band geek, but he had money, too, which was why the bracelet was a heavy, expensive thing loaded down with a dozen charms that jingled together. Daphne's nails scraped against one of the charms, a small heart, and more pink sparks of magic fluttered like fireflies in the air.

I held out the bag again, and Daphne dropped the bracelet inside. I closed the top and tied off the plastic, careful not to touch the jewelry itself. I didn't want another slide show into Daphne Cruz's psyche. The first one had almost made me feel sorry for her.

But any sympathy I might have had for Daphne vanished when the Valkyrie gave me the cold, haughty stare that so many mean girls before her had perfected.

"You tell anyone about this, Gwen Frost, and I'll strangle you with that ugly purple hoodie you're wearing. Understand me?"

"Sure," I said in a pleasant tone. "But you might want to pull yourself together before you go to your next class, Daphne. Your lip gloss is smeared."

The Valkyrie's eyes narrowed, but I ignored her venomous dirty look, unlocked the bathroom door, and left.